House of the Whispering Pines by Anna Katharine Green

Anna Katharine Green was born in Brooklyn, New York on November 11th, 1846.

Anna's initial ambition was to be a poet. However that path failed to ignite any significant interest and she turned to fiction writing. She published her first—and most famous work in 1878—'The Leavenworth Case'. Wilkie Collins praised it and it sold extremely well.

It led to Anna writing 40 novels and to becoming known as 'the mother of the detective novel.'

In helping to shape the genre she brought many other innovations including a series detective: her main character was detective Ebenezer Gryce of the New York Metropolitan Police Force, but in three novels he is assisted by the nosy society spinster Amelia Butterworth, another innovation and a prototype for Miss Marple, Miss Silver and others.

She also invented the 'girl detective': in the character of Violet Strange, a debutante with a secret life as a sleuth. Anna's other innovations included the now familiar dead bodies in libraries, newspaper clippings as "clews," the coroner's inquest, and expert witnesses. Yale Law School once used her books to demonstrate how damaging it can be to rely on circumstantial evidence.

Her career was now well advanced and she was much admired.

On November 25, 1884, Green married the actor and stove designer, and later noted furniture maker, Charles Rohlfs, who was seven years her junior. They had three children; Rosamund, Roland and Sterling.

Although Anna was a progressive she did not approve of many of her feminist contemporaries, and was opposed to women's suffrage.

On November 25, 1884, Anna married the actor and noted furniture maker, Charles Rohlfs, who was seven years her junior. They had three children; Rosamund, Roland and Sterling.

Anna Katharine Green died on April 11, 1935 in Buffalo, New York, at the age of 88.

Index of Contents

BOOK ONE

SMOKE

CHAPTER I

THE HESITATING STEP

To have reared a towering scheme of happiness, and to behold it razed,
Were nothing: all men hope, and see their hopes Frustrate, and grieve awhile, and hope anew;
But—

A Blot in the 'Scutcheon.

The moon rode high; but ominous clouds were rushing towards it—clouds heavy with snow. I watched these clouds as I drove recklessly, desperately, over the winter roads. I had just missed the desire of my life, the one precious treasure which I coveted with my whole undisciplined heart, and not being what you call a man of self-restraint, I was chafed by my defeat far beyond the bounds I have usually set for myself.

The moon—with the wild skurry of clouds hastening to blot it out of sight—seemed to mirror the chaos threatening my better impulses; and, idly keeping it in view, I rode on, hardly conscious of my course till the rapid recurrence of several well-known landmarks warned me that I had taken the longest route home, and that in another moment I should be skirting the grounds of The Whispering Pines, our country clubhouse. I had taken? Let me rather say, my horse; for he and I had traversed this road many times together, and he had no means of knowing that the season was over and the club-house closed. I did not think of it myself at the moment, and was recklessly questioning whether I should not drive in and end my disappointment in a wild carouse, when, the great stack of chimneys coming suddenly into view against the broad disk of the still unclouded moon, I perceived a thin trail of smoke soaring up from their midst and realised, with a shock, that there should be no such sign of life in a house I myself had closed, locked, and barred that very day.

I was the president of the club and felt responsible. Pausing only long enough to make sure that I had yielded to no delusion, and that fire of some kind was burning on one of the club-house's deserted hearths, I turned in at the lower gateway. For reasons which I need not now state, there were no bells attached to my cutter and consequently my approach was noiseless. I was careful that it should be so, also careful to stop short of the front door and leave my horse and sleigh in the black depths of the pine-grove pressing up to the walls on either side. I was sure that all was not as it should be inside these walls, but, as God lives, I had no idea what was amiss or how deeply my own destiny was involved in the step I was about to take.

Our club-house stands, as it may be necessary to remind you, on a knoll thickly wooded with the ancient trees I have mentioned. These trees—all pines and of a growth unusual and of an aspect well-nigh hoary—extend only to the rear end of the house, where a wide stretch of gently undulating ground opens at once upon the eye, suggesting to all lovers of golf the admirable use to which it is put from early spring to latest fall. Now, links, as well as parterres and driveways, are lying under an even blanket of winter snow, and even the building, with its picturesque gables and rows of be-diamonded windows, is well-nigh indistinguishable in the shadows cast by the heavy pines, which soar above it and twist their limbs over its roof and about its forsaken corners, with a moan and a whisper always desolate to the sensitive ear, but from this night on, simply appalling.

No other building stood within a half-mile in any direction. It was veritably a country club, gay and full of life in the season, but isolated and lonesome beyond description after winter had set in and buried flower and leaf under a wide waste of untrodden snow.

I felt this isolation as I stepped from the edge of the trees and prepared to cross the few feet of open space leading to the main door. The sudden darkness instantly enveloping me, as the clouds, whose advancing mass I had been watching, made their final rush upon the moon, added its physical shock to this inner sense of desolation and, in some moods, I should have paused and thought twice before attempting the door, behind which lurked the unknown with its naturally accompanying suggestion of peril. But rage and disappointment, working hotly within me, had left no space for fear. Rather rejoicing in the doubtfulness of the adventure, I pushed my way over the snow until my feet struck the steps. Here, instinct caused me to stop and glance quickly up and down the building either way. Not a gleam of light met my eye from the smallest scintillating pane. Was the house as soundless as it was dark?

I listened but heard nothing. I listened again and still heard nothing. Then I proceeded boldly up the steps and laid my hand on the door.

It was unlatched and yielded to my touch. Light or no light, sound or no sound there was some one within. The fire which had sent its attenuated streak of smoke up into the moonlit air, was burning yet on one of the many hearths within, and before it I should presently see—

Whom?

What?

The question scarcely interested me.

Nevertheless I proceeded to enter and close the door carefully behind me. As I did so, I cast an involuntary glance without. The sky was inky and a few wandering flakes of the now rapidly advancing storm came whirling in, biting my cheeks and stinging my forehead.

Once inside, I stopped short, possibly to listen again, possibly to assure myself as to what I had best do next. The silence was profound. Not a sound disturbed the great, empty building. My own footfall, as I stirred, seemed to wake extraordinary echoes. I had moved but a few steps, yet to my heightened senses, the noise seemed loud enough to wake the dead. Instinctively I stopped and stood stock-still. There was no answering cessation of movement. Darkness, silence everywhere. Yet not quite absolute darkness. As my eyes grew accustomed to the place, I found it possible to discern the outlines of the windows and locate the stairs and the arches where the side halls opened. I was even able to pick out the exact spot where the great antlers spread themselves above the hatrack, and presently the rack itself came into view, with its row of empty pegs, yesterday so full, to-day quite empty. That rack interested me,—I hardly knew why,—and regardless of the noise I made, I crossed over to it and ran my hand along the wall underneath. The result was startling. A man's coat and hat hung from one of the pegs.

I knew my business as president of this club. I also knew that no one should be in the house at this time—that no one could be in it on any honest errand. Some secret and sinister business must be at the bottom of this mysterious intrusion immediately after the place had been shut for the winter. Would this hat and coat identify the intruder? I would strike a light and see. But this involved difficulties. The gas had been turned off that very morning and I had no matches in my pocket. But I remembered where they could be found. I had seen them when I passed through the kitchen earlier in the day. They were very accessible from the end of the hall where I stood. I had but to feel my way through a passage or two and I should come to the kitchen door.

I began to move that way, and presently came creeping back, with a match-box half full of matches in my hand. But I did not strike one then. I had just made a move to do so, when the unmistakable sound of a door opening somewhere in the house made me draw back into as quiet and dark a place as I could find. This lay in the rear and at the right of the staircase, and as the sound had appeared to come from above, it was the most natural retreat that offered. And a good one I found it.

I had hardly taken up my stand when the darkness above gave way to a faint glimmer, and a step became audible coming from some one of the many small rooms in the second story, but so slowly and with such evident hesitation that my imagination had ample time to work and fill my mind with varying anticipations, each more disconcerting than the last. Now I seemed to be listening to the movements of an intoxicated man seeking an issue out of strange quarters, then to the wary approach of one who had his own reasons for dread and was as conscious of my presence as I was of his.

But the light, steadily increasing with each lagging but surely advancing step, soon gave the lie to this latter supposition, since no sane man, afraid of an ambush, would be likely to offer such odds to the one lying in wait for him, as his own face illumined by a flaming candle, and I was yielding to the bewilderment of the moment when the uncertain step paused and a sob came faintly to my ears, wrung from lips so stiff with human anguish that my fears took on new shape and the event a significance which in my present mood of personal suffering and preoccupation was anything but welcome. Indeed, I was coward enough to contemplate flight and might in another moment have yielded to the unworthy impulse if the sound of a second sigh had not struck shudderingly on my ear, followed by the renewal of the step and the almost immediate appearance on the stairs of a young girl holding a candle in one hand and shielding her left cheek with the other.

Life offers few such shocks to any man, whatever his story or whatever his temperament. I had been prepared by the sob I had heard to see a woman, but not this woman. Nothing could have prepared me for an encounter with this woman anywhere that night, after what had passed between us and the wreck she had made of my life. But here! in a place so remote and desolate I had hesitated to enter it myself! What was I to think? How was I to reconcile so inconceivable a fact with what I knew of her in the past, with what I hoped from her in the future.

To steady my thoughts and bring my whirling brain again under control, I fixed my eyes on her well-known form and features as upon a stranger's whom I would understand and judge. I have called her a woman and certainly I had loved her as such, but as, in this moment of strange detachment, I watched her descend, swaying foot following swaying foot falteringly down the stairs, I was able to see that only the emotions which denaturalised her expression were a woman's; that her features, her pose, and the peculiar childlike contour of the one cheek open to view were those of one whose yesterday was in the playroom.

But beautiful! You do not often see such beauty. Under all the disfigurement of an agitation so great as to daunt me and make me question if I were its sole cause, her face shone with an individual charm which marked her out as one of the few who are the making or marring of men, sometimes of nations. This is the heritage she was born to, this her lot, not to be shirked, not to be evaded even now at her early age of seventeen. So much any one could see even in a momentary scrutiny of her face and figure. But what was not so clear, not even to myself with the consciousness of what had passed between us during the last few hours, was why her heart should have so outrun her years, and the emotion I beheld betray such shuddering depths. Some grisly fear, some staring horror had met her in this strange retreat. Simple grief speaks with a different language from that which I read in her distorted features and tottering, slowly creeping form. What had happened above? She had escaped me to run upon what? My lips refused to ask, my limbs refused to move, and if I breathed at all, I did so with such fierceness of restraint that her eyes never turned my way, not even when she had reached the lowest step and paused for a moment there, oscillating in pain or uncertainty. Her face was turned more fully towards me now, and I had just begun to discern something in it besides its tragic beauty, when she made a quick move and blew out the candle she held. One moment that magical picture of superhuman loveliness, then darkness, I might say silence, for I do not think either of us so much as stirred for several instants. Then there came a crash, followed by the sound of flying feet. She had flung the candlestick out of her hand and was hurriedly crossing the hail. I thought she was coming my way, and instinctively drew back against the wall. But she stopped far short of me, and I heard her groping about, then give a sudden spring towards the front door. It opened and the wind soughed in. I felt the chill of snow upon my face, and realised the tempest. Then all was quiet and dark again. She had slid quickly out and the door had swung to behind her. Another instant and I heard the click of the key as it turned in the lock, heard it and made no outcry, such the spell, such the bewilderment of my faculties! But once the act was accomplished and egress made difficult, nay, for the moment, impossible, I felt all lesser emotions give way to an anxiety which demanded immediate action, for the girl had gone out without wraps or covering for her head, and my experience of the evening had told me how cold it was. I must follow and find her and rescue her if possible from the snow. The distance was long to town, the cold would seize and perhaps prostrate her, after which, the wind and snow would do the rest.

Throwing myself against the door, I shook it violently. It was immovable. Then I flew to the windows. Their fastenings yielded readily enough, but not the windows themselves; one had a broken cord, another seemed glued to its frame, and I was still struggling with the latter when I heard a sound which lifted the hair on my head and turned my whole attention back to what lay behind and above me. There was still some one in the house. I had forgotten everything in this apparition of the woman I have described in a place so disassociated with any conception I could possibly have of her whereabouts on this especial evening. But this noise, short, sharp, but too distant to be altogether recognisable, roused doubts which once awakened changed the whole tenor of my thoughts and would not let me rest till I had probed the house from top to bottom. To find Carmel Cumberland alone in this desolation was a mystifying discovery to which I had found it hard enough to reconcile myself. But Carmel here in company with another at the very moment when I had expected the fruition of my own joy,—ah, that was to open hell's door in my breast; a possibility too intolerable to remain unsettled for an instant. Though she had passed out before my eyes in a drooping, almost agonised condition, not she, dear as she was, and great as were my fears in her regard, was to be sought out first, but the man! The man who was back of all this, possibly back of my disappointment; the man whose work I may have witnessed, but at whose identity I could not even guess.

Leaving the window, I groped my way along the wall until I reached the rack where the man's coat and hat hung. Whether it was my intention to carry them away and hide them, in my anxiety to secure this intruder and hold him to a bitter account for the misery he was causing me, or whether I only meant to satisfy myself that they were the habiliments of a stranger and not those of some sneaking member of the club, is of little importance in the light of the fact which presently burst upon me. The hat and coat were gone. Nothing hung from the rack. The wall was free from end to end. She had taken these articles of male apparel with her; she had not gone forth into the driving snow, unprotected, but—

I did not know what to think. No acquaintanceship with her girlish impulses, nothing that had occurred between us before or during this night, had prepared me for a freak of this nature. I felt backward along the wall; I felt forward; I even handled the pegs and counted them as I passed to and fro, touching every one; but I could not alter the fact. The groping she had done had been in this direction. She was searching for this hat and coat (a man's hat,—a derby, as I had been careful to assure myself at the first handling) and, in them, she had gone home as she had probably come, and there was no man in the case, or if there were—

The doubt drove me to the staircase. Making no further effort to unravel the puzzle which only beclouded my faculties, I began my wary ascent. I had not the slightest fear, I was too full of cold rage for that.

The arrangement of rooms on the second floor was well known to me. I understood every nook and corner and could find my way about the whole place without a light. I took but one precaution—that of slipping off my shoes at the foot of the stairs. I wished to surprise the intruder. I was willing to resort to any expedient to accomplish this. The matches I carried in my pocket would make this possible if once I heard him breathing. I held my own breath as I stole softly up, and waited for an instant at the top of the stairs to listen. There was an awesome silence everywhere, and I was hesitating whether to attack the front rooms first or to follow up a certain narrow hall leading to a rear staircase, when I remembered the thin line of smoke which, rising from one of the chimneys, had first attracted my attention to the house. In that was my clue. There was but one room on this floor where a fire could be lit. It lay a few feet beyond me down the narrow hall I have just mentioned. Why had I trusted everything to my ears when my nose would have been a better guide? As I took the few steps necessary, a slight smell of smoke became very perceptible, and no longer in doubt of my course, I pushed boldly on and entering the half-open door, struck a match and peered anxiously about.

Emptiness here just as everywhere else. A few chairs, a dresser,—it was a ladies' dressing-room,—some smouldering ashes on the hearth, a lounge piled up with cushions. But no person. The sound I had heard had not issued from this room, yet something withheld me from seeking further. Chilled to the bone, with teeth chattering in spite of myself, I paused just inside the door, and when the match went out in my hand remained shivering there in the darkness, a prey to sensations more nearly approaching those of fear than any I had ever before experienced in my whole life.

CHAPTER II

IT WAS SHE—SHE INDEED!

Look on death itself!—up, up, and see
The great doom's visage!

Macbeth.

Why, I did not know. There seemed to be no reason for this excess of feeling. I had no dread of attack; my apprehension was of another sort. Besides, any attack here must come from the rear—from the open doorway in which I stood—and my dread lay before me, in the room itself, which, as I have already said, appeared to be totally empty. What could occasion my doubts, and why did I not fly the place? There were passage-ways yet to search, why linger here like a gaby in the dark when perhaps the man I believed to be in hiding somewhere within these walls, was improving the opportunity to escape?

If I asked myself this question, I did not answer it, but I doubt if I asked it then. I had forgotten the intruder; the interest which had carried me thus far had become lost in a fresher one of which the beginning and ending lay hidden within the four walls I now stared upon, unseeing. Not to see and yet to feel—did that make the horror? If so, another lighted match must help me out. I struck one while the thought was hot within me, and again took a look at the room.

I noted but one thing new, but that made me reel back till I was half way into the hall. Then a certain dogged persistency I possess came to my rescue, and I re-entered the room at a leap and stood before the lounge and its pile of cushions. They were numerous,—all that the room contained, and more! Chairs had been stripped, window-seats denuded, and the whole collection disposed here in a set way which struck me as unnatural. Was this the janitor's idea? I hardly thought so, and was about to pluck one of these cushions off, when that most unreasonable horror seized me again and I found myself looking back over my shoulder at the fireplace from which rose a fading streak of smoke which some passing gust, perhaps, had blown out into the room.

I felt sick. Was it the smell? It was not that of burning wood, hardly of burning paper, I—but here my second match went out.

Thoroughly roused now (you will say, by what?) I felt my way out of the room and to the head of the staircase. I remembered the candle and candlestick I had heard thrown down on the lower floor by Carmel Cumberland. I would secure them and come back and settle these uncanny doubts. It might be the veriest fool business, but my mind was disturbed and must be set at ease. Nothing else seemed so important, yet I was not without anxiety for the lovely and delicate woman wandering the snow-covered roads in the teeth of a furious gale, any more than I was dead to the fact that I should never forgive myself if I allowed the man to escape whom I believed to be hiding somewhere in the rear of this house.

I had a hunt for the candlestick and a still longer one for the candle, but finally I recovered both, and, lighting the latter, felt myself, for the first time, more or less master of the situation.

Rapidly regaining the room in which my interest was now centred, I set the candlestick down on the dresser, and approached the lounge. Hardly knowing what I feared, or what I expected to find, I tore off one of the cushions and flung it behind me. More cushions were revealed—but that was not all.

Escaping from the edge of one of them I saw a shiny tress of woman's hair. I gave a gasp and pulled off more cushions, then I fell on my knees, struck down by the greatest horror which a man can feel. Death lay before me—violent, uncalled-for death—and the victim was a woman. But it was not that. Though the head was not yet revealed, I thought I knew the woman and that she—Did seconds pass or many minutes before I lifted that last cushion? I shall never know. It was an eternity to me and I am not of a sentimental cast, but I have some sort of a conscience and during that interval it awoke. It has never quite slept since.

The cushion had not concealed the hands, but I did not look at them—I did not dare. I must first see the face. But I did not twitch this pillow off; I drew it aside slowly, as though held by the restraining clutch of some one behind me. And I was so held, but not by what was visible—rather by the terrors which gather in the soul at the summons of some dreadful doom. I could not meet the certainty without some preparation. I released another strand of hair; then the side of a cheek, half buried out of sight in the loosened locks and bulging pillows; then, with prayers to God for mercy, an icy brow; two staring eyes—which having seen I let the cushion drop, for mercy was not to be mine.

It was she, she, indeed! and judgment was glassed in the look I met—judgment and nothing more kindly, however I might appeal to Heaven for mercy or whatever the need of my fiercely startled and repentant soul.

Dead! Adelaide! the woman I had planned to wrong that very night, and who had thus wronged me! For a moment I could take in nothing but this one astounding fact, then the how and the why woke in maddening curiosity within me, and seizing the cushion, I dragged it aside and stared down into the pitiful and accusing features thus revealed, as though to tear from them the story of the crime which had released me as I would not have been released, no, not to have had my heart's desire in all the fulness with which I had contemplated it a few short hours before.

But beyond the ever accusing, protuberant stare, those features told nothing; and steeling myself to the situation, I made what observation I could of her condition and the surrounding circumstances. For this was my betrothed wife. Whatever my intentions, however far my love had strayed under the spell cast over me by her sister,—the young girl who had just passed out,—Adelaide and I had been engaged for many months; our wedding day was even set.

But that was all over now—ended as her life was ended: suddenly, incomprehensibly, and by no stroke of God. Even the jewel on her finger was gone, the token of our betrothal. This was to be expected. She would be apt to take it off before committing herself to a fate that proclaimed me a traitor to this symbol. I should see that ring again. I should find it in a letter filled with bitter words. I would not think of it or of them now. I would try to learn how she had committed this act, whether by poison or—

It must have been by poison; no other means would suggest themselves to one of her refined sense; but if so, why those marks on her neck, growing darker and darker as I stared at them!

My senses reeled as I scrutinised those marks. Small, delicate but deadly, they stared upon me from either side of her white neck till nature could endure no more and I tottered back against the further wall, beholding no longer room, nor lounge, nor recumbent body, but a young girl's exquisite face, set in lines which belied her seventeen years, and made futile any attempt on my part at self-deception when my reason inexorably demanded an explanation of this death. As suicide it was comprehensible, as murder, not, unless—

And it had been murder!

I sank to the floor as I fully realised this.

CHAPTER III

"OPEN!"

PRINCE—Bring forth the parties of suspicion.

FRIAR—I am the greatest, as the time and place Doth make against me, of this direful murder; And here I stand, both to impeach and purge. Myself condemned and myself excused.

Romeo and Juliet.

I have mentioned poison as my first thought. It was a natural one, the result undoubtedly of having noticed two small cordial glasses standing on a little table over against the fireplace. When I was conscious again of my own fears, I crossed to the table and peered into these glasses. They were both empty. However, they had not been so long. In each I found traces of anisette cordial, and though no bottle stood near I was very confident that it could readily be found somewhere in the room. What had preceded and followed the drinking of this cordial?

As I raised my head from bending over these glasses—not club glasses, by the way—I caught sight of my face in the mantel mirror. It gave me maddening thoughts. In this same mirror there had been reflected but a little while before, two other faces, for a sight of whose expression at that fatal moment I would gladly risk my soul.

How had she looked—how that other? Would not the story of those awful, those irrevocable moments be plain to my eye, if the quickly responsive glass could but retain the impressions it receives and give back at need what had once informed its surface with moving life!

I stared at the senseless glass, appealed to it with unreasoning frenzy, as to something which could give up its secret if it would, but only to meet my own features in every guise of fury and despair—features I no longer knew—features which insensibly increased my horror till I tore myself wildly from the spot, and cast about for further clues to enlightenment, before yielding to the conviction which was making a turmoil in mind, heart, and conscience. Alas! there was but little more to see. A pair of curling-irons lay on the hearth, but I had no sooner lifted them than I dropped them with a shudder of unspeakable loathing, only to start at the noise they made in striking the tiles. For it was the self-same noise I had heard when listening from below. These tongs, set up against the side of the fireplace had been jarred down by the forcible shutting of the large front door, and no man other than myself was in the house, or had been in the house; only the two women. But the time when this discovery would have brought comfort was passed. Better a hundred times that a man—I had almost said any man—should have been with them here, than that they should be closeted together in a spot so secluded, with rancour and cause for complaint in one heart, and a biting, deadly flame in the other, which once reaching up must from its very nature leave behind it a corrosive impress. I saw,-I felt,—but I did not desist from my investigations. A stick or two still smouldered on the hearthstone. In the ashes lay some scattered fragments of paper which crumbled at my touch. On the floor in front I espied only a stray hair-pin; everything else was in place throughout the room except the cushions and that horror on the lounge, waiting the second look I had so far refrained from giving it.

That look I could no longer withhold. I must know the depth of the gulf over which I hung. I must not wrong with a thought one who had smiled upon me like an angel of light—a young girl, too, with the dew of innocence on her beauty to every eye but mine and only not to mine within—shall I say ten awful minutes? It seemed ages,—all of my life and more. Yet that lovely breast had heaved not so many times since I looked upon her as a deified mortal, and now two small spots on another woman's pulseless throat had drawn a veil of blood over that beauty, and given to a child the attributes of a Medusa. Yet hope was not quite stilled. I would look again and perhaps discover that my own eyes had been at fault, that there were no marks, or if marks, not just the ones my fancy had painted there.

Turning, I let my glance fall first on the feet. I had not noted them before, and I was startled to see that the arctics in which they were clad were filled all around with snow. She had walked then, as the other was walking now; she, who detested every effort and was of such delicate make that exertion of unusual kind could not readily be associated with her. Had she come alone or in Carmel's company, and if in Carmel's company, on what ostensible errand if not that of death? Her dress, which was of dark wool, showed that she had changed her garments for this trip. I had seen her at dinner, and this was not the gown she had worn then—the gown in which she had confronted me during those few intolerable minutes when I could not meet her eyes. Fatal cowardice! A moment of realisation then and we might all have been saved this horror of sin and death and shameful retribution.

And yet who knows? Not understanding what I saw, how could I measure the might-have-beens! I would proceed with my task—note if she wore the diamond brooch I had given her. No, she was without ornament; I had never seen her so plainly clad. Might I draw a hope from this? Even the pins which had fallen from her hair were such as she wore when least adorned. Nothing spoke of the dinner party or of her having been dragged here unaware; but all of previous intent and premeditation. Surely hope was getting uppermost. If I had dreamed the marks—

But no! There they were, unmistakable and damning, just where the breath struggles up. I put my own thumbs on these two dark spots to see if—when what was it? A lightning stroke or a call of fate which one must answer while sense remains? I felt my head pulled around by some unseen force from behind, and met staring into mine through the glass of the window a pair of burning eyes. Or was it fantasy? For in another moment they were gone, nor was I in the condition just then to dissociate the real from the unreal. But the possibility of a person having seen me in this position before the dead was enough to startle me to my feet, and though in another instant I became convinced that I had been the victim of hallucination, I nevertheless made haste to cross to the window and take a look through its dismal panes. A gale of blinding snow was sweeping past, making all things indistinguishable, but the absence of balcony outside was reassuring and I stepped hastily back, asking myself for the first time what I should do and where I should now go to ensure myself from being called as a witness to the awful occurrence which had just taken place in this house. Should I go home and by some sort of subterfuge now unthought of, try to deceive my servants as to the time of my return, or attempt to create an alibi elsewhere? Something I must do to save myself the anguish and Carmel the danger of my testimony in this matter. She must never know, the world must never know that I had seen her here.

I had lost at a blow everything that gives zest or meaning to life, but I might still be spared the bottommost depth of misery—be saved the utterance of the word which would sink that erring but delicate soul into the hell yawning beneath her. It was my one thought now—though I knew that the woman who had fallen victim to her childish hate had loved me deeply and was well worth my avenging.

I could not be the death of two women; the loss of one weighed heavily enough upon my conscience. I would fly the place—I would leave this ghastly find to tell its own story. The night was stormy, the hour late, the spot a remote one, and the road to it but little used. I could easily escape and when the morrow came—but it was the present I must think of now, this hour, this moment. How came I to stay so long! In feverish haste, I began to throw the pillows back over the quiet limbs, the accusing face. Shudderingly I hid those eyes (I understood their strange protuberance now) and recklessly bent on flight, was half way across the floor when my feet were stayed—I wonder that my reason was not unseated—by a sudden and tremendous attack on the great door below, mingled with loud cries to open which ran thundering through the house, calling up innumerable echoes from its dead and hidden corners.

It was the police. The wild night, the biting storm had been of no avail. An alarm had reached headquarters, and all hope of escape on my part was at an end. Yet because at such crises instinct rises superior to reason, I blew out the candle and softly made my way into the hall. I had remembered a window opening over a shed at the head of the kitchen staircase. I could reach it from this rear hall by just a turn or two, and once on that shed, a short leap would land me on the ground; after which I could easily trust to the storm to conceal my flight across the open golf-links. It was worth trying at least; anything was better than being found in the house with my murdered betrothed.

I had no reason to think that I was being sought, or that my presence in this building was even suspected. It might well be that the police were even ignorant of the tragedy awaiting them across the threshold of the door they seemed intent on battering down. The gleam of a candle burning in this closed-up house, or even the tale told by the rising smoke, may have drawn them from the road to investigate. Such coincidences had been. Such untoward happenings had misled people into useless self-betrayal. My case was too desperate for such weakness. Flight at this moment might save all; I would at least attempt it. The door was shaking on its hinges; these intruders seemed determined to enter.

With a spring I reached the window by which I hoped to escape, and quickly raised it. A torrent of snow swept in, covering my face and breast in a moment. It did something more: it cleared my brain, and I remembered my poor horse standing in this blinding gale under cover of the snow-packed pines. Every one knew my horse. I could commit no greater folly than to flee by the rear fields while such a witness to my presence remained in full view in front. With the sensation of a trapped animal, I reclosed the window and cast about for a safe corner where I could lie concealed until I learned what had brought these men here and how much I really had to fear from their presence.

I had but little time in which to choose. The door below had just given way and a party of at least three men were already stamping their feet free from snow in the hall. I did not like the tone of their voices, it was too low and steady to suit me. I had rather have heard drunken cries or a burst of wild hilarity than these stern and purposeful whispers. Men of resolution could have but one errand here. My doom was closing round me. I could only put off the fatal moment. But it was better to do this than to plunge headlong into the unknown fate awaiting me.

I knew of a possible place of concealment. It was in the ballroom not far from where I stood. I remembered the spot well. It was at the top of a little staircase leading to the musicians' gallery. A balustrade guarded this gallery, supported by a boarding wide enough to hide a man lying behind it at his full length. If the search I was endeavouring to evade was not minute enough to lead them to look behind this boarding, it would offer me the double advantage of concealment and an unobstructed view of what went on in the hall, through the main doorway opening directly opposite. I could reach this ballroom and its terminal gallery without going around to this door. A smaller one communicated directly with the corridor in which I was then lurking, and towards this I now made my way with all the precaution suggested by my desperate situation. No man ever moved more lightly. The shoes which I had taken off in the lower hall were yet in my hand. I had caught them up after replacing the cushions on Adelaide's body. Even to my own straining ears I made no perceptible sound. I reached the balcony and had stretched myself out at full length behind the boarding, before the men below had left the lower floor.

An interval of heart-torture and wearing suspense now followed. They were ransacking the rooms below by the aid of their own lanterns, as I could tell from their assured manner. That they had not made at once for the scene of crime brought me some small sense of comfort, but not much. They were too resolute in their movements and much too thorough and methodical in their search, for me to dream of their confining their investigations to the first floor. Unless I very much mistook their purpose, I should soon hear them ascending the stairs, after which, instinct, if not the faint smell of smoke still lingering in the air, would lead them to the room where my poor Adelaide lay.

And thus it proved. More quickly than I expected, the total darkness in which I lay, brightened under an advancing lantern, and I heard the steps of two men coming down the hall. It was a steady if not rapid approach, and I was quite prepared for their presence when they finally reached the doorway opposite and stopped to look in at what must have appeared to them a vast and empty space. They were officials, true enough—one hasty glance through the balustrade assured me of that. I even knew one of them by name—he was a sergeant of police and a highly trustworthy man. But how they had been drawn to this place at a moment so critical, I could not surmise. Do men of this stamp scent crime as a hound scents out prey? They had the look of hounds. Even in the momentary glimpse I got of them, I noted the tense and expectant look with which they endeavoured to pierce the dim spaces between us. The chase was on. It was something more than curiosity or a chance exercise of their duty which had brought them here. Their object was definite, and if the sight of the low gallery in which I lay, should suggest to them all its possibilities as a hiding-place, I should know in just one moment more what it is for the helpless quarry to feel the clutch of the captor.

But the moment passed without any attempt at approach on their part, and when I lifted my head again it was to catch a glimpse of their side faces as they turned to look elsewhere for what they were plainly in search of. An oath, muffled but stern, which was the first word above a whisper that I had heard issue from their lips, told me that they had reached the room and had come upon the horror which lay there. What would they say to it! Would they know who she was—her name, her quality, her story—and respect her dead as they certainly must have respected her living? I listened but caught only a low murmur as they conferred together. I imagined their movements; saw them in my mind's eye leaning over that death-tenanted couch, pointing with accusing finger at those two dark marks, and consulting each other with side-long looks, as they passed from one detail of her appearance to another. I even imagined them crossing the floor and lifting the two cordial glasses just as I had done, and then slowly setting them down again, with perhaps a lift of the brows or a suggestive shake of the head; and maddened by my own intolerable position, drawn by a power I felt it impossible to resist, I crept to my feet and took my staggering way down the half-dozen steps of the gallery and thence along by the left-hand wall towards the further doorway, and through it to where these men stood weighing the chances in which my life and honour were involved, and those of one other of whom I dared not think and would not have these men think for all that was left me of hope and happiness.

It was dark in the ballroom, and it was only a little less so in the corridor. All the light was in that room; but I still slid along the wall like a thief, with eyes set and ears agape for any chance word which might reach me. Suddenly I heard one. It was this, uttered with a decision which had the strange effect of lifting my head and making a man of me again:

"That settles it. He will find it hard to escape after this."

He! I had been dreading to hear a she. Yet why? Who on God's earth, save myself, could know that Carmel had been within these woeful walls to-night. He! I never stopped to question who was meant by this definite pronoun. I was not even conscious of caring very much. I was in a coil of threatening troubles, but I was in it alone, and, greatly relieved by the discovery, I drew myself up and stepped quickly forward into the room where the two officials stood.

Their faces, as they wheeled sharply about and took in my shoeless and more or less dishevelled figure, told me with an eloquence which made my heart sink, the unfortunate impression which my presence made upon them. It was but a fleeting look, for these men were both by nature and training easy masters of themselves; but its language was unmistakable and I knew that if I were to hold my own with them, I must get all the support I could from the truth, save where it would involve her—from the truth and my own consciousness of innocence, if I had any such consciousness. I was not sure that I had, for my falseness had precipitated this tragedy,—how I might never know, but a knowledge of the how was not necessary to my self-condemnation. Nevertheless my hands were clean of this murder, and allowing the surety of this fact to take a foremost place in my mind, I faced these men and with real feeling, but as little display of it as possible, I observed:

"You have come to my aid in a critical moment. This is my betrothed wife—the woman I was to marry—and I find her lying here dead, in this closed and lonely house. What does it mean? I know no more than you do."

CHAPTER IV

THE ODD CANDLESTICK

It is a damned and a bloody work;
The graceless action of a heavy hand,
If that it be the work of any hand.

King John.

The two men eyed me quietly, then Hexford pointed to my shoeless feet and sternly retorted:

"Permit us to doubt your last assertion. You seem to be in better position than ourselves to explain the circumstances which puzzle you."

They were right. It was for me to talk, not for them. I conceded the point in these words:

"Perhaps—but you cannot always trust appearances. I can explain my own presence here and the condition in which you find me, but I cannot explain this tragedy, near and dear as Miss Cumberland was to me. I did not know she was in the building, alive or dead. I came upon her here covered with the cushions just as you found her. I have felt the shock. I do not look like myself—I do not feel like myself; it was enough—" Here real emotion seized me and I almost broke down. I was in a position much more dreadful than any they could imagine or should be allowed to.

Their silence led me to examine their faces. Hexford's mouth had settled into a stiff, straight line and the other man's wore a cynical smile I did not like. At this presage of the difficulties awaiting me, I felt one strand of the rope sustaining me above this yawning gulf of shame and ignominy crack and give way. Oh, for a better record in the past!—a staff on which to lean in such an hour as this! But while nothing serious clouded my name, I had more to blush for than to pride myself upon in my career as prince of good fellows,—and these men knew it, both of them, and let it weigh in the scale already tipped far off its balance by coincidences which a better man than myself would have found it embarrassing to explain. I recognised all this, I say, in the momentary glance I cast at their stern and unresponsive figures; but the courage which had served me in lesser extremities did not fail me now, and, kneeling down before my dead betrothed, I kissed her cold white hand with sincere compunction, before attempting the garbled and probably totally incoherent story with which I endeavoured to explain the inexplainable situation.

They listened—I will do them that much justice; but it was with such an air of incredulity that my words fell with less and less continuity and finally lost themselves in a confused stammer as I reached the point where I pulled the cushions from the couch and made my ghastly discovery.

"You see—see for yourselves—what confronted me. My betrothed—a dainty, delicate woman—dead—alone—in this solitary, far-away spot—the victim of what? I asked myself then—I ask myself now. I cannot understand it—or those glasses yonder—or those marks!" They were black by this time—unmistakable—not to be ignored by them or by me.

"We understand those marks, and you ought to," came from the second man, the one I did not know.

My head fell forward; my lips refused to speak the words. I saw as in a flash, a picture of the one woman bending over the other; terror, reproach, anguish in the eyes whose fixed stare would never more leave my consciousness, an access of rage or some such sadden passion animating the other whose every curve spoke tenderness, whose every look up to this awful day had been as an angel's look to me. The vision was a maddening one. I shook myself free from it by starting to my feet." It's—it's—" I gasped.

"She has been strangled," quoth Hexford, doggedly.

"A dog's death," mumbled the other.

My hands came together involuntarily. At that instant, with the memory before me of the vision I have just described, I almost wished that it had been my hate, my anger which had brought those tell-tale marks out upon that livid skin. I should have suffered less. I should only have had to pay the penalty of my crime and not be forced to think of Carmel with terrible revulsion, as I was now thinking, minute by minute, fight with it as I would.

"You had better sit down," Hexford suddenly suggested, pushing a chair my way. "Clarke, look up the telephone and ask for three more men. I am going into this matter thoroughly. Perhaps you will tell us where the telephone is," he asked, turning my way.

It was some little time before I took in these words. When I did, I became conscious of his keen look, also of a change in my own expression. I had forgotten the telephone. It had not yet been taken out. If only I had remembered this before these men came—I might have saved—No, nothing could have saved her or me, except the snow, except the snow. That may already have saved her. All this time I was trying to tell where the telephone was.

That I succeeded at last I judged from the fact that the second man left the room. As he did so, Hexford lit the candle. Idly watching, for nothing now could make me look at the lounge again, I noticed the candlestick. It was of brass and rare in style and workmanship—a candlestick to be remembered; one of a pair perhaps. I felt my hair stir as I took in the details of its shape and ornamentation. If its mate were in her house—No, no, no! I would not have it so. I could not control my emotion if I let my imagination stray too far. The candlestick must be the property of the club. I had only forgotten. It was bought when? While thinking, planning, I was conscious of Hexford's eyes fixed steadily upon me.

"Did you go into the kitchen in your wanderings below?" he asked.

"No," I began, but seeing that I had made a mistake, I bungled and added weakly: "Yes; after matches."

"Only matches?"

"That's all."

"And did you get them?"

"Yes."

"In the dark? You must have had trouble in finding them?"

"Not at all. Only safety matches are allowed here, and they are put in a receptacle at the side of each door. I had but to open the kitchen door, feel along the jamb, find this receptacle, and pull the box out. I'm well used to all parts of the house."

"And you did this?"

"I have said so."

"May I ask which door you allude to?"

"The one communicating with the front hall."

"Where did you light your first match?"

"Upstairs."

"Not in the kitchen?"

"No, sir."

"You are sure?"

"Quite sure."

"That's a pity. I thought you might be able to tell me how so many wine and whiskey bottles came to be standing on the kitchen table."

I stared at him, dazed. Then I remembered the two small glasses on the little table across the room, and instinctively glanced at them. But no whiskey had been drunk out of them—the odor of anisette is unmistakable.

"You carry the key to the wine-cellar?" he asked.

I considered a moment. I did not know what to make of bottles on the kitchen table. These women and bottles! They abhorred wine; they had reason to, God knows; T remembered the dinner and all that had signalised it, and felt my confusion grow. But a question had been asked, and I must answer it. It would not do for me to hesitate about a matter of this kind. Only what was the question. Something about a key. I had no key; the cellar had been ransacked without my help; should I acknowledge this?

"The keys were given up by the janitor yesterday," I managed to stammer at last. "But I did not bring them here to-night. They are in my rooms at home."

I finished with a gasp. I had suddenly remembered that these keys were not in my rooms. I had had them with me at Miss Cumberland's and being given to fooling with something when embarrassed, I had fooled with them and dropped them while talking with Adelaide and watching Carmel. I had meant to pick them up but I forgot and—

"You need say nothing more about it," remarked Hexford. "I have no right to question you at all." And stepping across the room, he took up the glasses one after the other and smelled of them. "Some sweet stuff," he remarked. "Cordial, I should say anisette. There wasn't anything like that on the kitchen table. Let us see what there is in here," he added, stepping into the adjoining small room into which I had simply peered in my own investigation of the place.

As he did so, a keen blast blew in; a window in the adjoining room was open. He cast me a hurried glance and with the door in his hand, made the following remark:

"Your lady love—the victim here—could not have come through the snow with no more clothing on her than we see now. She must have worn a hat and coat or furs or something of that nature. Let us look for them."

I rose, stumbling. I saw that he did not mean to leave me alone for a moment. Indeed, I did not wish to be so left. Better any companionship than that of my own thoughts and of her white upturned face. As I followed him into this closet he pushed the door wide, pulling out an electric torch as he did so. By its light we saw almost at first glance the coat and hat he professed to seek, lying in a corner of the floor, beside an overturned chair.

"Good!" left my companion's lips. "That's all straight. You recognise these garments?"

I nodded, speechless. A thousand memories rushed upon me at the sight of the long plush coat which I had so often buttoned about her, with a troubled heart. How her eyes would seek mine as we stood thus close together, searching, searching for the old love or the fancied love of which the ashes only remained. Torment, all torment to remember now, as Hexford must have seen, if the keenness of his intelligence equalled that of his eye at this moment.

The window which stood open was a small one,-a mere slit in the wall; but it let in a stream of zero air and I saw Hexford shiver as he stepped towards it and looked out. But I felt hot rather than cold, and when I instinctively put my hand to my forehead, it came away wet.

CHAPTER V

A SCRAP OF PAPER

Look to the lady:—
And when we have our naked frailties hid,
That suffer in exposure, let us meet,
And question this most bloody piece of work,
To know it further. Fears and scruples shake us;
In the great hand of God I stand; and, thence,
Against the undivulg'd pretence I fight
Of treasonous malice.

Macbeth.

Shortly after this, a fresh relay of police arrived and I could hear the whole house being ransacked. I had found my shoes, and was sitting in my own private room before a fire which had been lighted for me on the hearth. I was in a state of stupor now, and if my body shook, as it did from time to time, it was not from cold, nor do I think from any special horror of mind or soul (I felt too dull for that), but in response to the shuddering pines which pressed up close to the house at this point and soughed and tapped at the walls and muttered among themselves with an insistence which I could not ignore, notwithstanding my many reasons for self-absorption.

The storm, which had been exceedingly fierce while it lasted, had quieted down to a steady fall of snow. Had its mission been to serve as a blanket to this crime by wiping out from the old snow all tell-tale footsteps and such other records as simplify cases of this kind for the detectives, it could not have happened more apropos to the event. From the complaints which had already reached my ears from the two policemen, I was quite aware that even as early as their first arrival, they had found a clean page where possibly a few minutes before the whole secret of this tragedy may have been written in unmistakable characters; and while this tilled me with relief in one way, it added to my care in another, for the storm which could accomplish so much in so short a time was a bitter one for a young girl to meet, and Carmel must have met it at its worst, in her lonesome struggle homeward.

Where was she? Living or dead, where was she now and where was Adelaide—the two women who for the last six weeks had filled my life with so many unhallowed and conflicting emotions? The conjecture passed incessantly through my brain, but it passed idly also and was not answered even in thought. Indeed, I seemed incapable of sustaining any line of thought for more than an instant, and when after an indefinite length of time the door behind me opened, the look I turned upon the gentleman who entered must have been a strange and far from encouraging one.

He brought a lantern with him. So far the room had had no other illumination than such as came from the fire, and when he had set this lantern down on the mantel and turned to face me, I perceived, with a sort of sluggish hope, that he was Dr. Perry, once a practising physician and my father's intimate friend, now a county official of no ordinary intelligence and, what was better, of no ordinary feeling.

His attachment to my father had not descended to me and, for the moment, he treated me like a stranger.

"I am the coroner of this district," said he. "I have left my bed to have a few words with you and learn if your detention here is warranted. You are the president of this club, and the lady whose violent death in this place I have been called upon to investigate, is Miss Cumberland, your affianced wife?"

My assent, though hardly audible, was not to be misunderstood. Drawing up a chair, he sat down and something in his manner which was not wholly without sympathy, heartened me still more, dispelling some of the cloudiness which had hitherto befogged my faculties.

"They have told me what you had to say in explanation of your presence here where a crime of some nature has taken place. But I should like to hear the story from your own lips. I feel that I owe you this consideration. At all events, I am disposed to show it. This is no common case of violence and the parties to it are not of the common order. Miss Cumberland's virtue and social standing no one can question, while you are the son of a man who has deservedly been regarded as an honour to the town. You have been intending to marry Miss Cumberland?"

"Yes." I looked the man directly in the eye. "Our wedding-day was set."

"Did you love her? Pardon me; if I am to be of any benefit to you at this crisis I must strike at the root of things. If you do not wish to answer, say so, Mr. Ranelagh."

"I do wish." This was a lie, but what was I to do, knowing how dangerous it would be for Carmel to have it publicly known where my affections were really centred and what a secret tragedy of heart-struggle and jealous passion underlay this open one of foul and murderous death. "I am in no position to conceal anything from you. I did love Miss Cumberland. We have been engaged for a year. She was a woman of fortune but I am not without means of my own and could have chosen a penniless girl and still been called prosperous."

"I see, and she returned your love?"

"Sincerely." Was the room light enough to reveal my guilty flush? She had loved me only too well, too jealously, too absorbingly for her happiness or mine.

"And the sister?"

It was gently but gravely put, and instantly I knew that our secret was out, however safe we had considered it. This man was cognisant of it, and if he, why not others! Why not the whole town! A danger which up to this moment I had heard whispered only by the pines, was opening in a gulf beneath our feet. Its imminence steadied me. I had kept my glance on Coroner Perry, and I do not think it changed. My tone, I am quite assured, was almost as quiet and grave as his as I made my reply in these words:

"Her sister is her sister. I hardly think that either of us would be apt to forget that. Have you heard otherwise, sir?"

He was prepared for equivocation, possibly for denial, but not for attack. His manner changed and showed distrust and I saw that I had lost rather than made by this venturous move.

"Is this your writing?" he suddenly asked, showing me a morsel of paper which he had drawn from his vest pocket.

I looked, and felt that I now understood what the pines had been trying to tell me for the last few hours. That compromising scrap of writing had not been destroyed. It existed for her and my undoing! Then doubt came. Fate could not juggle thus with human souls and purposes. I had simply imagined myself to have recognised the words lengthening and losing themselves in a blur before my eyes. Carmel was no fool even if she had wild and demoniacal moments. This could not be my note to her,—that fatal note which would make all denial of our mutual passion unavailing.

"Is it your writing?" my watchful inquisitor repeated.

I looked again. The scrap was smaller than my note had been when it left my hands. If it were the same, then some of the words were gone. Were they the first ones or the last? It would make a difference in the reading, or rather, in the conclusions to be drawn from what remained. If only the mist would clear from before my eyes, or he would hold the slip of paper nearer! The room was very dark. The—the—

"Is it your writing?" Coroner Perry asked for the third time.

There was no denying it. My writing was peculiar and quite unmistakable. I should gain nothing by saying no.

"It looks like it," I admitted reluctantly. "But I cannot be sure in this light. May I ask what this bit of paper is and where you found it?"

"Its contents I think you know. As for the last question I think you can answer that also if you will."

Saying which, he quietly replaced the scrap of paper in his pocket-book.

I followed the action with my eyes. I caught a fresh glimpse of a darkened edge, and realised the cause of the faint odour which I had hitherto experienced without being conscious of it. The scrap had been plucked out of the chimney. She had tried to burn it. I remembered the fire and the smouldering bits of paper which crumbled at my touch. And this one, this, the most important—the only important one of them all, had flown, half-scorched, up the chimney and clung there within easy reach.

The whole incident was plain to me, and I could even fix upon the moment when Hexford or Clarke discovered this invaluable bit of evidence. It was just before I burst in upon them from the ballroom, and it was the undoubted occasion of the remark I then overheard:

"This settles it. He cannot escape us now."

During the momentary silence which now ensued, I tried to remember the exact words which had composed this note. They were few—-sparks from my very heart—I ought to be able to recollect them.

"To-night—10:30 train—we will be married at P—. Come, come, my darling, my life. She will forgive when all is done. Hesitation will only undo us. To-night at 10 30. Do not fail me. I shall never marry any one but you."

Was that all? I had an indistinct remembrance of having added some wild and incoherent words of passionate affection affixed to her name. Her name! But it may be that in the hurry and flurry of the moment, these terms of endearment simply passed through my mind and found no expression on paper. I could not be sure, any more than I could be positive from the half glimpse I got of these lines, which portion had been burned off,—the top in which the word train occurred, or the final words, emphasising a time of meeting and my determination to marry no one but the person addressed. The first gone, the latter might take on any sinister meaning. The latter gone, the first might prove a safeguard, corroborating my statement that an errand had taken me into town.

I was oppressed by the uncertainty of my position. Even if I carried off this detail successfully, others of equal importance might be awaiting explanation. My poor, maddened, guilt-haunted girl had made the irreparable mistake of letting this note of mine fly unconsumed up the chimney, and she might have made others equally incriminating. It would be hard to find an alibi for her if suspicion once turned her way. She had not met me at the train. The unknown but doubtless easily-to-be-found man who had handed me her note could swear to that fact.

Then the note itself! I had destroyed it, it is true, but its phrases were so present to my mind—had been so branded into it by the terrors of the tragedy which they appeared to foreshadow, that I had a dreadful feeling that this man's eye could read them there. I remember that under the compelling power of this fancy, my hand rose to my brow outspread and concealing, as if to interpose a barrier between him and them. Is my folly past belief? Possibly. But then I have not told you the words of this fatal communication. They were these—innocent, if she were innocent, but how suggestive in the light of her probable guilt:

"I cannot. Wait till to-morrow. Then you will see the depth of my love for you—what I owe you—what I owe Adelaide."

I should see!

I was seeing.

Suddenly I dropped my hand; a new thought had come to me. Had Carmel been discovered on the road leading from this place?

You perceive that by this time I had become the prey of every threatening possibility; even of that which made the present a nightmare from which I should yet wake to old conditions and old struggles, bad enough, God knows, but not like this—not like this.

Meantime I was conscious that not a look or movement of mine had escaped the considerate but watchful eye of the man before me.

"You do not relish my questions," he dryly observed. "Perhaps you would rather tell your story without interruption. If so, I beg you to be as explicit as possible. The circumstances are serious enough for perfect candour on your part."

He was wrong. They were too serious for that. Perfect candour would involve Carmel. Seeming candour was all I could indulge in. I took a quick resolve. I would appear to throw discretion to the winds; to confide to him what men usually hold sacred; to risk my reputation as a gentleman, rather than incur a suspicion which might involve others more than it did myself. Perhaps I should yet win through and save her from an ignominy she possibly deserved but which she must never receive at my hands.

"I will give you an account of my evening," said I. "It will not aid you much, but will prove my good faith. You asked me a short time ago if I loved the lady whom I was engaged to marry and whose dead body I most unexpectedly came upon in this house some time before midnight. I answered yes, and you showed that you doubted me. You were justified in your doubts. I did love her once, or thought so, but my feelings changed. A great temptation came into my life. Carmel returned from school and—you know her beauty, her fascination. A week in her presence, and marriage with Adelaide became impossible. But how evade it? I only knew the coward's way; to lure this inexperienced young girl, fresh from school, into a runaway match. A change which now became perceptible in Miss Cumberland's manner, only egged me on. It was not sufficiently marked in character to call for open explanation, yet it was unmistakable to one on the watch as I was, and betokened a day of speedy reckoning for which I was little prepared. I know what the manly course would have been, but I preferred to skulk. I acknowledge it now; it is the only retribution I have to offer for a past I am ashamed of. Without losing one particle of my intention, I governed more carefully my looks and actions, and thought I had succeeded in blinding Adelaide to my real feelings and purpose. Whether I did or not, I cannot say. I have no means of knowing now. She has not been her natural self for these last few days, but she had other causes for worry, and I have been willing enough to think that these were the occasion of her restless ways and short, sharp speech and the blankness with which she met all my attempts to soothe and encourage her. This evening"—I choked at the word. The day had been one string of extraordinary experiences, accumulating in intensity to the one ghastly discovery which had overtopped and overwhelmed all the rest. "This evening," I falteringly continued, "I had set as the limit to my endurance of the intolerable situation. During a minute of solitude preceding the dinner at Miss Cumberland's house on the Hill, I wrote a few lines to her sister, urging her to trust me with her fate and meet me at the station in time for the ten-thirty train. I meant to carry her at once to P—, where I had a friend in the ministry who would at once unite us in marriage. I was very peremptory, for my nerves were giving way under the secret strain to which they had been subjected for so long, and she herself was looking worn with her own silent and uncommunicated conflict.

"To write this note was easy, but to deliver it involved difficulties. Miss Cumberland's eyes seemed to be more upon me than usual. Mine were obliged to respond and Carmel seeing this, kept hers on her plate or on the one other person seated at the table, her brother Arthur. But the opportunity came as we all rose and passed together into the drawing-room. Carmel fell into place at my side and I slipped the note into her hand. She had not expected it and I fear that the action was observed, for when I took my leave of Miss Cumberland shortly after, I was struck by her expression. I had never seen such a look on her face before, nor can I conceive of one presenting a more extraordinary contrast to the few and commonplace words with which she bade me good evening. I could not forget that look. I continued to see those pinched features and burning eyes all the way home where I went to get my grip-sack, and I saw them all the way to the station, though my thoughts were with her sister and the joys I had planned for myself. Man's egotism, Dr. Perry. I neither knew Adelaide nor did I know the girl whose love I had so over-estimated. She failed me, Dr. Perry. I was met at the station not by herself, but by a letter—a few hurried lines given me by an unknown man—in which she stated that I had asked too much of her, that she could not so wrong her sister who had brought her up and done everything for her since her mother died. I have not that letter now, or I would show it to you. In my raging disappointment I tore it up on the place where I received it, and threw the pieces away. I had staked my whole future on one desperate throw and I had lost. If I had had a pistol—" I stopped, warned by an uneasy movement on the part of the man I addressed, that I had better not dilate too much upon my feelings. Indeed, I had forgotten to whom I was talking. I realised nothing, thought of nothing but the misery I was describing. His action recalled me to the infinitely deeper misery of my present situation, and conscious of the conclusions which might be drawn from such impulsive utterances, I pulled myself together and proceeded to finish my story with greater directness.

"I did not leave the station till the ten-thirty train had gone. I had hopes, still, of seeing her, or possibly I dreaded the long ride back to my apartments. It was from sheer preoccupation of mind that I drove this way instead of straight out by Marshall Avenue. I had no intention of stopping here; the club-house was formally closed yesterday, as you may know, and I did not even have the keys with me. But, as I reached the bend in the road where you get your first sight of the buildings, I saw a thin streak of smoke rising from one of its chimneys, and anxious as to its meaning, I drove in—"

"Wait, Mr. Ranelagh, I am sorry to interrupt you, but by which gate did you enter?"

"By the lower one."

"Was it snowing at this time?"

"Not yet. It was just before the clouds rushed upon the moon. I could see everything quite plainly."

My companion nodded and I went breathlessly on. Any question of his staggered me. I was so ignorant of the facts at his command, of the facts at any one's command outside my own experience and observation, that the simplest admission I made might lead directly to some clew of whose very existence I was unaware. I was not even able to conjecture by what chance or at whose suggestion the police had raided the place and discovered the tragedy which had given point to that raid. No one had told me, and I had met with no encouragement to ask. I felt myself sliding amid pitfalls. My own act might precipitate the very doom I sought to avert. Yet I must preserve my self-possession and answer all questions as truthfully as possible lest I stumble into a web from which no skill of my own or of another could extricate me.

"Fastening my horse to one of the pine trees in the thickest clump I saw—he is there now, I suppose—I crept up to the house, and tried the door. It was on the latch and I stole in. There was no light on the lower floor, and after listening for any signs of life, I began to feel my way about the house, searching for the intruder. As I did not wish to attract attention to myself, I took off my shoes. I went through the lower rooms, and then I came upstairs. It was some time before I reached the—the room where a fire had been lit; but when I did I knew—not," I hastily corrected, as I caught his quick concentrated glance, "what had happened or whom I should find there, but that this was the spot where the intruder had been, possibly was now, and I determined to grapple with him. What—what have I said?" I asked in anguish, as I caught a look on the coroner's face of irrepressible repulsion and disgust, slight and soon gone but unmistakable so long as it lasted.

"Nothing," he replied, "go on."

But his tone, considerate as it had been from the first, did not deceive me. I knew that I had been detected in some slip or prevarication. As I had omitted all mention of the most serious part of my adventure—had said nothing of my vision of Carmel or the terrible conclusions which her presence there had awakened—my conscience was in a state of perturbation which added greatly to my confusion. For a moment I did not know where I stood, and I am afraid I betrayed a sense of my position. He had to recall me to myself by an unimportant question or two before I could go on. When I did proceed, it was with less connection of ideas and a haste in speaking which was not due altogether to the harrowing nature of the tale itself.

"I had matches in my pocket and I struck one," I began. "Afterwards I lit the candle. The emptiness of the room did not alarm me. I experienced the sense of tragedy. Seeing the pillows heaped high and too regularly for chance along a lounge ordinarily holding only two, I tore them off. I saw a foot, a hand, a tress of bright hair. Even then I did not think of her. Why should I? Not till I uncovered the face did I know the terrors of my discovery, and then, the confusion of it all unmanned me and I fell on my knees—"

"Go on! Go on!"

The impetuosity, the suspense in the words astounded me. I stared at the coroner and lost the thread of my story—What had I to say more? How account for what must be ever unaccountable to him, to the world, to my own self, if in obedience to the demands of the situation I subdued my own memory and blotted out all I had seen but that which it was safe to confess to?

"There is no more to say," I murmured. "The horror of that moment made a chaos in my mind. I looked at the dead body of her who lay there as I have looked at everything since; as I looked at the police when they came—as I look at you now. But I know nothing. It is all a phantasmagoria to me—with no more meaning than a nightmare. She is dead—I know that—but beyond that, all is doubt—confusion—what the world and all its passing show is to a blind man. I can neither understand nor explain."

CHAPTER VI

COMMENTS AND REFLECTIONS

There is no agony and no solace left;
Earth can console,
Heaven can torment, no more

Prometheus Unbound

The coroner's intent look which had more or less sustained me through this ordeal, remained fixed upon my face as though he were still anxious to see me exonerate myself. How much did he know? That was the question. How much did he know?

Having no means of telling, I was forced to keep silent. I had revealed all I dared to. As I came to this conclusion, his eyes fell and I knew that the favorable minute had passed.

The question he now asked proved it.

"You say that you were not blind to surrounding objects, even if they conveyed but little meaning to you. You must have seen, then, that the room where Miss Cumberland lay contained two small cordial glasses, both still moist with some liqueur."

"I noticed that, yes."

"Some one must have drunk with her?"

"I cannot contradict you."

"Was Miss Cumberland fond of that sort of thing?"

"She detested liquor of all kinds. She never drank I never saw a woman so averse to wine." I spoke before I thought. I might better have been less emphatic, but the mystery of those glasses had affected me from the first. Neither she nor Carmel ever allowed themselves so much as a social glass, yet those glasses had been drained. "Perhaps the cold—"

"There was a third glass. We found it in the adjoining closet. It had not been used. That third glass has a meaning if only we could find it out."

A possibility which had risen in my mind faded at these words.

"Three glasses," I dully repeated.

"And a small flask of cordial. The latter seems pure enough."

"I cannot understand it." The phrase had become stereotyped. No other suggested itself to me.

"The problem would be simple enough if it were not for those-marks on her neck. You saw those, too, I take it?"

"Yes. Who made them? What man—"

The lie, or rather the suggestion of a lie, flushed my face. I was conscious of this, but it did not trouble me. I was panting for relief. I could not rest till I knew the nature of the doubt in this man's mind. If these words, or any words I could use, would serve to surprise his secret, then welcome the lie or suggestion of a lie. "It was a brute's act," I went on, bungling with my sentences in anxiety to see if my conclusions fitted in with his own. "Who was the brute? Do you know, Dr. Perry?"

"There were three glasses in those rooms. Only two were drank from," he answered, steadily. "Tomorrow I may be in a position to answer your question. I am not to-night."

Why did I take heart? Not a change, not the flicker of one had passed over his countenance at my utterance of the word man. Either his official habit had stood him in wonderful stead, or the police had failed so far to see any connection between this murder and the young girl whose footprints, for all I knew, still lingered on the stairs.

Would the morrow arm them with completer knowledge? As I turned from his retreating figure and flung myself down before the hearth, this was the question I continually propounded to myself, in vain repetition. Would the morrow reveal the fact that Adelaide's young sister had been with her in the hour of death, or would the fates propitiously aid her in preserving this secret as they had already aided her in selecting for the one man who shared it, him who of all others was bound by honour and personal consideration for her not to divulge what he knew.

Thus the hours between two and seven passed when I fell into a fitful sleep, from which I was rudely wakened by a loud rattle at my door, followed by the entrance of the officer who had walked up and down the corridor all night.

"The waggon is here," said he. "Breakfast will be given you at the station."

To which Hexford, looking over his shoulder, added: "I'm sorry to say that we have here the warrant for your arrest. Can I do anything for you?"

"Warrant!" I burst out, "what do you want of a warrant? It is as a witness you seek to detain me, I presume?"

"No," was his brusque reply. "The charge upon which you are arrested is one of murder. You will have to appear before a magistrate. I'm sorry to be the one to tell you this, but the evidence against you is very strong, and the police must do their duty."

"But I am innocent, absolutely innocent," I protested, the perspiration starting from every pore as the full meaning of the charge burst upon me. "What I have told you was correct. I, myself, found her dead—"

Hexford gave me a look.

"Don't talk," he kindly suggested. "Leave that to the lawyers." Then, as the other man turned aside for a moment, he whispered in my ear, "It's no go; one of our men saw you with your fingers on her throat. He had clambered into a pine tree and the shade of the window was up. You had better come quietly. Not a soul believes you innocent."

This, then, was what had doomed me from the start; this, and that partly burned letter. I understood now why the kind-hearted coroner, who loved my father, had urged me to tell my tale, hoping that I would explain this act and give him some opportunity to indulge in a doubt. And I had failed to respond to the hint he had given me. The act itself must appear so sinister and the impulse which drove me to it so incomprehensible, without the heart-rending explanation I dare not subjoin, that I never questioned the wisdom of silence in its regard.

Yet this silence had undone me. I had been seen fingering my dead betrothed's throat, and nothing I could now say or do would ever convince people that she was dead before my hands touched her, strangled by another's clutch. One person only in the whole world would know and feel how false this accusation was. And yesterday that one's trust in my guiltlessness would have thrown a ray of light upon the deepest infamy which could befall me. But to-day there had settled over that once innocent spirit, a cloud of too impenetrable a nature for any light to struggle to and fro between us.

I could not contemplate that cloud. I could not dwell upon her misery, or upon the revulsion of feeling which follows such impetuous acts. And it had been an impetuous act—the result of one of her rages. I had been told of these rages. I had even seen her in one. When they passed she was her lovable self once more and very penitent and very downcast. If all I feared were true, she was suffering acutely now. But I gave no thought to this. I could dream of but one thing—how to save her from the penalty of crime, a penalty I might be forced to suffer myself and would prefer to suffer rather than see it fall upon one so young and so angelically beautiful.

Turning to the officer next me, I put the question which had been burning in my mind for hours:

"Tell me, how you came to know there was trouble here? What brought you to this house? There can be nothing wrong in telling me that."

"Well, if you don't know—" he began.

"I do not," I broke in.

"I guess you'd better wait till the chief has had a word with you."

I suppressed all tokens of my disappointment, and by a not unnatural reaction, perhaps, began to take in, and busy myself with, the very considerations I had hitherto shunned. Where was Carmel, and how was she enduring these awful hours? Had repentance come, and with it a desire to own her guilt? Did she think of me and the effect this unlooked-for death would have upon my feelings? That I should suffer arrest for her crime could not have entered her mind. I had seen her, but she had not seen me, in the dark hall which I must now traverse as a prisoner and a suspect. No intimation of my dubious position or its inevitable consequences had reached her yet. When it did, what would she do? I did not know her well enough to tell. The attraction she had felt for me had not been strong enough to lead her to accommodate herself to my wishes and marry me off-hand, but it had been strong enough to nerve her arm in whatever altercation she may have had with her jealous-minded sister. It was the temper and not the strength of the love which would tell in a strait like this. Would it prove of a generous kind? Should I have to combat her desire to take upon herself the full blame of her deed, with all its shames and penalties? Or should I have the still deeper misery of finding her callous to my position and welcoming any chance which diverted suspicion from herself? Either supposition might be possible, according to my judgment in this evil hour. All communication between us, in spite of our ardent and ungovernable passion, had been so casual and so slight. Looks, a whispered word or so, one furtive clasp in which our hands seemed to grow together, were all I had to go upon as tests of her feeling towards me. Her character I had judged from her face, which was lovely. But faces deceive, and the loveliness of youth is not like the loveliness of age—an absolute mirror of the soul within. Was not Medusa captivating, for all her snaky locks? Hide those locks and one might have thought her a Daphne.

What would relieve my doubts? As Hexford drew near me again on our way to the head of the staircase, I summoned up courage to ask:

"Have you heard anything from the Hill? Has the news of this tragedy been communicated to Miss Cumberland's family, and if so, how are they bearing this affliction?"

His lip curled, and for a minute he hesitated; then something in my aspect or the straight-forward look I gave him, softened him and he answered frankly, if coldly:

"Word has gone there, of course, but only the servants are affected by it so far. Miss Cumberland, the younger, is very ill, and the boy—I don't know his name—has not shown up since last evening. He's very dissipated, they say, and may be in any one of the joints in the lower part of the town."

I stopped in dismay, clutching wildly at the railing of the stairs we were descending. I had hardly heard the latter words, all my mind was on what he had said first.

"Miss Carmel Cumberland ill?" I stammered, "too ill to be told?"

I was sufficiently master of myself to put it this way.

"Yes," he rejoined, kindly, as he urged me down the very stairs I had seen her descend in such a state of mind a few hours before. "A servant who had been out late, heard the fall of some heavy body as she was passing Miss Cumberland's rooms, and rushing in found Miss Carmel, as she called her, lying on the floor near the open fire. Her face had struck the bars of the grate in falling, and she was badly burned. But that was not all; she was delirious with fever, brought on, they think, by anxiety about her sister, whose name she was constantly repeating. They had a doctor for her and the whole house was up before ever the word came of what had happened here."

I thanked him with a look. I had no opportunity for more. Half a dozen officers were standing about the front door, and in another moment I was bustled into the conveyance provided and was being driven away from the death-haunted spot.

I had heard the last whisper of those pines for many, many days. But not in my dreams; it ever came back at night, sinister, awesome, haunted with dead hopes and breathing of an ever doubtful future.

CHAPTER VII

CLIFTON ACCEPTS MY CASE

This hand of mine Is yet a maiden and an innocent hand,
Not painted with the crimson spots of blood.
Within this bosom never enter'd yet
The dreadful motion of a murd'rous thought.

King John.

My first thought (when I could think at all) was this:

"She has some feeling, then! Her terror and remorse have maddened her. I can dwell upon her image with pity." The next, "Will they find her wet clothes and discover that she was out last night?" The latter possibility troubled me. My mind was the seat of strange contradictions.

As the day advanced and I began to realise that I, Elwood Ranelagh, easy-going man of the world, but with traditions of respectable living on both sides of my house and a list of friends of which any man might be proud, was in a place of detention on the awful charge of murder, I found that my keenest torment arose from the fact that I was shut off from the instant knowledge of what was going on in the house where all my thoughts, my fears, and shall I say it, latent hopes were centred. To know Carmel ill and not to know how ill! To feel the threatening arm of the law hovering constantly over her head and neither to know the instant of its fall nor be given the least opportunity to divert it. To realise that some small inadvertance on her part, some trivial but incriminating object left about, some heedless murmur or burst of unconscious frenzy might precipitate her doom, and I remain powerless, bearing my share of suspicion and ignominy, it is true, but not the chief share if matters befell as I have suggested, which they were liable to do at any hour, nay, at any minute.

My examination before the magistrate held one element of comfort. Nothing in its whole tenor went to show that, as yet, she was in the least suspected of any participation in my so-called crime. But the knowledge which came later, of how the police first learned of trouble at the club-house did not add to this sense of relief, whatever satisfaction it gave my curiosity. A cry of distress had come to them over the telephone; a wild cry, in a woman's choked and tremulous voice: "Help at The Whispering Pines! Help!" That was all, or all they revealed to me. In their endeavour to find out whether or not I was present when this call was made, I learned the nature of their own suspicions. They believed that Adelaide in some moment of prevision had managed to reach the telephone and send out this message. But what did I believe? What could I believe? All the incidents of the deadly struggle which must have preceded the fatal culminating act, were mysteries which my mind refused to penetrate. After hours of torturing uncertainty, and an evening which was the miserable precursor of a still more miserable night, I decided to drop conjecture and await the enlightenment which must come with the morrow.

It was, therefore, in a condition of mingled dread and expectation that I opened the paper which was brought me the next morning. Of the shock which it gave me to see my own name blotting the page with suggestions of hideous crime, I will not speak, but pass at once to the few gleams of added knowledge I was able to gather from those abominable columns. Arthur, the good-for-nothing brother, had returned from his wild carouse and had taken affairs in charge with something like spirit and a decent show of repentance for his own shortcomings and the mad taste for liquor which had led him away from home that night. Carmel was still ill, and likely to be so for many days to come. Her case was diagnosed as one of brain fever and of a most dangerous type. Doctors and nurses were busy at her bedside and little hope was held out of her being able to tell soon, if ever, what she knew of her sister's departure from the house on that fatal evening. That her testimony on this point would be invaluable was self-evident, for proofs were plenty of her having haunted her sister's rooms all the evening in a condition of more or less delirium. She was alone in the house and this may have added to her anxieties, all of the servants having gone to the policemen's ball. It was on their return in the early morning hours that she had been discovered, lying ill and injured before her sister's fireplace.

One fact was mentioned which set me thinking. The keys of the club-house had been found lying on a table in the side hall of the Cumberland mansion—the keys which I have already mentioned as missing from my pocket. An alarming discovery which might have acted as a clew to the suspicious I feared, if their presence there had not been explained by the waitress who had cleared the table after dinner. Coming upon these keys lying on the floor beside one of the chairs, she had carried them out into the hall and laid them where they would be more readily seen. She had not recognised the keys, but had taken it for granted that they belonged to Mr. Ranelagh who had dined at the house that night.

They were my keys, and I have already related how I came to drop them on the floor. Had they but stayed there! Adelaide, or was it Carmel, might not have seen them and been led by some strange, if not tragic, purpose, incomprehensible to us now and possibly never to find full explanation, to enter the secret and forsaken spot where I later found them, the one dead, the other fleeing in frenzy, but not in such a thoughtless frenzy as to forget these keys or to fail to lock the club-house door behind her. That she, on her return home, should have had sufficient presence of mind to toss these keys down in the same place from which she or her sister had taken them, argued well for her clear-headedness up to that moment. The fever must have come on later—a fever which with my knowledge of what had occurred at The Whispering Pines, seemed the only natural outcome of the situation.

The next paragraph detailed a fact startling enough to rouse my deepest interest. Zadok Brown, the Cumberlands' coachman, declared that Arthur's cutter and what he called the grey mare had been out that night. They were both in place when he returned to the stable towards early morning, but the signs were unmistakable that both had been out in the snow since he left the stable at about nine. He had locked the stable-door at that time, but the key always hung in the kitchen where any one could get it. This was on account of Arthur, who, if he wanted to go out late, sometimes harnessed a horse himself. Zadok judged that he had done so this night, though how the horse happened to be back and in her stall and no Mr. Arthur in the house, it would take wiser heads than his to explain. But he was sure the mare had been out.

There was some comment made on this, because Arthur had denied using his cutter that night. He declared instead that he had gone out on foot and designated the coachman's tale as all bosh. "I was not the only one who had a drop too much down-town," was the dogged assertion with which he met all questions on this subject. "I wouldn't give a snap of my finger for Zadok's opinion on any subject, after five hours of dancing and the necessary drinks. There were no signs of the mare having been out when I got home." As this was about noon the next day, his opinion on this point could not be said to count for much.

As for myself, I felt inclined to believe that the mare had been out, that one or both of the women had harnessed him and that it was by these means they had reached The Whispering Pines. The night was too cold, a storm too imminent, for them to have contemplated so long a walk on a road so remote as that leading to the club-house. Arthur was athletic but Adelaide was far from strong and never addicted to walking under the most favourable conditions. Of all the mysteries surrounding her dead presence in the club-house, the one which from the first had struck me as the most inexplicable was the manner of her reaching there. Now I could understand both that fact and how Carmel had succeeded in returning in safety to her home. She had ridden both ways—a theory which likewise explained how she came to wear a man's derby and possibly a man's overcoat. With her skirts covered by a bear-skin she would present a very fair figure of a man to any one who chanced to pass her. This was desirable in her case. A man and woman driving at a late hour through the city streets would attract little, if any, attention, while two women might. Having no wish to attract attention, they had resorted to subterfuge—or Carmel had; it was not like Adelaide to do so. She was always perfectly open, both in manner and speech.

These were my deductions drawn from my own knowledge. Would others who had not my knowledge be in any wise influenced to draw the same? Would the fact that the mare had been out during those mysterious hours when everybody had appeared to be absent from the house, saving the one young girl whom they afterwards found stark, staring mad with delirium, serve to awaken suspicion of her close and personal connection with this crime? There was nothing in this reporter's article to show that such an idea had dawned upon his mind, but the police are not readily hoodwinked and I dreaded the result of their inquiries, if they chose to follow this undoubted clew.

Yet, if they let this point slip, where should I be? Human nature is human all the way through, and I could not help having moments when I asked myself if this young girl were worth the sacrifice I contemplated making for her? She was lovely to look at, amiable and of womanly promise save at those rare and poignant moments when passion would seize her in a gust which drove everything before it. But were any of these considerations sufficient to justify me in letting my whole manhood slip for the sake of one who, whatever the provocation, had used the strength of her hands against the sister who had been as a mother to her for so many years. That she had had provocation I did not doubt. Adelaide, for all her virtues, was not an easy person to deal with. Upright and perfectly sincere herself, she had no sympathy with or commiseration for any lack of principle or any display of selfishness in others. A little cold, a little reserved, a little lacking in spontaneity, though always correct and always generous in her gifts and often in her acts, her whole nature would rise at any evidence of meanness or ingratitude, and though she said little, you would feel her disapprobation through and through. She would even change physically. Naturally pallid and of small inconspicuous features, her eyes on these occasions would so flame and her whole figure so dilate that she looked like another woman. I have seen her brother, six feet in height and weighty for his years, cringe under her few quiet words at these times till she absolutely seemed the taller of the two. It was only in these moments she was handsome, and had I loved her, I should probably have admired this passionate purity, this intolerance of all that was small or selfish or unworthy a good woman's esteem. But not loving her, I had merely cherished a wholesome fear of her displeasure, and could quite comprehend what a full display of anger on her part might call up in her sensitive, already deeply suffering sister. The scathing arraignment, the unbearable taunt—Well, well, it was all dream-work, but I had time to dream and opportunity for little else, and pictures, which till now I had sedulously kept in the background of my imagination, would come to the front as I harped on this topic and weighed in my disturbed mind the following question: Should I continue the course which I had instinctively taken out of a natural sense of chivalry, or face my calumniators with the truth and leave my cause and hers to the justice of men, rather than to the slow but righteous workings of Providence?

I struggled with the dilemma for hours, the more so, that I did not stand alone in the world. I had relatives and I had friends, some of whom had come to see me and gone away deeply grieved at my reticence. I was swayed, too, by another consideration. I had deeply loved my mother. She was dead, but I had her honour to think of. Should it be said she had a murderer for her son? In the height of my inner conflict, I had almost cried aloud the fierce denial which would arise at this thought. But ere the word could leave my lips, such a vision rose before me of a bewildering young face with wonderful eyes and a smile too innocent for guile and too loving for hypocrisy, that I forgot my late antagonistic feelings, forgot the claims of my dear, dead mother, and even those of my own future. Such passion and such devotion merited consideration from the man who had called them forth. I would not slight the claims of my dead mother but I would give this young girl a chance for her life. Let others ferret out the fact that she had visited the club-house with her sister; I would not proclaim it. It was enough for me to proclaim my innocence, and that I would do to the last.

I was in this frame of mind when Charles Clifton called and was allowed to see me. I had sent for him in one of my discouraged moods. He was my friend, but he was also my legal adviser, and it was as such I had summoned him, and it was as such he had now come. Cordial as our relations had been— though he was hardly one of my ilk—I noted no instinctive outstretching of his hand, and so did not reach out mine. Appearances had been too strong against me for any such spontaneous outburst from even my best friends. I realised that to expect otherwise from him or from any other man would be to play the fool; and this was no time for folly. The day for that was passed.

I was the first to speak.

"You see me where you have never thought to see a friend of yours. But we won't go into that. The police have good reasons for what they have done and I presume feel justified in my commitment. Notwithstanding, I am an innocent man so far as the attack made upon Miss Cumberland goes. I had no hand in her murder, if murder it is found out to be. My story which you have read in the papers and which I felt forced to give out, possibly to my own shame and that of another whom I would fain have saved, is an absolutely true one. I did not arrive at The Whispering Pines until after Miss Cumberland was dead. To this I am ready to swear and it is upon this fact you must rely, in any defence you may hereafter be called upon to make in my regard."

He listened as a lawyer would be apt to listen to such statements from the man who had summoned him to his aid. But I saw that I had made no impression on his convictions. He regarded me as a guilty man, and what was more to the point no doubt, as one for whom no plea could be made or any rational defence undertaken.

"You don't believe me," I went on, still without any great bitterness. "I am not surprised at it, after what the man Clarke has said of seeing me with my hands on her throat. Any man, friend or not, would take me for a villain after that. But, Charles, to you I will confess what cowardice kept me from owning to Dr. Perry at the proper, possibly at the only proper moment, that I did this out of a wild desire to see if those marks were really the marks of strangling fingers. I could not believe that she had been so killed and, led away by my doubts, I leaned over her and—You shall believe me, you must," I insisted, as I perceived his hard gaze remain unsoftened. "I don't ask it of the rest of the world. I hardly expect any one to give me credit for good impulses or even for speaking the plain truth after the discovery which has been made of my treacherous attitude towards these two virtuous and devoted women. But you—if you are to act as my counsel—must take this denial from me as gospel truth. I may disappoint you in other ways. I may try you and often make you regret that you undertook my case, but on this fact you may safely pin your faith. She was dead before I touched her. Had the police spy whose testimony is likely to hang me, climbed the tree a moment sooner than he did, he would have seen that. Are you ready to take my case?"

Clifton is a fair fellow and I knew if he once accepted the fact I thus urged upon him, he would work for me with all the skill and ability my desperate situation demanded. I, therefore, watched him with great anxiety for the least change in the constrained attitude and fixed, unpromising gaze with which he had listened to me, and was conscious of a great leap of heart as the set expression of his features relaxed, and he responded almost warmly:

"I will take your case, Ranelagh. God help me to make it good against all odds."

I was conscious of few hopes, but some of the oppression under which I laboured lifted at those words. I had assured one man of my innocence! It was like a great rock in the weary desert. My sigh of relief bespoke my feelings and I longed to take his hand, but the moment had not yet come. Something was wanting to a perfect confidence between us, and I was in too sensitive a frame of mind to risk the slightest rebuff.

He was ready to speak before I was. "Then, you had not been long on the scene of crime when the police arrived?"

"I had been in the room but a few minutes. I do not know how long I was searching the house."

"The police say that fully twenty minutes elapsed between the time they received Miss Cumberland's appeal for help and their arrival at the club-house. If you were there that long—"

"I cannot say. Moments are hours at such a crisis—I—"

My emotions were too much for me, and I confusedly stopped. He was surveying me with the old distrust. In a moment I saw why.

"You are not open with me," he protested. "Why should moments be hours to you previous to the instant when you stripped those pillows from the couch? You are not a fanciful man, nor have you any cowardly instincts. Why were you in such a turmoil going through a house where you could have expected to find nothing worse than some miserable sneak thief?"

This was a poser. I had laid myself open to suspicion by one thoughtless admission, and what was worse, it was but the beginning in all probability of many other possible mistakes. I had never taken the trouble to measure my words and the whole truth being impossible, I necessarily must make a slip now and then. He had better be warned of this. I did not wish him to undertake my cause blindfolded. He must understand its difficulties while believing in my innocence. Then, if he chose to draw back, well and good. I should have to face the situation alone.

"Charles," said I, as soon as I could perfectly control my speech, "you are quite just in your remark. I am not and can not be perfectly open with you. I shall tell you no lies, but beyond that I cannot promise. I am caught in a net not altogether of my own weaving. So far I will be frank with you. A common question may trip me up, others find me free and ready with my defence. You have chanced upon one of the former. I was in a turmoil of mind from the moment of my entrance into that fatal house, but I can give no reason for it unless I am, as you hinted, a coward."

He settled that supposition with a gesture I had rather not have seen. It would be better for him to consider me a poltroon than to suspect my real reasons for the agitation which I had acknowledged.

"You say you cannot be open with me. That means you have certain memories connected with that night which you cannot divulge."

"Right, Charles; but not memories of guilt—of active guilt, I mean. This I have previously insisted on, and this is what you must believe. I am not even an accessory before the fact. I am perfectly innocent so far as Adelaide's death is concerned. You may proceed on that basis without fear. That is, if you continue to take an interest in my case. If not, I shall be the last to blame you. Little honour is likely to accrue to you from defending me."

"I have accepted the case and I shall continue to interest myself in it," he assured me, with a dogged rather than genial persistence. "But I should like to know what I am to work upon, if it cannot be shown that her call for help came before you entered the building."

"That would be the best defence possible, of course," I replied; "but neither from your standpoint nor mine is it a feasible one. I have no proof of my assertion, I never looked at my watch from the time I left the station till I found it run down this very morning. The club-house clock has been out of order for some time and was not running. All I know and can swear to about the length of time I was in that building prior to the arrival of the police, is that it could not have been very long, since she was not only dead and buried under those accumulated cushions, but in a room some little distance from the telephone."

"That will do for me," said he, "but scarcely for those who are prejudiced against you. Everything points so indisputably to your guilt. The note which you say you wrote to Carmel to meet you at the station looks very much more like one to Miss Cumberland to meet you at the club-house."

It was thus I first learned which part of this letter had been burned off.[1]

[Footnote :1 It was the top portion, leaving the rest to read:

"Come, come my darling, my life. She will forgive when all is done. Hesitation will only undo us. To-night at 10:30. I shall never marry any one but you."

It was also evident that I had failed to add those expressions of affection linked to Carmel's name which had been in my mind and awakened my keenest apprehension.]

"Otherwise," he pursued, "what could have taken her there? Everybody who knew her will ask that. Such a night! so soon after seeing you! It is a mystery any way, but one entirely inconceivable without some such excuse for her. These lines said 'Come!' and she went, for reasons which may be clear to you who were acquainted with her weak as well as strong points. Went how? No one knows. By chance or by intention on her part or yours, every servant was out of the house by nine o'clock, and her brother, too. Only the sister remained, the sister whom you profess to have urged to leave the town with you that very evening; and she can tell us nothing,—may die without ever being able to do so. Some shock to her feelings—you may know its character and you may not—drove her from a state of apparent health into the wildest delirium in a few hours. It was not your letter—if your story is true about that letter—or she would have shown its effect immediately upon receiving it; that is, in the early evening. And she did not. Helen, one of the maids, declares that she saw her some time after you left the house, and that she wore anything but a troubled look; that, in fact, her countenance was beaming and so beautiful that, accustomed as the girl was to her young mistress's good looks, she was more than struck by her appearance and spoke of it afterwards at the ball. A telling circumstance against you, Ranelagh, not only contradicting your own story but showing that her after condition sprang from some sudden and extreme apprehension in connection with her sister. Did you speak?"

No, I had not spoken. I had nothing to say. I was too deeply shaken by what he had just told me, to experience anything but the utmost confusion of ideas. Carmel beaming and beautiful at an hour I had supposed her suffering and full of struggle! I could not reconcile it with the letter she had written me, or with that understanding with her sister which ended so hideously in The Whispering Pines.

The lawyer, seeing my helpless state, proceeded with his presentation of my case as it looked to unprejudiced eyes.

"Miss Cumberland comes to the club-house; so do you. You have not the keys and so go searching about the building till you find an unlocked window by which you both enter. There are those who say you purposely left this window unfastened when you went about the house the day before; that you dropped the keys in her house where they would be sure to be found, and drove down to the station and stood about there for a good half hour, in order to divert suspicion from yourself afterwards and create an alibi in case it should be wanted. I do not believe any of this myself, not since accepting your assurance of innocence, but there are those who do believe it firmly and discern in the whole affair a cool and premeditated murder. Your passion for Carmel, while not generally known, has not passed unsuspected by your or her intimates; and this in itself is enough to give colour to these suspicions, even if you had not gone so far as to admit its power over you and the extremes to which you were willing to go to secure the wife you wished. So much for the situation as it appears to outsiders. Of the circumstantial evidence which links you personally to this crime, we have already spoken. It is very strong and apparently unassailable. But truth is truth, and if you only felt free to bare your whole soul to me as you now decline to do, I should not despair of finding some weak link in the chain which seems so satisfactory to the police and, I am forced to add, to the general public."

"Charles—"

I was very near unbosoming myself to him at that moment. But I caught myself back in time. While Carmel lay ill and unconscious, I would not clear my name at her expense by so much as a suggestion.

"Charles," I repeated, but in a different tone and with a different purpose, "how do they account for the cordial that was drunk—the two emptied glasses and the flask which were found in the adjacent closet?"

"It's one of the affair's conceded incongruities. Miss Cumberland is a well-known temperance woman. Had the flask and glasses not come from her house, you would get no one to believe that she had had anything to do with them. Have you any hint to give on this point? It would be a welcome addition to our case."

Alas! I was as much puzzled by those emptied cordial glasses as he was, and told him so; also by the presence of the third unused one. As I dwelt in thought on the latter circumstance, I remembered the observation which Coroner Perry had made concerning it.

"Coroner Perry speaks of a third and unused glass which was found with the flask," I ventured, tentatively. "He seemed to consider it an important item, hiding some truth that would materially help this case. What do you think, or rather, what is the general opinion on this point?"

"I have not heard. I have seen the fact mentioned, but without comment. It is a curious circumstance. I will make a note of it. You have no suggestions to offer on the subject?"

"None."

"The clew is a small one," he smiled.

"So is the one offered by the array of bottles found on the kitchen table; yet the latter may lead directly to the truth. Adelaide never dug those out of the cellar where they were locked up, and I'm sure I did not. Yet I suppose I'm given credit for doing so."

"Naturally. The key to the wine-vault was the only key which was lacking from the bunch left at Miss Cumberland's. That it was used to open the wine-vault door is evident from the fact that it was found in the lock."

This was discouraging. Everything was against me. If the whole affair had been planned with an intent to inculpate me and me only, it could not have been done with more attention to detail, nor could I have found myself more completely enmeshed. Yet I knew, both from circumstances and my own instinct that no such planning had occurred. I was a victim, not of malice but of blind chance, or shall I say of Providence? As to this one key having been slipped from the rest and used to open the wine-vault for wine which nobody wanted and nobody drank—this must be classed with the other incongruities which might yet lead to my enlargement.

"You may add this coincidence to the other," I conceded, after I had gone thus far in my own mind. "I swear that I had nothing to do with that key."

Neither could I believe that it had been used or even carried there by Adelaide or Carmel, though I knew that the full ring of keys had been in their hands and that they had entered the building by means of one of them. So assured was I of their innocence in this regard that the idea which afterwards assumed such proportions in all our minds had, at this moment, its first dawning in mine, as well as its first outward expression.

"Some other man than myself was thirsty that night," I firmly declared. "We are getting on, Charles."

Evidently he did not consider the pace a very fast one, but being a cheerful fellow by nature, he simply expressed his dissatisfaction by an imperceptible shrug.

"Do you know exactly what the club-house's wine-vault contained?" he asked.

"An inventory was given me by the steward the morning we closed. It must be in my rooms."

"Your rooms have been examined. You expected that, didn't you? Probably this inventory has been found. I don't suppose it will help any."

"How should it?"

"Very true; how should it! No thoroughfare there, of course."

"No thoroughfare anywhere to-day," I exclaimed. "To-morrow some loop-hole of escape may suggest itself to me. I should like to sleep on the matter. I—I should like to sleep on it."

He saw that I had something in mind of which I had thus far given him no intimation, and he waited anxiously for me to reconsider my last words before he earnestly remarked:

"A day lost at a time like this is often a day never retrieved. Think well before you bid me leave you, unenlightened as to the direction in which you wish me to work."

But I was not ready, not by any means ready, and he detected this when I next spoke.

"I will see you to-morrow; any time to-morrow; meantime I will give you a commission which you are at liberty to perform yourself or to entrust to some capable detective. The letter, of which a portion remains, was written to Carmel, and she sent me a reply which was handed me on the station platform by a man who was a perfect stranger to me. I have hardly any memory of how the man looked, but it should be an easy task to find him and if you cannot do that, the smallest scrap of the note he gave me, and which unfortunately I tore up and scattered to the winds, would prove my veracity in this one particular and so make it easier for them to believe the rest."

His eye lightened. I presume the prospect of making any practical attempt in my behalf was welcome.

"One thing more," I now added. "My ring was missing from Miss Cumberland's hand when I took away those pillows. I have reason to think—or it is natural for me to think—that she planned to return it to me by some messenger or in some letter. Do you know if such messenger or such letter has been received at my apartments? Have you heard anything about this ring? It was a notable one and not to be confounded with any other. Any one who knew us or who had ever remarked it on her hand would be able to identify it."

"I have heard the ring mentioned," he replied, "I have even heard that the police are interested in finding it; but I have not heard that they have been successful. You encourage me much by assuring me that it was missing from her hand when you first saw her. That ring may prove our most valuable clew."

"Yes, but you must also remember that she may have taken it off before she started for the club-house."

"That is very true."

"You do not know whether they have looked for it at her home?"

"I do not."

"Will you find out, and will you see that I get all my letters?"

"I certainly will, but you must not expect to receive the latter unopened."

"I suppose not."

I said this with more cheerfulness than he evidently expected. My heart had been lightened of one load. The ring had not been discovered on Carmel as I had secretly feared.

"I will take good care of your interests from now on," he remarked, in a tone much more natural than any he had before used. "Be hopeful and show a brave front to the district attorney when he comes to interview you. I hear that he is expected home to-morrow. If you are innocent, you can face him and his whole office with calm assurance." Which showed how little he understood my real position.

There was comfort in this very thought, however, and I quietly remarked that I did not despair.

"And I will not," he emphasised, rising with an assumption of ease which left him as he remained hesitating before me.

It was my moment of advantage, and I improved it by proffering a request which had been more or less in my mind during the whole of this prolonged colloquy.

First thanking him for his disinterestedness, I remarked that he had shown me so much consideration as a lawyer, that I now felt emboldened to ask something from him as my friend.

"You are free," said I; "I am not. Miss Cumberland will be buried before I leave these four walls. I hate to think of her going to her grave without one token from the man to whom she has been only too good and who, whatever outrage he may have planned to her feelings, is not without reverence for her character and a heartfelt repentance for whatever he may have done to grieve her. Charles, a few flowers,—white—no wreath, just a few which can be placed on her breast or in her hand. You need not say whom they are from. It would seem a mockery to any one but her. Lilies, Charles. I shall feel happier to know that they are there. Will you do this for me?"

"I will."

"That is all."

Instinctively he held out his hand. I dropped mine in it; there was a slight pressure, some few more murmured words and he was gone.

I slept that night.

I entreat you then
From one that so imperfectly conjects,
You'd take no notice; nor build yourself a trouble
Out of his scattering and unsure observance:
It were not for your quiet, nor your good,
Nor for my manhood, honesty or wisdom,
To let you know my thoughts.

Othello

I slept, though a question of no small importance was agitating my mind, demanding instant consideration and a definite answer before I again saw this friend and adviser. I woke to ask if the suggestion which had come to me in our brief conversation about the bottles taken from the wine-vault, was the promising one it had then appeared, or only a fool's trick bound to end in disaster. I weighed the matter in every conceivable way, and ended by trusting to the instinct which impelled me to have resource to the one and only means by which the scent might be diverted from its original course, confusion be sown in the minds of the police, and Carmel, as well as myself, be saved from the pit gaping to receive us.

This was my plan. I would acknowledge to having seen a horse and cutter leave the club-house by the upper gateway, simultaneously with my entrance through the lower one. I would even describe the appearance of the person driving this cutter. No one by the greatest stretch of imagination would be apt to associate this description with Carmel; but it might set the authorities thinking, and if by any good chance a cutter containing a person wearing a derby hat and a coat with an extra high collar should have been seen on this portion of the road, or if, as I earnestly hoped, the snow had left any signs of another horse having been tethered in the clump of trees opposite the one where I had concealed my own, enough of the truth might be furnished to divide public opinion and start fresh inquiry.

That a woman's form had sought concealment under these masculine habiliments would not, could not, strike anybody's mind. Nothing in the crime had suggested a woman's presence, much less a woman's active agency.

On the contrary, all the appearances, save such as I believed known to myself alone, spoke so openly of a man's strength, a man's methods, a man's appetite, and a man's brutal daring that the suspicion which had naturally fallen on myself as the one and only person implicated, would in shifting pass straight to another man, and, if he could not be found, return to me, or be lost in a maze of speculation. This seemed so evident after a long and close study of the situation that I was ready with my confession when Mr. Clifton next came. I had even forestalled it in a short interview forced upon me by the assistant district attorney and Chief Hudson. That it had made an altogether greater impression upon the latter than I had expected, gave me additional courage when I came to discuss this new line of defence with the young lawyer. I was even able to tell him that, to all appearance, my long silence on a point so favourable to my own interests had not militated against me to the extent one would expect from men so alive to the subterfuges and plausible inventions of suspected criminals.

"Chief Hudson believes me, late as my statement is. I saw it in his eye." Thus I went on. "And the assistant district attorney, too. At least, the latter is willing to give me the benefit of the doubt, which was more than I expected. What do you suppose has happened? Some new discovery on their part? If so, I ought to know what it is. Believe me, Charles, I ought to know what it is."

"I have heard of no new discovery," he coldly replied, not quite pleased, as I could see, either with my words or my manner. "An old one may have served your purpose. If another cutter besides yours passed through the club-house grounds at the time you mention, it left tracks which all the fury of the storm would not have entirely obliterated in the fifteen minutes elapsing between that time and the arrival of the police. Perhaps they remember these tracks, and if you had been entirely frank that night—"

"I know, I know," I put in, "but I wasn't. Lay it to my confusion of mind—to the great shock I had received, to anything but my own blood-guiltiness, and take up the matter as it now stands. Can't you follow up my suggestion? A witness can certainly be found who encountered that cutter and its occupant somewhere on the long stretch of open road between The Whispering Pines and the resident district."

"Possibly. It would help. You have not asked for news from the Hill."

The trembling which seized and shook me at these words testified to the shock they gave me. "Carmel!" I cried. "She is worse—dead!"

"No. She's not worse and she's not dead. But the doctors say it will be weeks before they can allow a question of any importance to be put to her. You can see what that will do for us. Her testimony is too important to the case to be ignored. A delay will follow which may or may not be favourable to you. I am inclined to think now that it will redound to your interests. You are ready to swear to the sleigh you speak of; that you saw it leave the club-house grounds and turn north?"

"Quite ready; but you must not ask me to describe or in any way to identify its occupant. I saw nothing but the hat and coat I have told you about. It was just before the moon went under a cloud, or I could not have seen that much."

Is it so hard to preserve a natural aspect in telling or suggesting a lie that Charles's look should change as I uttered the last sentence? I do not easily flush, and since my self-control had been called upon by the dreadful experiences of the last few days, I had learned to conceal all other manifestations of feeling except under some exceptional shock. But a lie embodied in so many words, never came easy to my lips, and I suppose my voice fell, for his glance became suddenly penetrating, and his voice slightly sarcastic as he remarked:

"Those clouds obscured more than the moon, I fancy. I only wish that they had not risen between you and me. This is the blindest case that has ever been put in my hands. All the more credit to me if I see you through it, I suppose; but—"

"Tell me," I broke in, with equal desire to cut these recriminations short and to learn what was going on at the Cumberland house, "have you been to the Hill or seen anybody who has? Can't you give me some details of—of Carmel's condition; of the sort of nurse who cares for her, and how Arthur conducts himself under this double affliction?"

"I was there last night. Miss Clifford was in the house and received me. She told me that Arthur's state of mind was pitiful. He was never a very affectionate brother, you know, but now they cannot get him away from Carmel's door. He sits or stands all day just outside the threshold and casts jealous and beseeching looks at those who are allowed to enter. They say you wouldn't know him. I tried to get him to come down and see me, but he wouldn't leave his post."

"Doesn't he grieve for Adelaide? I always thought that of the two she had the greater influence over him."

"Yes, but they cannot get him to enter the place where she lies. His duty is to the living, he says; at least, his anxiety is there. He starts at every cry Carmel utters."

"She—cries out—then?"

"Very often. I could hear her from where I sat downstairs."

"And what does she say?"

"The one thing constantly. 'Lila! Lila!' Nothing more."

I kept my face in shadow. If he saw it at all, it must have looked as cold and hard as stone. After a moment, I went on with my queries:

"Does he—Arthur—mention me at all?"

"I did not discuss you greatly with Miss Clifford. I saw that she was prejudiced, and I preferred not to risk an argument; but she let fall this much: that Arthur felt very hard towards you and loudly insisted upon your guilt. She seemed to think him justified in this. You don't mind my telling you? It is better for you to know what is being said about you in town."

I understood his motive. He was trying to drive me into giving him my full confidence. But I would not be driven. I simply retorted quietly but in a way to stop all such future attempts:

"Miss Clifford is a very good girl and a true friend of the whole Cumberland family; but she is not the most discriminating person in the world, and even if she were, her opinion would not turn me from the course I have laid out for myself. Does the doctor—Dr. Carpenter, I presume,—venture to say how long Carmel's present delirium will hold?"

"He cannot, not knowing its real cause. Carmel fell ill before the news of her sister's death arrived at the house, you remember. Some frightful scene must have occurred between the two, previous to Adelaide's departure for The Whispering Pines. What that scene was can only be told by Carmel and for her account we must wait. Happily you have an alibi which will serve you in this instance. You were at the station during the time we are speaking of."

"Has that been proved?"

"Yes; several men saw you there."

"And the gentleman who brought me the—her letter?" It was more than difficult for me to speak Carmel's name. "He has not come forward?"

"Not yet; not to my knowledge, at least."

"And the ring?"

"No news."

"The nurse—you have told me nothing about her," I now urged, reverting to the topic of gravest interest to me. "Is she any one we know or an importation of the doctor's?"

"I did not busy myself with that. She's a competent woman, of course. I suppose that is what you mean?"

Could I tell him that this was not what I meant at all—that it was her qualities as woman rather than her qualifications as nurse which were important in this case? If she were of a suspicious, prying disposition, given to weighing every word and marking every gesture of a delirious patient, what might we not fear from her circumspection when Carmel's memory asserted itself and she grew more precise in the frenzy which now exhausted itself in unintelligible cries, or the ceaseless repetition of her sister's name. The question seemed of such importance to me that I was tempted to give expression to my secret apprehension on this score, but I bethought myself in time and passed the matter over with the final remark:

"Watch her, watch them all, and bring me each and every detail of the poor girl's sickness. You will never regret humouring me in this. You ordered the flowers for—Adelaide?"

"Yes; lilies, as you requested."

A short silence, then I observed:

"There will be no autopsy the papers say. The evidences of death by strangulation are too well defined."

"Very true. Yet I wonder at their laxity in this. There were signs of some other agency having been at work also. Those two empty glasses smelling of cordial—innocent perhaps—yet—"

"Don't! I can bear no more to-day. I shall be stronger to-morrow."

Another feeler turned aside. His cheek showed his displeasure, but the words were kind enough with which he speedily took his leave and left me to solitude and a long night of maddening thought.

BOOK TWO

SWEETWATER TO THE FRONT

CHAPTER IX

"WE KNOW OF NO SUCH LETTER"

O, he sits high in all the people's hearts;
And that, which would appear offence in us,
His countenance like richest alchemy
Will change to virtue, and to worthiness.

Julius Caesar.

And you still hold him?"

"Yes, but with growing uncertainty. He's one of those fellows who affect your judgment in spite of yourself. Handsome beyond the ordinary, a finished gentleman and all that, he has, in addition to these advantages, a way with him that goes straight to the heart in spite of prejudice and the claims of conscience. That's a dangerous factor in a case like this. It hampers a man in the exercise of his duties. You may escape the fascination, probably will; but at least you will understand my present position and why I telephoned to New York for an expert detective to help us on this job. I wish to give the son of my old friend a chance."

The man whom Coroner Perry thus addressed, leaned back in his chair and quietly replied:

"You're right; not because he's the son of your old friend, a handsome fellow and all that, but for the reason that every man should have his full chance, whatever the appearances against him. Personally, I have no fear of my judgment being affected by his attractions. I've had to do with too many handsome scamps for that. But I shall be as just to him as you will, simply because it seems an incredibly brutal crime for a gentleman to commit, and also because I lay greater stress than you do on the two or three minor points which seem to favour his latest declaration, that a man had preceded him in his visit to this lonely club-house,—a man whom he had himself seen leaving the grounds in a cutter just as he entered by the opposite driveway."

"Ah!" came in quick ejaculation from the coroner's lips, "I like to hear you say that. I was purposely careful not to lay emphasis on the facts you allude to. I wished you to draw your own inferences, without any aid from me. The police did find traces of a second horse and cutter having passed through the club-house grounds. It was snowing hard, and these traces were speedily obliterated, but Hexford and Clarke saw them in time to satisfy themselves that they extended from the northern clump of trees to the upper gateway where they took the direction of the Hill."

"That is not all. A grip-sack, packed for travelling, was in Mr. Ranelagh's cutter, showing that his story of an intended journey was not without some foundation."

"Yes. We have retained that grip-sack. It is not the only proof we have of his intention to leave the city for a while. He had made other arrangements, business arrangements—But that's neither here nor there. No one doubts that he planned an elopement with the beautiful Carmel; the question is, was his disappointment followed by the murder of the woman who stood in his way?"

District Attorney Fox (you will have guessed his identity before now) took his time, deliberating carefully with himself before venturing to reply. Then when the coroner's concealed impatience was about to disclose itself, he quietly remarked:

"I suppose that no conclusion can be drawn from the condition of the body when our men reached it. I judge that it was still warm."

"Yes, but so it would have been if she had met her fate several minutes earlier than was supposed. Clarke and Hexford differ about the length of time which intervened between the moment when the former looked into the room from the outside and that of their final entrance. But whether it was five minutes or ten, the period was long enough to render their testimony uncertain as to the exact length of time she had lain there dead. Had I been there—But it's useless to go into that. Let us take up something more tangible."

"Very good. Here it is. Of the six bottles of spirits which were surreptitiously taken from the club-house's wine-vault, four were found standing unopened on the kitchen table. Where are the other two?"

"That's it! That's the question I have put myself ever since I interrogated the steward and found him ready to swear to the correctness of his report and the disappearance of these two bottles. Ranelagh did not empty them, or the bottles themselves would have been found somewhere about the place. Now, who did?"

"No one within the club-house precincts. They were opened and emptied elsewhere. There's our clew and if the man you've got up from New York is worth his salt, he has his task ready to hand."

"A hard task for a stranger—and such a stranger! Not very prepossessing, to say the least. But he has a good eye, and will get along with the boys all right. Nothing assertive about him; not enough go, perhaps. Would you like to see him?"

"In a moment. I want to clear my mind in reference to these bottles. Only some one addicted to drink would drag those six bottles out of that cold, unlighted cellar."

"Yes, and a connoisseur at that. The two missing bottles held the choicest brand in the whole stock. They were kept far back too—hidden, as it were, behind the other bottles. Yet they were hauled to the front and carried off, as you say, and by some one who knows a good thing in spirits."

"What was in the four bottles found on the kitchen table?"

"Sherry, whiskey, and rum. Two bottles of rum and one each of sherry and whiskey."

"The thief meant to carry them all off, but had not time."

"The gentleman thief! No common man such as we are looking for, would make choice of just those bottles. So there we are again! Contradictions in every direction."

"Don't let us bother with the contradictions, but just follow the clew. Those bottles, full or empty, must be found. You know the labels?"

"Yes, and the shape and colour of the bottles, both of which are peculiar."

"Good! Now let us see your detective."

But Sweetwater was not called in yet. Just as Coroner Perry offered to touch his bell, the door opened and Mr. Clifton was ushered in. Well and favourably known to both men, he had no difficulty in stating his business and preferring his request.

"I am here in the interests of Elwood Ranelagh," said he. "He is willing to concede, and so am I, that under the circumstances his arrest was justifiable, but not his prolonged detention. He has little excuse to offer for the mistakes he has made, or the various offences of which he has been guilty. His best friends must condemn his hypocrisy and fast-and-loose treatment of Miss Cumberland; but he vows that he had no hand in her violent death, and in this regard I feel not only bound but forced to believe him. At all events, I am going to act on that conviction, and have come here to entreat your aid in clearing up one or two points which may affect your own opinion of his guilt.

"As his counsel I have been able to extract from him a fact or two which he has hitherto withheld from the police. Reticent as he has shown himself from the start,—and considering the character of the two women involved in this tragedy, this cannot be looked upon as entirely to his discredit,—he has confided to me a circumstance, which in the excitement attendant on Miss Carmel Cumberland's sudden illness, may have escaped the notice of the family and very naturally, of the police. It is this:

"The ring which Miss Cumberland wore as the sign and seal of her engagement to him was not on her hand when he came upon her, as he declares he did, dead. It was there at dinner-time—a curious ring which I have often noted myself and could accurately describe if required. If she took it off before starting for The Whispering Pines, it should be easily found. But if she did not, what a clew it offers to her unknown assailant! Up till now, Mr. Ranelagh has been anticipating receiving this ring back in a letter, written before she left her home. But he has heard of no such letter, and doubts now if you have. May I ask if he is correct in this surmise?"

"We know of no such letter. None has come to his rooms," replied the coroner.

"I thought not. The whereabouts of this ring, then, is still to be determined. You will pardon my having called your attention to it. As Mr. Ranelagh's legal adviser, I am very anxious to have that ring found."

"We are glad to receive your suggestion," replied the district attorney. "But you must remember that some of its force is lost by its having originated with the accused."

"Very true; but Mr. Ranelagh was only induced to speak of this matter after I had worked with him for an hour. There is a mystery in his attitude which I, for one, have not yet fathomed. You must have noticed this also, Coroner Perry? Your inquest, when you hold it, will reveal some curious facts; but I doubt if it will reveal the secret underlying this man's reticence. That we shall have to discover for ourselves."

"He has another secret, then, than the one involving his arrest as a suspected murderer?" was the subtle conclusion of the district attorney.

"Yes, or why does he balk so at the simplest inquiries? I have my notion as to its nature; but I'm not here to express notions unless you call my almost unfounded belief in him a notion. What I want to present to you is fact, and fact which can be utilised."

"In the cause of your client!"

"Which is equally the cause of justice."

"Possibly. We'll search for the ring, Mr. Clifton."

"Meanwhile, will you cast your eye over these fragments of a note which Mr. Ranelagh says he received from Miss Carmel Cumberland while waiting on the station platform for her coming."

Taking an envelope from his pocket, Mr. Clifton drew forth two small scraps of soiled and crumpled paper, one of which was the half of another envelope presenting very nearly the following appearance:

As he pointed this out, he remarked:

"Elwood is not so common a baptismal name, that there can be any doubt as to the person addressed."

The other scraps, also written in pencil and by the same hand, contained but two or three disconnected words; but one of those words was Adelaide.

"I spent an hour and a half in the yards adjoining the station before I found those two bits," explained the young lawyer with a simple earnestness not displeasing to the two seasoned men he addressed. "One was in hiding under a stacked-up pile of outgoing freight, and the other I picked out of a cart of stuff which had been swept up in the early morning. I offer them in corroboration of Mr. Ranelagh's statement that the 'Come!' used in the partially consumed letter found in the clubhouse chimney was addressed to Miss Carmel Cumberland and not to Adelaide, and that the place of meeting suggested by this word was the station platform, and not the spot since made terrible by death."

"You are acquainted with Miss Carmel Cumberland's handwriting?"

"If I am not, the town is full of people who are. I believe these words to have been written by Carmel Cumberland."

Mr. Fox placed the pieces back in their envelope and laid the whole carefully away.

"For a second time we are obliged to you," said he.

"You can cancel the obligation," was the quick retort, "by discovering the identity of the man who in derby hat and a coat with a very high collar, left the grounds of The Whispering Pines just as Mr. Ranelagh drove into them. I have no facilities for the job, and no desire to undertake it."

He had endeavoured to speak naturally, if not with an off-hand air; but he failed somehow—else why the quick glance of startled inquiry which Dr. Perry sent him from under his rather shaggy eyebrows.

"Well, we'll undertake that, too," promised the district attorney.

"I can ask no more," returned Charles Clifton, arising to depart. "The confronting of that man with Ranelagh will cause the latter to unseal his lips. Before you have finished with my client, you will esteem him much more highly than you do now."

The district attorney smiled at what seemed the callow enthusiasm of a youthful lawyer; but the coroner who knew his district well, looked very thoughtfully down at the table before which he sat, and failed to raise his head until the young man had vanished from the room and his place had been taken by another of very different appearance and deportment. Then he roused himself and introduced the newcomer to the prosecuting attorney as Caleb Sweetwater, of the New York police department.

Caleb Sweetwater was no beauty. He was plain-featured to the point of ugliness; so plain-featured that not even his quick, whimsical smile could make his face agreeable to one who did not know his many valuable qualities. His receding chin and far too projecting nose were not likely to create a favourable impression on one ignorant of his cheerful, modest, winsome disposition; and the district attorney, after eyeing him for a moment with ill-concealed disfavour, abruptly suggested:

"You have brought some credentials with you, I hope."

"Here is a letter from one of the department. Mr. Gryce wrote it," he added, with just a touch of pride.

"The letter is all right," hastily remarked Dr. Perry on looking it over. "Mr. Sweetwater is commended to us as a man of sagacity and becoming reserve."

"Very good. To business, then. The sooner we get to work on this new theory, the better. Mr. Sweetwater, we have some doubts if the man we have in hand is the man we really want. But first, how much do you know about this case?"

"All that's in the papers."

"Nothing more?"

"Very little. I've not been in town above an hour."

"Are you known here?"

"I don't think so; it's my first visit this way."

"Then you are as ignorant of the people as they are of you. Well, that has its disadvantages."

"And its advantages, if you will permit me to say so, sir. I have no prejudices, no preconceived notions to struggle against. I can take persons as I find them; and if there is any deep family secret to unearth, it's mighty fortunate for a man to have nothing stand in the way of his own instincts. No likings, I mean—no leanings this way or that, for humane or other purely unprofessional reasons."

The eye of District Attorney Fox stole towards that of his brother official, but did not meet it. The coroner had turned his attention to the table again, and, while betraying no embarrassment, was not quite his usual self. The district attorney's hand stole to his chin, which he softly rubbed with his lean forefinger as he again addressed Sweetwater.

"This tragedy—the most lamentable which has ever occurred in this town—is really, and without exaggeration, a tragedy in high life. The lady who was strangled by a brute's clutch, was a woman of the highest culture and most estimable character. Her sister, who is supposed to have been the unconscious cause of the crime, is a young girl of blameless record. Of the man who was seen bending over the victim with his hands on her throat, we cannot speak so well. He has the faults and has lived the life of a social favourite. Gifted in many ways, and popular with both men and women, he has swung on his course with an easy disregard of the claims of others, which, while leaving its traces no doubt in many a humble and uncomplaining heart, did not attract notice to his inherent lack of principle, until the horrors of this tragedy lifted him into public view stripped of all his charms. He's an egotist, of the first water; there is no getting over that. But did he strangle the woman? He says not; that he was only following some extraordinary impulse of the moment in laying his thumbs on the marks he saw on Miss Cumberland's neck. A fantastic story—told too late, besides, for perfect credence, and not worthy of the least attention if—"

The reasons which followed are too well known to us for repetition. Sweetwater listened with snapping eyes to all that was said; and when he had been given the various clews indicating the presence of a third—and as yet unknown—party on the scene of crime, he rose excitedly to his feet and, declaring that it was a most promising case, begged permission to make his own investigations at The Whispering Pines, after which he would be quite ready to begin his search for the man in the derby hat and high coat-collar, whose love for wine was so great that he chose and carried off the two choicest bottles that the club-house contained.

"A hardy act for any man, gentleman or otherwise, who had just strangled the life out of a fine woman like that. If he exists and the whole story is not a pure fabrication of the entrapped Ranelagh, he shouldn't be hard to find. What do you say, gentlemen? He shouldn't be hard to find."

"We have not found him," emphasised the district attorney, with the shortest possible glance at the coroner's face.

"Then the field is all before me," smiled Sweetwater. "Wish me luck, gentlemen. It's a blind job, but that's just in my line. A map of the town, a few general instructions, and I'm off."

Mr. Fox turned towards the coroner, and opened his lips; but closed them again without speaking. Did Sweetwater notice this act of self-restraint? If he did, he failed to show it.

CHAPTER X

"I CAN HELP YOU"

A subtle knave; a finder out of occasions;
That has an eye can stamp and counterfeit
Advantages though true advantage never presents Itself;
A devilish knave!

Othello.

A half hour spent with Hexford in and about the club-house, and Sweetwater was ready for the road. As he made his way through the northern gate, he cast a quick look back at the long, low building he had just left, with its tall chimneys and rows of sightless windows, half hidden, half revealed by the encroaching pines. The mystery of the place fascinated him. To his awakened imagination, there was a breathless suggestion in it—a suggestion which it was his foremost wish, just now, to understand.

And those pines—gaunt, restless, communicative! ready with their secret, if one could only interpret their language. How their heads came together as their garrulous tongues repeated the tale, which would never grow old to them until age nipped their hoary heads and laid them low in the dust, with their horror half expressed, their gruesome tale unfinished.

"Witnesses of it all," commented the young detective as he watched the swaying boughs rising and dipping before a certain window. "They were peering into that room long before Clarke stole the glimpse which has undone the unfortunate Ranelagh. If I had their knowledge, I'd do something more than whisper."

Thus musing, thus muttering, he plodded up the road, his insignificant figure an unpromising break in the monotonous white of the wintry landscape. But could the prisoner who had indirectly speeded this young detective on his present course, have read his thoughts and rightly estimated the force of his purpose, would he have viewed with so much confidence the entrance of this unprepossessing stranger upon the no-thoroughfare into which his own carefully studied admissions had blindly sent him?

As has been said before, this road was an outlying one and but little travelled save in the height of summer. Under ordinary circumstances Sweetwater would have met not more than a half-dozen carts or sledges between the club-house gates and the city streets. But to-day, the road was full of teams carrying all sorts of incongruous people, eager for a sight of the spot made forever notorious by a mysterious crime. He noted them all; the faces of the men, the gestures of the women; but he did not show any special interest till he came to that portion of the road where the long line of half-buried fences began to give way to a few scattered houses. Then his spirit woke, and be became quick, alert, and persuasive. He entered houses; he talked with the people. Though evidently not a dissipated man, he stopped at several saloons, taking his time with his glass and encouraging the chatter of all who chose to meet his advances. He was a natural talker and welcomed every topic, but his eye only sparkled at one. This he never introduced himself; he did not need to. Some one was always ready with the great theme; and once it was started, he did not let the conversation languish till every one present had given his or her quota of hearsay or opinion to the general fund.

It seemed a great waste of time, for nobody had anything to say worth the breath expended on it. But Sweetwater showed no impatience, and proceeded to engage the attention of the next man, woman, or child he encountered with undiminished zest and hopefulness.

He had left the country road behind, and had entered upon the jumble of sheds, shops, and streets which marked the beginnings of the town in this direction, when his quick and experienced eye fell on a woman standing with uncovered head in an open doorway, peering up the street in anxious expectation of some one not yet in sight. He liked the air and well-kept appearance of the woman; he appreciated the neatness of the house at her back and gauged at its proper value the interest she displayed in the expected arrival of one whom he hoped would delay that arrival long enough for him to get in the word which by this time dropped almost unconsciously from his lips.

But a second survey of the woman's face convinced him that his ordinary loquaciousness would not serve him here. There was a refinement in her aspect quite out of keeping with the locality in which she lived, and he was hesitating how to proceed, when fortune favoured him by driving against his knees a small lad on an ill-directed sled, bringing him almost to the ground and upsetting the child who began to scream vociferously.

It was the woman's child, for she made instantly for the gate which, for some reason, she found difficulty in opening. Sweetwater, seeing this, blessed his lucky stars. He was at his best with children, and catching the little fellow up, he soothed and fondled him and finally brought him with such a merry air of triumph straight to his mother's arms, that confidence between them was immediately established and conversation started.

He had in his pocket an ingenious little invention which he had exhibited all along the road as an indispensable article in every well-kept house. He wanted to show it to her, but it was too cold a day for her to stop outside. Wouldn't she allow him to step in and explain how her work could be materially lessened and her labour turned to play by a contrivance so simple that a child could run it?

It was all so ridiculous in face of this woman's quiet intelligence, that he laughed at his own words, and this laughter, echoed by the child and in another instant by the mother, made everything so pleasant for the moment that she insensibly drew back while he pulled open the gate, only remarking, as she led the way in:

"I was looking for my husband. He may come any minute and I'm afraid he won't care much about contrivances to save me work—that is, if they cost very much."

Sweetwater, whose hand was in his pocket, drew it hastily out.

"You were watching for your husband? Do you often stand in the open doorway, looking for him?"

Her surprised eyes met his with a stare that would have embarrassed the most venturesome book agent, but this man was of another ilk.

"If you do," he went on imperturbably, but with a good-humoured smile which deepened her favourable impression of him, "how much I would give if you had been standing there last Tuesday night when a certain cutter and horse went by on its way up the hill."

She was a self-contained woman, this wife of a master mechanic in one of the great shops hard by; but her jaw fell at this, and she forgot to chide or resist her child when he began to pull her towards the open kitchen door.

Sweetwater, sensitive to the least change in the human face, prayed that the husband might be detained, if only for five minutes longer, while he, Sweetwater, worked this promising mine.

"You were looking out," he ventured. "And you did see that horse and cutter. What luck! It may save a man's life."

"Save!" she repeated, staggering back a few steps and dragging the child with her. "Save a man's life! What do you mean by that?"

"Not much if it was any cutter and any horse, and at any hour. But if it was the horse and cutter which left The Whispering Pines at ten or half past ten that night, then it may mean life and death to the man now in jail under the dreadful charge of murder."

Catching up her child, she slid into the kitchen and sat down with it, in the first chair she came to. Sweetwater following her, took up his stand in the doorway, unobtrusive, but patiently waiting for her to speak. The steaming kettles and the table set for dinner gave warning of the expected presence for which she had been watching, but she seemed to have forgotten her husband; forgotten everything but her own emotions.

"Who are you?" she asked at length. "You have not told me your real business."

"No, madam, and I ask your pardon. I feared that my real business, if suddenly made known to you, might startle, perhaps frighten you. I am a detective on the look-out for evidence in the case I have just mentioned. I have a theory that a most important witness in the same, drove by here at the hour and on the night I have named. I want to substantiate that theory. Can you help me?"

A sensitiveness to, and quick appreciation of, the character of those he addressed was one of Sweetwater's most valuable attributes. No glossing of the truth, however skillfully applied, would have served him with this woman so well as this simple statement, followed by its equally simple and direct inquiry. Scrutinising him over the child's head, she gave but a casual glance at the badge he took pains to show her, then in as quiet and simple tones as he had himself used, she made this reply:

"I can help you some. You make it my duty, and I have never shrunk from duty. A horse and cutter did go by here on its way uphill, last Tuesday night at about eleven o'clock. I remember the hour because I was expecting my husband every minute, just as I am now. He had some extra work on hand that night which he expected to detain him till eleven or a quarter after. Supper was to be ready at a quarter after. To surprise him I had beaten up some biscuits, and I had just put them in the pan when I heard the clock strike the hour. Afraid that he would come before they were baked, I thrust the pan into the oven and ran to the front door to look out. It was snowing very hard, and the road looked white and empty, but as I stood there a horse and cutter came in sight, which, as it reached the gate, drew up in a great hurry, as if something was the matter. Frightened, because I'm always thinking of harm to my husband whose work is very dangerous, I ran out bare-headed to the gate, when I saw why the man in the sleigh was making me such wild gestures. His hat had blown off, and was lying close up against the fence in front of me. Anxious always to oblige, I made haste to snatch at it and carry it out to its owner. I received a sort of thank you, and would never have remembered the occurrence if it had not been for that murder and if—" She paused doubtfully, ran her fingers nervously over her child's head, looked again at Sweetwater waiting expectantly for her next word, and faltered painfully—"if I had not recognised the horse."

Sweetwater drew a deep breath; it was such a happy climax. Then, as she showed no signs of saying more, asked as quietly as his rapidly beating heart permitted:

"Didn't you recognise the man?"

Her answer was short but as candid as her expression.

"No. The snow was blinding; besides he wore a high collar, in which his head was sunk down almost out of sight."

"But the horse—"

"Was one which is often driven by here. I had rather not tell you whose it is. I have not told any one, not even my husband, about seeing it on the road that night. I couldn't somehow. But if it will save a man's life and make clear who killed that good woman, ask any one on the Hill, in what stable you can find a grey horse with a large black spot on his left shoulder, and you will know as much about it as I do. Isn't that enough, sir? Now, I must dish up my dinner."

"Yes, yes; it's almost enough. Just one question, madam. Was the hat what folks call a derby? Like this one, madam," he explained, drawing his own from behind his back.

"Yes, I think so. As well as I can remember, it was like that. I'm afraid I didn't do it any good by my handling. I had to clutch it quick and I'm sure I bent the brim, to say nothing of smearing it with flour-marks."

"How?" Sweetwater had started for the door, but stopped, all eagerness at this last remark.

"I had been cutting out biscuits, and my hands were white with flour," she explained, simply. "But that brushes off easily; I don't suppose it mattered."

"No, no," he hastily assented. Then while he smiled and waved his hand to the little urchin who had been his means of introduction to this possibly invaluable witness, he made one final plea and that was for her name.

"Eliza Simmons," was the straightforward reply; and this ended the interview.

The husband, whose anticipated approach had occasioned all this abruptness, was coming down the hill when Sweetwater left the gate. As this detective of ours was as careful in his finish as in all the rest of his work, he called out as he went by:

"I've just been trying to sell a wonderful contrivance of mine to the missus. But it was no go."

The man looked, smiled, and went in at his own gate with the air of one happy in wife, child, and home.

Sweetwater went on up the hill. Towards the top, he came upon a livery-stable. Stopping in his good-humoured way, he entered into talk with a man loitering inside the great door. Before he left him, he had asked him these questions:

"Any grey horse in town?"

"Yes, one."

"I think I've seen it—has a patch of black on its left shoulder."

"Yes."

"Whose is it? I've a mighty curiosity about the horse. Looks like a trick horse."

"I don't know what you mean by that. It belongs to a respectable family. A family you must have heard about if you ever heard anything. There's a funeral there to-day—"

"Not Miss Cumberland's?" exclaimed Sweetwater, all agog in a moment.

"Yes, Miss Cumberland's. I thought you might have heard the name."

"Yes, I've heard it."

The tone was dry, the words abrupt, but the detective's heart was dancing like a feather. The next turn he took was toward the handsome residence district crowning the hill.

CHAPTER XI

IN THE COACH HOUSE

All things that we ordained festival
Turn from their office to black funeral;
Our instruments to melancholy bells;
Our wedding cheer to a sad burial feast;
And all things change them to the contrary.

Romeo and Juliet.

Fifteen minutes later, he stood in a finely wooded street before an open gateway guarded by a policeman. Showing his badge, he passed in, and entered a long and slightly curved driveway. As he did so, he took a glance at the house. It was not as pretentious as he expected, but infinitely more inviting. Low and rambling, covered with vines, and nestling amid shrubbery which even in winter gave it a habitable air, it looked as much the abode of comfort as of luxury, and gave—in outward appearance at least—no hint of the dark shadow which had so lately fallen across it.

The ceremonies had been set for three o'clock, and it was now half past two. As Sweetwater reached the head of the driveway, he saw the first of a long file of carriages approaching up the street.

"Lucky that my business takes me to the stable," thought he. "What is the coachman's name? I ought to remember it. Ah—Zadok! Zadok Brown. There's a combination for you!"

He had reached this point in his soliloquy (a bad habit of his, for it sometimes took audible expression) when he ran against another policeman set to guard the side door. A moment's parley, and he left this man behind; but not before he had noted this door and the wide and hospitable verandah which separated it from the driveway.

"I am willing to go all odds that I shall find that verandah the most interesting part of the house," he remarked, in quiet conviction, to himself, as he noted its nearness to the stable and the ease with which one could step from it into a vehicle passing down the driveway.

It had another point of interest, or, rather the wing had to which it was attached. As his eye travelled back across this wing, in his lively walk towards the stable, he caught a passing glimpse of a nurse's face and figure in one of its upper windows. This located the sick chamber, and unconsciously he hushed his step and moved with the greatest caution, though he knew that this sickness was not one of the nerves, and that the loudest sound would fail to reach ears lapsed in a blessed, if alarming, unconsciousness.

Once around the corner, he resumed a more natural pace, and perceiving that the stable-door was closed but that a window well up the garden side was open, he cast a look towards the kitchen windows at his back, and, encountering no watchful eye, stepped up to the former one and peered in.

A man sat with his back to him, polishing a bit of harness. This was probably Zadok, the coachman. As his interest was less with him than with the stalls beyond, he let his eye travel on in their direction, when he suddenly experienced a momentary confusion by observing the head and shoulders of Hexford leaning towards him from an opposite window—in much the same fashion, and certainly with exactly the same intent, as himself. As their glances crossed, both flushed and drew back, only to return again, each to his several peep-hole. Neither meant to lose the advantage of the moment. Both had heard of the grey horse and wished to identify it; Hexford for his own satisfaction, Sweetwater as the first link of the chain leading him into the mysterious course mapped out for him by fate. That each was more or less under the surveillance of the other did not trouble either.

There were three stalls, and in each stall a horse stamped and fidgeted. Only one held their attention. This was a mare on the extreme left, a large grey animal with a curious black patch on its near shoulder. The faces of both men changed as they recognised this distinguishing mark, and instinctively their eyes met across the width of the open space separating them. Hexford's finger rose to his mouth, but Sweetwater needed no such hint. He stood, silent as his own shadow, while the coachman rubbed away with less and less purpose, until his hands stood quite still and his whole figure drooped in irresistible despondency. As he raised his face, moved perhaps by that sense of a watchful presence to which all of us are more or less susceptible, they were both surprised to see tears on it. The next instant he had started to his feet and the bit of harness had rattled from his hands to the floor.

"Who are you?" he asked, with a touch of anger, quite natural under the circumstances. "Can't you come in by the door, and not creep sneaking up to take a man at disadvantage?"

As he spoke, he dashed away the tears with which his cheeks were still wet.

"I thought a heap of my young mistress," he added, in evident apology for this display of what such men call weakness. "I didn't know that it was in me to cry for anything, but I find that I can cry for her."

Hexford left his window, and Sweetwater slid from his; next minute they met at the stable door.

"Had luck?" whispered the local officer.

"Enough to bring me here," acknowledged the other.

"Do you mean to this house or to this stable?"

"To this stable."

"Have you heard that the horse was out that night?"

"Yes, she was out."

"Who driving?"

"Ah, that's the question!"

"This man can't tell you."

A jerk of Hexford's thumb in Zadok's direction emphasised this statement.

"But I'm going to talk to him, for all that."

"He wasn't here that night; he was at a dance. He only knows that the mare was out."

"But I'm going to talk to him."

"May I come in, too? I'll not interrupt. I've just fifteen minutes to spare."

"You can do as you please. I've nothing to hide—from you, at any rate."

Which wasn't quite true; but Sweetwater wasn't a stickler for truth, except in the statements he gave his superiors.

Hexford threw open the stable-door, and they both walked in. The coachman was not visible, but they could hear him moving about above, grumbling to himself in none too encouraging a way.

Evidently he was in no mood for visitors.

"I'll be down in a minute," he called out, as their steps sounded on the hardwood floor.

Hexford sauntered over to the stalls. Sweetwater stopped near the doorway and glanced very carefully about him. Nothing seemed to escape his eye. He even took the trouble to peer into a waste-bin, and was just on the point of lifting down a bit of broken bottle from an open cupboard when Brown appeared on the staircase, dressed in his Sunday coat and carrying a bunch of fresh, hot-house roses.

He stopped midway as Sweetwater turned towards him from the cupboard, but immediately resumed his descent and was ready with his reply when Hexford accosted him from the other end of the stable:

"An odd beast, this. They don't drive her for her beauty, that's evident."

"She's fast and she's knowing," grumbled the coachman. "Reason enough for overlooking her spots. Who's that man?" he grunted, with a drop of his lantern jaws, and a slight gesture towards the unknown interloper.

"Another of us," replied Hexford, with a shrug. "We're both rather interested in this horse."

"Wouldn't another time do?" pleaded the coachman, looking gravely down at the flowers he held. "It's most time for the funeral and I don't feel like talking, indeed I don't, gentlemen."

"We won't keep you." It was Sweetwater who spoke. "The mare's company enough for us. She knows a lot, this mare. I can see it in her eye. I understand horses; we'll have a little chat, she and I, when you are gone."

Brown cast an uneasy glance at Hexford.

"He'd better not touch her," he cautioned. "He don't know the beast well enough for that."

"He won't touch her," Hexford assured him. "She does look knowing, don't she? Would like to tell us something, perhaps. Was out that night, I've heard you say. Curious! How did you know it?"

"I've said and said till I'm tired," Brown answered, with sudden heat. "This is pestering a man at a very unfortunate time. Look! the people are coming. I must go. My poor mistress! and poor Miss Carmel! I liked 'em, do ye understand? Liked 'em—and I do feel the trouble at the house, I do."

His distress was so genuine that Hexford was inclined to let him go; but Sweetwater with a cock of his keen eye put in his word and held the coachman where he was.

"The old gal is telling me all about it," muttered this sly, adaptable fellow. He had sidled up to the mare and their heads were certainly very close together. "Not touch her? See here!" Sweetwater had his arm round the filly's neck and was looking straight into her fiery and intelligent eye. "Shall I pass her story on?" he asked, with a magnetic smile at the astonished coachman, which not only softened him but seemed to give the watchful Hexford quite a new idea of this gawky interloper.

"You'll oblige me if you can put her knowledge into words," the man Zadok declared, with one fascinated eye on the horse and the other on the house where he evidently felt that his presence was wanted. "She was out that night, and I know it, as any coachman would know, who doesn't come home stone drunk. But where she was and who took her, get her to tell if you can, for I don't know no more 'n the dead."

"The dead!" flashed out Sweetwater, wheeling suddenly about and pointing straight through the open stable-door towards the house where the young mistress the old servant mourned, lay in her funeral casket. "Do you mean her—the lady who is about to be buried? Could she tell if her lips were not sealed by a murderer's hand?"

"She!" The word came low and awesomely. Rude and uncultured as the man was, he seemed to be strangely affected by this unexpected suggestion. "I haven't the wit to answer that," said he. "How can we tell what she knew. The man who killed her is in jail. He might talk to some purpose. Why don't you question him?"

"For a very good reason," replied Sweetwater, with an easy good-nature that was very reassuring. "He was arrested on the spot; so that it wasn't he who drove this mare home, unharnessed her, put her back in her stall, locked the stable-door and hung up the key in its place in the kitchen. Somebody else did that."

"That's true enough, and what does it show? That the mare was out on some other errand than the one which ended in blood and murder," was the coachman's unexpected retort.

"Is that so?" whispered Sweetwater into the mare's cocked ear. "She's not quite ready to commit herself," he drawled, with another enigmatical smile at the lingering Zadok. "She's keeping something back. Are you?" he pointedly inquired, leaving the stalls and walking briskly up to Zadok.

The coachman frowned and hastily retreated a step; but in another moment he leaped in a rage upon Sweetwater, when the sight of the flowers he held recalled him to himself and he let his hand fall again with the quiet remark:

"You're overstepping your dooty. I don't know who you are or what you want with me, but you're overstepping your dooty."

"He's right," muttered Hexford. "Better let the fellow go. See! one of the maids is beckoning to him."

"He shall go, and welcome, if he will tell me where he gets his taste for this especial brand of whiskey." Sweetwater had crossed to the cupboard and taken down the lower half of the broken bottle which had attracted his notice on his first entrance, and was now holding it out, with a quizzical look at the departing coachman.

Hexford was at his shoulder with a spring, and together they inspected the label still sticking to it—which was that of the very rare and expensive spirit found missing from the club-house vault.

"This is a find," muttered Hexford into his fellow detective's ear. Then, with a quick move towards Zadok, he shouted out:

"You'd better answer that question. Where did this bit of broken bottle come from? They don't give you whiskey like this to drink."

"That they don't," muttered the coachman, not so much abashed as they had expected. "And I wouldn't care for it if they did. I found that bit of bottle in the ash-barrel outside, and fished it out to put varnish in. I liked the shape."

"Broken this way?"

"Yes; it's just as good."

"Is it? Well, never mind, run along. We'll close the stable-door for you."

"I'd rather do it myself and carry in the key."

"Here then; we're going to the funeral, too. You'd like to?" This latter in a whisper to Sweetwater.

The answer was a fervent one. Nothing in all the world would please this protean-natured man quite so well.

CHAPTER XII

"LILA—LILA!"

O, treble woe
Fall ten times treble on that cursed head,
Whose wicked deed thy most ingenious sense
Depriv'd thee of!—Hold off the earth awhile,
Till I have caught her once more in my arms.

Hamlet.

"Let us enter by the side door," suggested Sweetwater, as the two moved towards the house. "And be sure you place me where I can see without being seen. I have no wish to attract attention to myself, or to be identified with the police until the necessity is forced upon me."

"Then we won't go in together," decided Hexford. "Find your own place; you won't have any difficulty. A crowd isn't expected. Miss Cumberland's condition forbids it."

Sweetwater nodded and slid in at the side door.

He found himself at once in a narrow hall, from the end of which opened a large room. A few people were to be seen in this latter place, and his first instinct was to join them; but finding that a few minutes yet remained before the hour set for the services, he decided to improve them by a rapid glance about this hall, which, for certain reasons hardly as yet formulated in his own mind, had a peculiar interest for him.

The most important object within view, according to his present judgment, was the staircase which connected it with the floor above; but if you had asked his reason for this conclusion, he would not have told you, as Ranelagh might have done, that it was because it was the most direct and convenient approach to Carmel Cumberland's room. His thoughts were far from this young girl, intimately connected as she was with this crime; which shows through what a blind maze he was insensibly working. With his finger on the thread which had been put in his hand, he was feeling his way along inch by inch. It had brought him to this staircase, and it led him next to a rack upon which hung several coats and a gentleman's hat.

He inspected the former and noted that one was finished with a high collar; but he passed the latter by—it was not a derby. The table stood next the rack, and on its top lay nothing more interesting than a clothes-brush and one or two other insignificant objects; but, with his memory for details, he had recalled the keys which one of the maids had picked up somewhere about this house, and laid on a hall table. If this were the hall and this the table, then was every inch of the latter's simple cloth-covered top of the greatest importance in his eyes.

He had no further time for even these cursory investigations; Hexford's step could be heard on the verandah, and Sweetwater was anxious to locate himself before the officer came in. Entering the room before him, he crossed to the small group clustered in its further doorway. There were several empty chairs in sight; but he passed around them all to a dark and inconspicuous corner, from which, without effort, he could take in every room on that floor—from the large parlour in which the casket stood, to the remotest region of the servants' hall.

The clergyman had not yet descended, and Sweetwater had time to observe the row of little girls sitting in front of the bearers, each with a small cluster of white flowers in her hand. Miss Cumberland's Sunday-school class, he conjectured, and conjectured rightly. He also perceived that some of these children loved her.

Near them sat a few relatives and friends. Among these was a very, very old man, whom he afterwards heard was a great-uncle and a centenarian. Between him and one of the little girls, there apparently existed a strong sympathy; for his hand reached out and drew her to him when the tears began to steal down her cheeks, and the looks which passed between the two had all the appeal and all the protection of a great love.

Sweetwater, who had many a soft spot in his breast, felt his heart warm at this one innocent display of natural feeling in an assemblage otherwise frozen by the horror of the occasion. His eyes dwelt lingeringly on the child, and still more lingeringly on the old, old man, before passing to that heaped-up mound of flowers, under which lay a murdered body and a bruised heart. He could not see the face, but the spectacle was sufficiently awe-compelling without that.

Would it have seemed yet more so, had he known at whose request the huge bunch of lilies had been placed over that silent heart?

The sister sick, the brother invisible, there was little more to hold his attention in this quarter; so he let it roam across the heads of the people about him, to the distant hall communicating with the kitchen.

Several persons were approaching from this direction, among them Zadok. The servants of the house, no doubt, for they came in all together and sat down, side by side, in the chairs Sweetwater had so carefully passed by. There were five persons in all: two men and three women. Only two interested him—Zadok, with whom he had already made a superficial acquaintance and had had one bout; and a smart, bright-eyed girl with a resolute mouth softened by an insistent dimple, who struck him as possessing excellent sense and some natural cleverness. A girl to know and a girl to talk to, was his instantaneous judgment. Then he forgot everything but the solemnity of the occasion, for the clergyman had entered and taken his place, and a great hush had fallen upon the rooms and upon every heart there present.

"I am the resurrection and the life."

Never had these consoling words sounded more solemn than when they rang above the remains of Adelaide Cumberland, in this home where she had reigned as mistress ever since her seventeenth year. The nature of the tragedy which had robbed the town of one of its most useful young women; the awful fate impending over its supposed author,—a man who had come and gone in these rooms with a spell of fascination to which many of those present had themselves succumbed—the brooding sense of illness, if not of impending death, in the room above; gave to these services a peculiar poignancy which in some breasts of greater susceptibility than the rest, took the form of a vague expectancy bordering on terror.

Sweetwater felt the poignancy, but did not suffer from the terror. His attention had been attracted in a new direction, and he found himself watching, with anxious curiosity, the attitude and absorbed expression of a good-looking young man whom he was far from suspecting to be the secret representative of the present suspect, whom nobody could forget, yet whom nobody wished to remember at this hallowed hour.

Had this attitude and this absorption been directed towards the casket over which the clergyman's words rose and fell with ever increasing impressiveness, he might have noted the man but would scarcely have been held by him. But this interest, sincere and strong as it undoubtedly was, centred not so much in the services, careful as he was to maintain a decorous attitude towards the same, but in the faint murmurs which now and then came down from above where unconsciousness reigned and the stricken brother watched over the delirious sister, with a concentration and abandonment to fear which made him oblivious of all other duties, and almost as unconscious of the rites then being held below over one who had been as a mother to him, as the sick girl herself with her ceaseless and importunate "Lila! Lila!" The detective, watching this preoccupied stranger, shared in some measure his secret emotions, and thus was prepared for the unexpected occurrence of a few minutes later.

No one else had the least forewarning of any break in the services. There had been nothing in the subdued but impressive rendering of the prayers to foreshadow a dramatic episode; yet it came, and in this manner:

The final words had been said, and the friends present invited to look their last on the calm face which, to many there, had never worn so sweet a smile in life. Some had hesitated; but most had obeyed the summons, among them Sweetwater. But he had not much time in which to fix those features in his mind; for the little girls, who had been waiting patiently for this moment, now came forward; and he stepped aside to watch them as they filed by, dropping as they did so, a tribute of fragrant flowers upon the quiet breast. They were followed by the servants, among whom Zadok had divided his roses. As the last cluster fell from the coachman's trembling hand, the undertaker advanced with the lid, and, pausing a moment to be sure that all were satisfied, began to screw it on.

Suddenly there was a cry, and the crowd about the door leading into the main hall started back, as wild steps were heard on the stairs and a young man rushed into the room where the casket stood, and advanced upon the officiating clergyman and the astonished undertaker with a fierceness which was not without its suggestion of authority.

"Take it off!" he cried, pointing at the lid which had just been fastened down. "I have not seen her—I must see her. Take it off!"

It was the brother, awake at last to the significance of the hour!

The clergyman, aghast at the sacrilegious look and tone of the intruder, stepped back, raising one arm in remonstrance, and instinctively shielding the casket with the other. But the undertaker saw in the frenzied eye fixed upon his own, that which warned him to comply with the request thus harshly and peremptorily uttered. Unscrewing the lid, he made way for the intruder, who, drawing near, pushed aside the roses which had fallen on the upturned face, and, laying his hand on the brow, muttered a few low words to himself. Then he withdrew his hand, and without glancing to right or left, staggered back to the door amid a hush as unbroken as that which reigned behind him in that open casket. Another moment and his white, haggard face and disordered figure would be blotted from sight by the door-jamb.

The minister recovered his poise and the bearers their breath; the men stirred in their seats and the women began to cast frightened looks at each other, and then at the children, some of whom had begun to whimper, when in an instant all were struck again into stone. The young man had turned and was facing them all, with his hands held out in a clench which in itself was horrible.

"If they let the man go," he called out in loud and threatening tones, "I will strangle him with these two hands."

The word, and not the shriek which burst irrepressibly from more than one woman before him, brought him to himself. With a ghastly look on his bloated features, he scanned for one moment the row of deeply shocked faces before him, then tottered back out of sight, and fled towards the staircase. All thought that an end had come to the harrowing scene, and minister and people faced each other once more; when, loud and sharp from above, there rang down the shrill cry of delirium, this time in articulate words which even the children could understand:

"Break it open, I say! break it open, and see if her heart is there!"

It was too awful. Men and women and children leaped to their feet and dashed away into the streets, uttering smothered cries and wild ejaculations. In vain the clergyman raised his voice and bade them respect the dead; the rooms were well-nigh empty before he had finished his appeal.

Only the very old uncle and the least of the children remained of all who had come there in memory of their departed kinswoman and friend.

The little one had fled to the old man's arms before he could rise, and was now held close to his aged and shaking knees, while he strove to comfort her and explain.

Soon these, too, were gone, and the casket was refastened and carried out by the shrinking bearers, leaving in those darkened rooms a trail of desolation which was only broken from time to time by the now faint and barely heard reiteration of the name of her who had just been borne away!

"Lila! Lila!"

CHAPTER XIII

"WHAT WE WANT IS HERE"

I'll tell you, by the way,
The greatest comfort in the world.
You said There was a clew to all.
Remember, Sweet,
He said there was a clew! I hold it. Come!

A Blot in the 'Scutcheon.

Sweetwater, however affected by this scene, had not lost control of himself or forgotten the claims of duty. He noted at a glance that, while the candid looking stranger, whose lead he had been following, was as much surprised as the rest at the nature of the interruption—which he had possibly anticipated and for which he was in some measure prepared—he was, of all present, the most deeply and peculiarly impressed by it. No element of fear had entered into his emotion; nor had it been heightened by any superstitious sense. Something deeper and more important by far had darkened his thoughtful eye and caused that ebb and flow of colour in a cheek unused, if Sweetwater read the man aright, to such quick and forcible changes.

Sweetwater took occasion, likewise, while the excitement was at its height, to mark what effect had been made on the servants by the action and conduct of young Cumberland. "They know him better than we do," was his inner comment; "what do they think of his words, and what do they think of him?"

It was not so easy to determine as the anxious detective might wish. Only one of them showed a simple emotion, and that one was, without any possibility of doubt, the cook. She was a Roman Catholic, and was simply horrified by the sacrilege of which she had been witness. There was no mistaking her feelings. But those of the other two women were more complex.

So were those of the men. Zadok specially watched each movement of his young master with open mistrust; and very nearly started upright, in his repugnance and dismay, when that intruding hand fell on the peaceful brow of her over whose fate, to his own surprise, he had been able to shed tears. Some personal prejudice lay back of this or some secret knowledge of the man from whose touch even the dead appeared to shrink.

And the women! Might not the same explanation account for that curious droop of the eye with which the two younger clutched at each other's hands, to keep from screaming, and interchanged whispered words which Sweetwater would have given considerable out of his carefully cherished hoard to have heard.

It was impossible to tell, at present; but he was confident that it would not be long before he understood these latter, at least. He had great confidence in his success with women, homely as he was. He was not so sure of himself with men; and he felt that some difficulties and not a few pitfalls lay between him and, for instance, the uncommunicative Zadok. "But I've the whole long evening before me," he added in quiet consolation to himself. "It will be a pity if I can't work some of them in that time."

The last thing he had remarked, before Carmel's unearthly cry had sent the horrified guests in disorder from the house, was the presence of Dr. Perry in a small room which Sweetwater had supposed empty, until the astonishing events I have endeavoured to describe brought its occupant to the door. What the detective then read in the countenance of the family's best friend, he kept to himself; but his own lost a trace of its former anxiety, as the official slipped back out of sight and remained so, even after the funeral cortege had started on its course.

Plans had been made for carrying the servants to the cemetery, and, despite the universal disturbance consequent upon these events, these plans were adhered to. Sweetwater watched them all ride away in the last two carriages.

This gave him the opportunity he wanted. Leaving his corner, he looked up Hexford, and asked who was left in the house.

"Dr. Perry, Mr. Clifton, the lawyer, Mr. Cumberland, his sick sister, and the nurse."

"Mr. Cumberland! Didn't he go to the grave?"

"Did you expect him to, after that?"

Sweetwater's shoulders rose, and his voice took on a tone of indifference.

"There's no telling. Where is he now, do you think? Upstairs?"

"Yes. It seems he spends all his time in a little alcove opposite his sister's door. They won't let him inside, for fear of disturbing the patient; so he just sits where I've told you, doing nothing but listening to every sound that comes through the door."

"Is he there now?"

"Yes, and shaking just like a leaf. I walked by him a moment ago and noticed particularly."

"Where's his room? In sight of the alcove you mention?"

"No; there's a partition or two between. If you go up by the side staircase, you can slip into it without any one seeing you. Coroner Perry and Mr. Clifton are in front."

"Is the side door locked?"

"No."

"Lock it. The back door, of course, is."

"Yes, the cook attended to that."

"I want a few minutes all by myself. Help me, Hexford. If Dr. Perry has given you no orders, take your stand upstairs where you can give me warning if Mr. Cumberland makes a move to leave his post, or the nurse her patient."

"I'm ready; but I've been in that room and I've found nothing."

"I don't know that I shall. You say that it is near the head of the stairs running up from the side door?"

"Just a few feet away."

"I would have sworn to that fact, even if you hadn't told me," muttered Sweetwater.

Five minutes later, he had slipped from sight; and for some time not even Hexford knew where he was.

"Dr. Perry, may I have a few words with you?"

The coroner turned quickly. Sweetwater was before him; but not the same Sweetwater he had interviewed some few hours before in his office. This was quite a different looking personage. Though nothing could change his features, the moment had come when their inharmonious lines no longer obtruded themselves upon the eye; and the anxious, nay, deeply troubled official whom he addressed, saw nothing but the ardour and quiet self-confidence they expressed.

"It'll not take long," he added, with a short significant glance in the direction of Mr. Clifton.

Dr. Perry nodded, excused himself to the lawyer and followed the detective into the small writing-room which he had occupied during the funeral. In the decision with which Sweetwater closed the door behind them there was something which caused the blood to mount to the coroner's brow.

"You have made some discovery?" said he.

"A very important one," was the quick, emphatic reply. And in a few brief words the detective related his interview with the master mechanic's wife on the highroad. Then with an eager, "Now let me show you something," he led the coroner through the dining-room into the side hall, where he paused before the staircase.

"Up?" queried the coroner, with an obvious shrinking from what he might encounter above.

"No," was the whispered reply. "What we want is here." And, pushing open a small door let into the under part of the stairway (if Ranelagh in his prison cell could have seen and understood this movement!), he disclosed a closet and in that closet a coat or two, and one derby hat. He took down the latter and, holding it out to the light, pointed to a spot on the under side of its brim.

The coroner staggered as he saw it, and glanced helplessly about him. He had known this family all their lives and the father had been his dearest friend. But he could say nothing in face of this evidence. The spot was a flour-mark, in which could almost be discerned the outline of a woman's thumb.

CHAPTER XIV

THE MOTIONLESS FIGURE

'S blood, there is something in this more than natural, if philosophy could find it out.

Hamlet.

"The coat is here, too," whispered Sweetwater, after a moment of considerate silence. "I had searched the hall-rack for them; I had searched his closets; and was about owning myself to be on a false trail, when I spied this little door. We had better lock it, now, had we not, till you make up your mind what to do with this conclusive bit of evidence."

"Yes, lock it. I'm not quite myself, Sweetwater. I'm no stranger to this house, or to the unfortunate young people in it. I wish I had not been re-elected last year. I shall never survive the strain if—" He turned away.

Sweetwater carefully returned the hat to its peg, turned the key in the door, and softly followed his superior back into the dining-room, and thence to their former retreat.

"I can see that it's likely to be a dreadful business," he ventured to remark, as the two stood face to face again. "But we've no choice. Facts are facts, and we've got to make the best of them. You mean me to go on?"

"Go on?"

"Following up the clews which you have yourself given me? I've only finished with one; there's another—"

"The bottles?"

"Yes, the bottles. I believe that I shall not fail there if you'll give me a little time. I'm a stranger in town, you remember, and cannot be expected to move as fast as a local detective."

"Sweetwater, you have but one duty—to follow both clews as far as they will take you. As for my duty, that is equally plain, to uphold you in all reasonable efforts and to shrink at nothing which will save the innocent and bring penalty to the guilty. Only be careful. Remember the evidence against Ranelagh. You will have to forge an exceedingly strong chain to hold your own against the facts which have brought this recreant lover to book. You see—O, I wish that poor girl could get ease!" he impetuously cried, as "Lila! Lila!" rang again through the house.

"There can never be any ease for her," murmured Sweetwater. "Whatever the truth, she's bound to suffer if ever she awakens to reality again. Do you agree with the reporters that she knew why and for what her unhappy sister left this house that night?"

"If not, why this fever?"

"That's sound."

"She—" the coroner was emphatic, "she is the only one who is wholly innocent in this whole business. Consider her at every point. Her life is invaluable to every one concerned. But she must not be roused to the fact; not yet. Nor must he be startled either; you know whom I mean. Quiet does it, Sweetwater. Quiet and a seeming deference to his wishes as the present head of the house."

"Is the place his? Has Miss Cumberland made a will?"

"Her will will be read to-morrow. For to-night, Arthur Cumberland's position here is the position of a master."

"I will respect it, sir, up to all reasonable bounds. I don't think he meditates giving any trouble. He's not at all impressed by our presence. All he seems to care about is what his sister may be led to say in her delirium."

"That's how you look at it?" The coroner's tone was one of gloom. Then, after a moment of silence: "You may call my carriage, Sweetwater. I can do nothing further here to-day. The atmosphere of this house stifles me. Dead flowers, dead hopes, and something worse than death lowering in the prospect. I remember my old friend—this was his desk. Let us go, I say."

Sweetwater threw open the door, but his wistful look did not escape the older man's eye.

"You're not ready to go? Wish to search the house, perhaps."

"Naturally."

"It has already been done in a general way."

"I wish to do it thoroughly."

The coroner sighed.

"I should be wrong to stand in your way. Get your warrant and the house is yours. But remember the sick girl."

"That's why I wish to do the job my self."

"You're a good fellow, Sweetwater." Then as he was passing out, "I'm going to rely on you to see this thing through, quietly if you can, openly and in the public eye if you must. The keys tell the tale—the keys and the hat. If the former had been left in the club-house and the latter found without the mark set on it by the mechanic's wife, Ranelagh's chances would look as slim to-day as they did immediately after the event. But with things as they are, he may well rest easily to-night; the clouds are lifting for him."

Which shows how little we poor mortals realise what makes for the peace even of those who are the nearest to us and whose lives and hearts we think we can read like an open book.

The coroner gone, Sweetwater made his way to the room where he had last seen Mr. Clifton. He found it empty and was soon told by Hexford that the lawyer had left. This was welcome news to him; he felt that he had a fair field before him now; and learning that it would be some fifteen minutes yet before he could hope to see the carriages back, he followed Hexford upstairs.

"I wish I had your advantages," he remarked as they reached the upper floor.

"What would you do?"

"I'd wander down that hall and take a long look at things."

"You would?"

"I'd like to see the girl and I'd like to see the brother when he thought no one was watching him."

"Why see the girl?"

"I don't know. I'm afraid that's just curiosity. I've heard she was a wonder for beauty."

"She was, once."

"And not now?"

"You cannot tell; they have bound up her cheeks with cloths. She fell on the grate and got burned."

"But I say that's dreadful, if she was so beautiful."

"Yes, it's bad, but there are worse things than that. I wonder what she meant by that wild cry of 'Tear it open! See if her heart is there?' Tear what open? the coffin?"

"Of course. What else could she have meant?"

"Well! delirium is a queer thing; makes a fellow feel creepy all over. I don't reckon on my nights here."

"Hexford, help me to a peep. I've got a difficult job before me and I need all the aid I can get."

"Oh, there's no trouble about that! Walk boldly along; he won't notice—"

"He won't notice?"

"No, he notices nothing but what comes from the sick room."

"I see." Sweetwater's jaw had fallen, but it righted itself at this last word.

"Listening, eh?"

"Yes—as a fellow never listened before."

"Expectant like?"

"Yes, I should call it expectant."

"Does the nurse know this?"

"The nurse is a puzzler."

"How so?"

"Half nurse and half—but go see for yourself. Here's a package to take in,—medicine from the drug store. Tell her there was no one else to bring it up. She'll show no surprise."

Muttering his thanks, Sweetwater seized the proffered package, and hastened with it down the hall. He had been as far as the turn before, but now he passed the turn to find, just as he expected, a closed door on the left and an open alcove on the right. The door led into Miss Cumberland's room; the alcove, circular in shape and lighted by several windows, projected from the rear of the extension, and had for its outlook the stable and the huge sycamore tree growing beside it.

Sweetwater's fingers passed thoughtfully across his chin as he remarked this and took in the expressive outline of its one occupant. He could not see his face; that was turned towards the table before which he sat. But his drooping head, rigid with desperate thinking; his relaxed hand closed around the neck of a decanter which, nevertheless, he did not lift, made upon Sweetwater an impression which nothing he saw afterwards ever quite effaced.

"When I come back, that whiskey will be half gone," thought he, and lingered to see the tumbler filled and the first draught taken.

But no. The hand slowly unclasped and fell away from the decanter; his head sank forward until his chin rested on his breast; and a sigh, startling to Sweetwater, fell from his lips. Hexford was right; only one thing could arouse him.

Sweetwater now tried that thing. He knocked softly on the sick-room door.

This reached the ear oblivious to all else. Young Cumberland started to his feet; and for a moment Sweetwater saw again the heavy features which, an hour before, had produced such a repulsive effect upon him in the rooms below. Then the nerveless figure sank again into place, with the same constraint in its lines, and the same dejection.

Sweetwater's hand, lifted in repetition of his knock, hung suspended. He had not expected quite such indifference as this. It upset his calculations just a trifle. As his hand fell, he reminded himself of the coroner's advice to go easy. "Easy it is," was his internal reply. "I'll walk as lightly as if eggshells were under my feet."

The door was opened to him, this time. As it swung back, he saw, first, a burst of rosy color as a room panelled in exquisite pink burst upon his sight; then the great picture of his life—the bloodless features of Carmel, calmed for the moment into sleep.

Perfect beauty is so rare, its effect so magical! Not even the bandage which swathed one cheek could hide the exquisite symmetry of the features, or take from the whole face its sweet and natural distinction. Frenzy, which had distorted the muscles and lit the eyes with a baleful glare, was lacking at this moment. Repose had quieted the soul and left the body free to express its natural harmonies.

Sweetwater gazed at the winsome, brown head over the nurse's shoulder, and felt that for him a new and important factor had entered into this case, with his recognition of this woman's great beauty. How deep a factor, he was far from suspecting, or he would not have met the nurse's eye with quite so cheery and self-confident a smile.

"Excuse the intrusion," he said. "We thought you might need these things. Hexford signed for them."

"I'm obliged to you. Are you—one of them?" she sharply asked.

"Would it disturb you if I were? I hope not. I've no wish to seem intrusive."

"What do you want? Something, I know. Give it a name before there's a change there."

She nodded towards the bed, and Sweetwater took advantage of the moment to scrutinise more closely the nurse herself. She was a robust, fine-looking woman, producing an impression of capability united to kindness. Strength of mind and rigid attendance to duty dominated the kindness, however. If crossed in what she considered best for her patient, possibly for herself, she could be severe, if not biting, in her speech and manner. So much Sweetwater read in the cold, clear eye and firm, self-satisfied mouth of the woman awaiting his response to the curt demand she had made.

"I want another good look at your patient, and I want your confidence since you and I may have to see much of each other before this matter is ended. You asked me to speak plainly and I have done so."

"You are from headquarters?"

"Coroner Perry sent me." Throwing back his coat, he showed his badge. "The coroner has returned to his office. He was quite upset by the outcry which came from this room at an unhappy moment during the funeral."

"I know. It was my fault; I opened the door just for an instant, and in that instant my patient broke through her torpor and spoke."

She had drawn him in, by this time, and, after another glance at her patient, softly closed the door behind him.

"I have nothing to report," said she, "but the one sentence everybody heard."

Sweetwater took in the little memorandum book and pencil which hung at her side, and understood her position and extraordinary amenability to his wishes. Unconsciously, a low exclamation escaped him. He was young and had not yet sunk the man entirely in the detective.

"A cruel necessity to watch so interesting a patient, for anything but her own good," he remarked. Yet, because he was a detective as well as a man, his eye went wandering all over the room as he spoke until it fell upon a peculiar-looking cabinet or closet, let into the wall directly opposite the bed. "What's that?" he asked.

"I don't know; I can't make it out, and I don't like to ask."

Sweetwater examined it for a moment from where he stood; then crossed over, and scrutinised it more particularly. It was a unique specimen. What it lacked in height—it could not have measured more than a foot from the bottom to the top—it made up in length, which must have exceeded five feet. The doors, of which it had two, were both tightly locked; but as they were made of transparent glass, the objects behind them were quite visible. It was the nature of these objects which made the mystery. The longer Sweetwater examined them, the less he understood the reason for their collection, much less for their preservation in a room which in all other respects, expressed the quintessence of taste.

At one end he saw a stuffed canary, not perched on a twig, but lying prone on its side. Near it was a doll, with scorched face and limbs half-consumed. Next this, the broken pieces of a china bowl and what looked like the torn remnants of some very fine lace. Further along, his eye lighted on a young girl's bonnet, exquisite in colour and nicety of material, but crushed out of all shape and only betraying its identity by its dangling strings. The next article, in this long array of totally unhomogeneous objects, was a metronome, with its pendulum wrenched half off and one of its sides lacking. He could not determine the character of what came next, and only gave a casual examination to the rest. The whole affair was a puzzle to him, and he had no time for puzzles disconnected with the very serious affair he was engaged in investigating.

"Some childish nonsense," he remarked, and moved towards the door. "The servants will be coming back, and I had rather not be found here. You'll see me again—I cannot tell just when. Perhaps you may want to send for me. If so, my name is Sweetwater."

His hand was on the knob, and he was almost out of the room when he started and looked back. A violent change in the patient had occurred. Disturbed by his voice or by some inner pulsation of the fever which devoured her, Carmel had risen from the pillow and now sat, staring straight before her with every feature working and lips opened as if to speak. Sweetwater held his breath, and the nurse leaped towards her and gently encircled her with protecting arms.

"Lie down," she prayed; "lie down. Everything is all right: I am looking after things. Lie down, little one, and rest."

The young girl drooped, and, yielding to the nurse's touch, sank slowly back on the pillow; but in an instant she was up again, and flinging out her hand, she cried out loudly just as she had cried an hour before:

"Break it open! Break the glass and look in. Her heart should be there—her heart—her heart!"

"Go, or I cannot quiet her!" ordered the nurse, and Sweetwater turned to obey.

But a new obstacle offered. The brother had heard this cry, and now stood in the doorway.

"Who are you?" he impatiently demanded, surveying Sweetwater in sudden anger.

"I brought up the drugs," was the quiet explanation of the ever-ready detective. "I didn't mean to alarm the young lady, and I don't think I did. It's the fever, sir, which makes her talk so wildly."

"We want no strangers here," was young Cumberland's response. "Remember, nurse, no strangers." His tone was actually peremptory.

Sweetwater observed him in real astonishment as he slid by and made his quiet escape. He was still more astonished when, on glancing towards the alcove, he perceived that, contrary to his own prognostication, the whiskey stood as high in the decanter as before.

"I've got a puzzler this time," was his comment, as he made his way downstairs. "Even Mr. Gryce would say that. I wonder how I'll come out. Uppermost!" he finished in secret emphasis to himself. "Uppermost! It would never do for me to fail in the first big affair I've undertaken on my own account."

CHAPTER XV

HELEN SURPRISES SWEETWATER

Lurk, lurk.

King Lear.

The returning servants drove up just as Sweetwater reached the lower floor. He was at the side door when they came in, and a single glance convinced him that all had gone off decorously at the grave, and that nothing further had occurred during their absence to disturb them.

He followed them as they filed away into the kitchen, and, waiting till the men had gone about their work, turned his attention to the girls who stood about very much as if they did not know just what to do with themselves.

"Sit, ladies," said he, drawing up chairs quite as if he were doing the honours of the house. Then with a sly, compassionate look into each woe-begone face, he artfully remarked: "You're all upset, you are, by what Mr. Cumberland said in such an unbecoming way at the funeral. He'd like to strangle Mr. Ranelagh! Why couldn't he wait for the sheriff. It looks as if that gentleman would have the job, all right."

"Oh! don't!" wailed out one of the girls, the impressionable, warm-hearted Maggie. "The horrors of this house'll kill me. I can't stand it a minute longer. I'll go—I'll go to-morrow."

"You won't; you're too kind-hearted to leave Mr. Cumberland and his sister in their desperate trouble," Sweetwater put in, with a decision as suggestive of admiration as he dared to assume.

Her eyes filled, and she said no more. Sweetwater shifted his attention to Helen. Working around by her side, he managed to drop these words into her ear:

"She talks most, but she doesn't feel her responsibilities any more than you do. I've had my experience with women, and you're of the sort that stays."

She rolled her eyes towards him, in a slow, surprised way, that would have abashed most men.

"I don't know your name, or your business here," said she; "but I do know that you take a good deal upon yourself when you say what I shall do or shan't do. I don't even know, myself."

"That's because your eye is not so keen to your own virtues as—well, I won't say as mine, but as those of any appreciative stranger. I can't help seeing what you are, you know."

She turned her shoulder but not before he caught a slight disdainful twitch of her rosy, non-communicative mouth.

"Ah, ah, my lady, not quick enough!" thought he; and, with the most innocent air in the world, he launched forth in a tirade against the man then in custody, as though his guilt were an accepted fact and nothing but the formalities of the law stood between him and his final doom. "It must make you all feel queer," he wound up, "to think you have waited on him and seen him tramping about these rooms for months, just as if he had no wicked feelings in his heart and meant to marry Miss Cumberland, not to kill her."

"Oh, oh," Maggie sobbed out. "And a perfect gentleman he was, too. I can't believe no bad of him. He wasn't like—" Her breath caught, and so suddenly that Sweetwater was always convinced that the more cautious Helen had twitched her by her skirt. "Like—like other gentlemen who came here. It was a kind word he had or a smile. I—I—" She made no attempt to finish but bounded to her feet, pulling up the more sedate Helen with her. "Let's go," she whispered, "I'm afeared of the man."

The other yielded and began to cross the floor behind the impetuous Maggie.

Sweetwater summoned up his courage.

"One moment," he prayed. "Will you not tell me, before you go, whether the candlestick I have noticed on the dining-room mantel is not one of a pair?"

"Yes, there were two—once," said Helen, resisting Maggie's effort to drag her out through the open door.

"Once," smiled Sweetwater; "by which you mean, three days ago."

A lowering of her head and a sudden make for the door.

Sweetwater changed his tone to one of simple inquiry.

"And was that where they always stood, the pair of them, one on each end of the dining-room mantel?"

She nodded; involuntarily, perhaps, but decisively.

Sweetwater hid his disappointment. The room mentioned was a thoroughfare for the whole family. Any member of it could have taken the candlestick.

"I'm obliged to you," said he; and might have ventured further had she given him the opportunity. But she was too near the door to resist the temptation of flight. In another moment she was gone, and Sweetwater found himself alone with his reflections.

They were not altogether unpleasing. He was sure that he read the evidences of struggle in her slowly working lips and changing impulses.

"So, so!" thought he. "The good seed has found its little corner of soil. I'll leave it to take root and sprout. Perhaps the coroner will profit by it. If not, I've a way of coaxing tender plants which should bring this one to fruit. We'll see."

The moon shone that night, much to Sweetwater's discomforture. As he moved about the stable-yard, he momentarily expected to see the window of the alcove thrown up and to hear Mr. Cumberland's voice raised in loud command for him to quit the premises. But no such interruption came. The lonely watcher, whose solitary figure he could just discern above the unshaded sill, remained immovable, with his head buried in his arms, but whether in sleep or in brooding misery, there was naught to tell.

The rest of the house presented an equally dolorous and forsaken appearance. There were lights in the kitchen and lights in the servants' rooms at the top of the house, but no sounds either of talking or laughing. All voices had sunk to a whisper, and if by chance a figure passed one of the windows, it was in a hurried, frightened way, which Sweetwater felt very ready to appreciate.

In the stable it was no better. Zadok had bought an evening paper, and was seeking solace from its columns. Sweetwater had attempted the sociable but had been met by a decided rebuff. The coachman could not forget his attitude before the funeral and nothing, not even the pitcher of beer the detective proposed to bring in, softened the forbidding air with which this old servant met the other's advances.

Soon Sweetwater realised that his work was over for the night and planned to leave. But there was one point to be settled first. Was there any other means of exit from these grounds save that offered by the ordinary driveway?

He had an impression that in one of his strolls about, he had detected the outlines of a door in what looked like a high brick wall in the extreme rear. If so, it were well worth his while to know where that door led. Working his way along in the shadow cast by the house and afterward by the stable itself, he came upon what was certainly a wall and a wall with a door in it. He could see the latter plainly from where he halted in the thick of the shadows. The moonlight shone broadly on it, and he could detect the very shape and size of its lock. It might be as well to try that lock, but he would have to cross a very wide strip of moonlight in order to do so, and he feared to attract attention to his extreme inquisitiveness. Yet who was there to notice him at this hour? Mr. Cumberland had not moved, the girls were upstairs, Zadok was busy with his paper, and the footman dozing over his pipe in his room over the stable. Sweetwater had just come from that room, and he knew.

A quiet stable-yard and a closed door only ten feet away! He glanced again at the latter, and made up his mind. Advancing in a quiet, sidelong way he had, he laid his hand on the small knob above the lock and quickly turned it. The door was unlocked and swung under his gentle push. An alley-way opened before him, leading to what appeared to be another residence street. He was about to test the truth of this surmise when he heard a step behind him, and turning, encountered the heavy figure of the coachman advancing towards him, with a key in his hand.

Zadok was of an easy turn, but he had been sorely tried that day, and his limit had been reached.

"You snooper!" he bawled. "What do you want here? Won't the run of the house content ye? Come! I want to lock that door. It's my last duty before going to bed."

Sweetwater assumed the innocent.

"And I was just going this way. It looks like a short road into town. It is, isn't it?"

"No! Yes," growled the other. "Whichever it is, it isn't your road to-night. That's private property, sir. The alley you see, belongs to our neighbours. No one passes through there but myself and—"

He caught himself in time, with a sullen grunt which may have been the result of fatigue or of that latent instinct of loyalty which is often the most difficult obstacle a detective has to encounter.

"And Mr. Ranelagh, I suppose you would say?" was Sweetwater's easy finish.

No answer; the coachman simply locked the door and put the key in his pocket.

Sweetwater made no effort to deter him. More than that he desisted from further questions though he was dying to ask where this key was kept at night, and whether it had been in its usual place on the evening of the murder. He had gone far enough, he thought. Another step and he might rouse this man's suspicion, if not his enmity. But he did not leave the shadows into which he again receded until he had satisfied himself that the key went into the stable with the coachman, where it probably remained for this night, at least.

It was after ten when Sweetwater re-entered the house to say good night to Hexford. He found him on watch in the upper hall, and the man, Clarke, below. He had a word with the former:

"What is the purpose of the little door in the wall back of the stable?"

"It connects these grounds with those of the Fultons. The Fultons live on Huested Street."

"Are the two families intimate?"

"Very. Mr. Cumberland is sweet on the young lady there. She was at the funeral to-day. She fainted when—you know when."

"I can guess. God! What complications arise! You don't say that any woman can care for him?"

Hexford gave a shrug. He had seen a good deal of life.

"He uses that door, then?" Sweetwater pursued, after a minute.

"Probably."

"Did he use it that night?"

"He didn't visit her"

"Where did he go?"

"We can't find out. He was first seen on Garden Street, coming home after a night of debauch. He had drunk hard. Asked where he got the liquor, he maundered out something about a saloon; but none of the places which he usually frequents had seen him that night. I have tried them all and some that weren't in his books. It was no good."

"That door is supposed to be locked at night. Zadok says that's his duty. Was it locked that night?"

"Can't say. Perhaps the coroner can. You see the inquiry ran in such a different direction, at first, that a small matter like that may have been overlooked."

Sweetwater subdued the natural retort, and, reverting to the subject of the saloons, got some specific information in regard to them. Then he passed thoughtfully down-stairs, only to come upon Helen who was just extinguishing the front-hall light.

"Good night!" he said, in passing.

"Good night, Mr. Sweetwater."

There was something in her tone which made him stop and look back. She had stepped into the library and was blowing out the lamp there. He paused a moment and sighed softly. Then he started towards the door, only to stop again and cast another look back. She was standing in one of the doorways, anxiously watching him and twisting her fingers in and out in an irresolute way truly significant in one of her disposition.

He felt his heart leap.

Returning softly, he took up his stand before her, looking her straight in the eye.

"Good night," he repeated, with an odd emphasis.

"Good night," she answered, with equal force and meaning.

But the next moment she was speaking rapidly, earnestly.

"I can't sleep," said she. "I never can when I'm not certain of my duty. Mr. Ranelagh is an injured man. Ask what was said and done at their last dinner here. I can't tell you. I didn't listen and I didn't see what happened, but it was something out of the ordinary. Three broken wineglasses lay on the tablecloth when I went in to clear away. I heard the clatter when they fell and smashed, but I said nothing. I have said nothing since; but I know there was a quarrel, and that Mr. Ranelagh was not in it, for his glass was the only one which remained unbroken. Am I wrong in telling you? I wouldn't if— if it were not for Mr. Ranelagh. He didn't do right by Miss Cumberland, but he don't deserve to be in prison; and so would Miss Carmel tell you if she knew what was going on and could speak. She loved him and—I've said enough; I've said enough," the agitated girl protested, as he leaned eagerly towards her. "I couldn't tell the priest any more. Good night."

And she was gone.

He hesitated a moment, then pursued his way to the side door, and so out of the house into the street. As he passed along the front of the now darkened building, he scanned it with a new interest and a new doubt. Soon he returned to his old habit of muttering to himself. "We don't know the half of what has taken place within those walls during the last four weeks," said he. "But one thing I will solve, and that is where this miserable fellow spent the hours between this dinner they speak of and the time of his return next day. Hexford has failed at it. Now we'll see what a blooming stranger can do."

CHAPTER XVI

62 CUTHBERT ROAD

Tush! I will stir about,
And all things will be well, I warrant thee.

Romeo and Juliet.

He was walking south and on the best lighted and most beautiful street in town, but his eyes were forever seeking a break in the long line of fence which marked off the grounds of a seemingly interminable stretch of neighbouring mansions, and when a corner was at last reached, he dashed around it and took a straight course for Huested Street, down which he passed with quickened steps and an air of growing assurance.

He was soon at the bottom of the hill where the street, taking a turn, plunged him at once into a thickly populated district. As this was still the residence quarter, he passed on until he gained the heart of the town and the region of the saloons. Here he slackened pace and consulted a memorandum he had made while talking to Hexford. "A big job," was his comment, sorry to find the hour quite so late. "But I'm not bound to finish it to-night. A start is all I can hope for, so here goes."

It was not his intention to revisit the places so thoroughly overhauled by the police. He carried another list, that of certain small groceries and quiet unobtrusive hotels where a man could find a private room in which to drink alone; it being Sweetwater's conviction that in such a place, and in such a place only, would be found the tokens of those solitary hours spent by Arthur Cumberland between the time of his sister's murder and his reappearance the next day. "Had they been spent in his old haunts or in any of the well-known drinking saloons of the city, some one would have peached on him before this," he went on, in silent argument with himself. "He's too well known, too much of a swell for all his lowering aspect and hang-dog look, to stroll along unnoticed through any of the principal streets, so soon after the news of his sister's murder had set the whole town agog. Yet he was not seen till he struck Garden Street, a good quarter of a mile from his usual resorts."

Here, Sweetwater glanced up at the corner gas-lamp beneath which he stood, and seeing that he was in Garden Street, tried to locate himself in the exact spot where this young man had first been seen on the notable morning in question. Then he looked carefully about him. Nothing in the street or its immediate neighbourhood suggested the low and secret den he was in search of.

"I shall have to make use of the list," he decided, and asked the first passer-by the way to Hubbell's Alley.

It was a mile off. "That settles it," muttered Sweetwater. "Besides, I doubt if he would go into an alley. The man has sunk low, but hardly so low as that. What's the next address I have? Cuthbert Road. Where's that?"

Espying a policeman eyeing him with more or less curiosity from the other side of the street, he crossed over and requested to be directed to Cuthbert Road.

"Cuthbert Road! That's where the markets are. They're closed at this time of night," was the somewhat suspicious reply.

Evidently the location was not a savoury one.

"Are there nothing but markets there?" inquired Sweetwater, innocently. It was his present desire not to be recognised as a detective even by the men on beat. "I'm looking up a friend. He keeps a grocery or some kind of small hotel. I have his number, but I don't know how to get to Cuthbert Road."

"Then turn straight about and go down the first street, and you'll reach it before the trolley-car you see up there can strike this corner. But first, sew up your pockets. There's a bad block between you and the markets."

Sweetwater slapped his trousers and laughed.

"I wasn't born yesterday," he cried; and following the officer's directions, made straight for the Road. "Worse than the alley," he muttered; "but too near to be slighted. I wonder if I shouldn't have borrowed somebody's old coat."

It had been wiser, certainly. In Garden Street all the houses had been closed and dark, but here they were open and often brightly lighted and noisy from cellar to roof. Men, women, and frequently children, jostled him on the pavement, and he felt his pockets touched more than once. But he wasn't Caleb Sweetwater of the New York department of police for nothing. He laughed, bantered, fought his way through and finally reached the quieter region and, at this hour, the almost deserted one, of the markets. Sixty-two was not far off, and, pausing a moment to consider his course, he mechanically took in the surroundings. He was surprised to find himself almost in the open country. The houses extending on his left were fronted by the booths and stalls of the market but beyond these were the fields. Interested in this discovery, and anxious to locate himself exactly, he took his stand under a favouring gas-lamp, and took out his map.

What he saw, sent him forward in haste. Shops had now taken the place of tenements, and as these were mostly closed, there were very few persons on the block, and those were quiet and unobtrusive. He reached a corner before coming to 62 and was still more interested to perceive that the street which branched off thus immediately from the markets was a wide and busy one, offering both a safe and easy approach to dealer and customer. "I'm on the track," he whispered almost aloud in his secret self-congratulation. "Sixty-two will prove a decent quiet resort which I may not be above patronising myself."

But he hesitated when he reached it. Some houses invite and some repel. This house repelled. Yet there was nothing shabby or mysterious about it. There was the decent entrance, lighted, but not too brilliantly; a row of dark windows over it; and, above it all, a sloping roof in which another sparkle of light drew his attention to an upper row of windows, this time, of the old dormer shape. An alley ran down one side of the house to the stables, now locked but later to be thrown open for the use of the farmers who begin to gather here as early as four o'clock. Nothing wrong in its appearance, everything ship-shape and yet—"I shall find some strange characters here," was the Sweetwater comment with which our detective opened the door and walked into the house.

It was an unusual hour for guests, and the woman whom he saw bending over a sort of desk in one corner of the room he strode into, looked up hastily, almost suspiciously.

"Well, and what is your business?" she asked, with her eye on his clothes, which while not fashionable, were evidently of the sort not often seen in that place.

"I want a room," he tipsily confided to her, "in which I can drink and drink till I cannot see. I'm in trouble I am; but I don't want to do any mischief; I only want to forget. I've money, and—" as he saw her mouth open, "and I've the stuff. Whiskey, just whiskey. Give me a room. I'll be quiet."

"I'll give you nothing." She was hot, angry, and full of distrust. "This house is not for such as you. It's a farmer's lodging; honest men, who'd stare and go mad to see a feller like you about. Go along, I tell you, or I'll call Jim. He'll know what to do with you."

"Then, he'll know mor'n I do myself," mumbled the detective, with a crushed and discouraged air. "Money and not a place to spend it in! Why can't I go in there?" he peevishly inquired with a tremulous gesture towards a half-open door through which a glimpse could be got of a neat little snuggery. "Nobody'll see me. Give me a glass and leave me till I rap for you in the morning. That's worth a fiver. Don't you think so, missus?—And we'll begin by passing over the fiver."

"No."

She was mighty peremptory and what was more, she was in a great hurry to get rid of him. This haste and the anxious ear she turned towards the hall enlightened him as to the situation. There was some one within hearing or liable to come within hearing, who possibly was not so stiff under temptation. Could it be her husband? If so, it might be worth his own while to await the good man's coming, if only he could manage to hold his own for the next few minutes.

Changing his tactics, he turned his back on the snuggery and surveyed the offended woman, with just a touch of maudlin sentiment.

"I say," he cried, just loud enough to attract the attention of any one within ear-shot. "You're a mighty fine woman and the boss of this here establishment; that's evident. I'd like to see the man who could say no to you. He's never sat in that 'ere cashier's seat where you be; of that I'm dead sure. He wouldn't care for fivers if you didn't, nor for tens either."

She was really a fine woman for her station, and a buxom, powerful one, too. But her glance wavered under these words and she showed a desire, with difficulty suppressed, to use the strength of her white but brawny arms, in shoving him out of the house. To aid her self-control, he, on his part, began to edge towards the door, always eyeing her and always speaking loudly in admirably acted tipsy unconsciousness of the fact.

"I'm a man who likes my own way as well as anybody," were the words with which he sought to save the situation, and further his own purposes. "But I never quarrel with a woman. Her whims are sacred to me. I may not believe in them; they may cost me money and comfort; but I yield, I do, when they are as strong in their wishes as you be. I'm going, missus —I'm going—Oh!"

The exclamation burst from him. He could not help it. The door behind him had opened, and a man stepped in, causing him so much astonishment that he forgot himself. The woman was big, bigger than most women who rule the roost and do the work in haunts where work calls for muscle and a good head behind it. She was also rosy and of a make to draw the eye, if not the heart. But the man who now entered was small almost to the point of being a manikin, and more than that, he was weazen of face and ill-balanced on his two tiny, ridiculous legs. Yet she trembled at his presence, and turned a shade paler as she uttered the feeble protest:

"Jim!"

"Is she making a fool of herself?" asked the little man in a voice as shrill as it was weak. "Do your business with me. Women are no good." And he stalked into the room as only little men can.

Sweetwater took out his ten; pointed to the snuggery, and tapped his breast-pocket. "Whiskey here," he confided. "Bring me a glass. I don't mind your farmers. They won't bother me. What I want is a locked door and a still mouth in your head."

The last he whispered in the husband's ear as the wife crossed reluctantly back to her books.

The man turned the bill he had received, over and over in his hand; then scrutinised Sweetwater, with his first show of hesitation.

"You don't want to kill yourself?" he asked.

Sweetwater laughed with a show of good humour that appeared to relieve the woman, if it did not the man.

"Oh, that's it," he cried. "That's what the missus was afraid of, was it? Well, I vow! And ten thousand dollars to my credit in the bank! No, I don't want to kill myself. I just want to booze to my heart's content, with nobody by to count the glasses. You've known such fellers before, and that cosey, little room over there has known them, too. Just add me to the list; it won't harm you."

The man's hand closed on the bill. Sweetwater noted the action out of the corner of his eye, but his direct glance was on the woman. Her back was to him, but she had started as he mentioned the snuggery and made as if to turn; but thought better of it, and bent lower over her books.

"I've struck the spot," he murmured, exultantly to himself. "This is the place I want and here I'll spend the night; but not to booze my wits away, oh, no."

Nevertheless it was a night virtually wasted. He learned nothing more than what was revealed by that one slight movement on the part of the woman.

Though the man came in and sat with him for an hour, and they drank together out of the flask Sweetwater had brought with him, he was as impervious to all Sweetwater's wiles and as blind to every bait he threw out, as any man the young detective had ever had to do with. When the door closed on him, and Sweetwater was left to sit out the tedious night alone, it was with small satisfaction to himself, and some regret for his sacrificed bill. The driving in of the farmers and the awakening of life in the market, and all the stir it occasioned inside the house and out, prevented sleep even if he had been inclined that way. He had to swallow his pill, and he did it with the best grace possible. Sooner than was expected of him, sooner than was wise, perhaps, he was on his feet and peering out of the one small window this most dismal day room contained. He had not mistaken the outlook. It gave on to the alley, and all that was visible from behind the curtains where he stood, was the high brick wall of the neighbouring house. This wall had not even a window in it; which in itself was a disappointment to one of his resources. He turned back into the room, disgusted; then crept to the window again, and, softly raising the sash, cast one of his lightning glances up and down the alley. Then he softly let the sash fall again and retreated to the centre of the room, where he stood for a moment with a growing smile of intelligence and hope on his face. He had detected close against the side of the wall, a box or hand-cart full of empty bottles. It gave him an idea. With an impetuosity he would have criticised in another man, he flung himself out of the room in which he had been for so many hours confined, and coming face to face with the landlady standing in unexpected watch before the door, found it a strain on his nerves to instantly assume the sullen, vaguely abused air with which he had decided to leave the house. Nevertheless, he made the attempt, and if he did not succeed to his own satisfaction, he evidently did to hers, for she made no effort to stop him as he stumbled out, and in her final look, which he managed with some address to intercept, he perceived nothing but relief. What had been in her mind? Fear for him or fear for themselves? He could not decide until he had rummaged that cart of bottles. But how was he to do this without attracting attention to himself in a way he still felt, to be undesirable. In his indecision, he paused on the sidewalk and let his glances wander vaguely over the busy scene before him. Before be knew it, his eye had left the market and travelled across the snow-covered fields to a building standing by itself in the far distance. Its appearance was not unfamiliar. Seizing hold of the first man who passed him, he pointed it out, crying:

"What building is that?"

"That? That's The Whispering Pines, the country club-house, where—"

He didn't wait for the end of the sentence, but plunged into the thickest group of people he could find, with a determination greater than ever to turn those bottles over before he ate.

His manner of going about this was characteristic. Lounging about the stalls until he found just the sort of old codger he wanted, he scraped up an acquaintance with him on the spot, and succeeded in making himself so agreeable that when the old fellow sauntered back to the stables to take a look at his horse, Sweetwater accompanied him. Hanging round the stable-door, he kept up his chatter, while sizing up the bottles heaped in the cart at his side. He even allowed himself to touch one or two in an absent way, and was meditating an accidental upset of the whole collection when a woman he had not seen before, thrust her head out of a rear window, shouting sharply:

"Leave those bottles alone. They're waiting for the old clothes man. He pays us money for them."

Sweetwater gaped and strolled away. He had used his eyes to purpose, and was quite assured that the bottle he wanted was not there. But the woman's words had given him his cue, and when later in the day a certain old Jew peddler went his rounds through this portion of the city, a disreputable-looking fellow accompanied him, whom even the sharp landlady in Cuthbert Road would have failed to recognise as the same man who had occupied the snuggery the night before. He was many hours on the route and had many new experiences with human nature. But he gained little else, and was considering with what words he should acknowledge his defeat at police headquarters, when he found himself again at the markets and a minute later in the alley where the cart stood, with the contents of which he had busied himself earlier in the day.

He had followed the peddler here because he had followed him to every other back door and alley. But he was tired and had small interest in the cart which looked quite undisturbed and in exactly the same condition as when he turned his back upon it in the morning. But when he drew nearer and began to lend a hand in removing the bottles to the waggon, he discovered that a bottle had been added to the pile, and that this bottle bore the label which marked it as being one of the two which had been taken from the club-house on the night of the murder.

CHAPTER XVII

"MUST I TELL THESE THINGS?"

Had I but died an hour before this chance,
I had liv'd a blessed time; for from this instant,
There's nothing serious in mortality:

All is but toys; renown, and grace is dead;
The wine of life is drawn, and the lees Is left this vault to brag of.

Macbeth.

The lamp in the coroner's room shone dully on the perturbed faces of three anxious men. They had been talking earnestly and long, but were now impatiently awaiting the appearance of a fourth party, as was shown by the glances which each threw from time to time towards the door leading into the main corridor.

The district attorney courted the light, and sat where he would be the first seen by any one entering. He had nothing to hide, being entirely engrossed in his duty.

Further back and rather behind the lamp than in front of it stood or sat, as his restlessness prompted, Coroner Perry, the old friend of Amasa Cumberland, with whose son he had now to do. Behind him, and still further in the shadow, could be seen the quiet figure of Sweetwater. All counted the minutes and all showed relief—the coroner by a loud sigh—when the door finally opened and an officer appeared, followed by the lounging form of Adelaide's brother.

Arthur Cumberland had come unwillingly, and his dissatisfaction did not improve his naturally heavy countenance. However, he brightened a little at sight of the two men sitting at the table, and, advancing, broke into speech before either of the two officials had planned their questions.

"I call this hard," he burst forth. "My place is at home and at the bedside of my suffering sister, and you drag me down here at nine o'clock at night to answer questions about things of which I am completely ignorant. I've said all I have to say about the trouble which has come into my family; but if another repetition of the same things will help to convict that scoundrel who has broken up my home and made me the wretchedest dog alive, then I'm ready to talk. So, fire ahead, Dr. Perry, and let's be done with it."

"Sit down," replied the district attorney, gravely, with a gesture of dismissal to the officer. "Mr. Cumberland, we have spared you up to this time, for two very good reasons. You were in great trouble, and you appeared to be in the possession of no testimony which would materially help us. But matters have changed since you held conversation with Dr. Perry on the day following your sister's decease. You have laid that sister away; the will which makes you an independent man for life has been read in your hearing; you are in as much ease of mind as you can be while your remaining sister's life hangs trembling in the balance; and, more important still, discoveries not made before the funeral, have been made since, rendering it very desirable for you to enter into particulars at this present moment, which were not thought necessary then."

"Particulars? What particulars? Don't you know enough, as it is, to hang the fellow? Wasn't he seen with his fingers on Adelaide's throat? What can I tell you that is any more damaging than that? Particulars!" The word seemed to irritate him beyond endurance. Never had he looked more unprepossessing or a less likely subject for sympathy, than when he stumbled into the chair set for him by the district attorney.

"Arthur!"

The word had a subtle ring. The coroner, who uttered it, waited to watch its effect. Seemingly it had none, after the first sullen glance thrown him by the young man; and the coroner sighed again, but this time softly, and as a prelude to the following speech:

"We can understand," said he, "why you should feel so strongly against one who has divided the hearts of your sisters, and played with one, if not with both. Few men could feel differently. You have reason for your enmity and we excuse it; but you must not carry it to the point of open denunciation before the full evidence is in and the fact of murder settled beyond all dispute. Whatever you may think, whatever we may think, it has not been so settled. There are missing links still to be supplied, and this is why we have summoned you here and ask you to be patient and give the district attorney a little clearer account of what went on in your own house, before you broke up that evening and you went to your debauch, and your sister Adelaide to her death at The Whispering Pines."

"I don't know what you mean." He brought his fist down on the table with each word. "Nothing went on. That is,—"

"Something went on at dinner-time. It was not a usual meal," put in the district attorney. "You and your sisters—"

"Stop!" He was at that point of passion which dulls the most self-controlled to all sense of propriety.

"Don't talk to me about that dinner. I want to forget that dinner. I want to forget everything but the two things I live for—to see that fellow hanged, and to—" The words choked him, and he let his head fall, but presently threw it up again. "That dastard, whom may God confound, passed a letter across Adelaide into Carmel's hand," he panted out. "I saw him, but I didn't take it in; I wasn't thinking. I was—"

"Who broke the glasses?" urged his relentless inquisitor. "One at your plate, one at Carmel's, and one at the head of the board where sat your sister Adelaide?"

"God! Must I tell these things?" He had started to his feet and his hand, violent in all it did, struck his forehead impulsively, as he uttered this exclamation. "Have it, then! Heaven knows I think of it enough not to be afraid to speak it out in words. Adelaide"—the name came with passion, but once uttered, produced its own calming effect, so that he went on with more restraint—"Adelaide never had much patience with me. She was a girl who only saw one way. 'The right! the right!' was what she dinned into my ears from the time I was a small boy and didn't know but that all youngsters were brought up by sisters. I grew to hate what she called 'the right,' I wanted pleasure, a free time, and a good drink whenever the fancy took me. You know what I am, Dr. Perry, and everybody in town knows; but the impulse which has always ruled me was not a downright evil one; or if it was, I called it natural independence, and let it go at that. But Adelaide suffered. I didn't understand it and I didn't care a fig for it, but she did suffer. God forgive me!"

He stopped and mopped his forehead. Sweetwater moved a trifle on his seat, but the others—men who had passed the meridian of life, who had known temptations, possibly had succumbed to them, from time to time—sat like two statues, one in full light and the other in as dark a shadow as he could find.

"That afternoon," young Cumberland presently resumed, "she was keyed up more than usual. She loved Ranelagh,—damn him!—and he had played or was playing her false. She watched him with eyes that madden me, now, when I think of them. She saw him look at Carmel, and she saw Carmel look at him. Then her eyes fell on me. I was angry; angry at them all, and I wanted a drink. It was not her habit to have wine on the table; but sometimes, when Ranelagh was there, she did. She was a slave to Ranelagh, and he could make her do whatever he wished, just as he can make you and everybody else."

Here he shot insolent glances at his two interlocutors, one of whom changed colour—which, happily, he did not see. "'Ring the bell,' I ordered, 'and have in the champagne. I want to drink to your marriage and the happy days in prospect for us all,' It was brutal and I knew it; but I was reckless and wild for the wine. So, I guess, was Ranelagh, for he smiled at her, and she rang for the champagne. When the glasses had been set beside each plate, she turned towards Carmel. 'We will all drink,' she said, 'to my coming marriage,' This made Carmel turn pale; for Adelaide had never been known to drink a drop of liquor in her life. I felt a little queer, myself; and not one of us spoke till the glasses were filled and the maid had left the dining-room and shut the door.

"Then Adelaide rose. 'We will drink standing,' said she, and never had I seen her look as she did then. I thought of my evil life when I should have been watching Ranelagh; and when she lifted the glass to her lips and looked at me, almost as earnestly as she did at Ranelagh,—but it was a different kind of earnestness,—I felt like—like—well, like the wretch I was and always had been; possibly, always will be. She drank;—we wouldn't call it drinking, for she just touched the wine with her lips; but to her it was debauch. Then she stood waiting, with the strangest gleam in her eyes, while Ranelagh drained his glass and I drained mine. Ranelagh thought she wanted some sentiment, and started to say something appropriate; but his eye fell on Carmel, who had tried to drink and couldn't, and he bungled over his words and at last came to a pause under the steady stare of Adelaide's eyes.

"'Never mind, Elwood,' she said; 'I know what you would like to say. But that's not what I am thinking of now. I am thinking of my brother, the boy who will soon be left to find his way through life without even the unwelcome restraint of my presence. I want him to remember this day. I want him to remember me as I stand here before him with this glass in my hand. You see wine in it, Arthur; but I see poison—poison—nothing else, for one like you who cannot refuse a friend, cannot refuse your own longing. Never from this day on shall another bottle be opened under my roof. Carmel, you have grieved as well as I over what has passed for pleasure in this house. Do as I do, and may Arthur see and remember.'

"Her fingers opened; the glass fell from her hand, and lay in broken fragments beside her plate. Carmel followed suit, and, before I knew it, my own fingers had opened, and my own glass lay in pieces on the table-cloth beneath me. Only Ranelagh's hand remained steady. He did not choose to please her, or he was planning his perfidy and had not caught her words or understood her action. She held her breath, watching that hand; and I can hear the gasp yet with which she saw him set his glass down quietly on the board. That's the story of those three broken glasses. If she had not died that night, I should be laughing at them now; but she did die and I don't laugh! I curse—curse her recreant lover, and sometimes myself! Do you want anything more of me? I'm eager to be gone, if you don't."

The district attorney sought out and lifted a paper from the others lying on the desk before him. It was the first movement he had made since Cumberland began his tale.

"I'm sorry," said he, with a rapid examination of the paper in his hand, "but I shall have to detain you a few minutes longer. What happened after the dinner? Where did you go from the table?"

"I went to my room to smoke. I was upset and thirsty as a fish."

"Have you liquor in your room?"

"Sometimes."

"Did you have any that night?"

"Not a drop. I didn't dare. I wanted that champagne bottle, but Adelaide had been too quick for me. It was thrown out—wasted—I do believe, wasted."

"So you did not drink? You only smoked in your room?"

"Smoked one cigar. That was all. Then I went down town."

His tone had grown sulky, the emotion which had buoyed him up till now, seemed suddenly to have left him. With it went the fire from his eye, the quiver from his lip, and it is necessary to add, everything else calculated to awaken sympathy. He was simply sullen now.

"May I ask by which door you left the house?"

"The side door—the one I always take."

"What overcoat did you wear?"

"I don't remember. The first one I came to, I suppose."

"But you can surely tell what hat?"

They expected a violent reply, and they got it.

"No, I can't. What has my hat got to do with the guilt of Elwood Ranelagh?"

"Nothing, we hope," was the imperturbable answer. "But we find it necessary to establish absolutely just what overcoat and what hat you wore down street that night."

"I've told you that I don't remember." The young man's colour was rising.

"Are not these the ones?" queried the district attorney, making a sign to Sweetwater, who immediately stepped forward, with a shabby old ulster over his arm, and a battered derby in his hand.

The young man started, rose, then sat again, shouting out with angry emphasis:

"No!"

"Yet you recognise these?"

"Why shouldn't I? They're mine. Only I don't wear them any more. They're done for. You must have rooted them out from some closet."

"We did; perhaps you can tell us what closet."

"I? No. What do I know about my old clothes? I leave that to the women."

The slight faltering observable in the latter word conveyed nothing to these men.

"Mr. Cumberland,"—the district attorney was very serious,—"this hat and this coat, old as they are, were worn into town from your house that night. This we know, absolutely. We can even trace them to the club-house."

Mechanically, not spontaneously this time, the young man rose to his feet, staring first at the man who had uttered these words, then at the garments which Sweetwater still held in view. No anger now; he was too deeply shaken for that, too shaken to answer at once—too shaken to be quite the master of his own faculties. But he rallied after an interval during which these three men devoured his face, each under his own special anxiety, and read there possibly what each least wanted to see.

"I don't know anything about it," were the words with which Arthur Cumberland sought to escape from the net which had been thus deftly cast about him. "I didn't wear the things. Anybody can tell you what clothes I came home in. Ranelagh may have borrowed—"

"Ranelagh wore his own coat and hat. We will let the subject of apparel drop, and come to a topic on which you may be better qualified to speak. Mr. Cumberland, you have told us that you didn't know at the time, and can't remember now, where you spent that night and most of the next morning. All you can remember is that it was in some place where they let you drink all you wished and leave when the fancy took you, and not before. This seemed strange to your friends, at the time; but it is easier for us to understand, now that you have told us what had occurred at your home-table. You dreaded to have your sister know how soon you could escape the influence of that moment. You wished to drink your fill and leave your family none the wiser. Am I not right?"

"Yes; it's plain enough, isn't it? Why harp on that string? Don't you see that it maddens me? Do you want to drive me to drink again?"

The coroner interposed. He had been very willing to leave the burden of this painful inquiry to the man who had no personal feelings to contend with; but at this indignant cry he started forward, and, with an air of fatherly persuasion, remarked kindly:

"You mustn't mind the official tone, or the official persistence. There is reason for all that Mr. Fox says. Answer him frankly, and this inquiry will terminate speedily. We have no wish to harry you— only to get at the truth."

"The truth? I thought you had that pat enough. The truth? The truth about what? Ranelagh or me? I should think it was about me, from the kind of questions you ask."

"It is, just now," resumed the district attorney, as his colleague drew back out of sight once more. "You cannot remember the saloon in which you drank. That's possible enough; but perhaps you can remember what they gave you. Was it whiskey, rum, absinthe, or what?"

The question took his irritable listener by surprise. Arthur gasped, and tried to steal some comfort from Coroner Perry's eye. But that old friend's face was too much in shadow, and the young man was forced to meet the district attorney's eye, instead, and answer the district attorney's question.

"I drank—absinthe," he cried, at last.

"From this bottle?" queried the other, motioning again to Sweetwater, who now brought forward the bottle he had picked up in Cuthbert Road.

Arthur Cumberland glanced at the bottle the detective held up, saw the label, saw the shape, and sank limply in his chair, his eyes starting, his jaw falling.

"Where did you get that?" he asked, pulling himself together with a sudden desperate self-possession that caused Sweetwater to cast a quick significant glance at the coroner, as he withdrew to his corner, leaving the bottle on the table.

"That," answered the district attorney, "was picked up at a small hotel on Cuthbert Road, just back of the markets."

"I don't know the place."

"It's not far from The Whispering Pines. In fact, you can see the club-house from the front door of this hotel."

"I don't know the place, I tell you."

"It's not a high-class resort; not select enough by a long shot, to have this brand of liquor in its cellar. They tell me that this is of very choice quality. That very few private families, even, indulge in it. That there were only two bottles of it left in the club-house when the inventory was last taken, that those two bottles are now gone, and that—"

"This is one of them? Is that what you want to say? Well, it may be for all I know. I didn't carry it there. I didn't have the drinking of it."

"We have seen the man and woman who keep that hotel. They will talk, if they have to."

"They will?" His dogged self-possession rather astonished them. "Well, that ought to please you. I've nothing to do with the matter."

A change had taken place in him. The irritability approaching to violence, which had attended every speech and infused itself into every movement since he came into the room, had left him. He spoke quietly, and with a touch of irony in his tone. He seemed more the man, but not a whit more prepossessing, and, if anything, less calculated to inspire confidence. The district attorney showed that he was baffled, and Dr. Perry moved uneasily in his seat, until Sweetwater, coming forward, took up the cue and spoke for the first time since young Cumberland entered the room.

"Then I have no doubt but you will do us this favour," he volunteered, in his pleasantest manner. "It's not a long walk from here. Will you go there in my company, with your coat-collar pulled up and your hat well down over your eyes, and ask for a seat in the snuggery and show them this bottle? They won't know that it's empty. The man is sharp and the woman intelligent. They will see that you are a stranger, and admit you readily. They are only shy of one man—the man who drank there on the night of your sister's murder."

"You 're a—" he began, with a touch of his old violence; but realising, perhaps, that his fingers were in a trap, he modified his manner again, and continued more quietly. "This is an odd request to make. I begin to feel as if my word were doubted here; as if my failings and reckless confession of the beastly way in which I spent that night, were making you feel that I have no good in me and am at once a liar and a sneak. I'm not. I won't go with you to that low drinking hell, unless you make me, but I'll swear—"

"Don't swear." It is unnecessary to say who spoke. "We wouldn't believe you, and it would be only adding perjury to the rest."

"You wouldn't believe me?"

"No; we have reasons, my boy. There were two bottles."

"Well?"

"The other has been found nearer your home."

"That's a trick. You're all up to tricks—"

"Not in this case, Arthur. Let me entreat you in memory of your father to be candid with us. We have arrested a man. He denies his guilt, but can produce no witnesses in support of his assertions. Yet such witnesses may exist. Indeed, we think that one such does exist. The man who took the bottles from the club-house's wine-vault did so within a few minutes of the time when this crime was perpetrated on your sister. He should be able to give valuable testimony for or against Elwood Ranelagh. Now, you can see why we are in search of this witness and why we think you can serve us in this secret and extraordinary matter. If you can't, say so; and we will desist from all further questions. But this will not help you. It will only show that, in our opinion, you have gained the rights of a man suspected of something more than shirking his duty as an unknown and hitherto unsuspected witness."

"This is awful!" Young Cumberland had risen to his feet and was swaying to and fro before them like a man struck between the eyes by some maddening blow.

"God! if I had only died that night!" he muttered, with his eyes upon the floor and every muscle tense with the shock of this last calamity. "Dr. Perry," he moaned suddenly, stretching out one hand in entreaty, and clutching at the table for support with the other, "let me go for to-night. Let me think. My brain is all in a whirl. I'll try to answer to-morrow." But even as he spoke he realised the futility of his request. His eye had fallen again on the bottle, and, in its shape and tell-tale label, he beheld a witness bound to testify against him if he kept silent himself.

"Don't answer," he went on, holding fast to the table, but letting his other hand fall. "I was always a fool. I'm nothing but a fool now. I may as well own the truth, and be done with it. I was in the clubhouse. I did rob the wine-vault; I did carry off the bottles to have a quiet spree, and it was to some place on Cuthbert Road I went. But, when I've admitted so much, I've admitted all. I saw nothing of my sister's murder; saw nothing of what went on in the rooms upstairs. I crept in by the open window at the top of the kitchen stairs, and I came out by the same. I only wanted the liquor, and when I got it, I slid out as quickly as I could, and made my way over the golf-links to the Road."

Wiping the sweat from his brow, he stood trembling. There was something in the silence surrounding him which seemed to go to his heart; for his free right hand rose unconsciously to his breast, and clung there. Sweetwater began to wish himself a million of miles away from this scene. This was not the enjoyable part of his work. This was the part from which he always shrunk with overpowering distaste.

The district attorney's voice sounded thin, almost piercing, as he made this remark:

"You entered by an open window. Why didn't you go in by the door?"

"I hadn't the key. I had only abstracted the one which opens the wine-vault. The rest I left on the ring. It was the sight of this key, lying on our hall-table, which first gave me the idea. I feel like a cad when I think of it, but that's of no account now. All I really care about is for you to believe what I tell you. I wasn't mixed up in that matter of my sister's death. I didn't know about it—I wish I had. Adelaide might have been saved; we might all have been saved; but it was not to be."

Flushed, he slowly sank back into his seat. No complaint, now, of being in a hurry, or of his anxiety to regain his sick sister's bedside. He seemed to have forgotten those fears in the perturbations of the moment. His mind and interest were here; everything else had grown dim with distance.

"Did you try the front door?"

"What was the use? I knew it to be locked."

"What was the use of trying the window? Wasn't it also, presumably, locked?"

The red mounted hot and feverish to his cheek.

"You'll think me no better than a street urchin or something worse," he exclaimed. "I knew that window; I had been through it before. You can move that lock with your knife-blade. I had calculated on entering that way."

"Mr. Ranelagh's story receives confirmation," commented the district attorney, wheeling suddenly towards the coroner. "He says that he found this window unlocked, when he approached it with the idea of escaping that way."

Arthur Cumberland remained unmoved.

The district attorney wheeled back.

"There were a number of bottles taken from the wine-vault; some half dozen were left on the kitchen table. Why did you trouble yourself to carry up so many?"

"Because my greed outran my convenience. I thought I could lug away an armful, but there are limits to one's ability. I realised this when I remembered how far I had to go, and so left the greater part of them behind."

"Why, when you had a team ready to carry you?"

"A—I had no team." But the denial cost him something. His cheek lost its ruddiness, and took on a sickly white which did not leave it again as long as the interview lasted.

"You had no team? How then did you manage to reach home in time to make your way back to Cuthbert Road by half-past eleven?"

"I didn't go home. I went straight across the golf-links. If fresh snow hadn't fallen, you would have seen my tracks all the way to Cuthbert Road."

"If fresh snow had not fallen, we should have known the whole story of that night before an hour had passed. How did you carry those bottles?"

"In my overcoat pockets. These pockets," he blurted out, clapping his hands on either side of him.

"Had it begun to snow when you left the clubhouse?"

"No."

"Was it dark?"

"I guess not; the links were bright as day, or I shouldn't have got over them as quickly as I did."

"Quickly? How quickly?" The district attorney stole a glance at the coroner, which made Sweetwater advance a step from his corner.

"I don't know. I don't understand these questions," was the sullen reply.

"You walked quickly. Does that mean you didn't look back?"

"How, look back?"

"Your sister lit a candle in the small room where her coat was found. This light should have been visible from the golf-links."

"I didn't see any light."

He was almost rough in these answers. He was showing himself now at his very worst.

A few more questions followed, but they were of minor import, and aroused less violent feeling. The serious portion of the examination, if thus it might be called, was over, and all parties showed the reaction which follows all unnatural restraint or subdued excitement.

The coroner glanced meaningly at the district attorney, who, tapping with his fingers on the table, hesitated for a moment before he finally turned again upon Arthur Cumberland.

"You wish to return to your sister? You are at liberty to do so; I will trouble you no more to-night. Your sleigh is at the door, I presume."

The young man nodded, then rising slowly, looked first at the district attorney, then at the coroner, with a glance of searching inquiry which did not escape the watchful eye of Sweetwater, lurking in the rear. There was no display of anger, scarcely of impatience, in him now. If he spoke, they did not hear him; and when he moved, it was heavily and with a drooping head. They watched him go, each as silent as he. The coroner tried to speak, but succeeded no better than the boy himself. When the door opened under his hand, they all showed relief, but were startled back into their former attention by his turning suddenly in the doorway with this final remark:

"What did you say about a bottle with a special label on it being found at our house? It never was, or, if it was, some fellow has been playing you a trick. I carried off those two bottles myself. One you see there; the other is—I can't tell where; but I didn't take it home. That you can bet on."

One more look, followed by a heavy frown and a low growling sound in his throat—which may have been his way of saying good-bye—and he was gone.

Sweetwater came forward and shut the door; then the three men drew more closely together, and the district attorney remarked:

"He is better at the house. I hadn't the heart on your account, Dr. Perry, to hurry matters faster than necessity compels. What a lout he is! Pardon me, but what a lout he is to have had two such uncommon and attractive sisters."

"And such a father," interposed the coroner.

"Just so—and such a father. Sweetwater? Hey! what's the matter? You don't look satisfied. Didn't I cover the ground?"

"Fully, sir, so far as I see now, but—"

"Well, well—out with it."

"I don't know what to out with. It's all right but—I guess I'm a fool, or tired, or something. Can I do anything more for you? If not, I should like to hunt up a bunk. A night's sleep will make a man of me again."

"Go then; that is, if Dr. Perry has no orders for you."

"None. I want my sleep, too." But Dr. Perry had not the aspect of one who expects to get it.

Sweetwater brightened. A few more words, some understanding as to the morrow, and he was gone. The district attorney and the coroner still sat, but very little passed between them. The clock overhead struck the hour; both looked up but neither moved. Another fifteen minutes, then the telephone rang. The coroner rose and lifted the receiver. The message could be heard by both gentlemen, in the extreme quiet of this midnight hour.

"Dr. Perry?"

"Yes, I'm listening."

"He came in at a quarter to twelve, greatly agitated and very white. I ran upon him in the lower hall, and he looked angry enough to knock me down; but he simply let out a curse and passed straight up to his sister's room. I waited till he came out; then I managed to get hold of the nurse and she told me this queer tale:

"He was all in a tremble when he came in, but she declares he had not been drinking. He went immediately to the bedside; but his sister was asleep, and he didn't stay there, but went over where the nurse was, and began to hang about her till suddenly she felt a twitch at her side and, looking quickly, saw the little book she carries there, falling back into place. He had lifted it, and probably read what she had written in it during his absence.

"She was displeased, but he laughed when he saw that he had been caught and said boldly: 'You are keeping a record of my sister's ravings. Well, I think I'm as interested in them as you are, and have as much right to read as you to write. Thank God! they are innocent enough. Even you must acknowledge that,' She made no answer, for they were innocent enough; but she'll keep the book away from him after this—of that you may be sure."

"And what is he doing now? Is he going into his own room to-night?"

"No. He went there but only to bring out his pillows. He will sleep in the alcove."

"Drink?"

"No, not a drop. He has ordered the whiskey locked up. I hear him moaning sometimes to himself as if he missed it awfully, but not a thimbleful has left the decanter."

"Goodnight, Hexford."

"Good night."

"You heard?" This to the district attorney.

"Every word."

Both went for their overcoats. Only on leaving did they speak again, and then it was to say:

"At ten o'clock to-morrow morning."

"At ten o'clock."

CHAPTER XVIII

ON IT WAS WRITTEN—

Can this avail thee?
Look to it!

Prometheus Bound.

The district attorney was right; Sweetwater was not happy. His night's rest had not benefited him. He had seemed natural enough when he first appeared at the coroner's office in the early morning, and equally natural all through the lengthy conference which followed; but a half hour later, any one who knew him well,—any of his fellow detectives in New York; especially Mr. Gryce, who had almost fathered him since he came among them, a raw and inexperienced recruit—would have seen at first glance that his spirits were no longer at par, and that the cheer he displayed in manner and look was entirely assumed, and likely to disappear as soon as he found himself alone.

And it did so disappear. When, at two o'clock, he entered the club-house grounds, it was without buoyancy or any of the natural animation with which he usually went about his work. Each step seemed weighted with thought, or, at least, heavy with inner dissatisfaction. But his eye was as keen as ever, and he began to use that eye from the moment he passed the gates. What was in his mind? Was he hunting for new clews, or was he merely seeking to establish the old?

The officers on guard knew him, by this time, and let him pass hither, thither, and where he would, unmolested. He walked up and down the driveways, peering continuously at the well-trodden snow. He studied the spaces between. He sauntered to the rear, and looked out over the golf-links. Then he began to study the ground in this direction, as he had already studied it in front. The few mutterings which left his lips continued to speak of discontent. "If I had only had Clarke's chance, or even Hexford's," was among his complaints. "But what can I hope now? The snow has been trampled till it is one solid cake of ice, to the very edge of the golf-links. Beyond that, the distance is too great for minute inspection. Yet it will have to be gone over, inch by inch, before I shall feel satisfied. I must know how much of his story is to be believed, and how much of it we can safely set aside."

He ended by wandering down on the golf-links. Taking out his watch, he satisfied himself that he had time for an experiment, and immediately started for Cuthbert Road. An hour later, he came wandering back, on a different line. He looked soured, disappointed. When near the building again, he cast his eye over its rear, and gazed long and earnestly at the window which had been pointed out to him as the one from which a possible light had shone forth that night. There were no trees on this side of the house—only vines. But the vines were bare of leaves and offered no obstruction to his view. "If there had been a light in that window, any one leaving this house by the rear would have seen it, unless he had been drunk or a fool," muttered Sweetwater, in contemptuous comment to himself. "Arthur Cumberland's story is one lie. I'll take the district attorney's suggestion and return to New York to-night. My work's done here."

Yet he hung about the links for a long time, and finally ended by entering the house, and taking up his stand beneath the long, narrow window of the closet overlooking the golf-links. With chin resting on his arms, he stared out over the sill and sought from the space before him, and from the intricacies of his own mind, the hint he lacked to make this present solution of the case satisfactory to all his instincts.

"Something is lacking." Thus he blurted out after a look behind him into the adjoining room of death. "I can't say what; nor can I explain my own unrest, or my disinclination to leave this spot. The district attorney is satisfied, and so, I'm afraid is the coroner; but I'm not, and I feel as guilty—"

Here he threw open the window for air, and, thrusting his head out, glanced over the links, then aside at the pines, showing beyond the line of the house on the southern end, and then out of mere idleness, down at the ground beneath him. "As guilty," he went on, "as Ranelagh appears to be, and some one really is. I—"

Starting, he leaned farther out. What was that he saw in the vines—not on the snow of the ground, but half way up in the tangle of small branches clinging close to the stone of the lower story, just beneath this window? He would see. Something that glistened, something that could only have got there by falling from this window. Could he reach it? No; he would have to climb up from below to do that. Well, that was easy enough. With the thought, he rushed from the room. In another minute he was beneath that window; had climbed, pulled, pushed his way up; had found the little pocket of netted vines observable from above; had thrust in his fingers and worked a small object out; had looked at it, uttered an exclamation curious in its mixture of suppressed emotions, and let himself down again into the midst of the two or three men who had scented the adventure and hastened to be witnesses of its outcome.

"A phial!" he exclaimed, "An empty phial, but—" Holding the little bottle up between his thumb and forefinger, he turned it slowly about until the label faced them.

On it was written one word, but it was a word which invariably carries alarm with it.

That word was: Poison.

Sweetwater did not return to New York that night.

CHAPTER XIX

"IT 'S NOT WHAT YOU WILL FIND"

I am not mad;—I would to heaven I were!
For then, 't is like I should forget myself:
O, if I could, what grief should I forget!—
Preach some philosophy to make me mad,
For being not mad, but sensible of grief,
My reasonable part produces reason
How I may be delivered of these woes.

King John.

"I regret to disturb you, Arthur; but my business is of great importance, and should be made known to you at once. This I say as a friend. I might have waited for the report to have reached you from hearsay, or through the evening papers; but I preferred to be the one to tell you. You can understand why."

Sullen and unmollified, the young man thus addressed eyed, apprehensively, his father's old friend, placed so unfortunately in his regard, and morosely exclaimed:

"Out with it! I'm a poor hand at guessing. What has happened now?"

"A discovery. A somewhat serious one I fear; at least, it will force the police to new action. Your sister may not have died entirely from strangulation; other causes may have been at work!"

"Now, what do you mean by that?" Arthur Cumberland was under his own roof and in presence of one who should have inspired his respect; but he made no effort to hide the fury which these words called up. "I should like to know what deviltry is in your minds now. Am I never to have peace?"

"Peace and tragedy do not often run together," came in the mild tones of his would-be friend. "A great crime has taken place. All the members of this family are involved—to say nothing of the man who lies, now, under the odium of suspicion, in our common county jail. Peace can only come with the complete clearing up of this crime, and the punishment of the guilty. But the clearing up must antedate the punishment. Mr. Ranelagh's assertion that he found Miss Cumberland dead when he approached her, may not be, as so many now believe, the reckless denial of a criminal, disturbed in his act. It may have had a basis in fact."

"I don't believe it. Nothing will make me believe it," stormed the other, jumping up, and wildly pacing the drawing-room floor. "It is all a scheme for saving the most popular man in society. Society! That for society!" he shouted out, snapping his fingers. "He is president of the club; the pet of women; the admired of all the dolts and gawks who are taken with his style, his easy laughter, and his knack at getting at men's hearts. He won't laugh so easily when he's up before a jury for murder; and he'll never again fool women or bulldoze men, even if they are weak enough to acquit him of this crime. Enough of the smirch will stick to prevent that. If it doesn't, I'll—"

Again his hands went out in the horribly suggestive way they had done at his sister's funeral. The coroner sat appalled,—confused, almost distracted between his doubts, his convictions, his sympathy for the man and his recoil from the passions he would be only too ready to pardon if he could feel quite sure of their real root and motive. Cumberland may have felt the other's silence, or he may have realised the imprudence of his own fury; for he dropped his hands with an impatient sigh, and blurted out:

"But you haven't told me your discovery. It seems to me it is a little late to make discoveries now."

"This was brought about by the persistence of Sweetwater. He seems to have an instinct for things. He was leaning out of the window at the rear of the clubhouse—the window of that small room where your sister's coat was found—and he saw, caught in the vines beneath, a—"

"Why don't you speak out? I cannot tell what he found unless you name it."

"A little bottle—an apothecary's phial. It was labelled 'Poison,' and it came from this house."

Arthur Cumberland reeled; then he caught himself up and stood, staring, with a very obvious intent of getting a grip on himself before he spoke.

The coroner waited, a slight flush deepening on his cheek.

"How do you know that phial came from this house?"

Dr. Perry looked up, astonished. He was prepared for the most frantic ebullitions of wrath, for violence even; or for dull, stupid, blank silence. But this calm, quiet questioning of fact took him by surprise. He dropped his anxious look, and replied:

"It has been seen on the shelves by more than one of your servants. Your sister kept it with her medicines, and the druggist with whom you deal remembers selling it some time ago to a member of your family."

"Which member? I don't believe this story; I don't believe any of your—" He was fast verging on violence now.

"You will have to, Arthur. Facts are facts, and we cannot go against them. The person who bought it was yourself. Perhaps you can recall the circumstance now."

"I cannot." He did not seem to be quite master of himself. "I don't know half the things I do; at least, I didn't use to. But what are you coming to? What's in your mind, and what are your intentions? Something to shame us further, I've no doubt. You're soft on Ranelagh and don't care how I feel, or how Carmel will feel when she comes to herself—poor girl. Are you going to call it suicide? You can't, with those marks on her throat."

"We're going to carry out our investigations to the full. We're going to hold the autopsy, which we didn't think necessary before. That's why I am here, Arthur. I thought it your due to know our intentions in regard to this matter. If you wish to be present, you have only to say so; if you do not, you may trust me to remember that she was your father's daughter, as well as my own highly esteemed friend."

Shaken to the core, the young man sat down amid innumerable tokens of the two near, if not dear, ones just mentioned; and for a moment had nothing to say. Gone was his violence, gone his self-assertion, and his insolent, captious attitude towards his visitor. The net had been drawn too tightly, or the blow fallen too heavily. He was no longer a man struggling with his misery, but a boy on whom had fallen a man's responsibilities, sufferings, and cares.

"My duty is here," he said at last. "I cannot leave Carmel."

"The autopsy will take place to-morrow. How is Carmel to-day?"

"No better." The words came with a shudder. "Doctor, I've been a brute to you. I am a brute! I have misused my life and have no strength with which to meet trouble. What you propose to do with—with Adelaide is horrible to me. I didn't love her much while she was living; I broke her heart and shamed her, from morning till night, every day of her life; but good-for-nothing as I am and good-for-nothing as I've always been, if I could save her body this last humiliation, I would willingly die right here and now, and be done with it. Must this autopsy take place?"

"It must."

"Then—" He raised his arm; the blood swept up, dyeing his cheeks, his brow, his very neck a vivid scarlet. "Tell them to lock up every bottle the house holds, or I cannot answer for myself. I should like to drink and drink till I knew nothing, cared for nothing, was a madman or a beast."

"You will not drink." The coroner's voice rang deep; he was greatly moved. "You will not drink, and you will come to the office at five o'clock to-morrow. We may have only good news to impart. We may find nothing to complicate the situation."

Arthur Cumberland shook his head. "It's not what you will find—" said he, and stopped, biting his lips and looking down.

The coroner uttered a few words of consolation forced from him by the painfulness of the situation. The young man did not seem to hear them. The only sign of life he gave was to rush away the moment the coroner had taken his leave, and regain his seat within sight and hearing of his still unconscious sister. As he did so, these words came to his ears through the door which separated them:

"Flowers—I smell flowers! Lila, you always loved flowers; but I never saw your hands so full of them."

Arthur uttered a sharp cry; then, bowing his face upon his aims, he broke into sobs which shook the table where he sat.

Twenty-four hours later, in the coroner's office, sat an anxious group discussing the great case and the possible revelations awaiting them. The district attorney, Mr. Clifton, the chief of police, and one or two others—among them Sweetwater—made up the group, and carried on the conversation. Dr. Perry only was absent. He had undertaken to make the autopsy and had been absent, for this purpose, several hours.

Five o'clock had struck, and they were momentarily looking for his reappearance; but, when the door opened, as it did at this time, it was to admit young Cumberland, whose white face and shaking limbs betrayed his suspense and nervous anxiety.

He was welcomed coldly, but not impolitely, and sat down in very much the same place he had occupied during his last visit, but in a very different, and much more quiet state of mind. To Sweetwater, his aspect was one of despair, but be made no remark upon it; only kept all his senses alert for the coming moment, of so much importance to them all. But even he failed to guess how important, until the door opened again, and the coroner appeared, looking not so much depressed as stunned. Picking out Arthur from the group, he advanced towards him with some commonplace remark; but desisted suddenly and turned upon the others instead.

"I have finished the autopsy," said he. "I knew just what poison the phial had held, and lost no time in my tests. A minute portion of this drug, which is dangerous only in large quantities, was found in the stomach of the deceased; but not enough to cause serious trouble, and she died, as we had already decided, from the effect of the murderous clutch upon her throat. But," he went on sternly, as young Cumberland moved, and showed signs of breaking in with one of his violent invectives against the supposed assassin, "I made another discovery of still greater purport. When we lifted the body out of its resting-place, something beside withered flowers slid from her breast and fell at our feet. The ring, gentlemen—the ring which Ranelagh says was missing from her hand when he came upon her, and which certainly was not on her finger when she was laid in the casket,—rolled to the floor when we moved her. Here it is; there is one person here, at least, who can identify it. But I do not ask that person to speak. That we may well spare him."

He laid the ring on the table, not too near Arthur, not within reach of his hand, but close enough for him to see it. Then he sat down, and hid his face in his hands. The last few days had told on him. He looked older, by ten years, than he had at the beginning of the month.

The silence which followed these words and this action, was memorable to everybody there concerned. Some had seen, and all had heard of young Cumberland's desperate interruption of the funeral, and the way his hand had invaded the flowers which the children had cast in upon her breast. As the picture, real or fancied, rose before their eyes, one man rose and left his place at the table; then another, and presently another. Even Charles Clifton drew back. The district attorney remained where he was, and so did young Cumberland. The latter had reached out his hand, but he had not touched the ring, and he sat thus, frozen. What went on in his heart, no man there could guess, and he did not enlighten them. When at last he looked up, it was with a dazed air and an almost humble mien:

"Providence has me this time," he muttered. "I don't understand these mysteries. You will have to deal with them as you think best." His eyes, still glued to the jewel, dilated and filled with fierce light as he said this. "Damn the ring, and damn the man who gave it to her! However it came into her casket, he's at the bottom of the business, just as he was at the bottom of her death. If you think anything else, you will think a lie."

Turning away, he made for the door. There was in his manner, desperation approaching to bravado, but no man made the least effort to detain him. Not till he was well out of the room did any one move, then the district attorney raised his finger, and Arthur Cumberland did not ride back to his home alone.

BOOK THREE

HIDDEN SURPRISES

CHAPTER XX

"HE OR YOU! THERE IS NO THIRD"

A heavy summons lies like lead upon me,
And yet I would not sleep Merciful powers!
Restrain in me the cursed thoughts that nature
Gives way to in repose.

Macbeth.

For several days I had been ill. They were merciful days to me since I was far too weak for thought. Then there came a period of conscious rest, then renewed interest in life and my own fate and reputation. What had happened during this interval?

I had a confused memory of having seen Clifton's face at my bedside, but I was sure that no words had passed between us. When would he come again? When should I hear about Carmel, and whether she were yet alive, or mercifully dead, like her sister? I might read the papers, but they had been carefully kept from me. Not one was in sight. The nurse would undoubtedly give me the information I desired, but, kind as she had been, I dreaded to consult a stranger about matters which involved my very existence and every remaining hope. Yet I must know; for I could not help thinking, now, and I dreaded to think amiss and pile up misery for myself when I needed support and consolation.

I would risk one question, but no more. I would ask about the inquest. Had it been held? If she said yes—ah, if she said yes!—I should know that Carmel was dead; and the news, coming thus, would kill me. So I asked nothing, and was lying in a sufficiently feverish condition when the doctor came in, saw my state, and thinking to cheer me up, remarked blandly:

"You are well enough this morning to hear good news. Do you recognise the room you are in?"

"I'm in the hospital, am I not?"

"Hardly. You are in one of Mr. O'Hagen's own rooms." (Mr. O'Hagen was the head keeper.) "You are detained, now, simply as a witness."

I was struck to the heart; terrified in an instant.

"What? Why? What has happened?" I questioned, rapidly, half starting up, then falling back on my pillow under his astonished eye.

"Nothing," he parried, seeing his mistake, and resorting to the soothing process. "They simply have had time to think. You're not the sort of man from which criminals are made."

"That's nonsense," I retorted, reckless of his opinion, and mad to know the truth, yet shrinking horribly from it. "Criminals are made from all kinds of men; neither are the police so philosophical.

Something has occurred. But don't tell me—" I protested inconsistently, as he opened his lips. "Send for Mr. Clifton. He's my friend; I can better bear—"

"Here he is," said the doctor, as the door softly opened under the nurse's careful hand.

I looked up, saw Charles's faithful face, and stretched out my hand without speaking. Never had I needed a friend more, and never had I been more constrained in my greeting. I feared to show my real heart, my real fears, my real reason for not hailing my release, as every one evidently expected me to!

With a gesture to the nurse, the doctor tiptoed out, muttering to Clifton, as he passed, some word of warning or casual instruction. The nurse followed, and Clifton, coming forward, took a seat at my side. He was cheerful but not too cheerful; and the air of slight constraint which tinged his manner, as much as it did mine, did not escape me.

"Well, old fellow," he began—

My hand went up in entreaty.

"Tell me why they have withdrawn their suspicions. I've heard nothing—read nothing—for days. I don't understand this move."

For reply, he laid his hand on mine.

"You're stanch," he began. "You have my regard, Elwood. Not many men would have stood the racket and sacrificed themselves as you have done. The fact is recognised, now, and your motive—"

I must have turned very white; for he stopped and sprang to his feet, searching for some restorative.

I felt the need of blinding him to my condition. With an effort, which shook me from head to foot, I lifted myself from the depths into which his words had plunged me, and fighting for self-control, faltered forth, feebly enough:

"Don't be frightened. I'm all right again; I guess I'm not very strong yet. Sit down; I don't need anything."

He turned and surveyed me carefully, and finding my colour restored, reseated himself, and proceeded, more circumspectly:

"Perhaps I had better wait till to-morrow before I satisfy your curiosity," said he.

"And leave me to imagine all sorts of horrors? No! Tell me at once. Is—is—has anything happened at the Cumberlands'?"

"Yes. What you feared has happened—No, no; Carmel is not dead. Did you think I meant that? Forgive me. I should have remembered that you had other causes for anxiety than the one weighing on our minds. She is holding her own—just holding it—but that is something, in one so young and naturally healthy."

I could see that I baffled him. It could not be helped. I did not dare to utter the question with which my whole soul was full. I could only look my entreaty. He misunderstood it, as was natural enough.

"She does not know yet what is in store for her," were his words; and I could only lie still, and look at him helplessly, and try not to show the despair that was sinking me deeper and deeper into semi-unconsciousness. "When she comes to herself, she will have to be told; but you will be on your feet, then, and will be allowed, no doubt, to soften the blow for her by your comfort and counsel. The fact that it must have been you, if not he—"

"He!" Did I shout it, or was the shout simply in my own mind? I trembled as I rose on my elbow. I searched his face in terror of my self-betrayal; but his showed only compassion and an eager desire to clear the air between us by telling me the exact facts.

"Yes—Arthur. His guilt has not been proven; he has not even been remanded; the sister's case is too pitiful and Coroner Perry too soft-hearted, where any of that family is involved. But no one doubts his guilt, and he does not deny it himself. You know—probably no one better—that he cannot very consistently do this, in face of the evidence accumulated against him, evidence stronger in many regards, than that accumulated against yourself. The ungrateful boy! The—the—Pardon me, I don't often indulge in invectives against unhappy men who have their punishment before them, but I was thinking of you and what you have suffered in this jail, where you have not belonged—no, not for a day."

"Don't think of me." The words came with a gasp. I was never so hard put to it—not when I first realised that I had been seen with my fingers on Adelaide's throat. Arthur! A booby and a boor, but certainly not the slayer of his sister, unless I had been woefully mistaken in all that had taken place in that club-house previous to my entrance into it on that fatal night. As I caught Clifton's eye fixed upon me, I repeated—though with more self-control, I hope: "Don't think of me. I'm not thinking of myself. You speak of evidence. What evidence? Give me details. Don't you see that I am burning with curiosity? I shan't be myself till I hear."

This alarmed him.

"It's a risk," said he. "The doctor told me to be careful not to excite you too much. But suspense is always more intolerable than certainty, and you have heard too much to be left in ignorance of the rest."

"Yes, yes," I agreed feverishly, pressing his hand.

"It all came about through you," he blundered on. "You told me of the fellow you saw riding away from The Whispering Pines at the time you entered the grounds. I passed the story on to the coroner, and he to a New York detective they have put on this case. He and Arthur's own surly nature did the rest."

I cringed where I lay. This was my work. The person who drove out of the club-house grounds while I stood in the club-house hall was Carmel—and the clew I had given, instead of baffling and confusing them, had led directly to Arthur!

Seeing nothing peculiar—or at all events, giving no evidence of having noted anything peculiar in my movement—Clifton went evenly on, pouring into my astonished ears the whole long story of this detective's investigations.

I heard of his visit at the mechanic's cottage and of the identification of the hat marked by Eliza Simmons's floury thumb, with an old one of Arthur's, fished out from one of the Cumberland closets;

then, as I lay dumb, in my secret dismay and perturbation, of Arthur's acknowledged visit to the club-house, and his abstraction of the bottles, which to all minds save my own, perhaps, connected him directly and well-nigh unmistakably, with the crime.

"The finger of God! Nothing else. Such coincidences cannot be natural," was my thought. And I braced myself to meet the further disclosures I saw awaiting me.

But when these disclosures were made, and Arthur's conduct at the funeral was given its natural explanation by the finding of the tell-tale ring in Adelaide's casket, I was so affected, both by the extraordinary nature of the facts and the doubtful position in which they seemed to place one whom, even now, I found it difficult to believe guilty of Adelaide's death, that Clifton, aroused, in spite of his own excitement, to a sudden realisation of my condition, bounded to his feet and impetuously cried out:

"I had to tell you. It was your due and you would not have been satisfied if I had not. But I fear that I rushed my narrative too suddenly upon you; that you needed more preparation, and that the greatest kindness I can show you now, is to leave before I do further mischief."

I believe I answered. I know that his idea of leaving was insupportable to me. That I wanted him to stay until I had had time to think and adjust myself to these new conditions. Instinctively, I did not feel as certain of Arthur's guilt as he did. My own case had taught me the insufficiency of circumstantial evidence to settle a mooted fact. Besides, I knew Arthur even better than I did his sisters. He was as full of faults, and as lacking in amiable and reliable traits as any fellow of my acquaintance. But he had not the inherent snap which makes for crime. He lacked the vigour which,—God forgive me the thought!—lay back of Carmers softer characteristics. I could not imagine him guilty; I could, for all my love, imagine his sister so, and did. The conviction would not leave my mind.

"Charles," said I, at last, struggling for calmness, and succeeding better in my task than either he or I expected; "what motive do they assign for this deed? Why should Arthur follow Adelaide to the club-house and kill her? Now, if he had followed me—"

"You were at dinner with them that night, and know what she did and what she vowed about the wine. He was very angry. Though he dropped his glass, and let it shiver on the board, he himself says that he was desperately put out with her, and could only drown his mad emotions in drink. He knew that she would hear of it if he went to any saloon in town; so he stole the key from your bunch, and went to help himself out of the club-house wine-vault. That's how he came to be there. What followed, who knows? He won't tell, and we can only conjecture. The ring, which she certainly wore that night, might give the secret away; but it is not gifted with speech, though as a silent witness it is exceedingly eloquent."

The episode of the ring confused me. I could make nothing out of it, could not connect it with what I myself knew of the confused experiences of that night. But I could recall the dinner and the sullen aspect, not unmixed with awe, with which this boy contemplated his sister when his own glass fell from his nerveless fingers. My own heart was not in the business; it was on the elopement I had planned; but I could not help seeing what I have just mentioned, and it recurred to me now with fatal distinctness. The awe was as great as the sullenness. Did that offer a good foundation for crime? I disliked Arthur. I had no use for the boy, and I wished with all my heart to detect guilt in his actions, rather than in those of the woman I loved; but I could not forget that tinge of awe on features too heavy to mirror very readily the nicer feelings of the human soul. It would come up, and, under the influence of this impression I said:

"Are you sure that he made no denial of this crime? That does not seem like Arthur, guilty or innocent."

"He made none in my presence and I was in the coroner's office when the ring was produced from its secret hiding-place and set down before him. There was no open accusation made, but he must have understood the silence of all present. He acknowledged some days ago, when confronted with the bottle found in Cuthbert Road, that he had taken both it and another from the club-house just before the storm began to rage that night."

"The hour, the very hour!" I muttered.

"He entered and left by that upper hall window, or so he says; but he is not to be believed in all his statements. Some of his declarations we know to be false."

"Which ones? Give me a specimen, Charlie. Mention something he has said that you know to be false."

"Well, it is hard to accuse a man of a direct lie. But he cannot be telling the truth when he says that he crossed the links immediately to Cuthbert Road, thus cutting out the ride home, of which we have such extraordinary proof."

Under the fear of betraying my thoughts, I hurriedly closed my eyes. I was in an extraordinary position, myself. What seemed falsehood to them, struck me as the absolute truth. Carmel had been the one to go home; he, without doubt, had crossed the links, as he said. As this conviction penetrated deeply and yet more deeply into my mind, I shrank inexpressibly from the renewed mental struggle into which it plunged me. To have suffered, myself,—to have fallen under the ban of suspicion and the disgrace of arrest—had certainly been hard; but it was nothing to beholding another in the same plight through my own rash and ill-advised attempt to better my position and Carmel's by what I had considered a totally harmless subterfuge.

I shuddered as I anticipated the sleepless hours of silent debate which lay before me. The voice which whispered that Arthur Cumberland was not over-gifted with sensitiveness and would not feel the shame of his position like another, did not carry with it an indisputable message, and could not impose on my conscience for more than a passing moment. The lout was human; and I could not stifle my convictions in his favour.

But Carmel!

I clenched my hands under the clothes. I wished it were not high noon, but dark night; that Clifton would only arise or turn his eyes away; that something or anything might happen to give me an instant of solitary contemplation, without the threatening possibility of beholding my thoughts and feelings reflected in another's mind.

Was this review instantaneous, or the work of many minutes? Forced by the doubt to open my eyes, I met Clifton's full look turned watchfully on me. The result was calming; even to my apprehensive gaze it betrayed no new enlightenment. My struggle had been all within; no token of it had reached him.

This he showed still more plainly when he spoke.

"There will be a close sifting of evidence at the inquest. You will not enjoy this; but the situation, hard as it may prove, has certainly improved so far as you are concerned. That should hasten your convalescence."

"Poor Arthur!" burst from my lips, and the cry was echoed in my heart. Then, because I could no longer endure the pusillanimity which kept me silent, I rose impulsively into a sitting posture, and, summoning all my faculties into full play, endeavoured to put my finger on the one weak point in the evidence thus raised against Carmel's brother.

"What sort of a man would you make Arthur out to be, when you accuse him of robbing the wine-vault on top of a murderous assault on his sister?"

"I know. It argues a brute, but he—"

"Arthur Cumberland is selfish, unresponsive, and hard, but he is not a brute. I'm disposed to give him the benefit of my good opinion to this extent, Charlie; I cannot believe he first poisoned and then choked that noble woman."

Clifton drew himself up in his turn, astonishment battling with renewed distrust.

"Either he or you, Ranelagh!" he exclaimed, firmly. "There is no third person. This you must realise."

CHAPTER XXI

CARMEL AWAKES

One woe doth tread upon another's heel,
So fast they follow.

Hamlet.

Later, I asked myself many questions, and wandered into mazes of speculation which only puzzled me and led nowhere. I remembered the bottles; I remembered the ring. I went back, in fancy, to the hour of my own entrance into the club-house, and, recalling each circumstance, endeavoured to fit the facts of Arthur's story with those of my own experience.

Was he in the building when I first stepped into it? It was just possible. I had been led to prevaricate as to the moment I entered the lower gateway, and he may have done the same as to the hour he left by the upper hall window. Whatever his denials on this or any subject, I was convinced that he knew, as well as I, that Carmel had been in the building with her sister, and was involved more or less personally in the crime committed there. Might it not be simply as his accessory after the fact? If only I could believe this! If my knowledge of him and of her would allow me to hug this forlorn hope, and behold, in this shock to her brain, and in her look and attitude on leaving the club-house, only a sister's horror at a wilful brother's crime!

But one fact stood in the way of this—a fact which nothing but some predetermined, underhanded purpose on her part could explain. She had gone in disguise to The Whispering Pines, and she had returned home in the same suspicious fashion. The wearing of her brother's hat and coat over her own womanly garments was no freak. There had been purpose in it—a purpose which demanded secrecy. That Adelaide should have accompanied her under these circumstances was a mystery. But then the whole affair was a mystery, totally out of keeping, in all its details, with the characters of these women, save—and what a fearful exception I here make—the awful end, which, alas! bespoke the fiery rush and impulse to destroy which marked Carmel's unbridled rages.

Of a less emotional attack she would be as incapable as any other good woman. Poison she would never use. Its presence there was due to another's forethought, another's determination. But the poison had not killed. Both glasses had been emptied, but—Ah! those glasses. What explanation had the police, now, for those two emptied glasses? They had hitherto supposed me to be the second person who had joined Adelaide in this totally uncharacteristic drinking.

To whom did they now attribute this act? To Arthur, the brother whose love for liquor in every form she had always decried, and had publicly rebuked only a few hours before? Knowing nothing of Carmel having been on the scene, they must ascribe this act either to him or to me; and when they came to dwell upon this point more particularly—when they came to study the exact character of the relations which had always subsisted between Adelaide and her brother—they must see the improbability of her drinking with him under any circumstances. Then their thoughts would recur to me, and I should find myself again a suspect. The monstrous suggestion that Arthur had brought the liquor there himself, had poured it out and forced her to drink it, poison and all, out of revenge for her action at the dinner-table a short time before, did not occur to me then, but if it had, there were the three glasses—he would not bring three; nor would Adelaide; nor, as I saw it, would Carmel.

Chaos! However one looked at it, chaos! Only one fact was clear—that Carmel knew the whole story and might communicate the same, if ever her brain cleared and she could be brought to reveal the mysteries of that hour. Did I desire such a consummation? Only God, who penetrates more deeply than ourselves into the hidden regions of the human heart, could tell. I only know that the fear and expectation of such an outcome made my anguish for the next two weeks.

Would she live? Would she die? The question was on every tongue. The crisis of her disease was approaching, and the next twenty-four hours would decide her fate, and in consequence, my own, if not her brother Arthur's. As I contemplated the suspense of these twenty-four hours, I revolted madly for the first time against the restrictions of my prison. I wanted air, movement, the rush into danger, which my horse or my automobile might afford. Anything which would drag my thoughts from that sick room, and the anticipated stir of that lovely form into conscious life and suffering. Her eyes—I could see her eyes wakening upon the world again, after her long wandering in the unknown and unimaginable intricacies of ungoverned thought and delirious suggestion. Eyes of violet colour and infinite expression; eyes which would make a man's joy if they smiled on him in innocence; but which, as I well knew, had burned more than once, in her short but strenuous life, with fiery passions; and might, at the instant of waking, betray this same unholy gleam under the curious gaze of the unsympathetic ones set in watch over her.

What would her first word be? Whither would her first thought fly? To Adelaide or to me; to Arthur or to her own frightened and appalled self? I maddened as I dwelt upon the possibilities of this moment. I envied Arthur; I envied the attendants; I envied even the servants in the house. They would all know sooner than I. Carmel! Carmel!

Sending for Clifton, I begged him to keep himself in communication with the house, or with the authorities. He promised to do what he could; then, perceiving the state I was in, he related all he knew of present conditions. No one was allowed in the sick room but the nurse and the doctor. Even Arthur was denied admission, and was wearing himself out in his own room as I was wearing myself out here, in restless inactivity. He expected her to sink and never to recover consciousness, and was loud in his expressions of rebellion against the men who dared to keep him from her bedside when her life was trembling in the balance. But the nurse had hopes and so had the doctor. As for Carmel's looks, they were greatly changed, but beautiful still in spite of the cruel scar left by her fall against the burning bars of her sister's grate. No delirium disturbed the rigid immobility in which she now lay. I could await her awakening with quiet confidence in the justice of God.

Thus Clifton, in his ignorance.

The day was a bleak one, dispiriting in itself even to those who could go about the streets and lose themselves in their tasks and round of duties. To me it was a dead blank, marked by such interruptions as necessarily took place under the prison routine. The evening hours which followed them were no better. The hands on my watch crawled. When the door finally opened, it came as a shock. I seemed to be prepared for anything but the termination of my suspense. I knew that it was Clifton who entered, but I could not meet his eye. I dug my nails into my palms, and waited for his first word. When it came, I felt my spirits go down, down—I had thought them at their lowest ebb before. He hesitated, and I started up:

"Tell me," I cried. "Carmel is dead!"

"Not dead," said he, "but silly. Her testimony is no more to be relied upon than that of any other wandering mind."

CHAPTER XXII

"BREAK IN THE GLASS!"

This inundation of mistempered humour
Rests by you only to be qualified.

King John.

It was some time before I learned the particulars of this awakening.

It had occurred at sunset. A level beam of light had shot across the bed, and the nurse had moved to close the blind, when a low exclamation from the doctor drew her back, to mark the first faint fluttering of the snowy lids over the long-closed eyes. Afterwards she remembered what a picture her youthful patient made, with the hue of renewed life creeping into her cheeks, in faint reflection of the nest of roseate colour in which she lay.

Carmel's hair was dark; so were her exquisitely pencilled eye-brows, and the long lashes which curled upward from her cheek. In her surroundings of pink—warm pink, such as lives in the heart of the sea-shell—their duskiness took on an added beauty; and nothing, not even the long, dark scar running from eye to chin could rob the face of its individuality and suggestion of charm. She was lovely; but it was the loveliness of line and tint, just as a child is lovely. Soul and mind were still asleep, but momentarily rousing, as all thought, to conscious being—and, if to conscious being, then to conscious suffering as well.

It was a solemn moment. If the man who loved her had been present—or even her brother, who, sullen as he was, must have felt the tie of close relationship rise superior even to his fears at an instant so critical,—it would have been more solemn yet. But with the exception of the doctor and possibly the nurse, only those interested in her as a witness in the most perplexing case on the police annals, were grouped in silent watchfulness about the room, waiting for the word or look which might cut the Gordian knot which none of them, as yet, had been able to untangle.

It came suddenly, as all great changes come. One moment her lids were down, her face calm, her whole figure quiet in its statue-like repose; the next, her big violet eyes had flashed open upon the world, and lips and limbs were moving feebly, but certainly, in their suddenly recovered freedom. It was then—and not at a later moment when consciousness had fully regained its seat—that her face, to those who stood nearest wore the aspect of an angel's. What she saw, or what vision remained to her from the mysterious world of which she had so long been a part, none ever knew—nor could she, perhaps, have told. But the rapture which informed her features and elevated her whole expression but poorly prepared them for the change which followed her first glance around on nurse and doctor. The beam which lay across the bed had been no brighter than her eye during that first tremulous instant of renewed life. But the clouds fell speedily and very human feelings peered from between those lids as she murmured, half petulantly:

"Why do you look at me so? Oh, I remember, I remember!"

And a flush, of which they little thought her weakened heart capable, spread over her features, hiding the scar and shaming her white lips. "What's the matter?" she complained again, as she tried to raise her hands, possibly to hide her face. "I cannot move as I used to do, and I feel—I feel—"

"You have been ill," came soothingly from the doctor. "You have been in bed many days; now you are better and will soon be well. This is your nurse." He said nothing of the others, who were so placed behind screens as to be invisible to her.

She continued to gaze, first at one, then at the other; confidently at the doctor, doubtfully at the nurse. As she did so, the flush faded and gave way to an anxious, troubled expression. Not just the expression anticipated by those who believed that, with returning consciousness, would come returning memory of the mysterious scene which had taken place between herself and sister, or between her sister and her brother, prior to Adelaide's departure for The Whispering Pines. Had they shared my knowledge—had they even so much as dreamed that their patient had been the companion of one or both of the others in this tragic escapade—how much greater would have been their wonder at the character of this awakening.

"You have the same kind look for me as always," were her next words, as her glance finally settled on the doctor. "But hers—Bring me the mirror," she cried. "Let me see with my own eyes what I have now to expect from every one who looks at me. I want to know before Lila comes in. Why isn't she here? Is she with—with—" She was breaking down, but caught herself back with surprising courage, and almost smiled, I was told. Then in the shrill tones which will not be denied, she demanded again, "The mirror!"

Nurse Unwin brought it. Her patient evidently remembered the fall she had had in her sister's room, and possibly the smart to her cheek when it touched the hot iron.

"I see only my forehead," she complained, as the nurse held the mirror before her. "Move it a little. Lower—lower," she commanded. Then suddenly "Oh!"

She was still for a long time, during which the nurse carried off the glass.

"I—I don't like it," she acknowledged quaintly to the doctor, as he leaned over her with compassionate words. "I shall have to get acquainted with myself all over again. And so I have been ill! I shouldn't have thought a little burn like that would make me ill. How Adelaide must have worried."

"Adelaide is—is not well herself. It distressed her to have been out when you fell. Don't you remember that she went out that night?"

"Did she? She was right. Adelaide must have every pleasure. She had earned her good times. I must be the one to stay home now, and look after things, and learn to be useful. I don't expect anything different. Call Adelaide, and let me tell her how—how satisfied I am."

"But she's ill. She cannot come. Wait till tomorrow, dear child. Rest is what you need now. Take these few drops and go to sleep again, and you'll not know yourself to-morrow."

"I don't know myself now," she repeated, glancing with slowly dilating eyes at the medicine glass he proffered. "I can't take it," she protested. "I forget now why, but I can't take anything more from a glass. I've promised not to, I think. Take it away; it makes me feel queer. Where is Adelaide?"

Her memory was defective. She could not seem to take in what the doctor told her. But he tried her again. Once more he spoke of illness as the cause of Adelaide's absence. Her attention wandered while he spoke of it.

"How it did hurt!" she cried. "But I didn't think much about it. I thought only of—" Next moment her voice rose in a shriek, thin but impetuous, and imbued with a note of excited feeling which made every person there start. "There should be two," she cried. "Two! Why is there only one?"

This sounded like raving. The doctor's face took on a look of concern, and the nurse stirred uneasily.

"One is not enough! That is why Adelaide is not satisfied; why she does not come and love and comfort me, as I expected her to. Tell her it is not too late yet, not too late yet, not too late—"

The doctor's hand was on her forehead. This "not too late," whatever she meant by it, was indescribably painful to the listeners, oppressed as they were by the knowledge that Adelaide lay in her grave, and that all fancies, all hopes, all meditated actions between these two were now, so far as this world goes, forever at an end.

"Rest," came in Dr. Carpenter's most soothing tones. "Rest, my little Carmel; forget everything and rest." He thought he knew the significance of her revolt from the glass he had offered her. She remembered the scene at the Cumberland dinner-table on that fatal night and shrank from anything that reminded her of it. Ordering the medicine put in a cup, he offered it to her again, and she drank it without question. As she quieted under its influence, the disappointed listeners, now tip-toeing carefully from the room, heard her murmur in final appeal:

"Cannot Adelaide spare one minute from—from her company downstairs, to wish me health and kiss me good night?"

Was it weakness, or a settled inability to remember anything but that which filled her own mind?

It proved to be a settled inability to take in any new ideas or even to remember much beyond the completion of that dinner. As the days passed and news of her condition came to me from time to time, I found that she had not only forgotten what had passed between herself and the rest of the family previous to their departure for the club-house, but all that had afterwards occurred at The Whispering Pines, even to her own presence there and the ride home. She could not even retain in her mind for any appreciable length of time the idea of Adelaide's death. Even after Dr. Carpenter, with infinite precautions, revealed to her the truth—not that Adelaide had been murdered, but that Adelaide had passed away during the period of her own illness, Carmel gave but one cry of grief, then immediately burst forth in her old complaint that Adelaide neglected her. She had lost her happiness and hope, and Adelaide would not spare her an hour.

This expression, when I heard of it, convinced me, as I believe it did some others, that her act of self-denial in not humouring my whim and flying from home and duty that night, had made a stronger impression on her mind than all that came after.

She never asked for Arthur. This may have grieved him; but, according to my faithful friend and attorney, it appeared to have the contrary effect, and to bring him positive relief. When it was borne in on him, as it was soon to be borne in on all, that her mind was not what it was, and that the beautiful Carmel had lost something besides her physical perfection in the awful calamity which had made shipwreck of the whole family, he grew noticeably more cheerful and less suspicious in his manner. Was it because the impending inquiry must go on without her, and proceedings, which had halted till now, be pushed with all possible speed to a finish? So those who watched him interpreted his changed mood, with a result not favourable to him.

With this new shock of Carmel's inability to explain her own part in this tragedy and thus release my testimony and make me a man again in my own eyes, I lost the sustaining power which had previously held me up. I became apathetic; no longer counting the hours, and thankful when they passed. Arthur had not been arrested; but he understood—or allowed others to see that he understood, the reason for the surveillance under which he was now strictly kept; and, though he showed less patience than myself under the shameful suspicion which this betokened, he did not break out into open conflict with the authorities, nor did he protest his innocence, or take any other stand than the one he had assumed from the first.

All this gave me much food for thought, but I declined to think. I had made up my mind from the moment I realised Carmel's condition, that there was nothing for me to do till after the inquest. The public investigation which this would involve, would show the trend of popular opinion, and thus enlighten me as to my duty. Meanwhile, I would keep to the old lines and do the best I could for myself without revealing the fact of Carmel's near interest in a matter she was in no better condition to discuss now than when in a state of complete unconsciousness.

Of that inquest, which was held in due course, I shall not say much. Only one new fact was elicited by its means, and that of interest solely as making clear how there came to be evidences of poison in Adelaide's stomach, without the quantity being great enough for more than a temporary disturbance.

Maggie, the second girl, had something to say about this when the phial which had held the poison was handed about for inspection. She had handled that phial many times on the shelf where it was kept. Once she had dropped it, and the cork coming out, some of the contents had escaped. Frightened at the mishap, she had filled the phial up with water, and put it, thus diluted, back on the shelf. No one had noticed the difference, and she had forgotten all about the matter until now. From her description, there must have been very little of the dangerous drug left in the phial; and the conclusions of Dr. Perry's autopsy received a confirmation which ended, after a mass of testimony tending rather to confuse than enlighten, the jury, in the non-committal verdict:

Death by strangulation at the hands of some person unknown.

I had expected this. The evidence, pointing as it did in two opposing directions, presented a problem which a coroner's jury could hardly be expected to solve. What followed, showed that not only they but the police authorities as well, acknowledged the dilemma. I was allowed one sweet half hour of freedom, then I was detained to await the action of the grand jury, and so was Arthur.

When I was informed of this latter fact, I made a solemn vow to myself. It was this: If it falls to my lot to be indicted for this murderous offence, I will continue to keep my own counsel, as I have already done, in face of lesser provocation and at less dangerous risk. But, if I escape and a true bill should be found against Arthur, then will I follow my better instinct, and reveal what I have hitherto kept concealed, even if the torment of the betrayal drive me to self-destruction afterwards. For I no longer cherished the smallest doubt, that to Carmel's sudden rage and to that alone, the death of Adelaide was due.

My reason for this change from troubled to absolute conviction can be easily explained. It dated from the inquest, and will best appear in the relation of an interview I held with my attorney, Charles Clifton, very soon after my second incarceration.

We had discussed the situation till there seemed to be nothing left to discuss. I understood him, and he thought he understood me. He believed Arthur guilty, and credited me with the same convictions. Thus only could he explain my inconceivable reticence on certain points he was very well assured I could make clear if I would. That he was not the only man who had drawn these same conclusions from my attitude both before and during the inquest, troubled me greatly and deeply disturbed my conscience, but I could indulge in no protests—or, rather would indulge in no protests—as yet. There was an unsolved doubt connected with some facts which had come out at the inquest—or perhaps, I should call it a circumstance not as yet fully explained—which disturbed me more than did my conscience, and upon this circumstance I must have light before I let my counsel leave me.

I introduced the topic thus:

"You remember the detached sentences taken down by the nurse during the period of Carmel's unconsciousness. They were regarded as senseless ravings, and such they doubtless were; but there was one of them which attracted my attention, and of which I should like an explanation. I wish I had that woman's little book here; I should like to read for myself those wandering utterances."

"You can," was the unexpected and welcome reply. "I took them all down in shorthand as they fell from Dr. Perry's lips. I have not had time since to transcribe them, but I can read some of them to you, if you will give me an idea as to which ones you want."

"Read the first—what she said on the day of the funeral. I do not think the rest matter very much."

Clifton took a paper from his pocket, and, after only a short delay, read out these words:

"December the fifth: Her sister's name, uttered many times and with greatly varied expression—now in reproach, now in terror, now in what seemed to me in tones of wild pleading and even despair. This continued at intervals all through the day.

"At three P.M., just as people were gathering for the funeral, the quick, glad cry: 'I smell flowers, sweet, sweet flowers!'"

Alas! she did.

"At three-forty P.M., as the services neared their close, a violent change took place in her appearance, and she uttered in shrill tones those astonishing words which horrified all below and made us feel that she had a clairvoyant knowledge of the closing of the casket, then taking place:

"'Break it open! Break it open! and see if her heart is there!'"

"Pause there," I said; "that is what I mean. It was not the only time she uttered that cry. If you will glance further down, you will come across a second exclamation of the like character."

"Yes; here it is. It was while the ubiquitous Sweetwater was mousing about the room."

"Read the very words he heard. I have a reason, Clifton. Humour me for this once."

"Certainly—no trouble. She cried, this time: 'Break it open! Break the glass and look in. Her heart should be there—her heart—her heart!" Horrible! but you insisted, Ranelagh."

"I thought I heard that word glass," I muttered, more to myself than to him. Then, with a choking fear of giving away my thought, but unable to resist the opportunity of settling my own fears, I asked: "Was there glass in the casket lid?"

"No; there never is."

"But she may have thought there was," I suggested hastily. "I'm much obliged to you, Clifton. I had to hear those sentences again. Morbidness, no doubt; the experience of the last three weeks would affect a stronger-minded man than myself." Then before he could reply: "What do you think the nurse meant by a violent change in her patient?"

"Why, she roused up, I suppose—moved, or made some wild or feverish gesture."

"That is what I should like to know. I may seem foolish and unnecessarily exacting about trifles; but I would give a great deal to learn precisely where she looked, and what she did at the moment she uttered those wild words. Is the detective Sweetwater still in town?"

"I believe so. Came up for the inquest but goes back to-night."

"See him, Clifton. Ask him to relate this scene. He was present, you know. Get him to talk about it. You can, and without rousing his suspicion, keen as they all say he is. And when he talks, listen and remember what he says. But don't ask questions. Do this for me, Clifton. Some day I may be able to explain my request, but not now."

"I'm at your service," he replied; but he looked hurt at being thus set to work in the dark, and I dared say nothing to ease the situation. I did not dare even to prolong the conversation on this subject, or on any other subject. In consequence, he departed speedily, and I spent the afternoon wondering whether he would return before the day ended, or leave me to the endurance of a night of suspense. I was spared this final distress. He came in again towards evening, and this was what he told me:

"I have seen Sweetwater, and was more fortunate in my interview than I expected. He talked freely, and in the course of the conversation, described the very occurrence in which you are so interested. Carmel had been lying quietly previous to this outbreak, but suddenly started into feverish life and, raising herself up in her bed, pointed straight before her and uttered the words we have so often repeated. That's all there was to it, and I don't see for my part, what you have gained by a repetition of the same, or why you lay so much stress upon her gesture. What she said was the thing, though even that is immaterial from a legal point of view—which is the only view of any importance to you or to me, at this juncture."

"You're a true friend to me," I answered, "and never more so than in this instance. Forgive me that I cannot show my appreciation of your goodness, or thank you properly for your performance of an uncongenial task. I am sunk deep in trouble. I'm not myself and cannot be till I know what action will be taken by the grand jury."

If he replied, I have no remembrance of it; neither do I recall his leave-taking. But I was presently aware that I was alone and could think out my hideous thought, undisturbed.

Carmel had pointed straight before her, shouting out: "Break in the glass!"

I knew her room; I had been taken in there once by Adelaide, as a sequence to a long conversation about Carmel, shortly after her first return from school. Adelaide wished to show me the cabinet in the wall, the cabinet at which Carmel undoubtedly pointed, if her bed stood as it had stood then. It was not quite full, at that time. It did not contain Adelaide's heart among the other broken toys which Carmel had destroyed with her own hand or foot, in her moments of frenzied passion—the canary, that would not pick from her hand, the hat she hated, the bowl which held only bread and milk when she wanted meat or cake. Adelaide had kept them all, locked behind glass and in full view of the child's eyes night and day, that the shame of those past destructive moments might guard her from their repetition and help her to understand her temper and herself. I had always thought it cruel of Adelaide, one of the evidences of the flint-like streak which ran through her otherwise generous and upright nature. But its awful prophecy was what affected me most now; for destruction had fallen on something more tender than aught that cabinet held.

Adelaide's heart! And Carmel acknowledged it—acknowledged that it should be there, with what else she had trampled upon and crushed in her white heat of rage. I could not doubt her guilt, after this. Whatever peace her forgetfulness had brought—whatever innocent longing after Adelaide—the wild cry of those first few hours, ere yet the impressions of her awful experience had succumbed to disease, revealed her secret and showed the workings of her conscience. It had not been understood; it had passed as an awesome episode. But for me, since hearing of it, she stood evermore convicted out of her own mouth—that lovely mouth which angels might kiss in her hours of joyous serenity; but from whose caress friends would fly, when the passion reigned in her heart and she must break, crush, kill, or go mad.

CHAPTER XXIII

AT TEN INSTEAD OF TWELVE

Forget the world around you.
Meantime friendship

Shall keep strict vigils for you, anxious, active,
Only be manageable when that friendship
Points you the road to full accomplishment.

Coleridge.

"I don't care a rush what you do to me. If you are so besotted by your prejudices that you refuse to see the nose before your face; if you don't believe your own officer who swore he saw Ranelagh's hands upon my sister's throat, then this world is all a jumble and it makes very little difference to me whether I'm alive or dead."

When these words of Arthur Cumberland were repeated to me, I echoed them in my inmost soul. I, too, cared very little whether I lived or died.

The grand jury reeled off its cases and finally took up ours. To the last I hoped—sincerely I think—that I should be the man to suffer indictment. But I hoped in vain. A true bill was brought against Arthur, and his trial was set for the eighteenth of January.

The first use I made of my liberty was to visit Adelaide's grave. In that sacred place I could best review my past and gather strength for the future. The future! Was it under my control? Did Arthur's fate hang upon my word? I believed so. But had I strength to speak that word? I had expected to; I had seen my duty clearly enough before the sitting of the grand jury. But now that Arthur was indicted—now that it was an accepted fact that he would have to stand trial instead of myself, I was conscious of such a recoil from my contemplated action that I lost all confidence in myself and my stoical adherence to what I considered the claims of justice.

Standing in the cemetery grounds with my eyes upon the snow-covered mound beneath which lay the doubly injured Adelaide, I had it out with myself, for good and all.

I trusted Arthur; I distrusted Carmel. But she had claims to consideration, which he lacked. She was a woman. Her fall would mean infinitely more to her than any disgrace to him. Even he had seemed to recognise this. Miserable and half-hearted as his life had been, he had shown himself man enough not to implicate his young sister in the crime laid to his charge. What then was I that I should presume to disregard his lead in the difficult maze in which we were both lost. Yet, because of the self-restraint he manifested, he had my sympathy and when I left the cemetery and took my mournful way back into town, it was with the secret resolution to stand his friend if I saw the case really going against him. Till then, I would consider the helpless girl, tongue-tied by her condition, and injured enough already by my misplaced love and its direful consequences.

The only change I now allowed myself was an occasional midnight stroll up Huested Street. This was as near as I dared approach Carmel's windows. I feared some watchful police spy. Perhaps I feared my own hardly-to-be-restrained longings.

Mr. Fulton's house and extensive grounds lay between this street and the dismal walls beyond the huge sycamore which lifted itself like a beacon above the Cumberland estate. But I allowed myself the doubtful pleasure of traversing this course, and this course only, and if I obtained one glimpse through bush and tree of the spot whither all my thoughts ran continuously, I went home satisfied.

This was before Carmel left with her nurse for Lakewood. After that event, I turned my head no more, in taking my midnight stroll. I was not told the day or hour of her departure. Happily, perhaps, for us both, for I could never have kept away from the station. I should have risked everything for one glimpse of her face, if only to satisfy my own judgment as to whether she would ever recognise me again, or remember what had occurred on that doleful night when the light of her intellect set in the darkness of sin and trouble.

The police had the same idea, I think, for I heard later that she was deliberately driven past The Whispering Pines, though the other road was more direct and less free, if anything, from possible spectators. They thought, no doubt, that a sight of the place might reawaken whatever memories remained of the last desperate scene preceding her brother and sister's departure for this out-of-the-way spot. They little knew how cruel was the test, or what a storm of realisation might have overwhelmed her mind as her eye fell on those accursed walls, peering from their bower of snow-laden, pines. But I did, and I never rested till I learned how she had borne herself in her slow drive by the two guarded gateways: merrily, it seems, and with no sign of the remembrances I feared. The test, if it were meant for such, availed them nothing; no more, indeed, than an encounter with her on the road, or at the station would have availed me. For the veil she begged for had shrouded her features completely, and it was only from her manner that those who accompanied her, perceived her light-heartedness and delight in this change.

One sentence, and one only, reached my ears of all she said before she disappeared from town.

"If Adelaide were only going, too! But I suppose I shall meet her and Mr. Ranelagh somewhere before my return. She must be very happy. But not so peaceful as I am. She will see that when we meet. I can hardly wait for the day."

Words which set me thinking; but which I was bound to acknowledge could be only the idle maunderings of a diseased mind from which all impressions had fled, save those of innocence and futile hope.

One incident more before I enter upon the serious business of the trial. I had no purpose in what I did. I merely followed the impulse of the moment, as I had so often done before in my selfish and thoughtless life, when I started one night for my walk at ten o'clock instead of twelve. I went the old way; and the old longing recurring at the one charmed spot on the road, I cast a quick look at the towering sycamore and the desolated house beneath, which, short as it was, roused feelings which kept my head lowered for the remainder of my walk north and to the very moment, when, on my return, the same chimneys and overhanging roofs came again into view through the wintry branches. Then habit lifted my head, and I paused to look again, when the low sound of a human voice, suppressed into a moan or sob, caused me to glance about for the woman or child who had uttered this note of sorrow. No one was in sight; but as I started to move on, I heard my name uttered in choked tones from behind the hedge separating the Fulton grounds from the city sidewalk.

I halted instantly. A lamp from the opposite side of the street threw a broad illumination across the walk where I stood, but the gate-posts behind threw a shadow. Had the voice issued from this isolated point of darkness? I went back to see. A pitiful figure was crouching there, a frail, agitated little being, whom I had no sooner recognised than my manner instantly assumed an air of friendly interest, called out by her timid and appealing attitude.

"Ella Fulton!" I exclaimed. "You wish to speak to me?"

"Hush!" she prayed, with a frightened gesture towards the house. "No one knows I am here. Mamma thinks me in bed, and papa, who is out, may come home any minute. Oh, Mr. Ranelagh, I'm in such misery and no one but you can give me any help. I have watched you go by night after night, and I have wanted to call out and beg you to come in and see me, or let me go and meet you somewhere, and I have not dared, it was so late. To-night you have come earlier, and I have slipped out and—O, Elwood, you won't think badly of me? It's all about Arthur, and I shall die if some one does not help me and tell me how I can reach him with a message."

As she spoke the last words, she caught at the gatepost which was too broad and ponderous to offer her any hold. Gravely I held out my arm, which she took; we were old friends and felt no necessity of standing on any sort of ceremony.

"You don't wish to bother," was her sensitive cry. "You had rather not stop; rather not listen to my troubles."

Had I shown my feelings so plainly as that? I felt mortified. She was a girl of puny physique and nervous manner—the last sort of person you would expect Arthur Cumberland to admire or even to have patience with, and the very last sort who could be expected to endure his rough ways, or find anything congenial to herself in his dissipated and purposeless life. But the freaks of youthful passion are endless, and it was evident that they loved each other sincerely.

Her tremulous condition and meek complaint went to my heart, notwithstanding my growing dread of any conversation between us on this all-absorbing but equally peace-destroying topic. Reassuringly pressing her hand, I was startled to find a small piece of paper clutched convulsively within it.

"For Arthur," she explained under her breath. "I thought you might find some way of getting it to him. Father and mother are so prejudiced. They have never liked him, and now they believe the very worst. They would lock me up if they knew I was speaking to you about him. Mother is very stern and says that all this nonsense between Arthur and myself must stop. That we must never—no matter whether he is cleared or—or—" Silence, then a little gasp, after which she added with an emphasis which bespoke the death of every hope: "She is very decided about it, Elwood."

I hardly blamed the mother.

"I—I love Arthur. I don't think him guilty and I would gladly stand by him if they would let me. I want him to know this. I want him to get such comfort as he can out of my belief and my desire to serve him. I want to sacrifice myself. But I can't, I can't," she moaned. "You don't know how mother frightens me. When she looks at me, the words falter on my tongue and I feel as if it would be easier to die than to acknowledge what is in my heart."

I could believe her. Mrs. Fulton was a notable woman, whom many men shrank from encountering needlessly. It was not her tongue, though that could be bitter enough, but a certain way she had of infusing her displeasure into attitude, tone, and manner, which insensibly sapped your self-confidence and forced you to accept her bad opinion of you as your rightful due. This, whether your judgment coincided with hers or not.

"Yet your mother is your very best friend," I ventured gently, with a realisation of my responsibility which did not add much to my self-possession.

She seemed startled.

"Not in this, not in this," she objected, with a renewal of her anxious glances, this time up and down the street. "I must get a word to Arthur. I must."

I saw that she had some deeper reason than appeared, for desiring communication with him. I was debating how best to meet the situation and set her right as to my ability to serve her, without breaking down her spirit too seriously, when I felt her feverish hand pressing her little note into my unwilling palm.

"Don't read it," she whispered, innocent of all offence and only anxious to secure my good offices. "It's for Arthur. I've used the thinnest paper, so that you can secrete it in something he will be sure to get. Don't disappoint me. I was sorry for you, too, and glad when they let you out. Both of you are old playmates of mine, but Arthur—"

I had to tell her; I had to dash her small hopes to the ground.

"Forgive me, Ella," I said, "but I cannot carry him this message or even get it to him secretly. I am watched myself; I know it, though I have never really detected the man doing it."

"Oh!" she ejaculated, terror-stricken at once. "Is there any one here, behind these trees or in the street on the other side of the hedge-row?"

I hastened to reassure her.

"No, no. If I've been followed, it was not so near as that. I cannot do what you ask for several reasons. Arthur will credit you with the best of impulses without your incurring any such risk."

"Yes, yes, but that's not enough. What shall I do? What shall I do?"

I strove to help her.

"There is a man," said I, "who sees him constantly and may be induced to assure Arthur of your belief and continued interest in him. That man is his lawyer, Mr. Moffat. Any one will tell you how to reach him."

"No, no," she disclaimed, hurriedly, breathlessly. "My last hope was in you. You wouldn't think the worse of me for—for what I've done; or let mother know. I couldn't tell a stranger even if he went right to Arthur with it. I'm not made that way. I couldn't stand the shame." Drawing back a step she wrung her small hands together, exclaiming, "What an unhappy girl I am!" Then stepping up to my side, she whispered in my ear: "There is something I could say which might—"

I stopped her. Right or wrong, I stopped her. I hadn't the courage just then to face the possibilities of what lay at the end of this simple sentence. She possessed evidence, or thought she did, which might help to clear Arthur. Evidence of what? Evidence which would implicate Carmel? The very thought unnerved me.

"I had rather not be the recipient of this confidence if it is at all important or at all in the line of testimony. Remember the man I mentioned. He will be glad to hear of anything helpful to his client."

Her distress mounted to passion.

"It's—it's something that will destroy my mother's confidence in me. I disobeyed her. I did what she would never have let me do if she had known. I—I used to meet Arthur in the driveway back by the barns. I had a key made to the little side door so that I could do it. I used to meet him late. I would get up out of bed when mother was asleep, and dress myself and sit at the window until I heard him come up the street. Then I would steal down and catch him on his way to the stables. I—I had a good reason for this, Elwood. He knew I would be there, and it brought him home earlier and not quite so—so full of liquor. If he was very bad, he would come up the other way and I would sit waiting and crying till three o'clock struck, then creep into my bed and try to sleep. Nights and nights I have done this. Nothing else in life seemed so important, for it did hold him back a little. But not so much as if he had loved me more. He loved me some, but he couldn't have loved me very much, or he would have sent me some word, or seen me, if but for a minute, since Adelaide's death. And he hasn't, he hasn't! and that makes it harder for me to acknowledge the watch I kept on him, and how I know he never went through our grounds for the second time that night. He went once, about nine, but not later. I am certain of this, for I was looking out for him till three in the morning. If he came back and then returned afterwards to town, it was through his own street, and that takes so long, he would never have been able to get to the place they said he did at the time they have agreed upon. Oh! I have studied every word of the case, to see if what I had to tell would help him any. Father cannot bear to see me with a newspaper in my hand, and mother comes and takes them out of my room; but I have managed to read every word since they accused him of being at the club-house that night, and I know that he needs some one to come out boldly in his cause, and I want to be that some one, and I will be, too, whatever happens to me, if—if I must," she faintly added.

I was dumb, but not from lack of interest, God knows, or from unsympathetic feeling for this brave-hearted girl. The significance of the situation was what held me speechless. Here was help for Arthur without my braving all the horrors of Carmel's downfall by any impulsive act of my own. For a moment, hope in one burning and renewing flame soared high in my breast. I was willing to accept my release in this way. I was willing to shift the load from my own back to the delicate shoulders of this shrinking but ardent girl. Then reason returned, if consideration halted, and I asked myself: "But is the help she offers of any practical worth? Would her timid declarations, trembling as she was between her awe of her parents and her desire to serve the man she loved, weigh in the balance against the evidence accumulated by the district attorney?"

It seemed doubtful. She would not be believed, and I should have to back up her statement with my own hitherto suppressed testimony. It was a hard case, any way I looked at it. A woman to be sacrificed whichever course I took. Contemplating the tremulous, half-fainting figure drooping in the shadows before me, such native chivalry as remained to me, urged me to spare this little friend of mine, so ungifted by nature, so innocent in intention, so sensitive and so shrinking in temperament and habit. Then Carmel's image rose before me, glorious, impassioned, driven by the fierce onrush of some mighty inherent force into violent deeds undreamed of by most women; but when thus undriven, gentle in manner, elevated in thought, refined as only a few rare characters are refined; and my heart stood still again with doubt, and I could not say: "It is your duty to save him at all hazards. Brave your father, brave your mother, brave public opinion and possibly the wrecking of your whole future, but tell the truth, and rid your days of doubt, your nights of remorse." I could not say this. So many things might happen to save Arthur, to save Carmel, to save the little woman before me. I would trust that future, temporise a bit and give such advice as would relieve us both from immediate fear without compromising Arthur's undoubted rights to justice.

Meanwhile, Ella Fulton had become distracted by new fears. The sound of sleigh-bells could be heard on the hill. It might be her father. Should she try to reach the house, or hide her small body, like a trapped animal's, on the dark side of the hedge? I was conscious of her thoughts, shared her uncertainties, notwithstanding the struggle then going on in my own mind. But I remained quiet and so did she, and the sleigh ultimately flew past us up the road. The sigh which broke from her lips as this terror subsided, brought my disordered thoughts to a focus. I must not keep her longer. Something must be said at once. As soon as she looked my way again, I spoke:

"Ella, this is no easy problem you have offered me. You are right in thinking that this testimony of yours might be of benefit to Arthur, and that you ought to give it in case of extremity. But I cannot advise you to obtrude it yet. I understand what it would cost you, and the sacrifice you would make is too great for the doubtful good which might follow. Neither must you trust me to act for you in this matter. My own position is too unstable for me to be of assistance to any one. I can sympathise with you, possibly as no one else can; but I cannot reach Arthur, either by word or by message. Your father is the man to appeal to in case interference becomes necessary and you must speak. You have not quite the same fear of him that you have of your mother. Take him into your confidence—not now but later when things press and you must have a friend. He's a just man. You may shock his fatherly susceptibilities, you may even lose some of his regard, but he will do the right thing by you and Arthur. Have confidence that this is so, and rest, little friend, in the hope and help it gives you. Will you?"

"I will try. I could only tell father on my knees, but I will do it if—if I must," she faltered out, unconsciously repeating her former phrase. "Now, I must go. You have been good; only I asked too much." And with no other farewell she left me and disappeared up the walk.

I lingered till I heard the faint click of her key in the door she had secretly made her own; then I moved on. As I did so, I heard a rustle somewhere about me on street or lawn. I never knew whence it came, but I felt assured that neither her fears nor mine had been quite unfounded; that a listener had been posted somewhere near us and that a part, if not all, we had said had been overheard. I was furious for an instant, then the soothing thought came that possibly Providence had ordained that the Gordian knot should be cut in just this way.

But the event bore no ostensible fruit. The week ended, and the case of the People against Arthur Cumberland was moved for trial.

CHAPTER XXIV

ALL THIS STOOD

It's fit this royal session do proceed;
And that, without delay, their arguments
Be now produc'd and heard

King Henry VIII.

There was difficulty, as you will conceive, in selecting an unprejudiced jury. But this once having been accomplished, the case went quickly and smoothly on under the able guidance of the prosecuting attorney.

I shall spare you the opening details, also much of the preliminary testimony. Enough that at the close of the sixth day, the outlook was a serious one for Arthur Cumberland. The prosecution appeared to be making good its claims. The quiet and unexpectedly dignified way in which, at the beginning, the defendant had faced the whole antagonistic court-room, with the simple plea of "Not Guilty," was being slowly but surely forgotten in the accumulated proofs of his discontented life under his sister's dominating influence, his desire for independence and a free use of the money held in trust for him by this sister under their father's will, the quarrels which such a situation would naturally evoke between characters cast in such different moulds and actuated by such opposing tastes and principles, and the final culmination of the same at the dinner-table when Adelaide forced him, as it were, to subscribe to her prohibition of all further use of liquor in their house. Following this evidence of motive, came the still more damaging one of opportunity. He was shown to have been in the club-house at or near the time of Adelaide's death. The matter of the bottles was gone into and the event in Cuthbert Road. Then I was called to the stand, and my testimony asked for.

I had prepared myself for the ordeal and faced it unflinchingly. That I might keep intact the one point necessary to Carmel's safety, I met my inquisitors, now as before, with the utmost candour in all other respects. Indeed, in one particular I was even more exact in my details than at any previous examination. Anxious to explain my agitated and hesitating advance through the club-house, prior to my discovery of the crime which had been committed there, I acknowledged what I had hitherto concealed, that in my first entrance into the building, I had come upon a man's derby hat and coat hanging in the lower hall, and when questioned more minutely on the subject, allowed it to appear that it was owing to the disappearance of these articles during my stay upstairs, that I had been led into saying that some one had driven away from The Whispering Pines before the coming of the police.

This, as you will see, was in open contradiction of my former statements that I had seen an unknown party, thus attired, driving away through the upper gateway just as I entered by the lower. But it was a contradiction which while noted by Mr. Moffat, failed to injure me with the jury, and much less with the spectators. The impression had become so firmly fixed in the public mind and in that of certain officials as well, that my early hesitations and misstatements were owing to a brotherly anxiety to distract attention from Arthur whose clothing they believed me to have recognised in these articles I have mentioned—that I rather gained than lost by what, under other circumstances would have seriously damaged my testimony. That I should prevaricate even to my own detriment, at a preliminary examination, only to tell the truth openly and like a man when in court and under the sanctity of an oath was, in the popular estimation, something to my credit; and Mr. Moffat, whose chief recommendation as counsel lay in his quick appreciation of the exigencies of the moment, did not press me too sharply on this point when he came to his cross-examination.

But in other respects he drove me hard. An effort was made by him, first of all, to discredit me as a witness. My lack of appreciation for Adelaide and my secret but absorbing love for Carmel were inexorably brought out: also the easy, happy-go-lucky tenor of my life, and my dogged persistence in any course I thought consistent with my happiness. My character was well known in this town of my birth, and it would have been folly for me to attempt to gloss it over. I had not even the desire to do so. If my sins exacted penance, I would pay it here and now and to the full. Only Carmel should not suffer. I refused to admit that she had given any evidences of returning my reckless passion. My tongue would not speak the necessary words, and it was not made to. It was not her character but mine which Mr. Moffat was endeavouring to assail.

But though I was thus shown up for what I was, in a manner most public and undesirable, neither the rulings of the court, nor the attitude of the jury betrayed any loss of confidence in me as a credible witness, and seeing this, the wily lawyer shifted his ground and confined himself to an endeavour to shake me on certain definite and important points. How were the pillows heaped upon the couch? What ones at top, what ones at bottom? Which did I remove first, and why did I remove any of them? What had I expected to find? These questions answered, the still more-to-be-dreaded ones followed of just how my betrothed looked at the moment I uncovered her face. Were the marks very plain upon her throat? How plain; and what did I mean by saying that I felt forced to lay my thumbs upon them? Was that a natural thing to do? Where was the candle at that moment? How many feet away? A candle does not give much light at that distance, was I sure that I saw those marks immediately; that they were dark enough and visible enough to draw my eyes from her face which would naturally attract my gaze first? It was horrible, devilish, but I won through, only to meet the still more disturbing question as to whether I saw any other evidences of strangulation besides the marks. I could only mention the appearance of the eyes; and when Mr. Moffat found that he could not shake me on this point, he branched off into a less harrowing topic and cross-examined me in regard to the ring. I had said that it was on her hand when I bade good-bye to her in her own house, and that it was not there when I came upon her dead. Had the fact made me curious to examine her hand? No. Then I could not tell whether the finger on which she wore it gave any evidence of this ring having been pulled off with violence? No. I could not swear that in my opinion it was? I could not.

The small flask of cordial and the three glasses, one clean and the others showing signs of having been used, were next taken up, but with no result for the defence. I had told all I knew about these in my direct examination; also about such matters as the bottles found on the kitchen table, the leaving of my keys at the Cumberland house, and the fact, well known, that the two bottles of wine left in the wine-vault and tabulated by the steward as so left in the list found in my apartments, were of an exclusive brand unlikely to be found anywhere else in town. I could add nothing more, and, having spoken the exact truth concerning them, from the very first, I ran no chance of contradicting myself even under the close fire of the opposing counsel.

But there was a matter I dreaded to see him approach, and, which, I was equally sure, with an insight unshared I believe by any one else in the whole courtroom, was equally dreaded by the prisoner.

This was the presence in the club-house chimney of the half-burned letter I had long ago been compelled, in my own defence, to acknowledge having written to the victim's young sister, Carmel Cumberland. As I saw District Attorney Fox about to enter upon this topic, I gathered myself together to meet the onslaught, for in this matter I could not be strictly truthful, since the least slip on my part might awaken the whole world to the fact that it could only have come there through the agency of Carmel herself.

What Mr. Moffat thought of it—what he hoped to prove in the prisoner's behalf by raking this subject over—it was left for me to discover later. The prisoner was an innocent man, in his eyes. I was not; and, while the time had not come for him to make this openly apparent, he was not above showing even now that the case contained a factor which weakened the prosecution—a factor totally dissociated with the openly accepted theory that the crime was simply the result of personal cupidity and drunken spite.

And in this he was right. It did weaken it—weakened it to the point of collapse, if the counsel for the defence had fully acted up to his opportunity. But something withheld him. Just at the moment when I feared the truth must come out, he hesitated and veered gradually away from this subject. In his nervous pacings to and fro before the witness stand, his eye had rested for a moment on Arthur's, and with this result. The situation was saved, but at a great loss to the defendant.

I began to cherish softened feelings towards Arthur Cumberland, from this moment. Was it then, or later, that he began in his turn to cherish new and less hostile feelings towards myself? He had hated me and vowed my death if I escaped the fate he could now dimly see opening out before himself; yet I could see that he was glad to see me slip from my tormentor's hands with my story unimpeached, and that he drew his breath more deeply and with much more evidence of freedom, now that my testimony had been thoroughly sifted and nothing had come to light implicating Carmel. I even thought I caught a kindly gleam in his eye as it met mine at this critical juncture, and by its light I understood my man and what he hoped from me. He wished me at any risk to himself, to unite with him in saving Carmel's good name. That I should accede to this; that I should respect his generous wishes and let him go to unmerited destruction for even so imperative an obligation as we both lay under, was a question for the morrow. I could not decide upon it to-day—not while the smallest hope remained that he would yet escape conviction by other means than the one which would wreck the life we were both intent on saving.

Several short examinations followed mine, all telling in their nature, all calculated to fix in the minds of the jury the following facts:

(Pray pardon the repetition. It is necessary to present the case to you just as it stood at this period of my greatest struggle.)

1—That Arthur, swayed by cupidity and moved to rage by the scene at the dinner-table, had, by some unknown means of a more or less violent character, prevailed upon Adelaide to accompany him to The Whispering Pines, in the small cutter, to which, in the absence of every servant about the place, he himself had harnessed the grey mare.

2—That in preparation for this visit to a spot remote from observation and closed against all visitors, they, still for some unknown reason, had carried between them a candlestick and candle, a flask of cordial, three glasses, and a small bottle marked "Poison"; also some papers, letters, or scraps of correspondence, among them the compromising line I had written to Carmel.

3—That, while in this building, at an hour not yet settled, a second altercation had arisen between them, or some attempt been made by the brother which had alarmed Adelaide and sent her flying to the telephone, in great agitation, with an appeal to the police for help. This telephone was in a front room and the jury was led to judge that she had gained access to it while her companion ransacked the wine-vault and brought the six bottles of spirit up from the cellar.

4—That her outcry had alarmed the prisoner in his turn, causing him to leave most of the bottles below, and hasten up to the room, where he completed the deed with which he had previously threatened her.

5—That poison having failed, he resorted to strangulation; after which—or before—came the robbery of her ring, the piling up of the cushions over the body in a vain endeavour to hide the deed, or to prolong the search for the victim. Then the departure—the locking of the front door behind the perpetrator; the flight of the grey horse and cutter through the blinding storm; the blowing off of the driver's hat; the identification of the same by means of the flour-mark left on its brim by the mechanic's wife; the presence of a portion of one of the two abstracted bottles in the stable where the horse was put up; and the appearance of Arthur with the other bottle at the door of the inn in Cuthbert Road, just as the clock was striking half-past eleven.

This latter fact might have been regarded as proving an alibi, owing to the length of road between the Cumberland house and the place just mentioned, if there had not been a short cut to town open to him by means of a door in the wall separating the Cumberland and Fulton grounds—a door which was found unlocked, and with the key in it, by Zadok Brown, the coachman, when he came home about three next morning.

All this stood; not an item of this testimony could be shaken. Most of it was true; some of it false; but what was false, so unassailable by any ordinary means, that, as I have already said, the clouds seemed settling heavily over Arthur Cumberland when, at the end of the sixth day, the proceedings closed.

The night that followed was a heavy one for me. Then came the fateful morrow, and, after that, the day of days destined to make a life-long impression on all who attended this trial.

CHAPTER XXV

"I AM INNOCENT"

All is oblique,
There's nothing level in our cursed natures,
But direct villainy. Therefore, be abhorred
All feasts, societies, and throngs of men!
His semblable, yea, himself, Timon disdains.

Timon of Athens.

I was early in my seat. Feeling the momentousness of the occasion—for this day must decide my action for or against the prisoner—I searched the faces of the jury, of the several counsel, and of the judge. I was anxious to know what I had to expect from them, in case my conscience got the better of my devotion to Carmel's interests and led me into that declaration of the real facts which was forever faltering on my tongue, without having, as yet, received the final impetus which could only end in speech.

To give him his rightful precedence, the judge showed an impenetrable countenance but little changed from that with which he had faced us all from the start. He, like most of the men involved in these proceedings, had been a close friend of the prisoner's father, and, in his capacity of judge in this momentous trial, had had to contend with his personal predilections, possibly with concealed sympathies, if not with equally well-concealed prejudices. This had lent to his aspect a sternness never observable in it before; but no man, even the captious Mr. Moffat, had seriously questioned his rulings; and, whatever the cost to himself, he had, up to this time, held the scales of justice so evenly that it would have taken an audacious mind to have ventured on an interpretation of his real attitude or mental leaning in this case.

From this imposing presence, nobly sustained by a well-proportioned figure and a head and face indicative of intellect and every kindly attribute, I turned to gaze upon Mr. Fox and his colleagues. One spirit seemed to animate them—confidence in their case, and unqualified satisfaction at its present status.

I was conscious of a certain ironic impulse to smile, as I noted the eager whisper and the bustle of preparation with which they settled upon their next witness and prepared to open their batteries upon him. How easily I could call down that high look, and into what a turmoil I could throw them all by an ingenuous demand to be recalled to the stand!

But the psychological moment had not yet come, and I subdued the momentary impulse and proceeded with my scrutiny of the people about me. The jury looked tired, with the exception of one especially alert little man who drank in even the most uninteresting details with avidity. But they all had good faces, and none could doubt their interest, or that they were fully alive to the significance of the occasion.

Mr. Moffat, leading counsel for the defendant, was a spare man of unusual height, modified a little, and only a little, by the forward droop of his shoulders. Nervous in manner, quick, short, sometimes rasping in speech, he had the changeful eye and mobile expression of a very sensitive nature; and from him, if from any one, I might hope to learn how much or how little Arthur had to fear from the day's proceedings. But Mr. Moffat's countenance was not as readable as usual. He looked preoccupied—a strange thing for him; and, instead of keeping his eye on the witness, as was his habitual practice, he allowed it to wander over the sea of heads before him, with a curious expectant interest which aroused my own curiosity, and led me to hunt about for its cause.

My first glance was unproductive. I saw only the usual public, such as had confronted us the whole week, with curious and increasing interest. But as I searched further, I discerned in an inconspicuous corner, the bowed head, veiled almost beyond recognition, of Ella Fulton. It was her first appearance in court. Each day I had anticipated her presence, and each day I had failed to see my anticipations realised. But she was here now, and so were her father and her cold and dominating mother; and, beholding her thus accompanied, I fancied I understood Mr. Moffat's poorly concealed excitement. But another glance at Mrs. Fulton assured me that I was mistaken in this hasty surmise. No such serious purpose, as I feared, lay back of their presence here to-day. Curiosity alone explained it; and as I realised what this meant, and how little understanding it betokened of the fierce struggle then going on in the timid breast of their distracted child, a sickening sense of my own responsibility drove Carmel's beauty, and Carmel's claims temporarily from my mind, and following the direction of Ella's thoughts, if not her glances, I sought in the face of the prisoner a recognition of her presence, if not of the promise this presence brought him.

His eye had just fallen on her. I was assured of this by the sudden softening of his expression—the first real softening I had ever seen in it. It was but a momentary flash, but it was unmistakable in its character, as was his speedy return to his former stolidity. Whatever his thoughts were at sight of his little sweetheart, he meant to hide them even from his counsel—most of all from his counsel, I decided after further contemplation of them both. If Mr. Moffat still showed nervousness, it was for some other reason than anxiety about this little body hiding from sight behind the proudly held figures of father and mother.

The opening testimony of the day, while not vital, was favourable to the prosecution in that it showed Arthur's conduct since the murder to have been inconsistent with perfect innocence. His belated return at noon the next day, raging against the man who had been found in an incriminating position on the scene of crime, while at the same time failing to betray his own presence there till driven to it by accumulating circumstances and the persistent inquiries of the police; the care he took to avoid drink, though constant tippling was habitual to him and formed the great cause of quarrel between himself and the murdered Adelaide; his haunting of Carmel's door and anxious listening for any words she might let fall in her delirium; the suspicion which he constantly betrayed of the nurse when for any reason he was led to conclude that she had heard something which he had not; his behaviour at the funeral and finally his action in demanding to have the casket-lid removed that he might look again at the face he had made no effort to gaze upon when opportunity offered and time and place were seemly: these facts and many more were brought forward in grim array against the prisoner, with but little opposition from his counsel and small betrayal of feeling on the part of Arthur himself. His stolid face had remained stolid even when the ring which had fallen out of his sister's casket was shown to the jury and the connection made between its presence there and the intrusion of his hand into the same, on the occasion above mentioned. This once thoughtless, pleasure-loving, and hopelessly dissipated boy had not miscalculated his nerve. It was sufficient for an ordeal which might have tried the courage and self-possession of the most hardened criminal.

Then came the great event of the day, in anticipation of which the court-room had been packed, and every heart within it awakened by slow degrees to a state of great nervous expectancy. The prosecution rested and the junior counsel for the defence opened his case to the jury.

If I had hoped for any startling disclosure, calculated to establish his client's alleged alibi, or otherwise to free the same from the definite charge of murder, I had reason to be greatly disappointed by this maiden effort of a young and inexperienced lawyer. If not exactly weak, there was an unexpected vagueness in its statements which seemed quite out of keeping with the emphatic declaration which he made of the prisoner's innocence.

Even Arthur was sensible of the bad effect made by this preliminary address. More than once during its delivery and notably at its conclusion, he turned to Mr. Moffat, with a bitter remark, which was not without effect on that gentleman's cheek, and at once called forth a retort stinging enough to cause Arthur to sink back into his place, with the first sign of restlessness I had observed in him.

"Moffat is sly. Moffat has something up his sleeve. I will wait till he sees fit to show it," was my thought; then, as I caught a wild and pleading look from Ella, I added in positive assertion to myself, "And so must she."

Answering her unspoken appeal with an admonitory shake of the head, I carelessly let my fingers rest upon my mouth until I saw that she understood me and was prepared to follow my lead for a little while longer.

My satisfaction at this was curtailed by the calling of Arthur Cumberland to the stand to witness in his own defence.

I had dreaded this contingency. I saw that for some reason, both his counsel and associate counsel, were not without their own misgivings as to the result of their somewhat doubtful experiment.

A change was observable in this degenerate son of the Cumberlands since many there had confronted him face to face. Physically he was improved. Enough time had elapsed since his sudden dropping of old habits, for him to have risen above its first effects and to have acquired that tone of personal dignity which follows a successful issue to any moral conflict. But otherwise the difference was such as to arouse doubt as to the real man lurking behind his dogged, uncommunicative manner.

Even with the knowledge of his motives which I believed myself to possess, I was at a loss to understand his indifference to self and the immobility of manner he maintained under all circumstances and during every fluctuation which took place in the presentation of his case, or in the temper of the people surrounding him. I felt that beyond the one fact that he could be relied upon to protect Carmel's name and Carmel's character, even to the jeopardising of his case, he was not to be counted on, and might yet startle many of us, and most notably of all, the little woman waiting to hear what he had to say in his own defence before she threw herself into the breach and made that devoted attempt to save him, in his own despite, which had been my terror from the first and was my terror now.

Perjury! but not in his own defence—rather in opposition to it—that is what his counsel had to fear; and I wondered if they knew it. My attention became absorbed in the puzzle. Carmel's fate, if not

Ella's—and certainly my own—hung upon the issue. This I knew, and this I faced, calmly, but very surely, as, the preliminary questions having been answered, Mr. Moffat proceeded.

The witness's name having been demanded and given and some other preliminary formalities gone through, he was asked:

"Mr. Cumberland, did you have any quarrel with your sister during the afternoon or evening of December the second?"

"I did." Then, as if not satisfied with this simple statement, he blurted forth: "And it wasn't the first. I hated the discipline she imposed upon me, and the disapproval she showed of my ways and the manner in which I chose to spend my money."

A straightforward expression of feeling, but hardly a judicious one.

Judge Edwards glanced, in some surprise, from Mr. Moffat to the daring man who could choose thus to usher in his defence; and then, forgetting his own emotions, in his instinctive desire for order, rapped sharply with his gavel in correction of the audible expression of a like feeling on the part of the expectant audience.

Mr. Moffat, apparently unaffected by this result of his daring move, pursued his course, with the quiet determination of one who sees his goal and is working deliberately towards it.

"Do you mind particularising? Of what did she especially disapprove in your conduct or way of spending money?"

"She disapproved of my fondness for drink. She didn't like my late hours, or the condition in which I frequently came home. I did not like her expressions of displeasure, or the way she frequently cut me short when I wanted to have a good time with my friends. We never agreed. I made her suffer often and unnecessarily. I regret it now; she was a better sister to me than I could then understand."

This was uttered slowly and with a quiet emphasis which reawakened that excited hum the judge had been at such pains to quell a moment before. But he did not quell it now; he seemed to have forgotten his duty in the strong interest called up by these admissions from the tongue of the most imperturbable prisoner he had had before him in years.

Mr. Moffat, with an eye on District Attorney Fox, who had shown his surprise at the trend the examination was taking by a slight indication of uneasiness, grateful enough, no doubt, to the daring counsellor, went on with his examination:

"Mr. Cumberland, will you tell us when you first felt this change of opinion in regard to your sister?"

Mr. Fox leaped to his feet. Then he slowly reseated himself. Evidently he thought it best to let the prisoner have his full say. Possibly he may have regretted his leniency the next moment when, with a solemn lowering of his head, Arthur answered:

"When I saw my home desolated in one dreadful night. With one sister dead in the house, the victim of violence, and another delirious from fright or some other analogous cause, I had ample time to think—and I used that time. That's all."

Simple words, read or repeated; but in that crowded court-room, with every ear strained to catch the lie which seemed the only refuge for the man so hemmed in by circumstance, these words, uttered without the least attempt at effect, fell with a force which gave new life to such as wished to see this man acquitted.

His counsel, as if anxious to take advantage of this very expectation to heighten the effect of what followed, proceeded immediately to inquire:

"When did you see your sister Adelaide for the last time alive?"

A searching question. What would be his reply?

A very quiet one.

"That night at the dinner-table. When I left the room, I turned to look at her. She was not looking at me; so I slammed the door and went upstairs. In an hour or so, I had left the house to get a drink. I got the drink, but I never saw Adelaide again till I saw her in her coffin."

This blunt denial of the crime for which he stood there arraigned, fell on my heart with a weight which showed me how inextinguishable is the hope we cherish deep down under all surface convictions. I had been unconscious of this hope, but it was there. It seemed to die a double death at these words. For I believed him! Courage is needed for a lie. There were no signs visible in him, as yet, of his having drawn upon this last resource of the despairing. I should know it when he did; he could not hide the subtle change from me.

To others, this declaration came with greater or less force, according as it was viewed in the light of a dramatic trick of Mr. Moffat's, or as the natural outburst of a man fighting for his life in his own way and with his own weapons. I could not catch the eye of Ella cowering low in her seat, so could not judge what tender chords had been struck in her sensitive breast by these two assertions so dramatically offset against each other—the one, his antagonism to the dead; the other, his freedom from the crime in which that antagonism was supposed to have culminated.

Mr. Moffat, satisfied so far, put his next question with equal directness:

"Mr. Cumberland, you have mentioned seeing your sister in her coffin. When was this?"

"At the close of her funeral, just before she was carried out."

"Was that the first and only time you had seen her so placed?"

"It was."

"Had you seen the casket itself prior to this moment of which you speak?"

"I had not."

"Had you been near it? Had you handled it in any way?"

"No, sir."

"Mr. Cumberland, you have heard mention made of a ring worn by your sister in life, but missing from her finger after death?"

"I have."

"You remember this ring?"

"I do."

"Is this it?"

"It is, so far as I can judge at this distance."

"Hand the ring to the witness," ordered the judge.

The ring was so handed.

He glanced at it, and said bitterly: "I recognise it. It was her engagement ring."

"Was this ring on her finger that night at the dinner-table?"

"I cannot say, positively, but I believe so. I should have noticed its absence."

"Why, may I ask?"

For the first time the prisoner flushed and the look he darted at his counsel had the sting of a reproach in it. Yet he answered: "It was the token of an engagement I didn't believe in or like. I should have hailed any proof that this engagement was off."

Mr. Moffat smiled enigmatically.

"Mr. Cumberland, if you are not sure of having seen this ring then, when did you see it and where?"

A rustle from end to end of that crowded court-room. This was an audacious move. What was coming? What would be the answer of the man who was believed not only to have made himself the possessor of this ring, but to have taken a most strange and uncanny method of disposing of it afterward? In the breathless hush which followed this first involuntary expression of feeling, Arthur's voice rose, harsh but steady in this reply:

"I saw it when the police showed it to me, and asked me if I could identify it."

"Was that the only time you have seen it up to the present moment?"

Instinctively, the witness's right hand rose; it was as if he were mentally repeating his oath before he uttered coldly and with emphasis, though without any show of emotion:

"It is."

The universal silence gave way to a universal sigh of excitement and relief. District Attorney Fox's lips curled with an imperceptible smile of disdain, which might have impressed the jury if they had been looking his way; but they were all looking with eager and interested eyes at the prisoner, who had just uttered this second distinct and unequivocal denial.

Mr. Moffat noted this, and his own lip curled, but with a very different show of feeling from that which had animated his distinguished opponent. Without waiting for the present sentiment to cool, he proceeded immediately with his examination:

"You swear that you have seen this ring but once since the night of your sister's death, and that was when it was shown you in the coroner's office?"

"I do."

"Does this mean that it was not in your possession at any time during that interim?"

"It certainly does."

"Mr. Cumberland, more than one witness has testified to the fact of your having been seen to place your hand in the casket of your sister, before the eyes of the minister and of others attending her funeral. Is this true?"

"It is."

"Was not this a most unusual thing to do?"

"Perhaps. I was not thinking about that. I had a duty to perform, and I performed it."

"A duty? Will you explain to the jury what duty?"

The witness's head rose, then sank. He, as well as every one else, seemed to be impressed by the solemnity of the moment. Though the intensity of my own interest would not allow my eyes to wander from his face, I could imagine the strained look in Ella's, as she awaited his words.

They came in another instant, but with less steadiness than he had shown before. I even thought I could detect a tremor in his muscles, as well as in his voice:

"I had rebelled against my sister's wishes; I had grieved and deceived her up to the very night of her foul and unnatural death—and all through drink."

Here his eye flashed, and for that fleeting moment he looked a man. "I wished to take an oath—an oath I would remember. It was for this purpose I ordered the casket opened, and thrust my fingers through the flowers I found there. When my fingers touched my sister's brow, I inwardly swore never to taste liquor again. I have kept that oath. Difficult as it was, in my state of mind, and with all my troubles, I have kept it—and been misunderstood in doing so," he added, in lower tones, and with just a touch of bitterness.

It was such an unexpected explanation, and so calculated to cause a decided and favourable reaction in the minds of those who had looked upon this especial act of his as an irrefutable proof of guilt, that it was but natural that some show of public feeling should follow. But this was checked almost immediately, and Mr. Moffat's voice was heard rising again in his strange but telling examination:

"When you thrust your hand in to take this oath, did you drop anything into your sister's casket?"

"I did not. My hand was empty. I held no ring, and dropped none in. I simply touched her forehead."

This added to the feeling; and, in another instant, the excitement might have risen into hubbub, had not the emotions of one little woman found vent in a low and sobbing cry which relieved the tension and gave just the relief needed to hold in check the overstrained feelings of the crowd. I knew the voice and cast one quick glance that way, in time to see Ella sinking affrightedly out of sight under the dismayed looks of father and mother; then, anxious to note whether the prisoner had recognised her, too, looked hastily back to find him standing quietly and unmoved, with his eyes on his counsel and his lips set in the stern line which was slowly changing his expression.

That counsel, strangely alive to the temper and feelings of his audience, waited just long enough for the few simple and solemn words uttered by the accused man to produce their full effect, then with a side glance at Mr. Fox, whose equanimity he had at last succeeded in disturbing, and whose cross-examination of the prisoner he had still to fear, continued his own examination by demanding why, when the ring was discovered in Adelaide's casket and he saw what inferences would be drawn from the fact, he had not made an immediate public explanation of his conduct and the reasons he had had for putting his hand there.

"I'm not a muff," shot from the prisoner's lips, in his old manner. "A man who would take such an oath, in such a way, and at such a time, is not the man to talk about it until he is forced to. I would not talk about it now—"

He was checked at this point; but the glimpse we thus obtained of the natural man, in this indignant and sullen outburst, following so quickly upon the solemn declarations of the moment before, did more for him in the minds of those present than the suavest and most discreet answer given under the instigation of his counsel. Every face showed pleasure, and for a short space, if for no longer, all who listened were disposed to accept his assertions and accord the benefit of doubt to this wayward son of an esteemed father.

To me, who had hoped nothing from Moffat's efforts, the substantial nature of the defence thus openly made manifest, brought reanimation and an unexpected confidence in the future.

The question as to who had dropped the ring into the casket if Arthur had not—the innocent children, the grieving servants—was latent, of course, in every breast, but it had not yet reached the point demanding expression.

Meanwhile, the examination proceeded.

"Mr. Cumberland, you have stated that you did not personally drop this ring into the place where it was ultimately found. Can you tell us of your own knowledge who did?"

"I cannot. I know nothing about the ring. I was much surprised, probably more surprised than any one else, to hear of its discovery in that place."

The slip—and it was a slip for him to introduce that more—was immediately taken advantage of by his counsel.

"You say 'more,' Why should it be more of a surprise to you than to any one else to learn where this missing engagement ring of your sister's had been found?"

Again that look of displeasure directed towards his questioner, and a certain additional hardness in his reply, when he finally made it.

"I was her brother. I had a brother's antipathies and rightful suspicions. I could not see how that ring came to be where it was, when the only one interested in its restoration was in prison."

This was a direct blow at myself, and of course called Mr. Fox to his feet, with a motion to strike out this answer. An altercation followed between him and Mr. Moffat, which, deeply as it involved my life and reputation, failed to impress me, as it might otherwise have done, if my whole mind had not been engaged in reconciling the difficulty about this ring with what I knew of Carmel and the probability which existed of her having been responsible for its removal from her sister's hand. But Carmel had been ill since, desperately ill and unconscious. She could have had nothing to do with its disposal afterwards among the flowers at her sister's funeral. Nor had she been in a condition to delegate this act of concealment to another. Who, then, had been the intermediary in this business? The question was no longer a latent one in my mind; it was an insistent one, compelling me either to discredit Arthur's explanation (in which case anything might be believed of him) or to accept for good and all this new theory that some person of unknown identity had played an accessory's part in this crime, whose full burden I had hitherto laid upon the shoulders of the impetuous Carmel. Either hypothesis brought light. I began to breathe again the air of hope, and if observed at that moment, must have presented the odd spectacle of a man rejoicing in his own shame and accepting with positive uplift, the inevitable stigma cast upon his honour by the suggestive sentence just hurled at him by an indignant witness.

The point raised by the district attorney having been ruled upon and sustained by the court, Mr. Moffat made no effort to carry his inquiries any further in the direction indicated; but I could see, with all my inexperience of the law and the ways of attorneys before a jury, that the episode had produced its inevitable result, and that my position, as a man released from suspicion, had received a shock, the results of which I might yet be made to feel.

A moment's pause followed, during which some of Mr. Moffat's nervousness returned. He eyed the prisoner doubtfully, found him stoical and as self-contained as at the beginning of his examination, and plunged into a topic which most people had expected him to avoid. I certainly had, and felt all the uncertainty and secret alarm which an unexpected move occasions where the issue is momentous with life or death. I was filled with terror, not for the man on trial, but for my secret. Was it shared by the defence? Was Mr. Moffat armed with the knowledge I thought confined to myself and Arthur? Had the latter betrayed the cause I had been led to believe he was ready to risk his life to defend? Had I mistaken his gratitude to myself; or had I underrated Mr. Moffat's insight or powers of persuasion? We had just been made witness to one triumph on the part of this able lawyer in a quarter deemed unassailable by the prosecution. Were we about to be made witnesses of another? I felt the sweat start on my forehead, and was only able to force myself into some show of self-possession by the evident lack of perfect assurance with which this same lawyer now addressed his client.

The topic which had awakened in me these doubts and consequent agitation will appear from the opening question.

"Mr. Cumberland, to return to the night of your sister's death. Can you tell us what overcoat you put on when leaving your house?"

Arthur was as astonished and certainly as disconcerted, if not as seriously alarmed, as I was, by this extraordinary move. Surprise, anger, then some deeper feeling rang in his voice as he replied:

"I cannot. I took down the first I saw and the first hat."

The emphasis placed on the last three words may have been meant as a warning to his audacious counsel, but if so, it was not heeded.

"Took down? Took down from where?"

"From the rack in the hall where I hang my things; the side hall leading to the door where we usually go out."

"Have you many coats—overcoats, I mean?"

"More than one."

"And you do not know which one you put on that cold night?"

"I do not."

"But you know what one you wore back?"

"No."

Short, sharp, and threatening was this no. A war was on between this man and his counsel, and the wonder it occasioned was visible in every eye. Perhaps Mr. Moffat realised this; this was what he had dreaded, perhaps. At all events, he proceeded with his strange task, in apparent oblivion of everything but his own purpose.

"You do not know what one you wore back?"

"I do not."

"You have seen the hat and coat which have been shown here and sworn to as being the ones in which you appeared on your return to the house, the day following your sister's murder?"

"I have."

"Also the hat and coat found on a remote hook in the closet under the stairs, bearing the flour-mark on its under brim?"

"Yes, that too."

"Yet cannot say which of these two overcoats you put on when you left your home, an hour or so after finishing your dinner?"

Trapped by his own lawyer—visibly and remorselessly trapped! The blood, shooting suddenly into the astounded prisoner's face, was reflected on the cheeks of the other lawyers present. Even Mr. Fox betrayed his surprise; but it was a surprise not untinged by apprehension. Mr. Moffat must feel very sure of himself to venture thus far. I, who feared to ask myself the cause of this assurance, could only wait and search the partially visible face of little Ella for an enlightenment, which was no more to be found there than in the swollen features of the outraged Arthur. The excitement which this event caused, afforded the latter some few moments in which to quell his own indignation; and when he spoke, it was passionately, yet not without some effort at restraint.

"I cannot. I was in no condition to notice. I was bent on going into town, and immediately upon coming downstairs went straight to the rack and pulled on the first things that offered."

It appeared to be a perfect give-a-way. And it was, but it was a give-a-way which, I feared, threatened Carmel rather than her brother.

Mr. Moffat, still nervous, still avoiding the prisoner's eye, relentlessly pursued his course, unmindful—wilfully so, it appeared—of the harm he was doing himself, as well as the witness.

"Mr. Cumberland, were a coat and hat all that you took from that hall?"

"No, I took a key—a key from the bunch which I saw lying on the table."

"Did you recognise this key?"

"I did."

"What key was it?"

"It belonged to Mr. Ranelagh, and was the key to the club-house wine-vault."

"Where did you put it after taking it up?"

"In my trousers' pocket."

"What did you do then?"

"Went out, of course."

"Without seeing anybody?"

"Of course. Whom should I see?"

It was angrily said, and the flush, which had begun to die away, slowly made its way back into his cheeks.

"Are you willing to repeat that you saw no one?"

"There was no one."

A lie! All knew it, all felt it. The man was perjuring himself, under his own counsel's persistent questioning on a point which that counsel had evidently been warned by him to avoid. I was assured of this by the way Moffat failed to meet Arthur's eye, as he pressed on hastily, and in a way to forestall all opposition.

"There are two ways of leaving your house for the city. Which way did you take?"

"The shortest. I went through my neighbour's grounds to Huested Street."

"Immediately?"

"As soon as I could. I don't know what you mean by immediately."

"Didn't you stop at the stable?"

A pause, during which more than one person present sat breathless. These questions were what might be expected from Mr. Fox in cross-examination. They seemed totally unsuited to a direct examination at the hands of his own counsel. What did such an innovation mean?

"Yes, I stopped at the stable."

"What to do?"

"To look at the horses."

"Why?"

"One of them had gone lame. I wanted to see his condition."

"Was it the grey mare?"

Had the defence changed places with the prosecution? It looked like it; and Arthur looked as if he considered Mr. Moffat guilty of the unheard of, inexplainable act, of cross-examining his own witness. The situation was too tempting for Mr. Fox to resist calling additional attention to it. With an assumption of extreme consideration, he leaned forward and muttered under his breath to his nearest colleague, but still loud enough for those about him to hear:

"The prisoner must know that he is not bound to answer questions when such answers tend to criminate him.".

A lightning glance, shot in his direction, was the eloquent advocate's sole reply.

But Arthur, nettled into speaking, answered the question put him, in a loud, quick tone: "It was not the grey mare; but I went up to the grey mare before going out; I patted her and bade her be a good girl."

"Where was she then?"

"Where she belonged—in her stall."

The tones had sunk; so had the previously lifted head; he no longer commanded universal sympathy or credence. The effect of his former avowals was almost gone.

Yet Mr. Moffat could smile. As I noticed this, and recognised the satisfaction it evinced, my heart went down, in great trouble. This esteemed advocate, the hero of a hundred cases, was not afraid to have it known that Arthur had harnessed that mare; he even wanted it known. Why? There could be but one answer to that—or, so I thought, at the moment. The next, I did not know what to think; for he failed to pursue this subject, and simply asked Arthur if, upon leaving, he had locked the stable-door.

"Yes—no,—I don't remember," was the bungling, and greatly confused reply.

Mr. Moffat glanced at the jury, the smile still on his lips. Did he wish to impress that body with the embarrassment of his client?

"Relate what followed. I am sure the jury will be glad to hear your story from your own lips."

"It's a beastly one, but if I've got to tell it, here it is: I went straight down to Cuthbert Road and across the fields to the club-house. I had not taken the key to the front door, because I knew of a window I could shake loose. I did this and went immediately down to the wine-vault. I used an electric torch of my own for light. I pulled out several bottles, and carried them up into the kitchen, meaning to light the gas, kindle a fire, and have a good time generally. But I soon found that I must do without light if I stayed there. The meter had been taken out; and to drink by the flash of an electric torch was anything but a pleasing prospect. Besides—" here he flashed at his counsel a glance, which for a moment took that gentleman aback—"I had heard certain vague sounds in the house which alarmed me, as well as roused my curiosity. Choosing the bottle I liked best, I went to investigate these sounds."

Mr. Moffat started. His witness was having his revenge. Kept in ignorance of his counsel's plan of defence, he was evidently advancing testimony new to that counsel. I had not thought the lad so subtle, and quaked in secret contemplation of the consequences. So did some others; but the interest was intense. He had heard sounds—he acknowledged it. But what sounds?

Observing the excitement he had caused, and gratified, perhaps, that he had succeeded in driving that faint but unwelcome smile from Mr. Moffat's lips, Arthur hastened to add:

"But I did not complete my investigations. Arrived at the top of the stairs, I heard what drove me from the house at once. It was my sister's voice—Adelaide's. She was in the building, and I stood almost on a level with her, with a bottle in my pocket. It did not take me a minute to clamber through the window. I did not stop to wonder, or ask why she was there, or to whom she was speaking. I just fled and made my way as well as I could across the golf-links to a little hotel on Cuthbert Road, where I had been once before. There I emptied my bottle, and was so overcome by it that I did not return home till noon the next day. It was on the way to the Hill that I was told of the awful occurrence which had taken place in the club-house after I had left it. That sobered me. I have been sober ever since."

Mr. Moffat's smile came back. One might have said that he had been rather pleased than otherwise by the introduction of this unexpected testimony.

But I doubt if any one but myself witnessed this evidence of good-humour on his part. Arthur's attitude and Arthur's manner had drawn all eyes to himself. As the last words I have recorded left his lips, he had raised his head and confronted the jury with a straightforward gaze. The sturdiness and immobility of his aspect were impressive, in spite of his plain features and the still unmistakable signs of long cherished discontent and habitual dissipation. He had struck bottom with his feet, and there he would stand,—or so I thought as I levelled my own glances at him.

But I had not fully sounded all of Alonzo Moffat's resources. That inscrutable lawyer and not-easily-to-be-understood man seemed determined to mar every good impression his unfortunate client managed to make.

Ignoring the new facts just given, undoubtedly thinking that they would be amply sifted in the coming cross-examination, he drew the attention of the prisoner to himself by the following question:

"Will you tell us again how many bottles of wine you took from the club-house?"

"One. No—I'm not sure about that—I'm not sure of anything. I had only one when at the inn in Cuthbert Road."

"You remember but one?"

"I had but one. One was enough. I had trouble in carrying that."

"Was the ground slippery?"

"It was snowy and it was uneven. I stumbled more than once in crossing the links."

"Mr. Cumberland, is there anything you would like to say in your own defence before I close this examination?"

The prisoner thus appealed to, let his eye rest for a moment on the judge, then on the jury, and finally on one little white face lifted from the crowd before him as if to meet and absorb his look. Then he straightened himself, and in a quiet and perfectly natural voice, uttered these simple words:

"Nothing but this: I am innocent."

CHAPTER XXVI

THE SYLLABLE OF DOOM

I alit
On a great ship lightning-split,
And speeded hither on the sigh
Of one who gave an enemy
His plank, then plunged aside to die.

Prometheus Unbound.

Recess followed. Clifton and I had the opportunity of exchanging a few words. He was voluble; I was reticent. I felt obliged to hide from him the true cause of the deep agitation under which I was labouring. Attached as he was to me, keenly as he must have felt my anomalous position, he was too full of Moffat's unwarrantable introduction of testimony damaging to his client, to think or talk of anything else.

"He has laid him open to attack on every side. Fox has but to follow his lead, and the thing is done. Poor Arthur may be guilty, but he certainly should have every chance a careful lawyer could give him. You can see—he makes it very evident—that he has no further use for Moffat. I wonder under whose advice he chose him for his counsel. I have never thought much of Moffat, myself. He wins his cases but—"

"He will win this," I muttered.

Clifton started; looked at me very closely for a minute, paled a little—I fear that I was very pale myself—but did not ask the question rising to his lips.

"There is method in the madness of a man like that," I pursued with a gloom I could not entirely conceal. "He has come upon some evidence which he has not even communicated to his client. At least, I fear so. We must be prepared for any untoward event." Then, noticing Clifton's alarm and wishing to confine it within safe bounds, I added: "I feel that I am almost as much on trial as Arthur himself. Naturally I am anxious at the appearance of anything I do not understand."

Clifton frowned. We were quite alone. Leaning forward, he touched my arm.

"Elwood," said he, "you've not been quite open with me."

I smiled. If half the bitterness and sorrow in my heart went into that smile, it must have been a sad and bitter one indeed.

"You have a right to reproach me," said I, "but not wholly. I did not deceive you in essentials. You may still believe me as guiltless of Adelaide's violent death as a man can be who drove her and hers into misery which death alone could end."

"I will believe it," he muttered, "I must." And he dropped the subject, as he made me see, forever.

I drew a deep breath of relief. I had come very near to revealing my secret.

When we returned to the court-room, we found it already packed with a very subdued and breathless crowd. It differed somewhat from the one which had faced us in the morning; but Ella and her parents were there and many others of the acknowledged friends of the accused and of his family.

He, himself, wore the heavy and dogged air which became him least. Physically refreshed, he carried himself boldly, but it was a boldness which convinced me that any talk he may have had with his lawyer, had been no more productive of comfort than the one I had held with mine.

As he took the witness chair, and prepared to meet the cross-examination of the district attorney, a solemn hush settled upon the room. Would the coming ordeal rob his brow of its present effrontery, or would he continue to bear himself with the same surly dignity, which, misunderstood as it was, produced its own effect, and at certain moments seemed to shake even the confidence of Mr. Fox, settled as he seemed to be in his belief in the integrity of his cause and the rights of the prosecution.

Shaken or not, his attack was stern, swift, and to the point.

"Was the visit you made to the wine-vault on the evening of the second of December, the first one you had ever paid there?"

"No; I had been there once before. But I always paid for my depredations," he added, proudly.

"The categorical answer, Mr. Cumberland. Anything else is superfluous."

Arthur's lip curled, but only for an instant; and nothing could have exceeded the impassiveness of his manner as Mr. Fox went on.

"Then you knew the way?"

"Perfectly."

"And the lock?"

"Sufficiently well to open it without difficulty."

"How long do you think you were in entering the house and procuring these bottles?"

"I cannot say. I have no means of knowing; I never thought of looking at my watch."

"Not when you started? Not when you left Cuthbert Road?"

"No, sir."

"But you know when you left the club-house to go back?"

"Only by this—it had not yet begun to snow. I'm told that the first flakes fell that night at ten minutes to eleven. I was on the golf-links when this happened. You can fix the time yourself. Pardon me," he added, with decided ill-grace as he met Mr. Fox's frown. "I forgot your injunction."

Mr. Fox smiled an acrid smile, as he asked: "Whereabouts on the golf-links? They extend for some distance, you remember."

"They are six hundred yards across from first tee to the third hole, which is the nearest one to Cuthbert Road," Arthur particularised. "I was—no, I can't tell you just where I was at that moment. It was a good ways from the house. The snow came on very fiercely. For a little while I could not see my way."

"How, not see your way?"

"The snow flew into my eyes."

"Crossing the links?"

"Yes, sir, crossing the links."

"But the storm came from the west. It should have beaten against your back."

"Back or front, it bothered me. I could not get on as fast as I wished."

Mr. Fox cast a look at the jury. Did they remember the testimony of the landlord that Mr. Cumberland's coat was as thickly plastered with snow on the front as it had been on the back. He seemed to gather that they did, for he went on at once to say:

"You are accustomed to the links? You have crossed them often?"

"Yes, I play golf there all summer."

"I'm not alluding to the times when you play. I mean to ask whether or not you had ever before crossed them directly to Cuthbert Road?"

"Yes, I had."

"In a storm?"

"No, not in a storm."

"How long did it take you that time to reach Cuthbert Road from The Whispering Pines?"

Mr. Moffat bounded to his feet, but the prisoner had answered before he could speak.

"Just fifteen minutes."

"How came you to know the time so exactly?"

"Because that day I did look at my watch. I had an engagement in the lower town, and had only twenty minutes in which to keep it. I was on time."

Honest at the core. This boy was growing rapidly in my favour. But this frank but unwise answer was not pleasing to his counsel, who would have advised, no doubt, a more general and less precise reply. However, it had been made and Moffat was not a man to cry over spilled milk. He did not even wince when the district attorney proceeded to elicit from the prisoner that he was a good walker, not afraid in the least of snow-storms and had often walked, in the teeth of the gale twice that distance in less than half an hour. Now, as the storm that night had been at his back, and he was in a hurry to reach his destination, it was evidently incumbent upon him to explain how he had managed to use up the intervening time of forty minutes before entering the hotel at half-past eleven.

"Did you stop in the midst of the storm to take a drink?" asked the district attorney.

As the testimony of the landlord in Cuthbert Road had been explicit as to the fact of his having himself uncorked the bottle which the prisoner had brought into the hotel, Arthur could not plead yes. He must say no, and he did.

"I drank nothing; I was too busy thinking. I was so busy thinking I wandered all over those links."

"In the blinding snow?"

"Yes, in the snow. What did I care for the snow? I did not understand my sister being in the club-house. I did not like it; I was tempted at times to go back."

"And why didn't you?"

"Because I was more of a brute than a brother—because Cuthbert Road drew me in spite of myself—because—" He stopped with the first hint of emotion we had seen in him since the morning. "I did not know what was going on there or I should have gone back," he flashed out, with a defiant look at his counsel.

Again sympathy was with him. Mr. Fox had won but little in this first attempt. He seemed to realise this, and shifted his attack to a point more vulnerable.

"When you heard your sister's voice in the club-house, how did you think she had got into the building?"

"By means of the keys Ranelagh had left at the house."

"When, instead of taking the whole bunch, you took the one key you wanted from the ring, did you do so with any idea she might want to make use of the rest?"

"No, I never thought of it. I never thought of her at all."

"You took your one key, and let the rest lie?"

"You've said it."

"Was this before or after you put on your overcoat?"

"I'm not sure; after, I think. Yes, it was after; for I remember that I had a deuce of a time unbuttoning my coat to get at my trousers' pocket."

"You dropped this key into your trousers' pocket?"

"I did."

"Mr. Cumberland, let me ask you to fix your memory on the moments you spent in the hall. Did you put on your hat before you pocketed the key, or afterwards?"

"My hat? How can I tell? My mind wasn't on my hat. I don't know when I put it on."

"You absolutely do not remember?"

"No."

"Nor where you took it from?"

"No."

"Whether you saw the keys first, and then went for your hat; or having pocketed the key, waited—"

"I did not wait."

"Did not stand by the table thinking?"

"No, I was in too much of a hurry."

"So that you went straight out?"

"Yes, as quickly as I could."

The district attorney paused, to be sure of the attention of the jury. When he saw that every eye of that now thoroughly aroused body was on him, he proceeded to ask: "Does that mean immediately, or as soon as you could after you had made certain preparations, or held certain talk with some one you called, or who called to you?"

"I called to nobody. I—I went out immediately."

It was evident that he lied; evident, too, that he had little hope from his lie. Uneasiness was taking the place of confidence in his youthful, untried, undisciplined mind. Carmel had spoken to him in the hall—I guessed it then, I knew it afterward—and he thought to deceive this court and blindfold a jury, whose attention had been drawn to this point by his own counsel.

District Attorney Fox smiled. "How then did you get into the stable?"

"The stable! Oh, I had no trouble in getting into the stable."

"Was it unlocked?"

A slow flush broke over the prisoner's whole face. He saw where he had been landed and took a minute to pull himself together before he replied: "I had the key to that door, too. I got it out of the kitchen."

"You have not spoken of going into the kitchen."

"I have not spoken of coming downstairs."

"You went into the kitchen?"

"Yes."

"When?"

"When I first came down."

"That is not in accordance with your direct testimony. On the contrary, you said that on coming downstairs you went straight to the rack for your overcoat. Stenographer read what the prisoner said on this topic."

A rustling of leaves, distinctly to be heard in the deathlike silence of the room, was followed by the reading of this reply and answer:

"Yet you cannot say which of these two overcoats you put on when you left your home an hour or so after finishing your dinner?"

"I cannot. I was in no condition to notice. I was bent on going into town and, on coming downstairs, I went straight to the rack and pulled on the first things that offered."

The prisoner stood immobile but with a deepening line gathering on his brow until the last word fell. Then he said: "I forgot. I went for the key before I put on my overcoat. I wanted to see how the sick horse looked."

"Did you drop this key into your pocket, too?"

"No, I carried it into the hall."

"What did you do with it there?"

"I don't know. Put it on the table, I suppose."

"Don't you remember? There were other keys lying on this table. Don't you remember what you did with the one in your hand while you took the club-house key from the midst of Mr. Ranelagh's bunch?"

"I laid it on the table. I must have—there was no other place to put it."

"Laid it down by itself?"

"Yes."

"And took it up when you went out?"

"Of course."

"Carrying it straight to the stable?"

"Naturally."

"What did you do with it when you came out?"

"I left it in the stable-door."

"You did? What excuse have you to give for that?"

"None. I was reckless, and didn't care for anything—that's all."

"Yet you took several minutes, for all your hurry and your indifference, to get the stable key and look in at a horse that wasn't sick enough to keep your coachman home from a dance."

The prisoner was silent.

"You have no further explanation to give on this subject?"

"No. All fellows who love horses will understand."

The district attorney shrugged this answer away before he went on to say: "You have listened to Zadok Brown's testimony. When he returned at three, he found the stable-door locked, and the key hanging up on its usual nail in the kitchen. How do you account for this?"

"There are two ways."

"Mention them, if you please."

"Zadok had been to a dance, and may not have been quite clear as to what he saw. Or, finding the stable door open, may have blamed himself for the fact and sought to cover up his fault with a lie."

"Have you ever caught him in a lie?"

"No; but there's always a first time."

"You would impeach his testimony then?"

"No. You asked me how this discrepancy could be explained, and I have tried to show you."

"Mr. Cumberland, the grey mare was out that night; this has been amply proved."

"If you believe Zadok, yes."

"You have heard other testimony corroborative of this fact. She was seen on the club-house road that night, by a person amply qualified to identify her."

"So I've been told."

"The person driving this horse wore a hat, identified as an old one of yours, which hat was afterwards found at your house on a remote peg in a seldom-used closet. If you were not this person, how can you explain the use of your horse, the use of your clothes, the locking of the stable-door—which you declare yourself to have left open—and the hanging up of the key on its own nail?"

It was a crucial question—how crucial no one knew but our two selves. If he answered at all, he must compromise Carmel. I had no fear of his doing this, but I had great fear of what Ella might do if he let this implication stand and made no effort to exonerate himself by denying his presence in the cutter, and consequent return to the Cumberland home. The quick side glances I here observed cast in her direction by both father and mother, showed that she had made some impulsive demonstration visible to them, if not to others and fearful of the consequences if I did not make some effort to hold her in check, I kept my eyes in her direction, and so lost Arthur's look and the look of his counsel as he answered, with just the word I had expected—a short and dogged:

"I cannot explain."

It was my death warrant. I realised this even while I held Ella's eye with mine and smoothed my countenance to meet the anguish in hers, in the effort to hold her back for a few minutes longer till I could quite satisfy myself that Arthur's case was really lost and that I must speak or feel myself his murderer.

The gloom which followed this recognition of his inability, real or fancied, to explain away the most damning feature of the case against him, taken with his own contradictions and growing despondency, could not escape my eye, accustomed as I was to the habitual expression of most every person there. But it was not yet the impenetrable gloom presaging conviction; and directing Ella's gaze towards Mr. Moffat, who seemed but little disturbed either by Mr. Fox's satisfaction or the prisoner's open despair, I took heart of grace and waited for the district attorney's next move. It was a fatal one. I began to recognise this very soon, simple as was the subject he now introduced.

"When you went into the kitchen, Mr. Cumberland, to get the stable-door key, was the gas lit, or did you have to light it?"

"It—it was lit, I think."

"Don't you know?"

"It was lit, but turned low. I could see well enough."

"Why, then, didn't you take both keys?"

"Both keys?"

"You have said you went down town by the short cut through your neighbour's yard. That cut is guarded by a door, which was locked that night. You needed the key to that door more than the one to the stable. Why didn't you take it?"

"I—I did."

"You haven't said so."

"I—I took it when I took the other."

"Are you sure?"

"Yes; they both hung on one nail. I grabbed them both at the same time."

"It does not appear so in your testimony. You mentioned a key, not keys, in all your answers to my questions."

"There were two; I didn't weigh my words. I needed both and I took both."

"Which of the two hung foremost?"

"I didn't notice."

"You took both?"

"Yes, I took both."

"And went straight out with them?"

"Yes, to the stable."

"And then where?"

"Through the adjoining grounds downtown."

"You are sure you went through Mr. Fulton's grounds at this early hour in the evening?"

"I am positive."

"Was it not at a later hour, much later, a little before eleven instead of a little before nine?"

"No, sir. I was on the golf-links then."

"But some one drove into the stable."

"So you say."

"Unharnessed the horse, drew up the cutter, locked the stable-door, and, entering the house, hung up the key where it belonged."

No answer this time.

"Mr. Cumberland, you admitted in your direct examination that you took with you out of the clubhouse only one bottle of the especial brand you favoured, although you carried up two into the kitchen?"

"No, I said that I only had one when I got to Cuthbert Road. I don't remember anything about the other."

"But you know where the other—or rather remnants of the other, was found?"

"In my own stable, taken there by my man Zadok Brown, who says he picked it out of one of our waste barrels."

"This is the part of bottle referred to. Do you recognise the label still adhering to it as similar to the one to be found on the bottle you emptied in Cuthbert Road?"

"It is like that one."

"Had you carried that other bottle off, and had it been broken as this has been broken would it not have presented an exactly similar appearance to this?"

"Possibly."

"Only possibly?"

"It would have looked the same. I cannot deny it. What's the use fooling?"

"Mr. Cumberland, the only two bottles known to contain this especial brand of wine were in the clubhouse at ten o'clock that night. How came one of them to get into the barrel outside your stable before your return the next day?"

"I cannot say."

"This barrel stood where?"

"In the passage behind the stable."

"The passage you pass through on your way to the door leading into your neighbour's grounds?"

"Yes."

The dreaded moment had come. This "Yes" had no sooner left Arthur's lips than I saw Ella throw out her innocent arms, and leap impetuously to her feet, with a loud "No, no, I can tell—"

She did not say what, for at the hubbub roused by this outbreak in open court, she fainted dead away and was carried out in her dismayed father's arms.

This necessarily caused a break in the proceedings. Mr. Fox suspended his cross-examination and in a few minutes more, the judge adjourned the court. As the prisoner rose and turned to pass out, I cast him a hurried glance to see what effect had been made upon him by this ingenuous outburst from one he had possibly just a little depreciated. A great one, evidently. His features were transformed, and he seemed almost as oblivious of the countless eyes upon him as she had been when she rose to testify for him in her self-forgetful enthusiasm. As I observed this and the satisfaction with which Mr. Moffat scented this new witness,—a satisfaction which promised little consideration for her if she ever came upon the stand—I surrendered to fate.

Inwardly committing Carmel's future to the God who made her and who knew better than we the story of her life and what her fiery temper had cost her, I drew a piece of paper from my pocket, and, while the courtroom was slowly emptying, hastily addressed the following lines to Mr. Moffat who had lingered to have a few words with his colleague:

"There is a witness in this building who can testify more clearly and definitely than Miss Fulton, that Arthur Cumberland, for all we have heard in seeming contradiction to the same, might have been on the golf-links at the time he swears to. That witness is myself.

"ELWOOD RANELAGH."

The time which elapsed between my passing over this note and his receiving and reading it, was to me like the last few moments of a condemned criminal. How gladly would I have changed places with Arthur, and with what sensations of despair I saw flitting before me in my mind's eye, the various visions of Carmel's loveliness which had charmed me out of myself. But the die had been cast, and I was ready to meet the surprised lawyer's look when his eve rose from the words I had written and settled steadily on my face. Next minute he was writing busily and in a second later I was reading these words:

"Do you absolutely wish to be recalled as a witness, and by the defence? M."

My answer was brief:

"I do. Not to make a confession of crime. I have no such confession to make. But I know who drove that horse. R."

I had sacrificed Carmel to my sense of right. Never had I loved her as I did at that moment.

CHAPTER XXVII

EXPECTANCY

*I see your end,
'T is my undoing.*

King Henry VIII.

A turning-point had been reached in the defence. That every one knew after the first glance at Mr. Moffat, on the opening of the next morning's session. As I noted the excitement which this occasioned even in quarters where self-control is usually most marked and such emotions suppressed, I marvelled at the subtle influence of one man's expectancy, and the powerful effect which can be produced on a feverish crowd by a well-ordered silence suggestive of coming action.

I, who knew the basis of this expectancy and the nature of the action with which Mr. Moffat anticipated startling the court, was the quietest person present. Since it was my hand and none other which must give this fresh turn to the wheel of justice, it were well for me to do it calmly and without any of the old maddening throb of heart. But the time seemed long before Arthur was released from further cross-examination, and the opportunity given Mr. Moffat to call his next witness.

Something in the attitude he now took, something in the way he bent over his client and whispered a few admonitory words, and still more the emotion with which these words were received and answered by some extraordinary protest, aroused expectation to a still greater pitch, and made my course seem even more painful to myself than I had foreseen when dreaming over and weighing the possibilities of this hour. With something like terror, I awaited the calling of my name; and, when it was delayed, it was with emotions inexplicable to myself that I looked up and saw Mr. Moffat holding open a door at the left of the judge, with that attitude of respect, which a man only assumes in the presence and under the dominating influence of woman.

"Ella!" thought I. "Instead of saving her by my contemplated sacrifice of Carmel, I have only added one sacrifice to another."

But when the timid faltering step we could faintly hear crossing the room beyond, had brought its possessor within sight, and I perceived the tall, black-robed, heavily veiled woman who reached for Mr. Moffat's sustaining arm, I did not need the startling picture of the prisoner, standing upright, with outheld and repellant hands, to realise that the impossible had happened, and that all which he, as well as I, had done and left undone, suffered and suppressed, had been in vain.

Mr. Moffat, with no eye for him or for me, conducted his witness to a chair; then, as she loosened her veil and let it drop in her lap, he cried in tones which rang from end to end of the court-room: "I summon Carmel Cumberland to the stand, to witness in her brother's defence."

The surprise was complete. It was a great moment for Mr. Moffat; but for me all was confusion, dread, a veil of misty darkness, through which shone her face, marred by its ineffaceable scar, but calm as I had never expected to see it again in this life, and beautiful with a smile under which her deeply shaken and hardly conscious brother sank slowly back into his seat, amid a silence as profound as the hold she had immediately taken upon all hearts.

CHAPTER XXVIII

"WHERE IS MY BROTHER?"

Let me see the writing.
My lord, 't is nothing.
No matter, then, who sees it;
I will be satisfied, let me see the writing.

Richard II.

What is the explanation of Carmel's reappearance in town and of this sensational introduction of her into the court-room, in a restored state of health of which no one, so far as known, had had any intimation save the man who was responsible for her appearance? The particulars are due you.

She had passed some weeks at Lakewood, under the eye of the nurse who was detailed to watch, as well as tend her. During these weeks she gave no sign of improvement mentally, though she constantly gained strength otherwise, and impressed everybody with the clear light in her eye and the absence of everything suggestive of gloom in her expression and language. There was the same complete loss of memory up to the time of the tragic occurrence which had desolated her home; the same harping at odd moments on Adelaide's happiness and her own prospect of seeing this dear sister very soon which had marked the opening days of her convalescence. But beyond and back of all this was some secret joy, unintelligible to the nurse, which helped rather than retarded the sick girl's recovery, and made Carmel appear at times as if she walked on air and breathed the very breath of Paradise—an anomaly which not only roused Miss Unwin's curiosity, but led her to regard with something like apprehension, any change in her patient's state of mind which would rob her of the strange and unseen delights which fed her secret soul and made her oblivious of the awful facts awaiting a restored memory.

Meanwhile Carmel was allowed such liberty as her condition required; but was never left alone for a moment after a certain day when her eye suddenly took on a strange look of confused inquiry, totally dissociated with anything she saw or heard. A stir had taken place in her brain, and her nurse wanted to take her back home. But this awakening—if such it could be called, was so short in its duration and was followed so immediately by a string of innocent questions about Adelaide, that Nurse Unwin concluded to remain a few days longer before risking this delicately balanced mind amid old scenes and the curious glances of her townspeople.

Alas! the awakening was to take place in Lakewood and under circumstances of the most ordinary nature. Carmel had been out and was just crossing the hall of her hotel to the elevator, when she stopped with a violent start and clutching the air, was caught by her nurse who had hurried up at the first intimation of anything unusual in the condition of her patient.

The cause of this agitation was immediately apparent. Near them sat two ladies, each with a small wine-glass in her hand. One was drinking, the other waiting and watching, but with every apparent intention of drinking when the other had ceased. A common sight enough, but it worked a revolution in Carmel's darkened mind. The light of youthful joyousness fled from her face; and the cheek, just pulsing softly with new life, blanched to the death-like hue of mortal suffering. Dropping her eyes from the women, who saw nothing and continued to sip their wine in happy ignorance of the soul-tragedy going on within ten feet of them, she looked down at her dress, then up at the walls about her; and then slowly, anxiously, and with unmistakable terror, at the woman in whose arms she felt herself supported.

"Explain," she murmured. "Where am I?"

"At Lakewood, in a hotel. You have been ill, and are only just recovering."

Her hand went up to her cheek, the one that had been burned, and still showed the deep traces of that accident.

"I remember," said she. Then with another glance at her dress, which had studiously been kept cheerful, she remarked, with deep reproach: "My sister is dead; why am I not in black?"

The nurse, realising her responsibility (she said afterwards that it was the most serious moment of her life), subdued her own astonishment at this proof of her young patient's knowledge of a crime of which she was universally supposed to be entirely ignorant, and, bestowing a reassuring smile on the agitated girl, observed softly:

"You wore too ill to be burdened with black. You are better now and may assume it if you will. I will help you buy your mourning."

"Yes, you look like a kind woman. What is your name, please, and are we here alone in this great hotel?"

Now, as a matter of expediency—to save Carmel from the unendurable curiosity of the crowd, and herself from the importunities of the New York reporters, Miss Unwin had registered herself and her charge under assumed names. She was, therefore, forced to reply:

"My name is Huckins, and we are here alone. But that need not worry you. I have watched over you night and day for many weeks."

"You have? Because of this slight burn?" Again Carmel's hand went to her cheek.

"Not on account of that only. You have had a serious illness quite apart from that injury. But you are better; you are almost well—well enough to go home, if you will."

"I cannot go home—not just yet. I'm—I'm not strong enough. But we shouldn't be here alone without some man to look after us. Miss Huckins, where is my brother?"

At this question, uttered with emphasis, with anxiety—with indignation even—Miss Unwin felt the emotion she had so successfully subdued up to this moment, betray itself in her voice as she answered, with a quiet motion towards the elevator: "Let us go up to our room. There I will answer all your questions."

But Carmel, with the waywardness of her years—or perhaps, with deeper reasoning powers than the other would be apt to attribute to her—broke softly away from Miss Unwin's detaining hand, and walking directly into the office, looked about for the newspaper stand. Miss Unwin, over-anxious not to make a scene, followed, but did not seek to deter her, until they were once again by themselves in the centre of the room. Then she ventured to speak again:

"We have all the papers in our room. Come up, and let me read them to you."

But Fate was making ready its great stroke. Just as Carmel seemed about to yield to this persuasion, some lingering doubt drew her eyes again to the stand, just at the very moment a boy stepped into view with the evening bulletin, on which had just been written these words:

The Last Juror Obtained in the Trial of Arthur Cumberland for the Murder of His Sister, Adelaide.

Carmel saw, and stood—a breathless image of horror. A couple of gentlemen came running; but the nurse waved them back, and herself caught Carmel and upheld her, in momentary dread of another mental, if not physical, collapse.

But Carmel had come back into the world of consciousness to stay. Accepting her nurse's support, but giving no sign of waning faculties or imperfect understanding of what she had seen, she spoke quite clearly and with her eyes fixed upon Miss Unwin:

"So that is why I am here, away from all my friends. Was I too ill to be told? Couldn't you make me know what was happening? You or the doctors or—or anybody?"

"You were much too ill," protested the nurse, leading her towards the elevator and so by degrees to her room. "I tried to arouse you after the crisis of your illness had passed; but you seemed to have forgotten everything which took place that night and the doctors warned me not to press you."

"And Arthur—poor Arthur, has been the sufferer! Tell me the whole story. I can bear it," she pleaded. "I can bear anything but not knowing. Why should he have fallen under suspicion? He was not even there. I must go to him! Pack up our clothing, Miss Huckins. I must go to him at once."

They were in their own room now, and Carmel was standing quite by herself in the full light of the setting sun. With the utterance of this determination, she had turned upon her companion; and that astute and experienced woman had every opportunity for observing her face. There was a woman's resolution in it. With the sudden rending of the clouds which had obscured her intellect, strange powers had awakened in this young girl, giving her a force of expression which, in connection with her inextinguishable beauty, formed a spectacle before which this older woman, in spite of her long experience, hesitated in doubt.

"You shall go—" began the nurse, and stopped.

Carmel was not listening. Another change of thought had come, and her features, as keenly alive now to every passing emotion as they had formerly been set in a dull placidity, mirrored doubts of her own, which had a deeper source than any which had disturbed the nurse, even in these moments of serious perplexity.

"How can I?" fell in unconscious betrayal from her lips. "How can I!" Then she stood silent, ghastly with lack of colour one minute, and rosy red with its excess the next, until it was hard to tell in which extreme her feeling spoke most truly.

What was the feeling? Nurse Unwin felt it imperative to know. Relying on the confidence shown her by this unfortunate girl, in her lonely position and unbearable distress, she approached Carmel, with renewed offers of help and such expressions of sympathy as she thought might lure her into open speech.

But discretion had come with fear, and Carmel, while not disdaining the other's kindness, instantly made it apparent that, whatever her burden, and however unsuited it was to her present weak condition, it was not one she felt willing to share.

"I must think," she murmured, as she finally followed the nurse's lead and seated herself on a lounge. "Arthur on trial for his life! Arthur on trial for his life! And Adelaide was not even murdered!"

"No?" gasped the nurse, intent on every word this long-silenced witness let fall.

"Had he no friend? Was there not some one to understand? Adelaide—" here her head fell till her face was lost to sight—"had—a—lover—"

"Yes. Mr. Elwood Ranelagh. He was the first to be arrested for the crime."

The soul in Carmel seemed to vanish at this word. The eyes, which had been so far-seeing the moment before, grew blank, and the lithe young body stiff with that death in life which is almost worse to look upon than death itself. She did not speak; but presently she arose, as an automaton might arise at the touch of some invisible spring, and so stood, staring, until the nurse, frightened at the result of her words and the complete overthrow which might follow them, sprang for a newspaper and thrust it into her patient's unwilling hand.

Was it too late? For a minute it seemed to be so; then the stony eyes softened and fell, the rigidity of her frame relaxed, and Carmel sank back again on the sofa and tried to read the headlines on the open sheet before her. But her eyes were unequal to the task. With a sob she dropped the paper and entreated the nurse to relate to her from her own knowledge, all that had passed, sparing her nothing that would make the situation perfectly clear to one who had been asleep during the worst crisis of her life.

Miss Unwin complied, but with reservations. She told of Adelaide having been found dead at The Whispering Pines by the police, whom she had evidently summoned during a moment of struggle or fear; of Ranelagh's presence there, and of the suspicions to which it gave rise; of his denial of the crime; of his strange reticence on certain points, which served to keep him incarcerated till a New York detective got to work and found so much evidence against her brother that Mr. Ranelagh was subsequently released and Arthur Cumberland indicted. But she said nothing about the marks on Adelaide's throat, or of the special reason which the police had for arresting Mr. Ranelagh. She did not dare. Strangulation was a horrible death to contemplate; and if this factor in the crime—she was not deceived by Carmel's exclamation that there had been no murder—was unknown as yet to her patient, as it must be from what she had said, and the absolute impossibility, as she thought, of her having known what went on in The Whispering Pines, then it had better remain unknown to her until circumstances forced it on her knowledge, or she had gotten sufficient strength to bear it.

Carmel received the account well. She started when she heard of the discovery of Ranelagh in the club-house on the entrance of the police, and seemed disposed to ask some questions. But though the nurse gave her an opportunity to do so, she appeared to hunt in vain for the necessary words, and the narrative proceeded without further interruption. When all was done, she sat quite still; then carefully, and with a show of more judgment than might be expected from one of her years, she propounded certain inquiries which brought out the main causes for her brother's arraignment. When she had these fully in mind, she looked up into the nurse's face again and repeated, quite calmly, but with immovable decision, the order of an hour before:

"We must return at once. You will pack up immediately."

Miss Unwin nodded, and began to open the trunks.

This, however, was a ruse. She did not intend to take her patient back that night. She was afraid to risk it. The next day would be soon enough. But she would calm her by making ready, and when the proper moment came, would find some complication of trains which would interfere with their immediate departure.

Meanwhile, she would communicate at the earliest moment with Mr. Fox. She had been in the habit of sending him frequent telegrams as to her patient's condition. They had been invariable so far: "No difference; mind still a blank," or some code word significant of the same. But a new word was necessary now. She must look it up, and formulate her telegram before she did anything else.

The code-book was in her top tray. She hunted and hunted for it, without being able to lay her hands on it. She grew very nervous. She was only human; she was in a very trying position, and she realised it. Where could that book be? Suddenly she espied it and, falling on her knees before the trunk, with her back still to Carmel, studied out the words she wanted. She was leaning over the tray to write these words in her note-book, when—no one ever knew how it happened—the lid of the heavy trunk fell forward and its iron edge struck her on the nape of the neck, with a keen blow which laid her senseless. When Carmel reached her side, she found herself the strong one and her stalwart nurse the patient.

When help had been summoned, the accident explained, and everything done for the unconscious woman which medical skill could suggest, Carmel, finding a moment to herself, stole to the trunk, and, lifting up the lid, looked in. She had been watchful of her nurse from the first, and was suspicious of the actions which had led to this untoward accident. Seeing the two little books, she took them out. The note-book lay open and on the page thus disclosed, she beheld written:

Ap Lox Fidestum Truhum

Ridiculous nonsense—until she consulted the code. Then these detached and meaningless words took on a significance which she could not afford to ignore:

Ap A change. Lox Makes remarkable statements. Fidestum   Shall we return? Trubum   Not tractable.

Carmel endeavoured to find out for whom this telegram was intended. There was nothing to inform her. A moment of indecision was followed by quick action. She had noticed that she had been invariably addressed as Miss Campbell by every one who had come into the room. Whether this was a proof of the care with which she had been guarded from the curiosity of strangers, or whether it was part of a system of deception springing from quite different causes, she felt that in the present emergency it was a fact to be thankful for and to be utilised.

Regaining her own room, which was on the other side of their common sitting-room, she collected a few necessary articles, and placed them in a bag which she thrust under her bed. Hunting for money, she found quite an adequate amount in her own purse, which was attached to her person. Satisfied thus far, she chose her most inconspicuous hat and coat, and putting them on, went out by her own door into the corridor.

The time—it was the dinner-hour—favoured her attempt. She found her way to the office unobserved, and, going frankly up to the clerk, informed him that she had some telegrams to send and that she would be out for some little time. Would he see that Miss Huckins was not neglected in her absence?

The clerk, startled at these evidences of sense and self-reliance in one he had been accustomed to see under the special protection of the very woman she was now confiding to his care, surveyed her eloquent features beaming with quiet resolve, and for a moment seemed at a loss how to take this change and control the strange situation. Perhaps she understood him, perhaps she only followed the impulses natural to her sex. She never knew; she only remembers that she smiled, and that his hesitation vanished at that smile.

"I will see to it," said he. Then, as she turned to go, he ventured to add, "It is quite dark now. If you would like one of the boys to go with you—". But he received no encouragement, and allowed his suggestion to remain unfinished.

She looked grateful for this, and was pulling down her veil when she perceived two or three men on the other side of the room, watching her in evident wonder. Stepping back to the desk, she addressed the clerk again, this time with a marked distinctness:

"I have been very ill, I know, and not always quite myself. But the shock of this accident to my nurse has cleared my brain and made me capable again of attending to my own affairs. You can trust me; I can do my errands all right; but perhaps I had better have one of the boys go with me."

The clerk, greatly relieved, rang his bell, and the gentlemen at the other end of the room sauntered elsewhere to exchange their impressions of an incident which was remarkable enough in itself, without the accentuation put upon it by the extreme beauty of the girl and the one conspicuous blemish to that beauty—her unfortunate scar. With what additional wonder would they have regarded the occurrence, had they known that the object of their interest was not an unknown Miss Campbell, but the much pitied, much talked-of Carmel Cumberland, sister of the man then on trial for his life in a New York town.

With her first step into the street, Carmel's freshly freed mind began its work. She knew she was in a place called Lakewood, but she knew little of its location, save that it was somewhere in New Jersey. Another strange thing! she did not recognise the streets. They were new to her. She did not remember ever having been in them before.

"Where is the railroad station?" she inquired of the boy who was trotting along at her side.

"Over there," he answered, vaguely.

"Take me to it."

He obeyed, and they threaded several streets whose lighted shops pleased her, notwithstanding her cares; such a joy it was to be alive to things once more, and capable of remembrance, even though remembrance brought visions at which she shuddered, and turned away, appalled.

The sight of the station, from which a train was just leaving, frightened her for a moment with its bustle and many lights; but she rallied under the stress of her purpose, and, entering, found the telegraph office, from which she sent this message, directed to her physician, at home, Dr. Carpenter:

"Look for me on early train. All is clear to me now, and I must return. Preserve silence till we meet."

This she signed with a pet name, known only to themselves, and dating back to her childish days.

Then she bought a ticket, and studied the time-table. When quite satisfied, she returned to the hotel. She was met in the doorway by the physician who was attending the so-called Miss Huckins. He paused when he saw her, and asked a few questions which she was penetrating enough to perceive were more for the purpose of testing her own condition than to express interest in his patient. She answered quietly, and was met by a surprise and curiosity which evinced that he was greatly drawn towards her case. This alarmed her. She did not wish to be the object of any one's notice. On the contrary, she desired to obliterate herself; to be counted out so far as all these people were concerned. But above all, she was anxious not to rouse suspicion. So she stopped and talked as naturally as she could about Miss Huckins's accident and what the prospects were for the night. These were favourable, or so the doctor declared, but the injured woman's condition called for great care and he would send over a capable nurse at-once. Meanwhile, the maid who was with her would do very well. She, herself, need have no worry. He would advise against worry, and suggested that she should have a good and nourishing dinner sent to her room, after which she should immediately retire and get what sleep she could by means of an anodyne he would send her.

Carmel exerted herself.

"You are very good," said she, "I need no anodyne. I am tired and when I once get to bed shall certainly sleep. I shall give orders not to be disturbed. Isn't that right?"

"Quite right. I will myself tell the nurse."

He was going, but turned to look at her again.

"Shall I accompany you to the door of your room?" he asked.

She shook her head, with a smile. This delay was a torment to her, but it must be endured.

"I am quite capable of finding my room. I hope Miss Huckins will be as well in a week from now as I am at this moment. But, doctor—" she had been struck by a strange possibility—"I should like to settle one little matter before we part. The money I have may not be quite safe in my hands. My memory might leave me again, and then Miss Huckins might suffer. If you will take charge of some of it on her account, I shall feel relieved."

"It would be a wise precaution," he admitted. "But you could just as well leave it at the desk."

"So I can," she smiled. Then, as his eye remained fixed on her: "You are wondering if I have friends. We both have and I have just come from telegraphing to one of them. You can leave us, with an easy mind. All that I dread is that Miss Huckins will worry about me if her consciousness should return during the night."

"It will not return so soon. Next week we may look for it. Then you can be by to reassure her if she asks for you."

Carmers eyes fell.

"I would not be a cause of distress to her for the world. She has been very good to me." Bowing, she turned in the direction of the office.

The doctor, lifting his hat, took his departure. The interview might have lasted five minutes. She felt as though it had lasted an hour.

She followed the doctor's advice and left half the money she had, in charge of the clerk. Then she went upstairs. She was not seen to come down again; but when the eight-forty-five train started out of the station that night, it had for a passenger, a young, heavily veiled girl, who went straight to her section. A balcony running by her window had favoured her escape. It led to a hall window at the head of a side staircase. She met no one on the staircase, and, once out of the door at its foot, her difficulties were over, and her escape effected.

She was missed the next morning, and an account of her erratic flight reached the papers, and was published far and wide. But the name of Miss Caroline Campbell conveyed nothing to the public, and the great trial went on without a soul suspecting the significance of this midnight flitting of an unknown and partially demented girl.

At the house of Dr. Carpenter she met Mr. Moffat. What she told him heartened him greatly for the struggle he saw before him. Indeed, it altered the whole tone of the defence. Perceiving from her story, and from what the doctor could tell him of their meeting at the station that her return to town was as yet a secret to every one but themselves, he begged that the secret should continue to be kept, in order that the coup d'etat which he meditated might lose none of its force by anticipation. Carmel, whose mind was full of her coming ordeal, was willing enough to hide her head until it came; while Dr. Carpenter, alarmed at all this excitement, would have insisted on it in any event.

Carmel wished her brother informed of her return, but the wily lawyer persuaded her to excuse him from taking Arthur into his confidence until the last moment. He knew that he would receive only opposition from his young and stubborn client; that Carmel's presence and Carmel's determination would have to be sprung upon Arthur even more than upon the prosecution; that the prisoner at the bar would struggle to the very last against Carmel's appearance in court, and make an infinite lot of trouble, if he did not actually endanger his own cause. One of the stipulations which he had made in securing Mr. Moffat for his counsel was that Carmel's name was to be kept as much as possible out of the proceedings; and to this Mr. Moffat had subscribed, notwithstanding his conviction that the crime laid to the defendant's charge was a result of Ranelagh's passion for Carmel, and, consequently, distinctly the work of Ranelagh's own hand.

He had thought that he could win his case by the powers of oratory and a somewhat free use of innuendo; but his view changed under the fresh enlightenment which he received in his conversation with Carmel. He saw unfolding before him a defence of unparalleled interest. True, it involved this interesting witness in a way that would be unpleasant to the brother; but he was not the man to sacrifice a client to any sentimental scruple—certainly not this client, whose worth he was just beginning to realise. Professional pride, as well as an inherent love of justice, led him to this conclusion. Nothing in God's world appealed to him, or ever had appealed to him, like a prisoner in the dock facing a fate from which only legal address, added to an orator's eloquence, could save him. His sympathies went out to a man so placed, even when he was a brute and his guilt far from doubtful. How much more, then, must he feel the claims of this surly but chivalrous-hearted boy, son of a good father and pious mother, who had been made the butt of circumstances, and of whose innocence he was hourly becoming more and more convinced.

Could he have probed the whole matter, examined and re-examined this new witness until every detail was his and the whole story of that night stood bare before him, he might have hesitated a little longer and asked himself some very serious questions. But Carmel was not strong enough for much talk. Dr. Carpenter would not allow it, and the continued clearness of her mind was too invaluable to his case for this far-seeing advocate to take any risk. She had told him enough to assure him that circumstances and not guilt had put Arthur where he was, and had added to the assurance, details of an unexpected nature—so unexpected, indeed, that the lawyer was led away by the prospect they offered of confounding the prosecution by a line of defence to which no clew had been given by anything that had appeared.

He planned then and there a dramatic climax which should take the breath away from his opponent, and change the whole feeling of the court towards the prisoner. It was a glorious prospect, and if the girl remained well—the bare possibility of her not doing so, drove him prematurely from her presence; and so it happened that, for the second time, the subject of Adelaide's death was discussed in her hearing without any mention being made of strangulation as its immediate cause. Would her action have been different had she known that this was a conceded fact?

Mr. Moffat did not repeat this visit. He was not willing to risk his secret by being seen too often at the doctor's house; but telephonic communication was kept up between him and her present guardian, and he was able to bear himself quietly and with confidence until the time drew near for the introduction of her testimony. Then he grew nervous, fearing that Nurse Unwin would come to herself and telegraph Carmel's escape, and so prepare the prosecution for his great stroke. But nothing of the kind happened; and, when the great day came, he had only to consider how he should prepare Arthur for the surprise awaiting him, and finally decided not to prepare him at all, but simply to state at the proper moment, and in the face of the whole court-room, that his sister had recovered and would soon take her place upon the stand. The restraint of the place would thus act as a guard between them, and Carmel's immediate entrance put an end to the reproaches of whose bitterness he could well judge from his former experience of them.

With all these anxieties and his deeply planned coup d'etat awaiting the moment of action, Ella's simple outburst and even Ranelagh's unexpected and somewhat startling suggestion lost much of their significance. All his mind and heart were on his next move. It was to be made with the queen, and must threaten checkmate. Yet he did not forget the two pawns, silent in their places—but guarding certain squares which the queen, for all her royal prerogatives, might not be able to reach.

BOOK FOUR

WHAT THE PINES WHISPERED

CHAPTER XXIX

"I REMEMBERED THE ROOM"

MERCURY—If thou mightst dwell among the Gods the while
Lapped in voluptuous joy?

PROMETHEUS—I would not quit
This bleak ravine, these unrepentant pains.

Prometheus Unbound.

Great moments, whether of pain, surprise, or terror, awaken in the startled breast very different emotions from those we are led to anticipate from the agitation caused by lesser experiences. As Carmel disclosed her features to the court, my one absorbing thought was: Would she look at me?

Could I hope for a glance of her eye? Did I wish it? My question was answered before Mr. Moffat had regained his place and turned to address the court.

As her gaze passed from her brother's face, it travelled slowly and with growing hesitation over the countenances of those near her, on and on past the judge, past the jury, until they reached the spot where I sat. There they seemed to falter, and the beating of my heart became so loud that I instinctively shrank away from my neighbour. By so doing, I drew her eye, which fell full upon mine for one overwhelming minute; then she shrank and looked away, but not before the colour had risen in a flood to her cheek.

The hope which had sprung to life under her first beautiful aspect, vanished in despair at sight of this flush. For it was not one of joy, or surprise, or even of unconscious sympathy. It was the banner of a deep, unendurable shame. Versed in her every expression, I could not mistake the language of her dismayed soul, at this, the most critical instant of her life. She had hoped to find me absent; she was overwhelmed to find me there. Could she, with a look, have transported me a thousand miles from this scene of personal humiliation and unknown, unimaginable outcome, she would have bestowed that look and ignored the consequences.

Nor was I behind her in the reckless passion of the moment. Could I, by means of a wish, have been transported those thousand miles, I should even now have been far from a spot where, in the face of a curious crowd, busy in associating us together, I must submit to the terror of hearing her speak and betray herself to these watchful lawyers, and to the just and impartial mind of the presiding judge.

But the days of magic had passed. I could not escape the spot; I could not escape her eye. The ordeal to which she was thus committed, I must share. As she advanced step by step upon her uncertain road, it would be my unhappy fate to advance with her, in terror of the same pitfalls, with our faces set towards the same precipice—slipping, fainting, experiencing agonies together. She knew my secret, and I, alas! knew hers. So I interpreted this intolerable, overwhelming blush.

Recoiling from the prospect, I buried my face in my hands, and so missed the surprising sight of this young girl, still in her teens, conquering a dismay which might well unnerve one of established years and untold experiences. In a few minutes, as I was afterward told by my friends, her features had settled into a strange placidity, undisturbed by the levelled gaze of a hundred eyes. Her whole attention was concentrated on her brother, and wavered only, when the duties of the occasion demanded a recognition of the various gentlemen concerned in the trial.

Mr. Moffat prefaced his examination by the following words:

"May it please your Honour, I wish to ask the indulgence of the court in my examination of this witness. She is just recovering from a long and dangerous illness; and while I shall endeavour to keep within the rules of examination, I shall be grateful for any consideration which may be shown her by your Honour and by the counsel on the other side."

Mr. Fox at once rose. He had by this time recovered from his astonishment at seeing before him, and in a fair state of health, the young girl whom he had every reason to believe to be still in a condition of partial forgetfulness at Lakewood, and under the care of a woman entirely in his confidence and under his express orders. He had also mastered his chagrin at the triumph which her presence here, and under these dramatic circumstances, had given his adversary. Moved, perhaps, by Miss Cumberland's beauty, which he saw for the first time—or, perhaps, by the spectacle of this beauty devoting its first hours of health to an attempt to save a brother, of whose precarious position before the law she had been ignorant up to this time—or more possibly yet, by a fear that it might be bad tactics to show harshness to so interesting a personality before she had uttered a word of testimony, he expressed in warmer tones than usual, his deep desire to extend every possible indulgence.

Mr. Moffat bowed his acknowledgments, and waited for his witness to take the oath, which she did with a simple grace which touched all hearts, even that of her constrained and unreconciled brother. Compelled by the silence and my own bounding pulses to look at her in my own despite, I caught the sweet and elevated look with which she laid her hand on the Book, and asked myself if her presence here was not a self-accusation, which would bring satisfaction to nobody—which would sink her and hers into an ignominy worse than the conviction of the brother whom she was supposedly there to save.

Tortured by this fear, I awaited events in indescribable agitation.

The cool voice of Mr. Moffat broke in upon my gloom. Carmel had reseated herself, after taking the oath, and the customary question could be heard:

"Your name, if you please."

"Carmel Cumberland."

"Do you recognise the prisoner, Miss Cumberland?"

"Yes; he is my brother."

A thrill ran through the room. The lingering tone, the tender accent, told. Some of the feeling she thus expressed seemed to pass into every heart which contemplated the two. From this moment on, he was looked upon with less harshness; people showed a disposition to discern innocence, where, perhaps, they had secretly desired, until now, to discover guilt.

"Miss Cumberland, will you be good enough to tell us where you were, at or near the hour of ten, on the evening of your sister's death?"

"I was in the club-house—in the house you call The Whispering Pines."

At this astounding reply, unexpected by every one present save myself and the unhappy prisoner, incredulity, seasoned with amazement, marked every countenance. Carmel Cumberland in the club-house that night—she who had been found at a late hour, in her own home, injured and unconscious! It was not to be believed—or it would not have been, if Arthur with less self-control than he had hitherto maintained, had not shown by his morose air and the silent drooping of his head that he accepted this statement, wild and improbable as it seemed. Mr. Fox, whose mind without doubt had been engaged in a debate from the first, as to the desirability of challenging the testimony of this young girl, whose faculties had so lately recovered from a condition of great shock and avowed forgetfulness that no word as yet had come to him of her restored health, started to arise at her words; but noting the prisoner's attitude, he hastily reseated himself, realising, perhaps, that evidence of which he had never dreamed lay at the bottom of the client's manner and the counsel's complacency. If so, then his own air of mingled disbelief and compassionate forbearance might strike the jury unfavourably; while, on the contrary, if his doubts were sound, and the witness were confounding the fancies of her late delirium with the actual incidents of this fatal night, then would he gain rather than lose by allowing her to proceed until her testimony fell of its own weight, or succumbed before the fire of his cross-examination.

Modifying his manner, he steadied himself for either exigency, and, in steadying himself, steadied his colleagues also.

Mr. Moffat, who saw everything, smiled slightly as he spoke encouragingly to his witness, and propounded his next question:

"Miss Cumberland, was your sister with you when you went to the club-house?"

"No; we went separately"

"How? Will you explain?"

"I drove there. I don't know how Adelaide went."

"You drove there?"

"Yes. I had Arthur harness up his horse for me and I drove there."

A moment of silence; then a slow awakening—on the part of judge, jury, and prosecution—to the fact that the case was taking a turn for which they were ill-prepared. To Mr. Moffat, it was a moment of intense self-congratulation, and something of the gratification he felt crept into his voice as he said:

"Miss Cumberland, will you describe this horse?"

"It was a grey horse. It has a large black spot on its left shoulder."

"To what vehicle was it attached?"

"To a cutter—my brother's cutter."

"Was that brother with you? Did he accompany you in your ride to The Whispering Pines?"

"No, I went quite alone."

Entrancement had now seized upon every mind. Even if her testimony were not true, but merely the wanderings of a mind not fully restored, the interest of it was intense. Mr. Fox, glancing at the jury, saw there would be small use in questioning at this time the mental capacity of the witness. This was a story which all wished to hear. Perhaps he wished to hear it, too.

Mr. Moffat rose to more than his accustomed height. The light which sometimes visited his face when feeling, or a sense of power, was strongest in him, shone from his eye and irradiated his whole aspect as he inquired tellingly:

"And how did you return? With whom, and by what means, did you regain your own house?"

The answer came, with simple directness:

"In the same way I went. I drove back in my brother's cutter and being all alone just as before, I put the horse away myself, and went into my empty home and up to Adelaide's room, where I lost consciousness."

The excitement, which had been seething, broke out as she ceased; but the judge did not need to use his gavel, or the officers of the court exert their authority. At Mr. Moffat's lifted hand, the turmoil ceased as if by magic.

"Miss Cumberland, do you often ride out alone on nights like that?"

"I never did before. I would not have dared to do it then, if I had not taken a certain precaution."

"And what was this precaution?"

"I wore an old coat of my brother's over my dress, and one of his hats on my head."

It was out—the fact for the suppression of which I had suffered arrest without a word; because of which Arthur had gone even further, and submitted to trial with the same constancy. Instinctively, his eyes and mine met, and, at that moment, there was established between us an understanding that was in strong contrast to the surrounding turmoil, which now exceeded all limits, as the highly wrought up spectators realised that these statements, if corroborated, destroyed one of the strongest points which had been made by the prosecution. This caused a stay in the proceedings until order was partially restored, and the judge's voice could be heard in a warning that the court-room would be cleared of all spectators if this break of decorum was repeated.

Meanwhile, my own mind had been busy. I had watched Arthur; I had watched Mr. Moffat. The discouragement of the former, the ill-concealed elation of the latter, proved the folly of any hope, on my part, that Carmel would be spared a full explanation of what I would have given worlds to leave in the darkness and ignorance of the present moment. To save Arthur, unwilling as he was, she was to be allowed to consummate the sacrifice which the real generosity of her heart drove her into making. Before these doors opened again and sent forth the crowd now pulsating under a preamble of whose terrible sequel none as yet dreamed, I should have to hear those sweet lips give utterance to the revelation which would consign her to opprobrium, and break, not only my heart, but her brother's.

Was there no way to stop it? The district attorney gave no evidence of suspecting any issue of this sort, nor did the friendly and humane judge. Only the scheming Moffat knew to what all this was tending, and Moffat could not be trusted. The case was his and he would gain it if he could. Tender and obliging as he was in his treatment of the witness, there was iron under the velvet of his glove. This was his reputation; and this I must now see exemplified before me, without the power to stop it. The consideration with which he approached his subject did not deceive me.

"Miss Cumberland, will you now give the jury the full particulars of that evening's occurrences, as witnessed by yourself. Begin your relation, if you please, with an account of the last meal you had together."

Carmel hesitated. Her youth—her conscience, perhaps—shrank in manifest distress from this inquisition.

"Ask me a question," she prayed. "I do not know how to begin."

"Very well. Who were seated at the dinner-table that night?"

"My sister, my brother, Mr. Ranelagh, and myself."

"Did anything uncommon happen during the meal?"

"Yes, my sister ordered wine, and had our glasses all filled. She never drank wine herself, but she had her glass filled also. Then she dismissed Helen, the waitress; and when the girl was gone, she rose and held up her glass, and invited us to do the same. 'We will drink to my coming marriage,' said she; but when we had done this, she turned upon Arthur, with bitter words about his habits, and, declaring that another bottle of wine should never be opened again in the house, unclosed her fingers and let her glass drop on the table where it broke. Arthur then let his fall, and I mine. We all three let our glasses fall and break."

"And Mr. Ranelagh?"

"He did not let his fall. He set it down on the cloth. He had not drank from it."

Clear, perfectly clear—tallying with what we had heard from other sources. As this fact forced itself in upon the minds of the jury, new light shone in every eye and each and all waited eagerly for the next question.

It came with a quiet, if not insinuating, intonation.

"Miss Cumberland, where were you looking when you let your glass fall?"

My heart gave a bound. I remembered that moment well. So did she, as could be seen from the tremulous flush and the determination with which she forced herself to speak.

"At Mr. Ranelagh," she answered, finally.

"Not at your brother?"

"No."

"And at whom was Mr. Ranelagh looking?"

"At—at me."

"Not at your sister?"

"No."

"Was anything said?"

"Not then. With the dropping of the glasses, we all drew back from the table, and walked towards a little room where we sometimes sat before going into the library. Arthur went first, and Mr. Ranelagh and I followed, Adelaide coming last. We—we went this way into the little room and—what other question do you wish to ask?" she finished, with a burning blush.

Mr. Moffat was equal to the appeal.

"Did anything happen? Did Mr. Ranelagh speak to you or you to him, or did your sister Adelaide speak?"

"No one spoke; but Mr. Ranelagh put a little slip of paper into my hand—a—a note. As he did this, my brother looked round. I don't know whether he saw the note or not; but his eye caught mine, and I may have blushed. Next moment he was looking past me; and presently he had flung himself out of the room, and I heard him going upstairs. Adelaide had joined me by this time, and Mr. Ranelagh turned to speak to her, and—and I went over to the book-shelves to read my note."

"And did you read it then?"

"No, I was afraid. I waited till Mr. Ranelagh was gone; then I went up to my room and read it. It was not a—a note to be glad of. I mean, proud of. I'm afraid I was a little glad of it at first. I was a wicked girl."

Mr. Moffat glanced at Mr. Fox; but that gentleman, passing over this artless expression of feeling, as unworthy an objection, he went steadily on:

"Miss Cumberland, before you tell us about this note, will you be good enough to inform us whether any words passed between you and your sister before you went upstairs?"

"Oh, yes; we talked. We all three talked, but it was about indifferent matters. The servants were going to a ball, and we spoke of that. Mr. Ranelagh did not stay long. Very soon he remarked that he had a busy evening before him, and took his leave. I was not in the room with them when he did this. I was in the adjoining one, but I heard his remark and saw him go. I did not wait to talk to Adelaide."

"Now, about the note?"

"I read it as soon as I reached my room. Then I sat still for a long time."

"Miss Cumberland, pardon my request, but will you tell us what was in that note?"

She lifted her patient eyes, and looked straight at her brother. He did not meet her gaze; but the dull flush which lit up the dead-white of his cheek showed how he suffered under this ordeal. At me she never glanced; this was the only mercy shown me that dreadful morning. I grew to be thankful for it as she went on.

"I do not remember the words," she said, finally, as her eyes fell again to her lap. "But I remember its meaning. It was an invitation for me to leave town with him that very evening and be married at some place he mentioned. He said it would be the best way to—to end—matters."

This brought Mr. Fox to his feet. For all his self-command, he had been perceptibly growing more and more nervous as the examination proceeded; and he found himself still in the dark as to his opponent's purpose and the character of the revelations he had to fear. Turning to the judge, he cried:

"This testimony is irrelevant and incompetent, and I ask to have it stricken out."

Mr. Moffat's voice, as he arose to answer this, was like honey poured upon gall.

"It is neither irrelevant nor incompetent, and, if it were, the objection comes too late. My friend should have objected to the question."

"The whole course of counsel has been very unusual," began Mr. Fox.

"Yes, but so is the case. I beg your Honour to believe that, in some of its features, this case is not only unusual, but almost without a precedent. That it may be lightly understood, and justice shown my client, a full knowledge of the whole family's experiences during those fatal hours is not only desirable, but absolutely essential. I beg, therefore, that my witness may be allowed to proceed and tell her story in all its details. Nothing will be introduced which will not ultimately be seen to have a direct bearing upon the attitude of my client towards the crime for which he stands here arraigned."

"The motion is denied," declared the judge.

Mr. Fox sat down, to the universal relief of all but the two persons most interested—Arthur and myself.

Mr. Moffat, generous enough or discreet enough to take no note of his opponent's discomfiture, lifted a paper from the table and held it towards the witness.

"Do you recognise these lines?" he asked, placing the remnants of my half-burned communication in her hands.

She started at sight of them. Evidently she had never expected to see them again.

"Yes," she answered, after a moment. "This is a portion of the note I have mentioned."

"You recognise it as such?"

"I do."

Her eyes lingered on the scrap, and followed it as it was passed back and marked as an exhibit.

Mr. Moffat recalled her to the matter in hand.

"What did you do next, Miss Cumberland?"

"I answered the note."

"May I ask to what effect?"

"I refused Mr. Ranelagh's request. I said that I could not do what he asked, and told him to wait till the next day, and he would see how I felt towards him and towards Adelaide. That was all. I could not write much. I was suffering greatly."

"Suffering in mind, or suffering in body?"

"Suffering in my mind. I was terrified, but that feeling did not last very long. Soon I grew happy, happier than I had been in weeks, happier than I had ever been in all my life before. I found that I loved Adelaide better than I did myself. This made everything easy, even the sending of the answer I have told you about to Mr. Ranelagh."

"Miss Cumberland, how did you get this answer to Mr. Ranelagh?"

"By means of a gentleman who was going away on the very train I had been asked to leave on. He was a guest next door, and I carried the note in to him."

"Did you do this openly?"

"No. I'm afraid not; I slipped out by the side door, in as careful a way as I could."

"Did this attempt at secrecy succeed? Were you able to go and come without meeting any one?"

"No. Adelaide was at the head of the stairs when I came back, standing there, very stiff and quiet."

"Did she speak to you?"

"No. She just looked at me; but it wasn't a common look. I shall never forget it."

"And what did you do then?"

"I went to my room."

"Miss Cumberland, did you sec anybody else when you came in at this time?"

"Yes, our maid Helen. She was just laying down a bunch of keys on the table in the lower hall. I stopped and looked at the keys. I had recognised them as the ones I had seen in Mr. Ranelagh's hands many times. He had gone, yet there were his keys. One of them unlocked the club-house. I noticed it among the others, but I didn't touch it then. Helen was still in the hall, and I ran straight upstairs, where I met my sister, as I have just told you."

"Miss Cumberland, continue the story. What did you do after re-entering your room?"

"I don't know what I did first. I was very excited—elated one minute, deeply wretched and very frightened the next. I must have sat down; for I was shaking very much, and felt a little sick. The sight of that key had brought up pictures of the club-house; and I thought and thought how quiet it was, and how far away and—how cold it was too, and how secret. I would go there for what I had to do; there! And then I saw in my fancy one of its rooms, with the moon in it, and—but I soon shut my eyes to that. I heard Arthur moving about his room, and this made me start up and go out into the hall again."

During all this Mr. Fox had sat by, understanding his right to object to the witness's mixed statements of fact and of feelings, and quite confident that his objections would be sustained. But he had determined long since that he would not interrupt the witness in her relation. The air of patience he assumed was sufficiently indicative of his displeasure, and he confined himself to this. Mr. Moffat understood, and testified his appreciation by a slight bow.

Carmel, who saw nothing, resumed her story.

"Arthur's room is near, and Adelaide's far off; but I went to Adelaide's first. Her door was shut and when I went to open it I found it locked. Calling her name, I said that I was tired and would be glad to say good night. She did not answer at once. When she did, her voice was strange, though what she said was very simple. I was to please myself; she was going to retire, too. And then she tried to say good night, but she only half said it, like one who is choked with tears or some other dreadful emotion. I cannot tell you how this made me feel—but you don't care for that. You want to know what I did—what Adelaide did. I will tell you, but I cannot hurry. Every act of the evening was so crowded with purpose; all meant so much. I can see the end, but the steps leading to it are not so clear."

"Take your time, Miss Cumberland; we have no wish to hurry you."

"I can go on now. The next thing I did was to knock at Arthur's door. I heard him getting ready to go out, and I wanted to speak to him before he went. When he heard me, he opened the door and let me in. He began at once on his grievances, but I could not listen to them. I wanted him to harness the grey mare for me and leave it standing in the stable. I explained the request by saying that it was necessary for me to see a certain friend of mine immediately, and that no one would notice me in the cutter under the bear-skins. He didn't approve, but I persuaded him. I even persuaded him to wait till Zadok was gone, so that Adelaide would know nothing about it. He looked glum, but he promised.

"He was going away when I heard Adelaide's steps in the adjoining room. This frightened me. The partition is very thin between these two rooms, and I was afraid she had heard me ask Arthur for the grey mare and cutter. I could hear her rattling the bottles in the medicine cabinet hanging on this very wall. Looking back at Arthur, I asked him how long Adelaide had been there. He said, 'For some time.' This sent me flying from the room. I would join her, and find out if she had heard. But I was too late. As I stepped into the hall I saw her disappearing round the corner leading to her own room. This convinced me that she had heard nothing, and, light of heart once more, I went back to my own room, where I collected such little articles as I needed for the expedition before me.

"I had hardly done this when I heard the servants on the walk outside, then Arthur going down. The impulse to see and speak to him again was irresistible. I flew after him and caught him in the lower hall. 'Arthur,' I cried, 'look at me, look at me well, and then—kiss me!' And he did kiss me—I'm glad when I think of it, though he did say, next minute: 'What is the matter with you? What are you going to do? To meet that villain?'

"I looked straight into his face. I waited till I saw I had his whole attention; then I said, as slowly and emphatically as I could: 'If you mean Elwood—no! I shall never meet him again, except in Adelaide's presence. He will not want to meet me. You may be at ease about that. To-morrow all will be well, and Adelaide very happy,'

"He shrugged his shoulders, and reached for his coat and hat. As he was putting them on, I said, 'Don't forget to harness up Jenny.' Jenny is the grey mare. 'And leave off the bells,' I urged. 'I don't want Adelaide to hear me go out.'

"He swung about at this. 'You and Adelaide are not very good friends it seems.' 'As good as you and she are,' I answered. Then I flung my arms about him. 'Don't go down street to-night,' I prayed. 'Stay home for this one night. Stay in the house with Adelaide; stay till I come home.' He stared, and I saw his colour change. Then he flung me off, but not rudely. 'Why don't you stay?' he asked. Then he laughed, and added, 'I'll go harness the mare.'

"'The key's in the kitchen,' I said. 'I'll go get it for you. I heard Zadok bring it in.' He did not answer, and I went for the key. I found two on the nail, and I brought them both; but I only handed him one, the key to the stable-door. 'Which way are you going?' I asked, as he looked at the key, then back towards the kitchen. 'The short way, of course,' 'Then here's the key to the Fulton grounds,'

"As he took the key, I prayed again, 'Don't do what's in your mind, Arthur. Don't drink to-night. He only laughed, and I said my last word: 'If you do, it will be for the last time. You'll never drink again after to-morrow.'

"He made no answer to this, and I went slowly upstairs. Everything was quiet—quiet as death—in the whole house. If Adelaide had heard us, she made no sign. Going to my own room, I waited until I heard Arthur come out of the stable and go away by the door in the rear wall. Then I stole out again. I carried a small bag with me, but no coat or hat.

"Pausing and listening again and again, I crept downstairs and halted at the table under the rack. The keys were still there. Putting them in my bag, I searched the rack for one of my brother's warm coats. But I took none I saw. I remembered an old one which Adelaide had put away in the closet under the stairs. Getting this, I put it on, and, finding a hat there too, I took that also; and when I had pulled it over my forehead and drawn up the collar of the coat, I was quite unrecognisable. I was going out, when I remembered there would be no light in the club-house. I had put a box of matches in my bag while I was upstairs, but I needed a candle. Slipping back, I took a candlestick and candle from the dining-room mantel, and finding that the bag would not hold them, thrust them into the pocket of the coat I wore, and quickly left the house. Jenny was in the stable, all harnessed; and hesitating no longer, I got in among the bear-skins and drove swiftly away."

There was a moment's silence. Carmel had paused, and was sitting with her hand on her heart, looking past judge, past jury, upon the lonely and desolate scene in which she at this moment moved and suffered. An inexpressible fatality had entered into her tones, always rich and resonant with feeling. No one who listened could fail to share the dread by which she was moved.

District Attorney Fox fumbled with his papers, and endeavoured to maintain his equanimity and show an indifference which his stern but fascinated glances at the youthful witness amply belied. He was biding his time, but biding it in decided perturbation of mind. Neither he nor any one else, unless it were Moffat, could tell whither this tale tended. While she held the straight course which had probably been laid out for her, he failed to object; but he could not prevent the subtle influence of her voice, her manner, and her supreme beauty on the entranced jury. Nevertheless, his pencil was busy; he was still sufficiently master of himself for that.

Mr. Moffat, quite aware of the effect which was being produced on every side, but equally careful to make no show of it, put in a commonplace question at this point, possibly to rouse the witness from her own abstraction, possibly to restore the judicial tone of the inquiry.

"How did you leave the stable-door?"

"Open."

"Can you tell us what time it was when you started?"

"No. I did not look. Time meant nothing to me. I drove as fast as I could, straight down the hill, and out towards The Whispering Pines. I had seen Adelaide in her window as I went flying by the house, but not a soul on the road, nor a sign of life, near or far. The whistle of a train blew as I stopped in the thicket near the club-house door. If it was the express train, you can tell—"

"Never mind the if" said Mr. Moffat. "It is enough that you heard the whistle. Go on with what you did."

"I tied up my horse; then I went into the house. I had used Mr. Ranelagh's key to open the door and for some reason I took it out of the lock when I got in, and put the whole bunch back into my satchel. But I did not lock the door. Then I lit my candle and then—I went upstairs."

Fainter and fainter the words fell, and slower and slower heaved the youthful breast under her heavily pressing palm. Mr. Moffat made a sign across the court-room, and I saw Dr. Carpenter get up and move nearer to the witness stand. But she stood in no need of his help. In an instant her cheek flushed; the eye I watched with such intensity of wonder that apprehension unconsciously left me, rose, glowed, and fixed itself at last—not on the judge, not on the prisoner, not even on that prisoner's counsel—but on me; and as the soft light filled my soul and awoke awe, where it had hitherto awakened passion, she quietly said:

"There is a room upstairs, in the club-house, where I have often been with Adelaide. It has a fireplace in it, and I had seen a box there, half filled with wood the day before. This is the room I went to, and here I built a fire. When it was quite bright, I took out something I had brought in my satchel, and thrust it into the flame. Then I got up and walked away. I—I did not feel very strong, and sank on my knees when I got to the couch, and buried my face in my arms. But I felt better when I came back to the fire again, and very brave till I caught a glimpse of my face in the mirror over the mantelpiece. That—that unnerved me, and I think I screamed. Some one screamed, and I think it was I. I know my hands went out—I saw them in the glass; then they fell straight down at my side, and I looked and looked at myself till I saw all the terror go out of my face, and when it was quite calm again, I stooped down and pulled out the little tongs I had been heating in the fire, and laid them quick—quick, before I could be sorry again—right across my cheek, and then—"

Uproar in the court. If she had screamed when she said she did, so some one cried out loudly now. I think that pitiful person was myself. They say I had been standing straight up in my place for the last two minutes.

CHAPTER XXX

"CHOOSE"

Let me have
A dram of poison; such soon speeding geer
As will disperse itself through all the veins,
That the life-weary taker may fall dead.

Come, bitter conduct, come unsavoury guide!
Thou desperate pilot, now at once run on
The dashing rocks thy sea-sick weary bark.

Romeo and Juliet

"I have not finished," were the first words we heard, when order was restored, and we were all in a condition to listen again.

"I had to relate what you have just heard, that you might understand what happened next. I was not used to pain, and I could never have kept on pressing those irons to my cheek if I had not had the strength given me by my own reflection in the glass. When I thought the burn was quite deep enough, I tore the tongs away, and was lifting them to the other cheek when I saw the door behind me open, inch by inch, as thought pushed by hesitating touches.

"Instantly, I forgot my pain, almost my purpose, watching that door. I saw it slowly swing to its full width, and disclose my sister standing in the gap, with a look and in an attitude which terrified me more than the fire had done. Dropping the tongs, I turned and faced her, covering my cheek instinctively with my hand.

"I saw her eyes run over my elaborate dinner dress—my little hand-bag, and the candle burning in a room made warm with a fire on the hearth. This, before she spoke a single word. Then, with a deep labouring breath, she looked me in the eye again, with the simple question:

"'And where is he?'"

Carmel's head had drooped at this, but she raised it almost instantly. Mine did not rise so readily.

"'Do you mean Elwood?' I asked. 'You know!' said she. 'The veil is down between us, Carmel; we will speak plainly now. I saw him give you the letter. I heard you ask Arthur to harness up the horse. I have demeaned myself to follow you, and we will have no subterfuges now. You expect him here?'

"'No,' I cried. 'I am not so bad as that, Adelaide—nor is he. Here is the note. You will see by it what he expects, and at what place I should have joined him, if I had been the selfish creature you think,' I had the note hidden in my breast. I took it out, and held it towards her. I did not feel the burn at all, but I kept it covered. She glanced down at the words; and I felt like falling at her feet, she looked so miserable. I am told that I must keep to fact, and must not express my feelings, or those of others. I will try to remember this; but it is hard for a sister, relating such a frightful scene.

"She glanced down at the paper and let it drop, almost immediately, from her hand, 'I cannot read his words!' she cried; 'I do not need to; we both know which of us he loves best. You cannot say that it is I, his engaged wife.' I was silent, and her face took on an awful pallor. 'Carmel,' said she, 'do you know what this man's love has been to me? You are a child, a warm-hearted and passionate child; but you do not know a woman's heart. Certainly, you do not know mine. I doubt if any one does— even he. Cares have warped my life. I do not quarrel with these cares; I only say that they have robbed me of what makes girlhood lovely. Duty is a stern task-master; and sternness, coming early into one's life, hardens its edges, but does not sap passion from the soul or devotion from the heart. I was ready for joy when it came, but I was no longer capable of bestowing it. I thought I was, but I soon saw my mistake. You showed it to me—you with your beauty, your freshness, your warm and untried heart. I have no charms to rival these; I have only love, such love as you cannot dream of at your age. And this is no longer desirable to him!'

"You see that I remember every word she spoke. They burned more fiercely than the iron. That did not burn at all, just then. I was cold instead—bitterly, awfully cold. My very heart seemed frozen, and the silence was dreadful. But I could not speak, I could not answer her.

"'You have everything,' she now went on. 'Why did you rob me of my one happiness? And you have robbed me. I have seen your smile when his head turned your way. It was the smile which runs before a promise. I know it; I have had that smile in my heart a long, long time—but it never reached my lips. Carmel, do you know why I am here?' I shook my head. Was it her teeth that were chattering or mine? 'I am here to end it all,' said she. 'With my hope gone, my heart laid waste, life has no prospect for me. I believe in God, and I know that my act is sinful; but I can no more live than can a tree stricken at the root. To-morrow he will not need to write notes; he can come and comfort you in our home. But never let him look at me. As we are sisters, and I almost a mother to you, shut my face away from his eyes—or I shall rise in my casket and the tangle of our lives will be renewed.'

"I tell you this—I bare my sister's broken heart to you, giving you her very words, sacred as they are to me and—and to others, who are present, and must listen to all I say—because it is right that you should understand her frenzy, and know all that passed between us in that awful hour."

This was irregular, highly irregular—but District Attorney Fox sat on, unmoved. Possibly he feared to prejudice the jury; possibly he recognised the danger of an interruption now, not only to the continuity of her testimony, but to the witness herself; or—what is just as likely—possibly he cherished a hope that, in giving her a free rein and allowing her to tell her story thus artlessly, she would herself supply the clew he needed to reconstruct his case on the new lines upon which it was being slowly forced by these unexpected revelations. Whatever the cause, he let these expressions of feeling pass.

At a gesture from Mr. Moffat, Carmel proceeded:

"I tottered at this threat; and she, a mother to me from my cradle, started instinctively to catch me; but the feeling left her before she had taken two steps, and she stopped still. 'Drop your hand,' she cried. 'I want to see your whole face while I ask you one last question. I could not read the note. Why did you come here? I dropped my hand, and she stood staring; then she uttered a cry and ran quickly towards me. 'What is it?' she cried. 'What has happened to you? Is it the shadow or—'

"I caught her by the hand. I could speak now. 'Adelaide,' said I, 'you are not the only one to love to the point of hurt. I love you. Let this little scar be witness,' Then, as her eyes opened and she staggered, I caught her to my breast and hid my face on her shoulder. 'You say that to-morrow I shall be free to receive notes. He will not wish to write them, tomorrow. The beauty he liked is gone. If it weighed overmuch with him, then you and I are on a plane again—or I am on an inferior one. Your joy will be sweeter for this break!'

"She started, raised my head from her shoulder, looked at me and shuddered—but no longer with hate. 'Carmel!' she whispered, 'the story—the story I read you of Francis the First and—'

"'Yes,' I agreed, 'that made me think,' Her knees bent under her; she sank at my feet, but her eyes never left my face. 'And—and Elwood?' 'He knows nothing. I did not make up my mind till to-night. Adelaide, it had to be. I hadn't the strength to—to leave you all, or—to say no, if he ever asked me to my face what he asked me in that note,'

"And then I tried to lift her; but she was kissing my feet, kissing my dress, sobbing out her life on my hands. Oh, I was happy! My future looked very simple to me. But my cheek began to burn, and instinctively I put up my hand. This brought her to her feet. 'You are suffering,' she cried. 'You must go home, at once, at once, while I telephone to Dr. Carpenter,' 'We will go together,' I said. 'We can telephone from there.' But at this, the awful look came back into her face, and seeing her forget my hurt, I forgot it, too, in dread of what she would say when she found strength to speak.

"It was worse than anything I had imagined; she refused absolutely to go back home. 'Carmel,' said she, 'I have done injustice to your youth. You love him, too—not like a child but a woman. The tangle is worse than I thought; your heart is caught in it, as well as mine, and you shall have your chance. My death will give it to you.' I shook my head, pointing to my cheek. She shook hers, and quietly, calmly said, 'You have never looked so beautiful. Should we go back together and take up the old life, the struggle which has undermined my conscience and my whole existence would only begin again. I cannot face that ordeal, Carmel. The morning light would bring me daily torture, the evening dusk a night of blasting dreams. We three cannot live in this world together. I am the least loved and so I should be the one to die. I am determined, Carmel. Life, with me, has come to this.'

"I tried to dissuade her. I urged every plea, even that of my own sacrifice. But she was no more her natural self. She had taken up the note and read it during my entreaties, and my words fell on deaf ears. 'Why, these words have killed me,' she cried crumpling the note in her hand. 'What will a little poison do? It can only finish what he has begun.'

"Poison! I remembered how I had heard her pushing about bottles in the medicine cabinet, and felt my legs grow weak and my head swim. 'You will not!' I cried, watching her hand, in terror of seeing it rise to her breast. 'You are crazed to-night; to-morrow you will feel differently.'

"But the fixed set look of her bleak face gave me no hope. 'I shall never feel differently. If I do not end it to-night, I shall do so soon. When a heart like mine goes down, it goes down forever,' I could only shudder. I did not know what to do, or which way to turn. She stood between me and the door, and her presence was terrible. 'When I came here,' she said, 'I brought a bottle of cordial with me and three glasses. I brought a little phial of poison too, once ordered for sickness. I expected to find Elwood here. If I had, I meant to drop the poison into one glass, and then fill them all up with the cordial. We should have drunk, each one of us his glass, and one of us would have fallen. I did not care which, you or Elwood or myself. But he is not here, and the cast of the die is between us two, unless you wish a certainty, Carmel,—in which case I will pour out but one glass and drink that myself.'

"She was in a fever, now, and desperate. Death was in the room; I felt it in my lifted hair, and in her strangely drawn face. If I screamed, who would hear me? I never thought of the telephone, and I doubt if she would have let me use it then. The power she had always exerted over me was very strong in her at this moment; and not till afterwards did it cross my mind that I had never asked her how she got to the house, or whether we were as much alone in the building as I believed.

"'Shall I drink alone?' she repeated, and I cried out 'No'; at which her hand went to her breast, as I had so long expected, and I saw the glitter of a little phial as she drew it forth.

"'Oh, Adelaide!' I began; but she heeded me no more than the dead.

"On leaving home, she had put on a long coat with pockets and this coat was still on her, and the pockets gaping. Thrusting her other hand into one of these, she drew out a little flask covered with wicker, and set it on a stand beside her. Then she pulled out two small glasses, and set them down also, and then she turned her back. I could hear the drop, drop of the liquor; and, dark as the room was, it seemed to turn darker, till I put out my hands like one groping in a sudden night. But everything cleared before me when she turned around again. Features set like hers force themselves to be seen.

"She advanced, a glass in either hand. As she came, the floor swayed, and the walls seemed to bow together; but they did not sway her. Step by step, she drew near, and when she reached my side she smiled in my face once. Then she said: 'Choose aright, dear heart. Leave the poisoned one for me.'

"Fascinated, I stared at one glass, then at the other. Had either of her hands trembled, I should have grasped at the glass it held; but not a tremor shook those icy fingers, nor did her eyes wander to the right hand or to the left. 'Adelaide!' I shrieked out. 'Toss them behind you. Let us live—live!' But she only reiterated that awful word: 'Choose!' and I dare not hesitate longer, lest I lose my chance to save her. Groping, I touched a glass—I never knew which one—and drawing it from her fingers, I lifted it to my mouth. Instantly her other hand rose. 'I don't know which is which, myself,' she said, and drank. That made me drink, also.

"The two glasses sent out a clicking sound as we set them back on the stand. Then we waited, looking at each other. 'Which?' her lips seemed to say. 'Which?' In another moment we knew. 'Your choice was the right one,' said she, and she sank back into a chair. 'Don't leave me!' she called out, for I was about to run shrieking out into the night. 'I—I am happy now that it is all settled; but I do not want to die alone. Oh, how hot I am!' And leaping up, she flung off her coat, and went gasping about the room for air. When she sank down again, it was on the lounge; and again I tried to fly for help, and again she would not let me. Suddenly she started up, and I saw a great change in her. The heavy, leaden look was gone; tenderness had come back to her eyes, and a human anxious expression to her whole face. 'I have been mad!' she cried. 'Carmel, Carmel, what have I done to you, my more than sister—my child, my child!'

"I tried to soothe her—to keep down my awful fear and soothe her. But the nearness of death had calmed her poor heart into its old love and habitual thoughtfulness. She was terrified at my position. She recalled our mother, and the oath she had taken at that mother's death-bed to protect me and care for me and my brother. 'And I have failed to do either,' she cried. 'Arthur, I have alienated, and you I am leaving to unknown trouble and danger,'

"She was not to be comforted. I saw her life ebbing and could do nothing. She clung to me while she called up all her powers, and made plans for me and showed me a way of escape. I was to burn the note, fling two of the glasses from the window and leave the other and the deadly phial near her hand. This, before I left the room. Then I was to call up the police and say there was something wrong at the club-house, but I was not to give my name or ever acknowledge I was there. 'Nothing can save trouble,' she said, 'but that trouble must not come near you. Swear that you will heed my words—swear that you will do what I say,'

"I swore. All that she asked I promised. I was almost dying, too; and had the light gone out and the rafters of the house fallen in and buried us both, it would have been better. But the light burned on, and the life in her eyes faded out, and the hands grasping mine relaxed. I heard one little gasp; then a low prayer: 'Tell Arthur never—never—again to—' Then—silence!"

Sobs—cries—veiled faces—then silence in the courtroom, too. It was broken but by one sound, a heartrending sigh from the prisoner. But nobody looked at him, and thank God!—nobody looked at me. Every eye was on the face of this young girl, whose story bore such an impress of truth, and yet was so contradictory of all former evidence. What revelations were yet to follow. It would seem that she was speaking of her sister's death.

But her sister had not died that way; her sister had been strangled. Could this dainty creature, with beauty scarred and yet powerfully triumphant, be the victim of an hallucination as to the cause of that scar and the awesome circumstances which attended its infliction? Or, harder still to believe, were these soul-compelling tones, these evidences of grief, this pathetic yielding to the rights of the law in face of the heart's natural shrinking from disclosures sacred as they were tragic—were these the medium by which she sought to mislead justice and to conceal truth?

Even I, with my memory of her looks as she faltered down the staircase on that memorable night— pale, staring, her left hand to her cheek and rocking from side to side in pain or terror—could not but ask if this heart-rending story did not involve a still more terrible sequel. I searched her face, and racked my very soul, in my effort to discern what lay beneath this angelic surface—beneath this recital which if it were true and the whole truth, would call not only for the devotion of a lifetime, but a respect transcending love and elevating it to worship.

But, in her cold and quiet features, I could detect nothing beyond the melancholy of grief; and the suspense from which all suffered, kept me also on the rack, until at a question from Mr. Moffat she spoke again, and we heard her say:

"Yes, she died that way, with her hands in mine. There was no one else by; we were quite alone."

That settled it, and for a moment the revulsion of feeling threatened to throw the court into tumult. But one thing restrained them. Not the look of astonishment on her face, not the startled uplift of Arthur's head, not the quiet complacency which in an instant replaced the defeated aspect of the district attorney; but the gesture and attitude of Mr. Moffat, the man who had put her on the stand, and who now from the very force of his personality, kept the storm in abeyance, and by his own composure, forced back attention to his witness and to his own confidence in his case. This result reached, he turned again towards Carmel, with renewed respect in his manner and a marked softening in his aspect and voice.

"Can you fix the hour of this occurrence?" he asked. "In any way can you locate the time?"

"No; for I did not move at once. I felt tied to that couch; I am very young, and I had never seen death before. When I did get up, I hobbled like an old woman and almost went distracted; but came to myself as I saw the note on the floor—the note I was told to burn. Lifting it, I moved towards the fireplace, but got a fright on the way, and stopped in the middle of the floor and looked back. I thought I had heard my sister speak!

"But the fancy passed as I saw how still she lay, and I went on, after a while, and threw the note into the one small flame which was all that was left of the fire. I saw it caught by a draught from the door behind me, and go flaming up the chimney.

"Some of my trouble seemed to go with it, but a great one yet remained. I didn't know how I could ever turn around again and see my sister lying there behind me, with her face fixed in death, for which I was, in a way, responsible. I was abjectly frightened, and knelt there a long time, praying and shuddering, before I could rise again to my feet and move about as I had to, since God had not stricken me and I must live my life and do what my sister had bidden me. Courage—such courage as I had had—was all gone from me now; and while I knew there was something else for me to do before I left the room, I could not remember what it was, and stood hesitating, dreading to lift my eyes and yet feeling that I ought to, if only to aid my memory by a look at my sister's face.

"Suddenly I did look up, but it did not aid my memory; and, realising that I could never think with that lifeless figure before me, I lifted a pillow from the window-seat near by and covered her face. I must have done more; I must have covered the whole lounge with pillows and cushions; for, presently my mind cleared again, and I recollected that it was something about the poison. I was to put the phial in her hand—or was I to throw it from the window? Something was to be thrown from the window—it must be the phial. But I couldn't lift the window, so having found the phial standing on the table beside the little flask, I carried it into the closet where there was a window opening inward, and I dropped it out of that, and thought I had done all. But when I came back and saw Adelaide's coat lying in a heap where she had thrown it, I recalled that she had said something about this but what, I didn't know. So I lifted it and put it in the closet—why, I cannot say. Then I set my mind on going home.

"But there was something to do first—something not in that room. It was a long time before it came to me; then the sight of the empty hall recalled it. The door by which Adelaide had come in had never been closed, and as I went towards it I remembered the telephone, and that I was to call up the police. Lifting the candle, I went creeping towards the front hall. Adelaide had commanded me, or I could never have accomplished this task. I had to open a door; and when it swung to behind me and latched, I turned around and looked at it, as if I never expected it to open again. I almost think I fainted, if one can faint standing, for when I knew anything, after the appalling latching of that door, I was in quite another part of the room and the candle which I still held, looked to my dazed eyes shorter than when I started with it from the place where my sister lay.

"I was wasting time. The thought drove me to the table. I caught up the receiver and when central answered, I said something about The Whispering Pines and wanting help. This is all I remember about that.

"Some time afterward—I don't know when—I was stumbling down the stairs on my way out. I had gone to—to the room again for my little bag; for the keys were in it, and I dared not leave them. But I didn't stay a minute, and I cast but one glance at the lounge. What happened afterward is like a dream to me. I found the horse; the horse found the road; and some time later I reached home. As I came within sight of the house I grew suddenly strong again. The open stable door reminded me of my duty, and driving in, I quickly unharnessed Jenny and put her away. Then I dragged the cutter into place, and hung up the harness. Lastly, I locked the door and carried the key with me into the house and hung it up on its usual nail in the kitchen. I had obeyed Adelaide, and now I would go to my room. That is what she would wish; but I don't know whether I did this or not. My mind was full of Adelaide till confusion came—then darkness—and then a perfect blank."

She had finished; she had done as she had been asked; she had told the story of that evening as she knew it, from the family dinner till her return home after midnight—and the mystery of Adelaide's death was as great as ever. Did she realise this? Had I wronged this lovely, tempestuous nature by suspicions which this story put to blush? I was happy to think so—madly, unreasonably happy. Whatever happened, whatever the future threatening Arthur or myself, it was rapture to be restored to right thinking as regards this captivating and youthful spirit, who had suffered and must suffer always—and all through me, who thought it a pleasant pastime to play with hearts, and awoke to find I was playing with souls, and those of the two noblest women I had ever known!

The cutting in of some half dozen questions from Mr. Moffat, which I scarcely heard and which did not at all affect the status of the case as it now stood, served to cool down the emotional element, which had almost superseded the judicial, in more minds than those of the jury; and having thus prepared his witness for an examination at other and less careful hands, he testified his satisfaction at her replies, and turned her over to the prosecution, with the time-worn phrase:

"Mr. District Attorney, the witness is yours."

Mr. Fox at once arose; the moment was ripe for conquest. He put his most vital question first:

"In all this interview with your sister, did you remark any discoloration on her throat?"

The witness's lips opened; surprise spoke from her every feature. "Discoloration?" she repeated. "I do not know what you mean."

"Any marks darker than the rest of her skin on her throat or neck?"

"No. Adelaide had a spotless skin. It looked like marble as she lay there. No, I saw no marks."

"Miss Cumberland, have you heard or read a full account of this trial?"

She was trembling, now. Was it from fear of the truth, or under that terror of the unknown embodied in this question.

"I do not know," said she. "What I heard was from my nurse and Mr. Moffat. I read very little, and that was only about the first days of the trial and the swearing in of jurors. This is the first time I have heard any mention made of marks, and I do not understand yet what you allude to."

District Attorney Fox cast at Mr. Moffat an eloquent glance, which that gentleman bore unmoved; then turning back to the witness, he addressed her in milder and more considerate tones than were usually heard from him in cross-examination, and asked: "Did you hold your sister's hands all the time she lay dying, as you thought, on the lounge?"

"Yes, yes."

"And did not see her raise them once?"

"No, no."

"How was it when you let go of them? Where did they fall then?"

"On her breast. I laid them down softly and crossed them. I did not leave her till I had done this and closed her eyes."

"And what did you do then?"

"I went for the note, to burn it."

"Miss Cumberland, in your direct examination, you said that you stopped still as you crossed the floor at the time, thinking that your sister called, and that you looked back at her to see."

"Yes, sir."

"Were her hands crossed then?"

"Yes, sir, just the same."

"And afterward, when you came from the fire after waiting some little time for courage?"

"Yes, yes. There were no signs of movement. Oh, she was dead—quite dead."

"No statements, Miss Cumberland. She looked the same, and you saw no change in the position of her hands?"

"None; they were just as I left them."

"Miss Cumberland, you have told us how, immediately after taking the poison, she staggered about the room, and sank first on a chair and then on the lounge. Were you watching her then?"

"Oh, yes—every moment."

"Her hands as well as her face?"

"I don't know about her hands. I should have observed it if she had done anything strange with them."

"Can you say she did not clutch or grip her throat during any of this time?"

"Yes, yes. I couldn't have forgotten it, if she had done that. I remember every move she made so well. She didn't do that."

Mr. Fox's eye stole towards the jury. To a man, they were alert, anxious for the next question, and serious, as the arbitrators of a man's life ought to be.

Satisfied, he put the question: "When, after telephoning, you returned to the room where your sister lay, you glanced at the lounge?"

"Yes, I could not help it."

"Was it in the same condition as when you left—the pillows, I mean?"

"I—I think so. I cannot say; I only half looked; I was terrified by it."

"Can you say they had not been disturbed?"

"No. I can say nothing. But what does—"

"Only the answer, Miss Cumberland. Can you tell us how those pillows were arranged?"

"I'm afraid not. I threw them down quickly, madly, just as I collected them. I only know that I put the window cushion down first. The rest fell anyhow; but they quite covered her—quite."

"Hands and face?"

"Her whole body."

"And did they cover her quite when you came back?"

"They must have—Wait—wait! I know I have no right to say that, but I cannot swear that I saw any change."

"Can you swear that there was no change—that the pillows and the window cushion lay just as they did when you left the room?"

She did not answer. Horror seemed to have seized hold of her. Her eyes, fixed on the attorney's face, wavered and, had they followed their natural impulse, would have turned towards her brother, but her fear—possibly her love—was her counsellor and she brought them back to Mr. Fox. Resolutely, but with a shuddering insight of the importance of her reply, she answered with that one weighty monosyllable which can crush so many hopes, and even wreck a life:

"No."

At the next moment she was in Dr. Carpenter's arms. Her strength had given way for the time, and the court was hastily adjourned, to give her opportunity for rest and recuperation.

CHAPTER XXXI

"WERE HER HANDS CROSSED THEN?"

Threescore and ten I can remember well:
Within the volume of which time, I have seen
Hours dreadful, and things strange; but this sore night
Hath trifled former knowledge.

Macbeth.

I shall say nothing about myself at this juncture. That will come later. I have something of quite different purport to relate.

When I left the court-room with the other witnesses, I noticed a man standing near the district attorney. He was a very plain man—with no especial claims to attention, that I could see, yet I looked at him longer than I did at any one else, and turned and looked at him again as I passed through the doorway.

Afterward I heard that he was Sweetwater, the detective from New York who had had so much to do in unearthing the testimony against Arthur,—testimony which in the light of this morning's revelations, had taken on quite a new aspect, as he was doubtless the first to acknowledge. It was the curious blending of professional disappointment and a personal and characteristic appreciation of the surprising situation, which made me observe him, I suppose. Certainly my heart and mind were full enough not to waste looks on a commonplace stranger unless there had been some such overpowering reason.

I left him still talking to Mr. Fox, and later received this account of the interview which followed between them and Dr. Perry.

"Is this girl telling the truth?" asked District Attorney Fox, as soon as the three were closeted and each could speak his own mind. "Doctor, what do you think?"

"I do not question her veracity in the least. A woman who for purely moral reasons could defy pain and risk the loss of a beauty universally acknowledged as transcendent, would never stoop to falsehood even in her desire to save a brother's life. I have every confidence in her. Fox, and I think you may safely have the same."

"You believe that she burnt herself—intentionally?"

"I wouldn't disbelieve it—you may think me sentimental; I knew and loved her father—for any fortune you might name."

"Say that you never knew her father; say that you had no more interest in the girl or the case, than the jurors have? What then—-?

"I should believe her for humanity's sake; for the sake of the happiness it gives one to find something true and strong in this sordid work-a-day world—a jewel in a dust-heap. Oh, I'm a sentimentalist, I acknowledge."

Mr. Fox turned to Sweetwater. "And you?"

"Mr. Fox, have you those tongs?"

"Yes, I forgot; they were brought to my office, with the other exhibits. I attached no importance to them, and you will probably find them just where I thrust them into the box marked 'Cumb.'"

They were in the district attorney's office, and Sweetwater at once rose and brought forward the tongs.

"There is my answer," he said pointing significantly at one of the legs.

The district attorney turned pale, and motioned Sweetwater to carry them back. He sat silent for a moment, and then showed that he was a man.

"Miss Cumberland has my respect," said he.

Sweetwater came back to his place.

Dr. Perry waited.

Finally Mr. Fox turned to him and put the anticipated question:

"You are satisfied with your autopsy? Miss Cumberland's death was due to strangulation and not to the poison she took?"

"That was what I swore to, and what I should have to swear to again if you placed me back on the stand. The poison, taken with her great excitement, robbed her of consciousness, but there was too little of it, or it was too old and weakened to cause death. She would probably have revived, in time; possibly did revive. But the clutch of those fingers was fatal; she could not survive it. It costs me more than you can ever understand to say this, but questions like yours must be answered. I should not be an honest man otherwise."

Sweetwater made a movement. Mr. Fox turned and looked at him critically.

"Speak out," said he.

But Sweetwater had nothing to say.

Neither had Dr. Perry. The oppression of an unsolved problem, involving lives of whose value each formed a different estimate, was upon them all; possibly heaviest upon the district attorney, the most serious portion of whose work lay still before him.

To the relief of all, Carmel was physically stronger than we expected when she came to retake the stand in the afternoon. But she had lost a little of her courage. Her expectation of clearing her brother at a word had left her, and with it the excitation of hope. Yet she made a noble picture as she sat there, meeting, without a blush, but with an air of sweet humility impossible to describe, the curious, all-devouring glances of the multitude, some of them anxious to repeat the experience of the morning; some of them new to the court, to her, and the cause for which she stood.

Mr. Fox kept nobody waiting. With a gentleness such as he seldom showed to any witness for the defence, he resumed his cross-examination by propounding the following question:

"Miss Cumberland, in your account of the final interview you had with your sister, you alluded to a story you had once read together. Will you tell us the name of this story?"

"It was called 'A Legend of Francis the First.' It was not a novel, but a little tale she found in some old magazine. It had a great effect upon us; I have never forgotten it."

"Can you relate this tale to us in a few words?"

"I will try. It was very simple; it merely told how a young girl marred her beauty to escape the attentions of the great king, and what respect he always showed her after that, even calling her sister."

Was the thrill in her voice or in my own heart, or in the story—emphasised as it was by her undeniable attempt upon her own beauty? As that last word fell so softly, yet with such tender suggestion, a sensation of sympathy passed between us for the first time; and I knew, from the purity of her look and the fearlessness of this covert appeal to one she could not address openly, that the doubts I had cherished of her up to this very moment were an outrage and that were it possible or seemly, I should be bowed down in the dust at her feet—in reality, as I was in spirit.

Others may have shared my feeling; for the glances which flew from her face to mine were laden with an appreciation of the situation, which for the moment drove the prisoner from the minds of all, and centred attention on this tragedy of souls, bared in so cruel a way to the curiosity of the crowd. I could not bear it. The triumph of my heart battled with the shame of my fault, and I might have been tempted into some act of manifest imprudence, if Mr. Fox had not cut my misery short by recalling attention to the witness, with a question of the most vital importance.

"While you were holding your sister's hands in what you supposed to be her final moments, did you observe whether or not she still wore on her finger the curious ring given her by Mr. Ranelagh, and known as her engagement ring?"

"Yes—I not only saw it, but felt it. It was the only one she wore on her left hand."

The district attorney paused. This was an admission unexpected, perhaps, by himself, which it was desirable to have sink into the minds of the jury. The ring had not been removed by Adelaide herself;

it was still on her finger as the last hour drew nigh. An awful fact, if established—telling seriously against Arthur. Involuntarily I glanced his way. He was looking at me. The mutual glance struck fire. What I thought, he thought—but possibly with a difference. The moment was surcharged with emotion for all but the witness herself. She was calm; perhaps she did not understand the significance of the occasion.

Mr. Fox pressed his advantage.

"And when you rose from the lounge and crossed your sister's hands?"

"It was still there; I put that hand uppermost."

"And left the ring on?"

"Oh, yes—oh, yes." Her whole attitude and face were full of protest.

"So that, to the best of your belief, it was still on your sister's finger when you left the room?"

"Certainly, sir, certainly."

There was alarm in her tone now, she was beginning to see that her testimony was not as entirely helpful to Arthur as she had been led to expect. In her helplessness, she cast a glance of entreaty at her brother's counsel. But he was busily occupied with pencil and paper, and she received no encouragement unless it was from his studiously composed manner and general air of unconcern. She did not know—nor did I know then—what uneasiness such an air may cover.

Mr. Fox had followed her glances, and perhaps understood his adversary better than she did; for he drew himself up with an appearance of satisfaction as he asked very quietly:

"What material did you use in lighting the fire on the club-house hearth?"

"Wood from the box, and a little kindling I found there."

"How large was this kindling?"

"Not very large; some few stray pieces of finer wood I picked out from she rest."

"And how did you light these?"

"With some scraps of paper I brought in my bag?"

"Oh—you brought scraps?"

"Yes. I had seen the box, seen the wood, but knew the wood would not kindle without paper. So I brought some."

"Did the fire light quickly?"

"Not very quickly."

"You had trouble with it?"

"Yes, sir. But I made it burn at last."

"Are you in the habit of kindling fires in your own home?"

"Yes, on the hearth."

"You understand them?"

"I have always found it a very simple matter, if you have paper and enough kindling."

"And the draught is good."

"Yes, sir."

"Wasn't the draught good at the club-house?"

"Not at first."

"Oh—not at first. When did you see a change?"

"When the note I was trying to burn flew up the chimney."

"I see. Was that after or before the door opened?"

"After."

"Did the opening of this door alter the temperature of the room?"

"I cannot say; I felt neither heat nor cold at any time."

"Didn't you feel the icy cold when you opened the dressing-closet window to throw out the phial?"

"I don't remember."

"Wouldn't you remember if you had?"

"I cannot say."

Can you say whether you noticed any especial chill in the hall when you went out to telephone?"

"My teeth were chattering but—"

"Had they chattered before?"

"They may have. I only noticed it then; but—"

"The facts, Miss Cumberland. Your teeth chattered while you were passing through the hall. Did this keep up after you entered the room where you found the telephone?"

"I don't remember; I was almost insensible."

"You don't remember that they did?"

"No, sir."

"But you do remember having shut the door behind you?"

"Yes."

An open window in the hall! That was what he was trying to prove—open at this time. From the expression of such faces of the jury as I could see, I think he had proved it. The next point he made was in the same line. Had she, in all the time she was in the building, heard any noises she could not account for?

"Yes, many times."

"Can you describe these noises?"

"No; they were of all kinds. The pines sighed continually; I knew it was the pines, but I had to listen. Once I heard a rushing sound—it was when the pines stopped swaying for an instant—but I don't know what it was. It was all very dreadful."

"Was this rushing sound such as a window might make on being opened?"

"Possibly. I didn't think of it at the time, but it might have been."

"From what direction did it come?"

"Back of me, for I turned my head about."

"Where were you at the time?"

"At the hearth. It was before Adelaide came in."

"A near sound, or a far?"

"Far, but I cannot locate it—indeed, I cannot. I forgot it in a moment."

"But you remember it now?"

"Yes."

"And cannot you remember now any other noises than those you speak of? That time you stepped into the hall—when your teeth chattered, you know—did you hear nothing then but the sighing of the pines?"

She looked startled. Her hands went up and one of them clutched at her throat, then they fell, and slowly—carefully—like one feeling his way—she answered:

"I had forgotten. I did hear something—a sound in one of the doorways. It was very faint—a sigh—a—a—I don't know what. It conveyed nothing to me then, and not much now. But you asked, and I have answered."

"You have done right, Miss Cumberland. The jury ought to know these facts. Was it a human sigh?"

"It wasn't the sigh of the pines."

"And you heard it in one of the doorways? Which doorway?"

"The one opposite the room in which I left my sister."

"The doorway to the large hall?"

"Yes, sir."

Oh, the sinister memories! The moments which I myself had spent there—after this time of her passing through the hall, thank God!—but not long after. And some one had been there before me! Was it Arthur? I hardly had the courage to interrogate his face, but when I did, I, like every one else who looked that way, met nothing but the quietude of a fully composed man. There was nothing to be learned from him now; the hour for self-betrayal was past. I began to have a hideous doubt.

Carmel being innocent, who could be guilty but he. I knew of no one. The misery under which I had suffered was only lightened, not removed. We were still to see evil days. The prosecution would prove its case, and—But there was Mr. Moffat. I must not reckon without Moffat. He had sprung one surprise. Was he not capable of springing another? Relieved, I fixed my mind again upon the proceedings. What was Mr. Fox asking her now?

"Miss Cumberland, are you ready to swear that you did not hear a step at that time?"

"Yes, sir."

"Or see a face?"

"Yes, sir."

"That you only heard a sigh?"

"A sigh, or something like one."

"Which made you stop—"

"No, I did not stop."

"You went right on?"

"Immediately."

"Entering the telephone room?"

"Yes."

"The door of which you shut?"

"Yes."

"Intentionally?"

"No, not intentionally."

"Did you shut that door yourself?"

"I do not know. I must have but I—"

"Never mind explanations. You do not know whether you shut it, or whether some one else shut it?"

"I do not."

The words fell weightily. They seemed to strike every heart.

"Miss Cumberland, you have said that you telephoned for the police."

"I telephoned to central."

"For help?"

"Yes, for help."

"You were some minutes doing this, you say?"

"I have reason to think so, but I don't know definitely. The candle seemed shorter when I went out than when I came in."

"Are you sure you telephoned for help?"

"Help was what I wanted—help for my sister. I do not remember my words."

"And then you left the building?"

"After going for my little bag."

"Did you see any one then?"

"No, sir."

"Hear any one?"

"No, sir."

"Did you see your sister again?"

"I have said that I just glanced at the couch."

"Were the pillows there?"

"Yes, sir."

"Just as you had left them?"

"I have said that I could not tell."

"Wouldn't you know if they had been disturbed?"

"No, sir—not from the look I gave them."

"Then they might have been disturbed—might even have been rearranged—-without your knowing it?"

"They might."

"Miss Cumberland, when you left the building, did you leave it alone?"

"I did."

"Was the moon shining?"

"No, it was snowing."

"Did the moon shine when you went to throw the phial out of the window?"

"Yes, very brightly."

"Bright enough for you to see the links?"

"I didn't look at the links."

"Where were you looking?"

"Behind me."

"When you threw the phial out?"

"Yes."

"What was there behind you?"

"A dead sister." Oh, the indescribable tone!

"Nothing else?"

"No."

"Forgive me, Miss Cumberland, I do not want to trouble you, but was there not something or some one in the adjoining room besides your dead sister, to make you look back?"

"I saw no one. But I looked back—I do not know why."

"And didn't you turn at all?"

"I do not think so."

"You threw the phial out without looking?"

"Yes."

"How do you know you threw it out?"

"I felt it slip from my hand."

"Where?"

"Over the window ledge. I had pulled the window open before I turned my head. I had only to feel for the sill. When I touched its edge, I opened my fingers."

Triumph for the defence. Cross-examination on this point had only served to elucidate a mysterious fact. The position of the phial, caught in the vines, was accounted for in a very natural manner.

Mr. Fox shifted his inquiries.

"You have said that you wore a hat and coat of your brother's in coming to the club-house? Did you keep these articles on?"

"No; I left them in the lower hall."

"Where in the lower hall?"

"On the rack there."

"Was your candle lit?"

"Not then, sir."

"Yet you found the rack?"

"I felt for it. I knew where it was."

"When did you light the candle?"

"After I hung up the coat."

"And when you came down? Did you have the candle then?"

"Yes, for a while. But I didn't have any light when I went for the coat and hat. I remember feeling all along the wall. I don't know what I did with the candlestick or the candle. I had them on the stairs; I didn't have them when I put on the coat and hat."

I knew what she did with them. She flung them out of her hand upon the marble floor. Should I ever forget the darkness swallowing up that face of mental horror and physical suffering.

"Miss Cumberland, you are sure about having telephoned for help, and that you mentioned The Whispering Pines in doing so?"

"Quite sure." Oh, what weariness was creeping into her voice!

"Then, of course, you left the door unlocked when you went out of the building?"

"No—no, I didn't. I had the key and I locked it. But I didn't realise this till I went to untie my horse; then I found the keys in my hand. But I didn't go back."

"Do you mean that you didn't know you locked the door?"

"I don't remember whether I knew or not at the time. I do remember being surprised and a little frightened when I saw the keys. But I didn't go back."

"Yet you had telephoned for the police?"

"Yes."

"And then locked them out?"

"I didn't care—I didn't care."

An infinite number of questions followed. The poor child was near fainting, but bore up wonderfully notwithstanding, contradicting herself but seldom; and then only from lack of understanding the question, or from sheer fatigue. Mr. Fox was considerate, and Mr. Moffat interrupted but seldom. All could see that this noble-hearted girl, this heroine of all hearts was trying to tell the truth, and sympathy was with her, even that of the prosecution. But certain facts had to be brought out, among them the blowing off of her hat on that hurried drive home through the ever thickening snow-storm—a fact easily accounted for, when one considered the thick coils of hair over which it had been drawn.

The circumstances connected with her arrival at the house were all carefully sifted, but nothing new came up, nor was her credibility as a witness shaken. The prosecution had lost much by this witness, but it had also gained. No doubt now remained that the ring was still on the victim's hand when she succumbed to the effects of the poison; and the possibility of another presence in the house during the fateful interview just recorded, had been strengthened, rather than lessened, by Carmel's hesitating admissions. And so the question hung poised, and I was expecting to see her dismissed from the stand, when the district attorney settled himself again into his accustomed attitude of inquiry, and launched this new question:

"When you went into the stable to unharness your horse, what did you do with the little bag you carried?"

"I took it out of the cutter."

"What, then?"

"Set it down somewhere."

"Was there anything in the bag?"

"Not now. I had left the tongs at the club-house, and the paper I had burned. I took nothing else."

"How about the candlestick?"

"That I carried in one of the pockets of my coat. That I left, too."

"Was that all you carried in your pockets?"

"Yes—the candlestick and the candle. The candlestick on one side and the candle on the other."

"And these you did not have on your return?"

"No, I left both."

"So that your pockets were empty—entirely empty—when you drove into your own gate?"

"Yes, sir, so far as I know. I never looked into them."

"And felt nothing there?"

"No, sir."

"Took nothing out?"

"No, sir."

"Then or when you unharnessed your horse, or afterward, as you passed back to the house?"

"No, sir."

"What path did you take in returning to the house?"

"There is only one."

"Did you walk straight through it?"

"As straight as I could. It was snowing heavily, and I was dizzy and felt strange, I may have zigzagged a little."

"Did you zigzag enough to go back of the stable?"

"Oh, no."

"You are sure that you did not wander in back of the stable?"

"As sure as I can be of anything."

"Miss Cumberland, I have but a few more questions to ask. Will you look at this portion of a broken bottle?"

"I see it, sir."

"Will you take it in your hand and examine it carefully?"

She reached out her hand; it was trembling visibly and her face expressed a deep distress, but she took the piece of broken bottle and looked at it before passing it back.

"Miss Cumberland, did you ever see that bit of broken glass before?"

She shook her head. Then she cast a quick look at her brother, and seemed to gain an instantaneous courage.

"No," said she. "I may have seen a whole bottle like that, at some time in the club-house, but I have no memory of this broken end—none at all."

"I am obliged to you, Miss Cumberland. I will trouble you no more to-day."

Then he threw up his head and smiled a slow, sarcastic smile at Mr. Moffat.

CHAPTER XXXII

AND I HAD SAID NOTHING!

O my soul's joy! If after every tempest come such calms
May the winds blow till they have wakened death!

Othello.

I had always loved her; that I knew even in the hour of my darkest suspicion—but now I felt free to worship her. As the thought penetrated my whole being, it made the night gladsome. Whatever awaited her, whatever awaited Arthur, whatever awaited me, she had regenerated me. A change took place that night in my whole nature, in my aspect of life and my view of women. One fact rode triumphant above all other considerations and possible distresses. Fate—I was more inclined now to call it Providence—had shown me the heart of a great and true woman; and I was free to expend all my best impulses in honouring her and loving her, whether she ever looked my way again, received or even acknowledged a homage growing out of such wrong as I had done her and her unfortunate sister. It set a star in my firmament. It turned down all the ill-written and besmirched leaves in my book of life and opened up a new page on which her name, written in letters of gold, demanded clean work in the future and a record which should not shame the aura surrounding that pure name. Sorrow for the past, dread of the future—both were lost in the glad rebound of my distracted soul. The night was dedicated to joy, and to joy alone.

The next day being Sunday, I had ample time for the reaction bound to follow hours of such exaltation. I had no wish for company. I even denied myself to Clifton. The sight of a human face was more than I could bear unless it were the one face; and that I could not hope for. But the desire to see her, to hear from her—if only to learn how she had endured the bitter ordeal of the day before—soon became unbearable. I must know this much at any cost to her feelings or to mine.

After many a struggle with myself, I called up Dr. Carpenter on the telephone. From him I learned that she was physically prostrated, but still clear in mind and satisfied of her brother's innocence. This latter statement might mean anything; but imparted by him to me, it seemed to be capable of but one interpretation. I must be prepared for whatever distrust of myself this confidence carried with it.

This was intolerable. I had to speak; I had to inquire if she had yet heard the real reason why I was the first to be arrested.

A decided "No," cut short that agony. I could breathe again and proffer a humble request.

"Doctor, I cannot approach her; I cannot even write,—it would seem too presumptuous. But tell her, as you find the opportunity, how I honour her. Do not let her remain under the impression that I am not capable of truly feeling what she has borne and must still bear."

"I will do what I can," was his reply, and he mercifully cut short the conversation.

This was the event of the morning.

In the afternoon I sat in my window thinking. My powers of reasoning had returned, and the insoluble problem of Adelaide's murder occupied my whole mind. With Carmel innocent, who was there left to suspect? Not Arthur. His fingers were as guiltless as my own of those marks on her throat. Of this I was convinced, difficult as it made my future. My mind refused to see guilt in a man who could meet my eye with just the look he gave me on leaving the courtroom, at the conclusion of his sister's triumphant examination. It was a momentary glance, but I read it, I am sure, quite truthfully.

"You are the man," it said; but not in the old, bitter, and revengeful way voiced by his tongue before we came together in the one effort to save Carmel from what, in our short-sightedness and misunderstanding of her character, we had looked upon as the worst of humiliations and the most desperate of perils. There was sadness in his conviction and an honest man's regret—which, if noted by those about us—was far more dangerous to my good name than the loudest of denunciations or the most acrimonious of assaults. It put me in the worst of positions. But one chance remained for me now.

The secret man of guilt might yet come to light; but how or through whose agency, I found myself unable to conceive. I had neither the wit nor the experience to untangle this confused web. Should I find the law in shape to deal with it? A few days would show. With the termination of Arthur's trial, the story of my future would begin. Meanwhile, I must have patience and such strength as could be got from the present.

And so the afternoon passed.

With the coming on of night, my mood changed. I wanted air, movement. The closeness of my rooms had become unbearable. As soon as the lamps were lit in the street, I started out and I went—toward the cemetery.

I had no motive in choosing this direction for my walk. The road was an open one, and I should neither avoid people nor escape the chilly blast blowing directly in my face from the northeast. Whim, or shall I not say, true feeling, carried me there though I was quite conscious, all the time, of a strong desire to see Ella Fulton and learn from her the condition of affairs—whether she was at peace, or in utter disgrace, with her parents.

It was a cold night, as I have said, and there were but few people in the streets. On the boulevard I met nobody. As I neared the cemetery, I passed one man; otherwise I was, to all appearance, alone on this remote avenue. The effect was sinister, or my mood made it so; yet I did not hasten my steps; the hours till midnight had to be lived through in some way, and why not in this? No companion would have been welcome, and had the solitude been less perfect, I should have murmured at the prospect of intrusion.

The cemetery gates were shut. This I had expected, but I did not need to enter the grounds to have a view of Adelaide's grave. The Cumberland lot occupied a knoll in close proximity to the fence, and my only intention had been to pass this spot and cast one look within, in memory of Adelaide. To reach the place, however, I had to turn a corner, and on doing so I saw good reason, as I thought, for not carrying out my intention at this especial time.

Some man—I could not recognise him from where I stood—had forestalled me. Though the night was a dark one, sufficient light shone from the scattered lamps on the opposite side of the way for me to discern his intent figure, crouching against the iron bars and gazing, with an intentness which made him entirely oblivious of my presence, at the very plot—and on the very grave—which had been the end of my own pilgrimage. So motionless he stood, and so motionless I myself became at this unexpected and significant sight, that I presently imagined I could hear his sighs in the dread quiet into which the whole scene had sunk.

Grief, deeper than mine, spoke in those labouring breaths. Adelaide was mourned by some one as I, for all my remorse, could never mourn her.

And I did not know the man.

Was not this strange enough to rouse my wonder?

I thought so, and was on the point of satisfying this wonder by a quick advance upon this stranger, when there happened an uncanny thing, which held me in check from sheer astonishment. I was so placed, in reference to one of the street lamps I have already mentioned, that my shadow fell before me plainly along the snow. This had not attracted my attention until, at the point of moving, I cast my eyes down and saw two shadows where only one should be.

As I had heard no one behind me, and had supposed myself entirely alone with the man absorbed in contemplation of Adelaide's grave, I experienced a curious sensation which, without being fear, held me still for a moment, with my eyes on this second shadow. It did not move, any more than mine did. This was significant, and I turned.

A man stood at my back—not looking at me but at the fellow in front of us. A quiet "hush!" sounded in my ear, and again I stood still. But only for an instant.

The man at the fence—aroused by my movement, perhaps—had turned, and, seeing our two figures, started to fly in the opposite direction. Instinctively I darted forward in pursuit, but was soon passed by the man behind me. This caused me to slacken; for I had recognised this latter, as he flew by, as Sweetwater, the detective, and knew that he would do this work better than myself.

But I reckoned without my host. He went only as far as the spot where the man had been standing. When, in my astonishment, I advanced upon him there, he wheeled about quite naturally in my direction and, accosting me by name, remarked, in his genial off-hand manner:

"There is no need for us to tire our legs in a chase after that man. I know him well enough."

"And who—" I began.

A quizzical smile answered me. The light was now in our faces, and I had a perfect view of his. Its expression quite disarmed me; but I knew, as well as if he had spoken, that I should receive no other reply to my half-formed question.

"Are you going back into town?" he asked, as I paused and looked down at the umbrella swinging in his hand. I was sure that he had not held this umbrella when he started by me on the run. "If so, will you allow me to walk beside you for a little way?"

I could not refuse him; besides, I was not sure that I wanted to. Homely as any man I had ever seen, there was a magnetic quality in his voice and manner that affected even one so fastidious as myself. I felt that I had rather talk to him, at that moment, than to any other person I knew. Of course, curiosity had something to do with it, and that community of interest which is the strongest bond that can link two people together.

"You are quite welcome," said I; and again cast my eye at the umbrella.

"You are wondering where I got this," he remarked, looking down at it in his turn. "I found it leaning against the fence. It gives me all the clue I need to our fleet-footed friend. Mr. Ranelagh, will you credit me with good intentions if I ask a question or two which you may or may not be willing to answer?"

"You may ask what you will," said I. "I have nothing to conceal, since hearing Miss Cumberland's explanation of her presence at The Whispering Pines."

"Ah!"

The ejaculation was eloquent. So was the silence which followed it. Without good reason, perhaps, I felt the strain upon my heart loosen a little. Was it possible that I should find a friend in this man?

"The question I am going to ask," he continued presently, "is one which you may consider unpardonable. Let me first express an opinion. You have not told all that you know of that evening's doings."

This called for no reply and I made none.

"I can understand your reticence, if your knowledge included the fact of Miss Cumberland's heroic act and her sister's manner of death at the club-house."

"But it did not," I asserted, with deliberate emphasis. "I knew nothing of either. My arrival happened later. Miss Cumberland's testimony gave me my first enlightenment on these points. But I did know that the two sisters were there together, for I had a glimpse of the younger as she was leaving the house."

"You had. And are willing to state it now?"

"Assuredly. But any testimony of that kind is for the defence, and your interests are all with the prosecution. Mr. Moffat is the man who should talk to me."

"Does he know it?"

"Yes."

"Who told him?"

"I did."

"You?"

"Yes, it was my duty."

"You are interested then in seeing young Cumberland freed?"

"I must be; he is innocent."

The man at my side turned, shot at me one glance which I met quite calmly, then, regulating his step by mine, moved on silently for a moment—thinking, as it appeared to me, some very serious thoughts. It was not until we had traversed a whole block in this way that he finally put his question. Whether it was the one he had first had in mind, I cannot say.

"Mr. Ranelagh, will you tell me why, when you found yourself in such a dire extremity as to be arrested for this crime, on evidence as startling as to call for all and every possible testimony to your innocence, you preserved silence in regard to a fact which you must have then felt would have secured you a most invaluable witness? I can understand why Mr. Cumberland has been loth to speak of his younger sister's presence in the club-house on that night; but his reason was not your reason. Yet you have been as hard to move on this point as he."

Then it was I regretted my thoughtless promise to be candid with this man. To answer were impossible, yet silence has its confidences, too. In my dilemma, I turned towards him and just then we stepped within the glare of an electric light pouring from some open doorway. I caught his eye, and was astonished at the change which took place in him.

"Don't answer," he muttered, volubly. "It isn't necessary. I understand the situation, now, and you shall never regret that you met Caleb Sweetwater on your walk this evening. Will you trust me, sir? A detective who loves his profession is no gabbler. Your secret is as safe with me as if you had buried it in the grave."

And I had said nothing!

He started to go, then he stopped suddenly and observed, with one of his wise smiles:

"I once spent several minutes in Miss Carmel Cumberland's room, and I saw a cabinet there which I found it very hard to understand. But its meaning came to me later. I could not rest till it did."

At the next moment he was half way around a corner, and in another, out of sight.

This was the evening's event.

CHAPTER XXXIII

THE ARROW OF DEATH

O if you rear this house against this house,
It will the wofulest division prove
That ever fell upon this cursed earth.

Prometheus Unbound.

In my first glance around the court-room the next morning, I sought first for Carmel and then for the detective Sweetwater. Neither was visible. But this was not true of Ella. She had come in on her father's arm, closely followed by the erect figure of her domineering mother. As I scrutinised the latter's bearing, I seemed to penetrate the mystery of her nature. Whatever humiliation she may have felt at the public revelation of her daughter's weakness, it had been absorbed by her love for that daughter, or had been forced, through the agency of her indomitable will, to become a ministrant to her pride which was unassailable. She had accepted the position exacted from her by the situation, and she looked for no loss of prestige, either on her daughter's or her own account. Such was the language of her eyes; and it was a language which should have assured Ella that she had a better friend in her mother than she had ever dreamed of. The entrance of the defendant cut short my contemplation of any mere spectator. The change in him was so marked that I was conscious of it before I really saw him. Every eye had reflected it, and it was no surprise to me when I noted the relieved, almost cheerful aspect of his countenance as he took his place and met his counsel's greeting with a smile—the first, I believe, which had been seen on his face since his sister's death. That counsel I had already noted. He was cheerful also, but with a restrained cheerfulness. His task was not yet over, and the grimness of Mr. Fox, and the non-committal aspect of the jurymen, proved that it was not to be made too easy for him.

The crier announced the opening of the court, and the defence proceeded by the calling of Ella Fulton to the witness stand.

I need not linger over her testimony. It was very short and contained but one surprise. She had stated under direct examination that she had waited and watched for Arthur's return that whole night, and was positive that he had not passed through their grounds again after that first time in the early evening. This was just what I had expected from her. But the prosecution remembered the snowfall, and in her cross-examination on this point, she acknowledged that it was very thick, much too thick for her to see her own gate distinctly; but added, that this only made her surer of the fact she had stated; for finding that she could not see, she had dressed herself for the storm and gone out into the driveway to watch there, and had so watched until the town clock struck three.

This did not help the prosecution. Sympathy could not fail to be with this young and tremulous girl, heroic in her love, if weak in other respects, and when on her departure from the stand, she cast one deprecatory glance at the man for whom she had thus sacrificed her pride, and, meeting his eye fixed upon her with anything but ingratitude, flushed and faltered till she with difficulty found her way, the sentiments of the onlookers became so apparent that the judge's gavel was called into requisition before order could be restored and the next witness summoned to testify.

This witness was no less a person than Arthur himself. Recalled by his counsel, he was reminded of his former statement that he had left the club-house in a hurry because he heard his sister Adelaide's voice, and was now asked if hers was the only voice he had heard.

His answer revealed much of his mind.

"No, I heard Carmel's answering her."

This satisfying Mr. Moffat, he was passed over to Mr. Fox, and a short cross-examination ensued on this point.

"You heard both your sisters speaking?"

"Yes, sir."

"Any of their words, or only their voices?"

"I heard one word."

"What word?"

"The word, 'Elwood.'"

"In which voice?"

"In that of my sister Adelaide."

"And you fled?"

"Immediately."

"Leaving your two sisters alone in this cold and out-of-the-way house?"

"I did not think they were alone."

"Who did you think was with them?"

"I have already mentioned the name."

"Yet you left them?"

"Yes, I've already explained that. I was engaged in a mean act. I was ashamed to be caught at it by Adelaide. I preferred flight. I had no premonition of tragedy—any such tragedy as afterwards occurred. I understood neither of my sisters and my thoughts were only for myself."

"Didn't you so much as try to account for their both being there?"

"Not then."

"Had you expected Adelaide to accompany your younger sister when you harnessed the horse for her?"

"No, sir."

"Had not this younger sister even enjoined secrecy upon you in asking you to harness the horse?"

"Yes, sir."

"Yet you heard the two together in this remote building without surprise?"

"No, I must have felt surprise, but I didn't stop to analyse my feelings. Afterward, I turned it over in my mind and tried to make something out of the whole thing. But that was when I was far out on the links."

A losing game thus far. This the district attorney seemed to feel; but he was not an ungenerous man though cursed (perhaps, I should say blessed, considering the position he held) by a tenacity which never let him lose his hold until the jury gave their verdict.

"You have a right to explain yourself fully," said he, after a momentary struggle in which his generosity triumphed over his pride. "When you did think of your sisters, what explanation did you give yourself of the facts we have just been considering?"

"I could not imagine the truth, so I just satisfied myself that Adelaide had discovered Carmel's intentions to ride into town and had insisted on accompanying her. They were having it out, I thought, in the presence of the man who had made all this trouble between them."

"And you left them to the task?"

"Yes, sir, but not without a struggle. I was minded several times to return. This I have testified to before."

"Did this struggle consume forty minutes?"

"It must have and more, if I entered the hold in Cuthbert Road at the hour they state."

Mr. Fox gave up the game, and I looked to be the next person called. But it was not a part of Mr. Moffat's plan to weaken the effect of Carmel's testimony by offering any weak corroboration of facts which nobody showed the least inclination to dispute. Satisfied with having given the jury an opportunity to contrast his client's present cheerfulness and manly aspect with the sullenness he had maintained while in doubt of Carmel's real connection with this crime, Mr. Moffat rested his case.

There was no testimony offered in rebuttal and the court took a recess.

When it reassembled I cast another anxious glance around. Still no Carmel, nor any signs of Sweetwater. I could understand her absence, but not his, and it was in a confusion of feeling which was fast getting the upper hand of me, that I turned my attention to Mr. Moffat and the plea he was about to make for his youthful client.

I do not wish to obtrude myself too much into this trial of another man for the murder of my betrothed. But when, after a wait during which the prisoner had a chance to show his mettle under the concentrated gaze of an expectant crowd, the senior counsel for the defence slowly rose, and, lifting his ungainly length till his shoulders lost their stoop and his whole presence acquired a dignity which had been entirely absent from it up to this decisive moment, I felt a sudden slow and creeping chill seize and shake me, as I have heard people say they experienced when uttering the common expression, "Some one is walking over my grave."

It was not that he glanced my way, for this he did not do; yet I received a subtle message from him, by some telepathic means I could neither understand nor respond to—a message of warning, or, possibly of simple preparation for what his coming speech might convey.

It laid my spirits low for a moment; then they rose as those of a better man might rise at the scent of danger. If he could warn, he could also withhold. I would trust him, or I would, at least, trust my fate. And so, good-bye to self. Arthur's life and Carmel's future peace were trembling in the balance. Surely these were worth the full attention of the man who loved the woman, who pitied the man.

At the next moment I heard these words, delivered in the slow and but slightly raised tones with which Mr. Moffat invariably began his address:

"May it please the court and gentlemen of the jury, my learned friend of the prosecution has shown great discretion in that, so far as appears from the trend of his examinations, he is planning no attempt to explain the many silences and the often forbidding attitude of my young client by any theory save the obvious one—the natural desire of a brother to hide his only remaining sister's connection with a tragedy of whose details he was ignorant, and concerning which he had formed a theory derogatory to her position as a young and well-bred woman.

"I am, therefore, spared the task of pressing upon your consideration these very natural and, I may add, laudable grounds for my client's many hesitations and suppressions—which, under other circumstances, would militate so deeply against him in the eyes of an upright and impartial jury. Any man with a heart in his breast, and a sense of honour in his soul, can understand why this man—whatever his record, and however impervious he may have seemed in the days of his prosperity and the wilfulness of his youth—should recoil from revelations which would attack the honour, if not the life, of a young and beautiful sister, sole remnant of a family eminent in station, and in all those moral and civic attributes which make for the honour of a town and lend distinction to its history.

"Fear for a loved one, even in one whom you will probably hear described as a dissipated man, of selfish tendencies and hitherto unbrotherly qualities, is a great miracle-worker. No sacrifice seems impossible which serves as a guard for one so situated and so threatened.

"Let us review his history. Let us disentangle, if we can, our knowledge of what occurred in the clubhouse, from his knowledge of it at the time he showed these unexpected traits of self-control and brotherly anxiety, which you will yet hear so severely scored by my able opponent. His was a nature in which honourable instincts had forever battled with the secret predilections of youth for independence and free living. He rebelled at all monition; but this did not make him altogether insensible to the secret ties of kinship, or the claims upon his protection of two highly gifted sisters.

Consciously or unconsciously, he kept watch upon the two; and when he saw that an extraneous influence was undermining their mutual confidence, he rebelled in his heart, whatever restraint he may have put upon his tongue and actions. Then came an evening, when, with heart already rasped by a personal humiliation, he saw a letter passed. You have heard the letter and listened to its answer; but he knew nothing beyond the fact—a fact which soon received a terrible significance from the events which so speedily followed."

Here Mr. Moffat recapitulated those events, but always from the standpoint of the defendant—a standpoint which necessarily brought before the jury the many excellent reasons which his client had for supposing this crime to have resulted solely from the conflicting interests represented by that furtively passed note, and the visit of two girls instead of one to The Whispering Pines. It was very convincing, especially his picture of Arthur's impulsive flight from the club-house at the first sound of his sisters' voices.

"The learned counsel for the people may call this unnatural," he cried. "He may say that no brother would leave the place under such circumstances, whether sober or not sober, alive to duty or dead to it—that curiosity would hold him there, if nothing else. But he forgets, if thus he thinks and thus would have you think, that the man who now confronts you from the bar is separated by an immense experience from the boy he was at that hour of surprise and selfish preoccupation.

"You who have heard the defendant tell how he could not remember if he carried up one or two bottles from the kitchen, can imagine the blank condition of this untutored mind at the moment when those voices fell upon his ear, calling him to responsibilities he had never before shouldered, and which he saw no way of shouldering now. In that first instant of inconsiderate escape, he was alarmed for himself,—afraid of the discovery of the sneaking act of which he had just been guilty—not fearful for his sisters. You would have done differently; but you are all men disciplined to forget yourselves and think first of others, taught, in the school of life to face responsibility rather than shirk it. But discipline had not yet reached this unhappy boy—the slave, so far, of his unfortunate habits. It began its work later; yet not much later. Before he had half crossed the golf-links, the sense of what he had done stopped him in middle course, and, reckless of the oncoming storm, he turned his back upon the place he was making for, only to switch around again, as craving got the better of his curiosity, or of that deeper feeling to which my experienced opponent will, no doubt, touchingly allude when he comes to survey this situation with you.

"The storm, continuing, obliterated his steps as fast as the ever whitening spaces beneath received them; but if it had stopped then and there, leaving those wandering imprints to tell their story, what a tale we might have read of the first secret conflict in this awakening soul! I leave you to imagine this history, and pass to the bitter hour when, racked by a night of dissipation, he was aroused, indeed, to the magnitude of his fault and the awful consequences of his self-indulgence, by the news of his elder sister's violent death and the hardly less pitiful condition of the younger.

"The younger!" The pause he here made was more eloquent than any words. "Is it for me to laud her virtues, or to seek to impress upon you in this connection, the overwhelming nature of the events which in reality had laid her mind and body low? You have seen her; you have heard her; and the memory of the tale she has here told will never leave you, or lose its hold upon your sympathies or your admiration. If everything else connected with this case is forgotten, the recollection of that will remain. You, and I, and all who wait upon your verdict, will in due time pass from among the living, and leave small print behind us on the sands of time. But her act will not die, and to it I now offer the homage of silence, since that would best please her heroic soul, which broke the bonds of womanly reserve only to save from an unmerited charge a falsely arraigned brother."

The restraint and yet the fire with which Mr. Moffat uttered these simple words, lifted all hearts and surcharged the atmosphere with an emotion rarely awakened in a court of law. Not in my pulses alone was started the electric current of renewed life. The jury, to a man, glowed with enthusiasm, and from the audience rose one long and suppressed sigh of answering feeling, which was all the tribute he needed for his eloquence—or Carmel for her uncalculating, self-sacrificing deed. I could have called upon the mountains to cover me; but—God be praised—no one thought of me in that hour. Every throb, every thought was for her.

At the proper moment of subsiding feeling, Mr. Moffat again raised his voice:

"Gentlemen of the jury, you have seen point after point of the prosecution's case demolished before your eyes by testimony which no one has had the temerity to attempt to controvert. What is left? Mr. Fox will tell you—three strong and unassailable facts. The ring found in the murdered woman's casket, the remnants of the tell-tale bottle discovered in the Cumberland stable, and the opportunity for crime given by the acknowledged presence of the defendant on or near the scene of death. He will harp on these facts; he will make much of them; and he will be justified in doing so, for they are the only links remaining of the strong chain forged so carefully against my client.

"But are these points so vital as they seem? Let us consider them, and see. My client has denied that he dropped anything into his sister's casket, much less the ring missing from that sister's finger. Dare you, then, convict on this point when, according to count, ten other persons were seen to drop flowers into this very place—any one of which might have carried this object with it?

"And the bit of broken bottle found in or near the defendant's own stable! Is he to be convicted on the similarity it offers to the one known to have come from the club-house wine-vault, while a reasonable doubt remains of his having been the hand which carried it there? No! Where there is a reasonable doubt, no high-minded jury will convict; and I claim that my client has made it plain that there is such a reasonable doubt."

All this and more did Mr. Moffat dilate upon. But I could no longer fix my mind on details, and much of this portion of his address escaped me.

But I do remember the startling picture with which he closed. His argument so far, had been based on the assumption of Arthur's ignorance of Carmers purpose in visiting the club-house, or of Adelaide's attempt at suicide. His client had left the building when he said he did, and knew no more of what happened there afterward than circumstances showed, or his own imagination conceived. But now the advocate took a sudden turn, and calmly asked the jury to consider with him the alternative outlined by the prosecution in the evidence set before them.

"My distinguished opponent," said he, "would have you believe that the defendant did not fly at the moment declared, but that he waited to fulfil the foul deed which is the only serious matter in dispute in his so nearly destroyed case. I hear as though he were now speaking, the attack which he will make upon my client when he comes to review this matter with you. Let me see if I cannot make you hear those words, too." And with a daring smile at his discomforted adversary, Alonzo Moffat launched forth into the following sarcasm:

"Arthur Cumberland, coming up the kitchen stairs, hears voices where he had expected total silence—sees light where he had left total darkness. He has two bottles in his hands, or in his large coat-pockets. If they are in his hands, he sets them down and steals forward to listen. He has recognised the voices. They are those of his two sisters, one of whom had ordered him to hitch up the cutter for her to escape, as he had every reason to believe, the other. Curiosity—or is it some nobler feeling—causes him to draw nearer and nearer to the room in which they have taken up their stand. He can hear their words now and what are the words he hears? Words that would thrill the most impervious heart, call for the interference of the most indifferent. But he is made of ice, welded together with steel. He sees—for no place save one from which he can watch and see, viz.: the dark dancing hall, would satisfy any man of such gigantic curiosity—Adelaide fall at Carmel's feet, in recognition of the great sacrifice she has made for her. But he does not move; he falls at no one's feet; he recognises no nobility, responds to no higher appeal. Stony and unmoved, he crouches there, and watches and watches—still curious, or still feeding his hate on the sufferings of the elder, the forbearance of the younger.

"And on what does he look? You have already heard, but consider it. Adelaide, despairing of happiness, decides on death for herself or sister. Both loving one man, one of the two must give way to the other. Carmel has done her part; she must now do hers. She has brought poison; she has brought glasses—three glasses, for three persons, but only two are on the scene, and so she fills but two. One has only cordial in it, but the other is, as she believes, deadly. Carmel is to have her choice; but who believes that Adelaide would ever have let her drink the poisoned glass?

"And this man looks on, as the two faces confront each other—one white with the overthrow of every earthly hope, the other under the stress of suffering and a fascination of horror sufficient to have laid her dead, without poison, at the other one's feet. This is what he sees—a brother!—and he makes no move, then or afterwards, when, the die cast, Adelaide succumbs to her fear and falls into a seemingly dying state on the couch.

"Does he go now? Is his hate or his cupidity satisfied? No! He remains and listens to the tender interchange of final words, and all the late precautions of the elder to guard the younger woman's good name. Still he is not softened; and when, the critical moment passed, Carmel rises and totters about the room in her endeavour to fulfil the tasks enjoined upon her by her sister, he gloats over a death which will give him independence and gluts himself with every evil thought which could blind him to the pitiful aspects of a tragedy such as few men in this world could see unmoved. A brother!

"But this is not the worst. The awful cup of human greed and hatred is but filled to the brim; it has not yet overflowed. Carmel leaves the room; she has a telephonic message to deliver. She may be gone a minute; she may be gone many. Little does he care which; he must see the dead, look down on the woman who has been like a mother to him, and see if her influence is forever removed, if his wealth is his, and his independence forever assured.

"Safe in the darkness of the gloomy recesses of the dancing hall, he steals slowly forward. Drawn as by a magnet, he enters the room of seeming death, draws up to the pillow-laden couch, pulls off first one cushion, and then another, till face and hands are bare and—

"Ah!—there is a movement! death has not, then, done its work. She lives—the hated one—lives! And he is no longer rich, no longer independent. With a clutch, he seizes her at the feeble seat of life; and as the breath ceases and her whole body becomes again inert, he stoops to pull off the ring, which can have no especial value or meaning for him—and then, repiling the cushions over her, creeps forth again, takes up the bottles, and disappears from the house.

"Gentlemen of the jury, this is what my opponent would have you believe. This will be his explanation of this extraordinary murder. But when his eloquence meets your ears—when you hear this arraignment, and the emphasis he will place upon the few points remaining to his broken case, then ask yourself if you see such a monster in the prisoner now confronting you from the bar. I do not believe it. I do not believe that such a monster lives.

"But you say, some one entered that room—some one stilled the fluttering life still remaining in that feeble breast. Some one may have, but that some one was not my client, and it is his guilt or innocence we are considering now, and it is his life and freedom for which you are responsible. No brother did that deed; no witness of the scene which hallowed this tragedy ever lifted hand against the fainting Adelaide, or choked back a life which kindly fate had spared.

"Go further for the guilty perpetrator of this most inhuman act; he stands not in the dock. Guilt shows no such relief as you see in him to-day. Guilt would remember that his sister's testimony, under the cross-examination of the people's prosecutor, left the charge of murder still hanging over the defendant's head. But the brother has forgotten this. His restored confidence in one who now represents to him father, mother, and sister has thrown his own fate into the background. Will you dim that joy—sustain this charge of murder?

"If in your sense of justice you do so, you forever place this degenerate son of a noble father, on the list of the most unimaginative and hate-driven criminals of all time. Is he such a demon? Is he such a madman? Look in his face to-day, and decide. I am willing to leave his cause in your hands. It could be placed in no better.

"May it please your Honour, and gentlemen of the jury, I am done."

If any one at that moment felt the arrow of death descending into his heart, it was not Arthur Cumberland.

CHAPTER XXXIV

"STEADY!"

I am a tainted wether of the flock,
Meetest for death; the weakest kind of fruit
Drops earliest to the ground, and so let me.
You cannot better be employ'd, Bassanio,
Than to live still, and write my epitaph.

Merchant of Venice.

Why linger over the result. Arthur Cumberland's case was won before Mr. Fox arose to his feet. The usual routine was gone through. The district attorney made the most of the three facts which he declared inconsistent with the prisoner's innocence, just as Mr. Moffat said he would; but the life was gone from his work, and the result was necessarily unsatisfactory.

The judge's charge was short, but studiously impartial. When the jury filed out, I said to myself, "They will return in fifteen minutes." They returned in ten, with a verdict of acquittal.

The demonstrations of joy which followed filled my ears, and doubtless left their impression upon my other senses; but my mind took in nothing but the apparition of my own form taking his place at the bar, under circumstances less favourable to acquittal than those which had exonerated him. It was a picture which set my brain whirling. A phantom judge, a phantom jury, a phantom circle of faces, lacking the consideration and confidence of those I saw before me; but not a phantom prisoner, or any mere dream of outrageous shame and suffering.

That shame and that suffering had already seized hold of me. With the relief of young Arthur's acquittal my faculties had cleared to the desperate position in which this very acquittal had placed me.

I saw, as never before, how the testimony which had reinstated Carmel in my heart and won for her and through her the sympathies of the whole people, had overthrown every specious reason which I and those interested in me had been able to advance in contradiction of the natural conclusion to be drawn from the damning fact of my having been seen with my fingers on Adelaide's throat.

Mr. Moffat's words rang in my ears: "Some one entered that room; some one stilled the fluttering life still remaining in that feeble breast; but that some one was not her brother. You must look further for the guilty perpetrator of this most inhuman act; some one who had not been a witness to the scene preceding this tragedy, some one—" he had not said this but every mind had supplied the omission,—"some one who had come in later, who came in after Carmel had gone, some one who knew nothing of the telephone message which was even then hastening the police to the spot; some one who had every reason for lifting those cushions and, on meeting life—"

The horror stifled me; I was reeling in my place on the edge of the crowd, when I heard a quiet voice in my ear:

"Steady! Their eyes will soon be off of Arthur, and then they will look at you."

It was Clifton, and his word came none too soon. I stiffened under its quiet force, and, taking his arm, let him lead me out of a side door, where the crowd was smaller and its attention even more absorbed.

I soon saw its cause—Carmel was entering the doorway from the street. She had come to greet her brother; and her face, quite unveiled, was beaming with beauty and joy. In an instant I forgot myself, forgot everything but her and the effect she produced upon those about her. No noisy demonstration here; admiration and love were shown in looks and the low-breathed prayer for her welfare which escaped from more than one pair of lips. She smiled and their hearts were hers; she essayed to move forward and the people crowded back as if at a queen's passage; but there was no noise.

When she reappeared, it was on Arthur's arm. I had not been able to move from the place in which we were hemmed; nor had I wished to. I was hungry for a glance of her eye. Would it turn my way, and, if it did, would it leave a curse or a blessing behind it? In anxiety for the blessing, I was willing to risk the curse; and I followed her every step with hungry glances, until she reached the doorway and turned to give another shake of the hand to Mr. Moffat, who had followed them. But she did not see me.

"I cannot miss it! I must catch her eye!" I whispered to Clifton. "Get me out of this; it will be several minutes before they can reach the sleigh. Let me see her, for one instant, face to face."

Clifton disapproved, and made me aware of it; but he did my bidding, nevertheless. In a few moments we were on the sidewalk, and quite by ourselves; so that, if she turned again she could not fail to observe me. I had small hope, however, that she would so turn. She and Arthur were within a few feet of the curb and their own sleigh.

I had just time to see this sleigh, and note the rejoicing face of Zadok leaning sideways from the box, when I beheld her pause and slowly turn her head around and peer eagerly—and with what divine anxiety in her eyes—back over the heads of those thronging about her, until her gaze rested fully and sweetly on mine. My heart leaped, then sank down, down into unutterable depths; for in that instant her face changed, horror seized upon her beauty, and shook her frantic hold on Arthur's arm.

I heard words uttered very near me, but I did not catch them. I did feel, however, the hand which was laid strongly and with authority upon my shoulder; and, tearing my eyes from her face only long enough to perceive that it was Sweetwater who had thus arrested me, I looked back at her, in time to see the questions leap from her lips to Arthur, whose answers I could well understand from the pitying movement in the crowd and the low hum of restrained voices which ran between her sinking figure and the spot where I stood apart, with the detective's hand on my shoulder.

She had never been told of the incriminating position in which I had been seen in the club-house. It had been carefully kept from her, and she had supposed that my acquittal in the public mind was as certain as Arthur's. Now she saw herself undeceived, and the reaction into doubt and misery was too much for her, and I saw her sinking under my eyes.

"Let me go to her!" I shrieked, utterly unconcerned with anything in the world but this tottering, fainting girl.

But Sweetwater's hand only tightened on my shoulder, while Arthur, with an awful look at me, caught his sister in his arms, just as she fell to the ground before the swaying multitude.

But he was not the only one to kneel there. With a sound of love and misery impossible to describe, Zadok had leaped from the box and had grovelled at those dear feet, kissing the insensible hands and praying for those shut eyes to open. Even after Arthur had lifted her into the sleigh, the man remained crouching where she had fallen, with his eyes roaming back and forth in a sightless stare from her to myself, muttering and groaning, and totally unheedful of Arthur's commands to mount the box and drive home. Finally some one else stepped from the crowd and mercifully took the reins. I caught one more glimpse of her face, with Arthur's bent tenderly over it; then the sleigh slipped away.

An officer shook Zadok by the arm and he got up and began to move aside. Then I had mind to face my own fate, and, looking up, I met Sweetwater's eye.

It was quietly apologetic.

"I only wished to congratulate you," said he, "on the conclusion of a case in which I know you are highly interested." Lifting his hat, he nodded affably and was gone before I could recover from my stupor.

It was for Clifton to show his indignation. I was past all feeling. Farce as an after-piece never appealed to me.

Would I have considered it farce if I could have heard the words which this detective was at that moment whispering into the district attorney's ears:

"Do you want to know who throttled Adelaide Cumberland? It was not her brother; it was not her lover; it was her old and trusted coachman."

CHAPTER XXXV

"AS IF IT WERE A MECCA"

—I have within my mind
A thousand raw tricks of these bragging Jacks
Which I will practise.

Merchant of Venice.

"Give me your reasons. They must be excellent ones, Sweetwater, or you would not risk making a second mistake in a case of this magnitude and publicity."

"Mr. Fox, they are excellent. But you shall judge of them. From the moment Miss Carmel Cumberland overthrew the very foundations of our case by her remarkable testimony, I have felt that my work was only half done. It was a strain on credulity to believe Arthur guilty of a crime so prefaced, and the alternative which Mr. Moffat believed in, which you were beginning to believe in, and perhaps are allowing yourself to believe in even now, never appealed to me.

"I allude to the very natural suspicion that the act beheld by your man Clarke was a criminal act, and that Ranelagh is the man really responsible for Miss Cumberland's death. Some instinct held me back from this conclusion, as well as the incontrovertible fact that he could have had no hand in carrying that piece of broken bottle into the Cumberland stable, or of dropping his engagement ring in the suggestive place where it was found. Where, then, should I look for the unknown, the unsuspected third party? Among the ten other persons who dropped something into that casket.

"Most of these were children, but I made the acquaintance of every one. I spent most of my Sunday that way; then, finding no clouded eye among them, I began a study of the Cumberland servants, naturally starting with Zadok. For two hours I sat at his stable fire, talking and turning him inside out, as only we detectives know how. I found him actually overwhelmed with grief; not the grief of a sane man, but of one in whom the very springs of life are poisoned by some dreadful remorse.

"He did not know he revealed this; he expressed himself as full of hope that his young master would be acquitted the next day; but I could see that this prospect could never still the worm working at his heart, and resolved to understand why. I left him ostensibly alone, but in reality shadowed him. The consequence was that, in the evening dusk, he led me to the cemetery, where he took up his watch at Miss Cumberland's grave, as if it were a Mecca and he a passionate devotee. I could hear his groans as he hung to the fence and spoke softly to the dead; and though I was too far away to catch a single word, I felt confident that I had at last struck the right track, and should soon see my way more clearly than at any time since this baffling case opened.

"But before I allowed my fancy to run away with me, I put in an evening of inquiry. If this man had an absolute alibi, what was the use of wasting effort upon him. But I could not find that he had, Mr. Fox. He went with the rest of the servants to the ball—which, you know, was held in Tibbitt's Hall, on Ford Street and he was seen there later, dancing and making merry in a way not usual to him. But there was a space of time dangerously tallying with that of the tragic scene at the club-house, when he was not seen by any one there, so far as I can make out; and this fact gave me courage to consider a certain point which had struck me, and of which I thought something might be made.

"Mr. Fox, after the fiasco I have made of this affair, it costs me something to go into petty details which must suggest my former failures and may not strike you with the force they did me. That broken bottle— or rather, that piece of broken bottle! Where was the rest of it? Sought for almost immediately after the tragedy, it had not been found at the Cumberland place or on the golf-links. It had been looked for carefully when the first thaw came; but, though glass was picked up, it was not the same glass. The task had become hopeless and ere long was abandoned.

"But with this idea of Zadok being the means of its transfer from The Whispering Pines to the house on the Hill, I felt the desire to look once more, and while court was in session this morning, I started a fresh search—this time not on the golf-links. Tibbitt's Hall communicates more quickly with The Whispering Pines by the club-house road than by the market one. So I directed my attention to the ground in front, and on the further side of the driveways. And I found the neck of that bottle!

"Yes, sir, I will show it to you later. I picked it up at some distance from the northern driveway, under a small tree, against the trunk of which it had evidently been struck off. This meant that the lower part had been carried away, broken.

"Now, who would do this but Zadok, who saw in it, he has said, a receptacle for some varnish which he had; and if Zadok, how had he carried it, if not in some pocket of his greatcoat. But glass edges make quick work with pockets; and if this piece of bottle had gone from The Whispering Pines to Tibbitt's Hall, and from there to the Hill, there should be some token of its work in Zadok's overcoat pocket.

"This led me to look for those tokens; and as I had by this time insinuated my way into his confidence by a free and cheerful manner which gave him a rest from his gloomy thoughts, I soon had a chance to see for myself the condition of those pockets. The result was quite satisfactory. In one of them I found a frayed lining, easily explainable on the theory I had advanced. That pocket can be seen by you.

"But Mr. Fox, I wanted some real proof. I wasn't willing to embarrass another man, or to risk my own reputation on a hazard so blind as this, without something really definite. A confession was what I wanted, or such a breakdown of the man as would warrant police action. How could I get this?

"I am a pupil of Mr. Gryce, and I remembered some of his methods.

"This man, guilty though he might be, loved this family, and was broken-hearted over the trouble in which he saw it plunged. Excused to-day from attendance at court, he was in constant telephonic communication with some friend of his, who kept him posted as to the conduct of the trial and the probabilities of a favourable verdict.

"If the case had gone against Arthur, we should have heard from his coachman—that I verily believe, but when we all saw that he was likely to be acquitted, I realised that some other course must be taken to shake Zadok from his new won complacency, and I chose the most obvious one.

"Just when everything looked most favourable to their restored peace and happiness, I shocked Miss Carmel and, through her, this Zadok, into the belief that the whole agony was to be gone over again, in the rearrest and consequent trial of the man she still loves, in spite of all that has happened to separate them.

"He was not proof against this new responsibility. As she fainted, he leaped from the box; and, could I have heard the words he muttered in her ear, I am sure that I should have that to give you which would settle this matter for all time. As it is, I can only say that my own convictions are absolute; the rest remains with you."

"We will go see the man," said District Attorney Fox.

CHAPTER XXXVI

THE SURCHARGED MOMENT

For Justice, when triumphant, will weep down
Pity, not punishment, on her own wrongs,
Too much avenged by those who err. I wait,
Enduring thus, the retributive hour
Which since we spake is even nearer now.

Prometheus Unbound.

The moment I felt Sweetwater's hand lifted from my shoulder I sprang into the first hack I could find, and bade the driver follow the Cumberland sleigh post-haste. I was determined to see Carmel and have Carmel see me. Whatever cold judgment might say against the meeting, I could not live in my present anxiety. If the thunderbolt which had struck her had spared her life and reason she must know from my own lips that I was not only a free man, but as innocent of the awful charge conveyed in Sweetwater's action as was the brother, who had just been acquitted of it by the verdict of his peers.

I must declare this, and she must believe me. Nothing else mattered—nothing else in all the world. That Arthur might stop me, that anything could stop me, did not disturb my mind for a minute. All that I dreaded was that I might find myself too late; that this second blow might have proved to be too much for her, and that I should find my darling dead or passed from me into that living death which were the harder punishment of the two. But I was spared this killing grief. When our two conveyances stopped, it was in the driveway of her old home; and as I bounded upon the walk, it was to see her again in Arthur's arms, but this time with open eyes and horror-drawn features.

"Carmel!" rushed in a cry from my lips. "Don't believe what they say. I cannot bear it—I cannot bear it!"

She roused; she looked my way, and struggling to her feet, held back Arthur with one hand while she searched my face—and possibly searched her own soul—for answer to my plea. Never was moment more surcharged. Further word I could not speak; I could only meet her eyes with the steady, demanding look of a despairing heart, while Arthur moved in every fibre of his awakened manhood, waited—thinking, perhaps, how few minutes had passed since he hung upon the words of a fellow being for his condemnation to death, or release to the freedom which he now enjoyed.

A moment! But what an eternity before I saw the rigid lines of her white, set face relax—before I marked the play of human, if not womanly, emotion break up the misery of her look and soften her youthful lips into some semblance of their old expression. Love might be dead—friendship, even, be a thing of the far past—but consideration was still alive and in another instant it spoke in these trembling sentences, uttered across a threshold made sacred by a tragedy involving our three lives:

"Come in and explain yourself. No man should go unheard. I know you will not come where Adelaide's spirit yet lingers, if you cannot bring hands clean from all actual violence."

I motioned my driver away, and as Carmel drew back out of sight, I caught at Arthur's arm and faced him with the query:

"Are you willing that I should enter? I only wish to declare to her, and to you, an innocence I have no means of proving, but which you cannot disbelieve if I swear it, here and now, by your sister Carmel's sacred disfigurement. Such depravity could not exist, as such a vow from the lips guilty of the crime you charge me with. Look at me, Arthur. I considered you—now consider me."

Quickly he stepped back. "Enter," said he.

It was some minutes later—I cannot say how many—that one of the servants disturbed us by asking if we knew anything about Zadok.

"He has not come home," said he, "and here is a man who wants him."

"What man?" asked Arthur.

"Oh, that detective chap. He never will leave us alone."

I arose. In an instant enlightenment had come to me. "It's nothing," said I with my eyes on Carmel; but the gesture I furtively made Arthur, said otherwise.

A few minutes later we were both in the driveway. "We are on the brink of a surprise," I whispered. "I think I understand this Sweetwater now."

Arthur looked bewildered, but he took the lead in the interview which followed with the man who had made him so much trouble and was now doing his best to make us all amends.

Zadok could not be found; he was wanted by the district attorney, who wished to put some questions to him. Were there any objections to his searching the stable-loft for indications of his whereabouts?

Arthur made none; and the detective, after sending the Cumberlands' second man before him to light up the stable, disappeared beneath the great door, whither we more slowly followed him.

"Not here!" came in a shout from above, as we stepped in from the night air; and in a few minutes the detective came running down the stairs, baffled and very ill at ease. Suddenly he encountered my eye. "Oh—I know!" he cried, and started for the gate.

"I am going to follow him," I confided to Arthur. "Look for me again to-night; or, at least, expect a message. If fortune favours us, as I now expect, we two shall sleep to-night as we have not slept for months." And waiting for no answer, not even to see if he comprehended my meaning, I made a run for the gate, and soon came up with Sweetwater.

"To the cemetery?" I asked.

"Yes, to the cemetery."

And there we found him, in the same place where we had seen him before, but not in the same position. He was sunken now to the ground; but his face was pressed against the rails, and in his stiff, cold hand was clutched a letter which afterwards we read.

Let it be read by you here. It will explain the mystery which came near destroying the lives of more than Adelaide.

No more unhappy wretch than I goes to his account. I killed her who had shown me only goodness, and will be the death of others if I do not confess my dreadful, my unsuspected secret. This is how it happened. I cannot give reasons; I cannot even ask for pardon.

That night, just as I was preparing to leave the stable to join the other servants on their ride to Tibbitt's Hall, the telephone rang and I heard Miss Cumberland's voice. "Zadok," she said—and at first I could hardly understand her,—"I am in trouble; I want help, and you are the only one who can aid me. Answer; do you hear me and are you quite alone in the stable?" I told her yes, and that I was listening to all she said. I suspected her trouble, and was ready to stand by her, if a man like me could do anything.

I had been with her many years, and I loved her as well as I could love anybody; though you won't think it when I tell you my whole story. What she wanted was this: I was to go to the ball just as if nothing had happened, but I was not to stay there. As soon as I could, I was to slip out, get a carriage from some near-by stable, and hurry back up the road to meet her and take her where she would tell me; or, if I did not meet her, to wait two houses below hers, till she came along. She would not want me long, and very soon I could go back and have as good a time as I pleased. But she would like me to be secret, for her errand was not one for gossip, even among her own servants.

It was the first time she had ever asked me to do anything for her which any one else might not have done, and I was proud of her confidence, and happy to do just what she asked. I even tried to do better, and be even more secret about it than she expected. Instead of going to a stable, I took one of the rigs which I found fastened up in the big shed alongside the hall; and being so fortunate as not to attract anybody's attention by this business, I was out on the road and half way to The Whispering Pines, before Helen and Maggie could wonder why I had not asked them to dance.

A few minutes later I was on the Hill, for the horse I had chosen was a fast one; and I was just turning into our street when I was passed by Mr. Arthur's grey mare and cutter. This made me pull up for a minute, for I hadn't expected this; but on looking ahead and seeing Miss Cumberland peering from our own gateway, I drove quickly on and took her up.

I was not so much astonished as you would think, to be ordered to follow fast after the mare and cutter, and to stop where it stopped. That was all she wanted—to follow that cutter, and to stop where it stopped. Well, it stopped at the club-house; and when she saw it turn in there, I heard her give a little gasp.

"Wait," she whispered. "Wait till she has had time to get out and go in; then drive in, too, and help me to find my way into the building after her."

And then I knew it was Miss Carmel we had been following. Before, I thought it was Mr. Arthur.

Presently, she pulled me by the sleeve. "I heard the door shut," said she—and I was a little frightened at her voice, but I was full of my importance, and went on doing just as she bade me. Driving in after the cutter, I drew up into the shadows where the grey mare was hid, and then, reaching out my hand to Miss Cumberland, I helped her out, and went with her as far as the door. "You may go back now," said she. "If I survive the night, I shall never forget this service, my good Zadok." And I saw her lift her hand to the door, then fall back white and trembling in the moonlight. "I can't," she whispered, over and over; "I can't—I can't."

"Shall I knock?" I asked.

"No, no," she whispered back. "I want to go in quietly; let's see if there's no other way. Run about the house, Zadok; I will submit to any humiliation; only find me some entrance other than this." She was shaking so and her face looked so ghastly in the moonlight that I was afraid to leave her; but she made me a gesture of such command that I ran quickly down the steps, and so round the house till I came to a shed over the top of which I saw a window partly open.

Could I get her up on to the shed? I thought I could, and went hurrying back to the big entrance where I had left her. She was still there, shivering with the cold, but just as determined as ever. "Come," I whispered; "I have found a way."

She gave me her hand and I led her around to the shed. She was like a snow woman and her touch was ice itself. "Wait till I get a box or board or something," I said. Hunting about, I found a box leaning against the kitchen side, and, bringing it, I helped her up and soon had her on a level with the window.

As she made her way in, she turned and whispered to me: "Go back now. Carmel has a horse, and will see me home. You have served me well, Zadok."

I nodded, and she vanished into the darkness. Then I should have gone; but my curiosity was too great. I wanted to know just a little more. Two women in this desolate and bitterly cold club-house! What did it mean?

I could not restrain myself from following her in and listening, for a few minutes, to what they had to say. But I did not catch much of it; and when I heard other sounds from some place below, and recognised these sounds as a man's heavy footsteps coming up the rear stairs, I got a fright at being where I should not be, and slipped into the first door I found, expecting this man to come out and join the ladies.

But he did not; he just lingered for a moment in the hall I had left, then I heard him clamber out of the window and go. I now know that this was Mr. Arthur. But I did not know it then, and I was frightened for the horse I had run off with, and so got out of the building as quickly as I could.

And all might yet have been well if I had not found, lying on the snow at the foot of the shed, a bottle of whiskey such as I had never drunk and did not know how to resist. Catching it up, I ran about the house to where I had left my rig. It was safe, and in my relief at finding it, I knocked off the head of the bottle and took a long drink.

Then I drank again; then I sat down in the snow and drank again. In short, I nearly finished it; then I became confused; I looked at the piece of broken bottle in my hand, took a fancy to its shape, and breaking off a bit more, thrust it into one of my big pockets. Then I staggered up to the horse; but I did not untie him.

Curiosity seized me again, and I thought I would take another look at the ladies—perhaps they might want me—perhaps—I was pretty well confused, but I went back and crawled once more into the window.

This time the place was silent—not a sound, not a breath,—but I could see a faint glimmer of light. I followed this glimmer. Still there was no sound.

I came to an open door. A couch was before me, heaped with cushions. A long ray of moonlight had shot in through a communicating door, and I could see everything by it. This was where the ladies had been when I listened before, but they were not here now.

Weren't they? Why did I tremble so, then, and stare and stare at those cushions? Why did I feel I must pull them away, as I presently did? I was mad with liquor and might easily have imagined what I there saw; but I did not think of this then. I believed what I saw instantly. Miss Cumberland was dead, and I had discovered the crime. She had killed herself—no, she had been killed!

Should I yell out murder? No, no; I could be sorry without that. I would not yell—mistresses were plenty. I had liked her, but I need not yell. There was something else I could do.

She had a ring on her finger—a ring that for months I had gloated over and watched, as I had never watched and gloated over any other beautiful thing in my life. I wanted it—I had always wanted it. It was before me, for the taking now—I should be a fool to leave it there for some other wretch to pilfer. I had loved her—I would love the ring.

Reaching down, I took it. I drew it from her finger; I put it in my pocket; I—God in heaven! The eyes I had seen glassed in death were looking at me.

She was not dead—she had been witness of the theft. Without a thought of what I was doing, my hands closed round her throat. It was drink—fright—terror at the look she gave me—which made me kill her; not my real self. My real self could have shrieked when, in another instant, I saw my work.

But shrieking would not bring her back and it would quite ruin me. Miss Carmel was somewhere near. I heard her now at the telephone; in another minute she would come out and meet me. I dared not linger.

Tossing back the pillows, I stumbled from the place. Why I was not heard by my young mistress, I do not know; her ears were deaf, just as my eyes were half-blind. In a half hour I was dancing with the maids, telling them of the pretty stranger with whom I had been sitting out an hour of fun in a quiet corner. They believed me, and not a particle of suspicion has any man ever had of me since.

But others have had to suffer, and that has made hell of my nights. I restored the ring to my poor mistress; but even that brought harm to one I had no quarrel with. But he has escaped conviction; and if I thought Mr. Ranelagh would also escape, I might have courage to live out my miserable life, and seek to make amends in the way she would have me.

But I fear for him; I fear for Miss Carmel. Never could I testify in another trial which threatened her peace of mind. I see that, instead of being the selfish stealer of her sister's happiness, as I had thought, she is an angel from whom all future suffering should be kept.

This is my way of sparing her. Perhaps it will help her sister to forgive me when we meet in the world to which I am now going.

Anna Katharine Green – A Concise Bibliography

The Leavenworth Case (1878)
A Strange Disappearance (1880)
The Sword of Damocles: A Story of New York Life (1881)
The Defence of the Bride, and other Poems (1882)
X Y Z: A Detective Story (1883)
Hand and Ring (1883)
The Mill Mystery (1886)
7 to 12: A Detective Story (1887)
Risifi's Daughter, A Drama (1887)
Behind Closed Doors (1888)
Forsaken Inn (1890)
A Matter of Millions (1891)
The Old Stone House and Other Stories (1891)
Cynthia Wakeham's Money (1892)
Marked "Personal" (1893)
Miss Hurd: An Enigma (1894)
The Doctor, His Wife, and the Clock (1895)
Doctor Izard (1895)
That Affair Next Door (1897)
Lost Man's Lane: A Second Episode in the Life of Amelia Butterworth (1898)
Agatha Webb (1899)
The Circular Study (1900)
A Difficult Problem (1900)
One of my Sons (1901)
The Filigree Ball: Being a Full and True Account of the Solution of the Mystery Concerning the Jeffrey-Moore Affair (1903)
The Amethyst Box (1905)
The House in the Mist (1905)
The Millionaire Baby (1905)
The Chief Legatee' (1906)
The Woman in the Alcove (1906)
The Mayor's Wife (1907)
The House of the Whispering Pines (1910)
Three Thousand Dollars (1910)
Initials Only (1911)
Masterpieces of Mystery (1913)
Dark Hollow (1914)
The Golden Slipper, and Other Problems for Violet Strange (1915)
To the Minute; Scarlet and Black: Two Tales of Life's Perplexities (1916)
The Mystery of the Hasty Arrow (1917)
The Step on the Stair (1923)

www.ingramcontent.com/pod-product-compliance
Lightning Source LLC
Chambersburg PA
CBHW070504260626
47161CB00004B/1442